GAMES of DEATH and DESIRE

EVA CHASE

RITES OF POSSESSION - BOOK 2

Games of Death and Desire

Book 2 in the Rites of Possession series

First Digital Edition, 2023

Copyright © 2023 Eva Chase

Cover design: Sanja Balan (Sanja's Covers)

Map design: Fictive Designs

Page Edge Designs: Painted Wings Publishing

Chapter Illustrations: Bojan Serafimovski

Ebook ISBN: 978-1-998752-55-3

Paperback ISBN: 978-1-998752-56-0

Hardcover ISBN: 978-1-998752-57-7

STARSIL RIVER

FLORIAN

HARBOR

TANGLESIDE

MIDDLE WARD

SILTSTON

CAPITAL PALACE

TEMPLE of the CROWN

SOVEREIGN COLLEGE

INSTITUTE FOR CHILD WELLNESS

the NIGHT'S CALLING

CROW'S CLOSE

CLOTH FACTORY

INNER WARDS

OLD CITY WALLS

SLAUGHTERWELL

OUTER WARDS

ONE

Ivy

A once exalted general is pointing a sword at me—and somehow that feels like the least of my problems.

Stavros's grip on the sword tightens enough that his light brown knuckles pale in the dim twilight. He takes a wary step up the curving staircase of the tower toward me.

Toward the woven vines I'm standing on that fill the gap where daimon smashed several of the stone stairs. The vines that my monstrous magic called forth.

The same magic twitches in my chest, tugging at me to let it push Stavros away, shatter his sword—defend me.

I clamp down hard on the urge. Releasing my power is what got me into this mess in the first place.

There's got to be a way we can all walk down from this tower alive.

My hand starts to lift toward the torn folds of fabric on my chest where a fall ripped open the bodice of my dress. Stavros twitches both his head and the sword.

"Don't move an inch," he says in a voice so low and dark it sends a shiver down my spine.

I suppose it wouldn't do any good to cover up the bare skin he's already seen—the smooth flesh between my breasts where nearly anyone else would bear a godlen brand. The absence of a brand means I shouldn't be able to wield any magic at all.

Other than the kind that'll get me executed, that is.

The massive man has always cut an imposing figure, but I've never felt so close to death, not even when he held a sword right against my throat. Through the rattle of my frantic pulse, I register that the sword he's holding now isn't his usual blade, which is still sheathed at his hip.

No, it's the short sword with the royal crest on its hilt that he gave to me just hours ago, when he told me all he wanted was to keep me safe.

As tense as I already am, my stomach balls even tighter.

I'm never going to hear sentiments like that from Stavros's lips again.

He takes another step, his gaze sliding past me for just a second. For long enough that even his unsteady vision will be able to pick out the body slumped on the platform just above me.

The man I nearly killed.

It was *nearly*, not completely. I can take a shred of pride in the self-control I held on to, even if the former general won't see the situation that way.

The words tumble out of me. "I didn't kill Wendos. I only— He was summoning daimon to attack the city."

I sense one of those spirit-creatures flitting past me with a ripple of my skirt, and then it's gone. The several daimon that pinned me down on Wendos's orders all appear to have fled.

"I had to stop him," I go on. "But the Crown's Watch

will still be able to question him, find out… find out who he was working with."

My voice falters with the hardening of Stavros's expression. I hadn't thought his stunningly chiseled features could get any fiercer than they already were, but I was wrong.

"What exactly did you do?" he demands.

My hands clench at my sides. I can't help glancing past him toward the other two men poised farther down the staircase.

Alek has managed to straighten up a little, though his bronze-brown hand is still braced against the wall as if he needs the support. It's always hard to judge the scholar's reactions with his polished leather mask covering most of his face, but his full lips are set in the stiffest line I've ever seen.

He jerks his hand down his front in a shaky gesture of the divinities—three fingers tapping forehead for sky, heart for sea, and gut for earth before they all fist over his sternum. I restrain a cringe at the thought of any more godly attention being drawn to us.

Casimir—the man who welcomed me from the start, who treated me like a friend and sometimes more—simply stares at me. His gorgeous face has drained of color, leaving his normally peachy skin as sallow as my own. None of his usual grace shows in his rigid stance.

They all know. They know what they're seeing, what this scene must signify.

Denying it will only make me look guiltier.

A rasp creeps into my voice. "I don't want to be what I am. I don't want this power. I don't *use* it—I haven't been using it—I tried everything and there was nothing else, and he was going to destroy the city. I managed not to hurt anyone but him."

Which would be a first.

The other participant in our standoff, the ghost who's an

uninvited guest inside my head, pipes up a little shakily. *Ivy, you're... you're riven?*

I hadn't wanted to say the word myself. I don't see the need to answer Julita. Even to a minor noblewoman who's barely been outside her own county and the capital city's royal college, the source of my godless magic must be obvious.

Stavros's sword hasn't wavered. He makes a scoffing sound. "And you expect us to believe you? Of course you'd claim all that now that you're caught."

It's a battle already lost. The riven are reviled throughout the continent, and Stavros hates magic like mine more than just about anyone.

Still, I can't stop myself from arguing. "Other than just now and keeping myself from *dying* yesterday, I haven't let my magic out in seven wretched years. I'd snuff the power right out of me if I knew how."

But the problem is how I'm torn already. The cracks in my soul that let endless magic seep through me, taking and sacrificing without limit if I give it free rein.

Alek finally speaks, his voice thin. "Riven sorcerers go mad with their power. It consumes them. That's what always happens."

I swallow thickly. "Well, apparently it's possible to at least delay that outcome for a while, if you're stubborn enough. Why do you think I've been refusing it? The magic would like me to bring it out every blasted moment I could. You can be sure it never shuts up about how disappointed it is."

Casimir eases up a step, his deep blue gaze gone pensive. "Is it because of your magic that Julita... Is *that* how her soul ended up inside you?"

Julita's presence shudders in the back of my skull. *Gods above, maybe it is.*

I answer both her and the courtesan at the same time. "I

don't know. I didn't use any magic when I tried to save her. If I had, she'd be alive and we wouldn't be here right now, and somehow I don't think you'd be upset about it then."

Stavros's lips draw back from his teeth in a silent snarl. "You wielded the power meant as divine punishment in the greatest temple in Silana—in the All-Giver's own fucking tower. Don't try to take the moral high ground."

My jaw sets on edge. "If the gods had a problem with it, I don't think one of them would have been egging me on."

"*What?*" Alek blurts out, swiping his messy black waves back from where they'd shaded his eyes.

"He told me to use it after I was stabbed. Practically ordered me to. I would have let myself die otherwise—I didn't even exactly *agree*—and he spoke to me again just now—"

Stavros cuts me off with a sputter of a laugh. "You *are* insane. If the gods even noticed you were here, they—"

Then his voice dies too, with a widening of his eyes and another subtle twitch to refocus his sight. At the same moment, Alek and Casimir freeze all over again.

Alek's lips part in apparent shock. Casimir's eyebrows jolt upward.

A tingling sensation like a waft of magic brings my own gaze down, to the spot on my chest they're staring at. My pulse lurches.

The skin between the torn flaps of my bodice was bare a moment ago. Now a godlen sigil shimmers there, an unearthly glow against the thickening darkness of the night.

Two lines arch from a central apex, with two smaller points poking from their peaks like little horns.

Kosmel's sigil.

Well, I figured he was the most likely of any of the nine lesser gods to support my riven magic. The godlen of luck and rebellion is known to appreciate a little chaos.

But I keep staring at the glowing mark just as the men are, my jaw gone slack. That's divine magic shining against my body.

Like I've been claimed, without any say in it.

Kosmel must be trying to help my case here. If he didn't want me dead from a knife wound, he won't want me ending up with a noose around my neck either. He's confirming my story.

Part of me recoils all the same. I didn't ask for this—I purposefully skipped my dedication ceremony. I've avoided the attention of our deities in every way I know how.

My soul's been ravaged by godly retribution enough without anyone else sticking their divine fingers in.

For the first time, Stavros's sword wavers. Even he isn't going to suggest that a riven sorcerer could get away with blasphemous fraud in the grandest building that bears all the gods' blessings.

He doesn't outright lower the blade either, though.

"You—" he starts, and Casimir's head jerks to the side with a ripple of his tawny hair.

"Someone's coming," he says quickly. "Probably the Crown's Watch. Stavros—we can't hand Ivy over to them. Not when Kosmel himself is watching over her. We should at least give her more of a chance to explain. She's never hurt any of us, and gods know she's had plenty of opportunity."

Alek purses his lips. "We need to understand exactly what's going on."

Stavros inhales with a hiss through his teeth, but his sword hand drops to his side. He glares at me while he answers the others. "What are we going to say happened here, then?"

As my spirits rise with the unexpected reprieve, fragments of an idea come together in my head. "Let me handle that. I'm the one who *was* here for most of it."

Stavros grimaces as if he's going to argue, but right then the sound of hurried footsteps reverberates from just around the bend in the stairs.

My pulse stutters for a different reason. "This battle isn't over. There are other scourge sorcerers out there. If they find out we were working together—"

I don't need to say any more. I doubt the former general cares about protecting my identity at this point, but he spins to charge down the stairs and meet the incoming brigade while motioning Alek and Casimir farther up the steps.

The glowing sigil has faded away. I snatch at the torn fabric of my bodice to cover my lack of dedication brand just as a familiar blond head comes into view beyond the other men.

"I've brought the full squadron of royal soldiers," Benedikt announces. The king's bastard half-nephew sounds a little ragged but still manages a jaunty lilt. "Although from the fact that all the shaking and crashing stopped a few minutes ago, I assume we're not quite as urgently needed as expected?"

A couple of men in the rich blue uniforms of the Crown's Watch appear behind him at the front of the squadron. I draw farther to the side where I'm less visible. My mouth has gone dry.

One word from Stavros, one swerve in his resolve back toward ridding the world of all illicit sorcery, and I'll be meeting the hangman tomorrow.

His voice comes out terse. "It appears everything is under control now. There's only one villain up here, and he's been subdued. You're welcome to bring him down the tower to take him into custody."

Benedikt lets out a soft huff. "Barely needed at all, then. Well, I was happy to lead the charge all the same."

One of the soldiers in view lets out a snort he doesn't even try to stifle. Benedikt's grin stiffens just for a second.

He turns toward the squadron. "The threat has been quelled. It's been an honor ushering you into battle even if it never happened."

The other soldier I can see barely spares Benedikt a glance, his attention focusing on Stavros. "Are you sure all's clear up here, General? This fop didn't seem to know much about anything."

The self-proclaimed "bastard's bastard" lets out a light chuckle as if he thinks the insult is a joke. Stavros taps his prosthetic hand against Benedikt's arm in a subtle gesture of solidarity.

"None of us was sure what we were going to be dealing with," he says. "But the immediate danger has passed. I need to speak with the king. If a few of you could go ahead and inform him that I'll require a private meeting—"

"I could—" Benedikt starts to volunteer.

But the first of the nearby soldiers is already turning away from him to shoulder down the stairs. Benedikt falls silent and gives an awkward shrug.

Stavros strides back up the steps and over the woven vines, I suppose to collect Wendos's unconscious body. But he pauses beside me just long enough to speak in a dark murmur.

"You'll come with me and follow my lead to the letter, or gods help me, Kosmel will find himself missing a Hand too."

Two

Stavros

The thief walks down the shadowy palace corridor with a meekness she's never shown in my presence before.

On our way down the tower, she picked up the cloak she must have discarded, and now she has it wrapped tight over her dress. Her head dips low beneath the hood that conceals her pale red-blond hair. Her shoulders have hunched as if she's drawing in on herself.

She's trying to make herself look weak. Fragile.

Because she's just proven herself to be the exact opposite to an extent I never could have imagined.

Not just a street-hardened petty criminal. Not even just the charitable vigilante the outer-warders dubbed the Hand of Kosmel.

Gods smite me, I've had one of the riven under my nose for weeks and never suspected.

As I walk a step behind where I can keep a careful eye on her, my fingers clench around the hilt of my sword. I can't

draw it, because the blasted royal bastard insisted on accompanying us to see King Konram in case his familial influence could be of use with his half-uncle, and he wouldn't understand why I'd like to keep a blade pointed Ivy's way.

I don't know if I should tell him. I don't know if I should already be planning how to run her through and explain why afterward.

The uncertainty gnaws at my gut.

I was coming to respect her. To appreciate her presence. To *want* to hear her snarky comebacks when I heckled her, to see the hesitant way she'd brighten when I offered a friendlier remark.

Great God help me, just remembering the moment when I handed her my old sword with its royal seal sets an unwelcome warmth blooming in my chest. I grit my teeth and smother the sensation.

How much of her mix of mettle and vulnerability was an act?

Just how wretched an imbecile have I been?

My wooden prosthetic feels like a dead weight on my arm. I didn't have time to swap it for a metal one shaped for combat, which would at least give me another advantage.

Bizarrely, I wish I hadn't sent Casimir and Aleksi back to the college. It was a split-second decision based on wanting to keep our group out of the public eye, as secret as this particular route through the palace is.

It isn't as if the scholar or the courtesan would be much help in a fight against a riven sorcerer. Fuck, *I* wouldn't be much use in that fight.

The only way you take down one of the riven is by surprise. Might to might, you'll always lose.

At least if they were here, the decision wouldn't rest entirely on me. Whether to lunge and bash her head against the plastered wall beside us or keep escorting her on, bringing one of the most dangerous beings in existence to a chat with the king.

I don't think even riven magic could harm him through the precautions he takes for an unguarded conversation, but who can say what a monster might be capable of?

Ivy is the only one who knows what happened when she confronted that prick Wendos. What he said about his scourge sorcerer colleagues and their plans.

Kill this riven woman, and we lose our best chance of stopping a whole horde of even viler villains.

But what lingers in my mind the most is the image of Kosmel's sigil glowing on her chest. The look that came over her face when she noticed it too, startled and then almost horrified.

She didn't ask for the godlen's blessing. He imposed it on her.

I'm not arrogant enough to argue with a divine being.

Aleksi is right. We need to figure out what this all means. Which requires that she stay alive for at least a little longer.

The back of her head has turned into a blur, as everything does if I hold my gaze in the same place for more than a second or two. As if I'm looking through a window that's hazed with condensation.

I flick my attention to the hall ahead and then back to this unpredictable woman for another brief moment of clarity.

Is Julita still in her head? I can't picture how our former ally would respond to the revelations we've just heard.

Whatever Julita thought of me when we worked together, I'd like to believe she'd understand if I have to end the scrap of a life she's managed to cling on to via her reluctant host.

Even with the thief's meek stance, there's still a confidence to the way she moves. As if she always knows exactly where she's putting her feet—and how she'd need to pivot at an unexpected interruption.

I have to yank my attention away before my appreciation of her subtle assurance brings my gaze skimming down her slim body. It's traveled that path before more times than I'd like to admit, with a flicker of heat I can't allow now.

When we reach the door to the king's most private meeting room, I push a little ahead of Ivy and Benedikt. I'm one of the few who knows how to handle the carving on the wooden surface to disengage the lock.

With a flash of flaring magical sconces, we step into a small, windowless sitting room that nonetheless demonstrates the palace's splendor. With a flick of my eyes, I take in the velvet cushions on the chairs and the gold gilding around the fireplace.

What matters most is the huge, gold-framed mirror that stands against the wall next to the fireplace, taller and broader than even me. I motion for Ivy and Benedikt to join me before it.

I don't know what gift allowed the creation of this mirror or how long it's been in the Melchiorek family. It's a fantastic trick, allowing King Konram to speak with trusted advisors without even a guard overhearing while remaining in the security of his personal chambers.

There must be something in the room that alerts him to our entry. Within a matter of seconds, our reflection on the mirror shudders and ripples away, replaced by the king's regal form.

In the first instant before my sight clouds, I take in the sternness of his deep-set eyes and the tight set of his thin lips. It's late in the day for handling official business, but a king's job is never truly done.

"Ster. Stavros and companions," Konram says with a slight nod of acknowledgment. Unlike his soldiers, he never makes the error of calling me by my lost military title. "It's been a tumultuous day, but I gather we're closer to answers than the last time we spoke?"

I draw my posture even straighter than it already was. Through months of practice, I hold my gaze steady on him as if my vision isn't hazed. I can see well enough to make out the basic shapes of his features if not the details.

I might not be serving under him as a general any longer —I might have fucked up not just my career but so many other things that mattered more as well—but he still values my input. I have to show I'm worthy of his generous trust.

"It appears that the scourge sorcerers I told you about were responsible for a great deal of the destruction today," I say, going over my mental inventory of that damage. Part of the college's Quadring building, a row of shops a few blocks away, a nobleman's home on another corner.

I gather myself before continuing with the part that makes me balk. "I mentioned that my assistant, Ivy, was helping us investigate. She confronted one of the sorcerers directly in the All-Giver's tower of the Temple of the Crown."

Konram's head turns so he can study Ivy. "You saw the supposed scourge sorcery first-hand?"

Ivy keeps her cloak close around her, but she lifts her chin with the fire I'm used to from her. "I saw enough to know it isn't 'supposed.' I found Wendos of Nikodi at the top of the tower, conducting a ritual. He had three accomplices with him—people whose power he was taking to bolster his own."

The king frowns. "And when you say taking, you mean…?"

Ivy's voice tightens. "It seems these scourge sorcerers are attempting to avoid the gods' retribution by using a slightly different strategy than the ones centuries ago. Rather than having people die in sacrifice, they're manipulating their accomplices into sacrificing every body part they can spare while remaining alive. Presumably so they have as large a gift as possible to lend the conspirators ongoing power."

My stomach roils at her words. Every part they could spare? The image her words stir in my mind is sickening.

I didn't see any accomplices with Wendos in the tower, but I'm not going to question her story while my king is in the middle of doing so himself.

"That does complicate matters," Konram says. "Do you know what the purpose of tonight's ritual was?"

Ivy dips her head. "Wendos said he was trying to combine his and his accomplices' powers with those of two other sorcerers who were working elsewhere in the city. They'd already been exerting some control over the daimon—I'm sure they encouraged the creatures to attack everyone at the ball the other night. This time they wanted a larger scale disaster, wreaking havoc throughout the inner wards and maybe the rest of the city too."

Konram hums to himself. "So we're dealing with at least two other members of this conspiracy then."

Ivy hesitates and then ventures, "From the way he was talking, I think it's quite a few more. Unfortunately, Wendos didn't mention any names… except Ster. Torstem. And I believe one of the sacrificial accomplices was an orphan Ster. Torstem groomed for the role. Possibly they all were."

She got confirmation about Torstem. A strange lurching sensation runs through me, half exhilarated, half queasy.

We're getting closer to the root of the conspiracy. But I never wanted to believe one of my fellow professors was involved.

With a slight tick of my eyes, I make out the furrowing of the king's brow before everything blurs again. "The law professor? I've looked into his past conduct—there's been nothing amiss."

Benedikt steps forward with a quick bob of a bow and a flash of a smile. "If I may, Your Highness, from what I've seen of Ivy over the past few weeks, she may be sharper than the rest of us combined. She wouldn't say a thing like that if she wasn't certain."

Konram barely spares the royal bastard a glance. "My certainty is what's more important."

"Wendos was very clear about Ster. Torstem's involvement before he even knew I was there to overhear," Ivy says, her tone mild but firm. "He was threatening one of the sacrificial accomplices that Torstem would take her back to where he'd hidden some of them away if she couldn't pull her weight. You'll be able to ask him yourself when he comes to."

The king's gaze swerves back to me. "This criminal is still alive, Stavros? Hasn't he already been questioned?"

"He's currently unconscious," I reply immediately. "The Crown's Watch took him into custody and are guarding him while medics see to his recovery."

Benedikt pipes up again before anyone else can speak. "If he clams up once he's awake, I could see what I can wheedle out of him. Disarm him in my own way, so to speak."

With another adjustment of my eyes, I make out Konram's faint grimace of distaste in the moment before he replies. "Were *you* there when the confrontation took place, Benedikt?"

The royal bastard hesitates. "Well, I—the commanding officer was in the middle of gathering troops when we got the summons. I volunteered to lead the way for the soldiers while Stavros and the others hurried ahead. It was lucky we weren't needed."

"If you didn't see anything there, then why exactly are you *here*?"

A hint of exasperation has crept into the king's even tone.

Benedikt lets out a nervous laugh, as if he shouldn't have been able to predict that his "influence" over the half-uncle who's barely acknowledged his existence would amount to nothing more than hot air.

Before he can come up with a suitable answer, Konram focuses on Ivy. "Let's hear the whole story from you. Everything from what made you check the All-Giver's tower in the first place to interrupting Wendos's magic. As succinctly as you can manage."

Ivy folds her arms over her chest, gripping her cloak. "I'll do my best."

I watch her blurred form with occasional ticks of my gaze to catch a clearer glimpse, my gut knotting. She's the only one who can tell him this part of the story—and I want to hear it too, even if the thought of what she's leaving out unsettles me.

With a quick glance toward me that might be apologetic, the thief explains how she left my quarters when she saw the Quadring starting to crumble, how she overheard a professor mentioning that the dorms would be unlocked and realized she could check Wendos's room, and the notes she found there that led to her deciding he must be using the tower for his spell.

My muscles tense more when she gets to the confrontation itself. How is she going to spin *that* story without revealing her own deviant magic?

"Once I realized what Wendos was trying to accomplish, I did everything I could to stop him," she says. "But he had quite a few daimon under his control protecting him. They stopped me from tackling him, and I was unlucky with the one knife I managed to throw—it only hit him in the shoulder. After that, the spirit-creatures pinned me down."

Konram motions for her to continue. "It sounds as though you fought valiantly."

Ivy's small smile doesn't reach her bright blue eyes. "The accomplices whose power he was stealing were more valiant. In the end, they broke free from the scourge sorcerers' influence and sacrificed themselves to stop him. They jumped off the tower and died when they hit the roof of the lower temple below—and the power of their sacrifice hit him hard. That's what knocked him out. They must have tried to fix the tower too, because vines grew over the steps the daimon broke."

I stare hazily at her for a second before yanking my attention back to the king. Her story sounds impressively reasonable... but I know a significant part of it is falsehood.

What *really* happened with the mutilated accomplices?

Konram is nodding. "I've heard reports of the bodies and the vines from the temple staff. Once we can identify the victims, they'll be given honorable funerals."

"How would you like us to move forward from here?" I have to ask. "If you plan to arrest Ster. Torstem, I may be able to—"

The king cuts me off with a shake of his head. "I don't think we can proceed to that step yet."

I will my tone to stay cool and collected. "No? Are Ivy's observations not enough?"

"They're enough for me that I wouldn't let the man within striking distance of me or my family, but she's also said she believes he has many other allies. He's the only one we can identify. There's no guarantee he'll reveal anything else to us if we attempt to force him to talk." Konram sighs. "From consultation with my chief magical advisor, I've gathered that there's no definite method to confirm a person has carried out scourge sorcery after the fact. Removing him does us little good if there are several others who'll continue attacking the city."

Ivy hasn't tempered her reaction quite as well as I have,

her voice taut with disbelief. "Then they *will* keep attacking the city—or sending the daimon they've harnessed to do it. They've already tried to kill your younger son, and for all we know they were responsible for Prince Dunstam's death years ago too."

My gaze flicks from her to Konram in time to catch the subtle tensing of his shoulders. I haven't mentioned the death of his eldest son and former heir in connection with the scourge sorcerers before. We haven't found any evidence they were involved in the illness that struck down Dunstam just a few days before his twelfth birthday.

"That was more than seven years ago," he says tersely.

I step in to draw his attention back to me. "We've traced Ster. Torstem's questionable activities farther back than that. It appears the conspiracy has been growing for more than a decade in the shadows."

Konram lifts his chin imperiously. "The gravity of the situation is clear. I'm not saying we'll do nothing. As soon as the medics are able to revive Wendos, he'll be questioned and given every reason to reveal his associates. And I'll have the Crown's Watch pursue our other leads. You said Ster. Torstem has been conscribing orphans into the conspiracy?"

"Yes. We've identified one orphanage where he's given funds and spoken to the wards, but there may be others."

Ivy clears her throat. "I know he was hiding at least some of the sacrificial accomplices at a brothel not far from there. That might be a common tactic of his. Anyone who'd see one of the victims would know immediately it wasn't a typical dedication sacrifice."

The king folds his arms over his chest. "Then we'll make arrangements for raiding brothels and monitoring this orphanage and others in the city. In the meantime, you three and your companions have proven yourselves adept at uncovering the conspiracy bit by bit. Ferret out whatever other information you can about their intentions. Ster. Torstem will reveal more if he doesn't know you suspect him."

It *will* be easier for us to investigate, being sure of Torstem's involvement and his connection to Wendos. But I can't help raising a careful protest of my own. "The daimon have already been rampaging. The students at the college may be afraid to—"

"We can rebuild the damage done quickly. I'm bringing in several clerics who are skilled at working with unsettled spirit-creatures to counteract the effects on the daimon— they should arrive tomorrow. I'll be traveling with most of the court for several days on a scheduled tour, but I plan to keep in close contact with my people here. If the situation escalates, I'll revise my strategy."

A little relief trickles through me with the knowledge that the royal family will be somewhat distant from the threat while we continue to grapple with it.

I don't like this situation any more than Ivy appears to. Skulking around hoping we can dig up more intelligence on the miscreants while the one we know of for certain walks free...

But at the same time, I can't deny the wisdom of Konram's approach. Scourge sorcerers build their magic by maiming and killing others. They're no strangers to sacrifice.

If we arrest Torstem, the odds of him lashing out to force his murder or simply offing himself seem far too high. Then we'd be left with no solid trail to follow at all.

Of course, the conspirators will know that *someone* foiled their plan tonight. I don't intend to let down anyone under my watch.

Konram sweeps his gaze over us with an even more commanding air than before. "You have your orders. I trust you can get on with them?"

I speak up before he officially dismisses us. "It's become increasingly difficult for us to meet and discuss our findings without our association being discovered. If you could offer any resources to allow greater ease of communication, that would be an immense help."

Konram rubs his chin. "I might be able to arrange just the thing. I'll confirm with you as soon as I have it ready."

I incline my head. "Thank you, Your Highness. We will do our best."

"We'll bring all the scourge sorcerers down," Benedikt puts in. After the king's earlier dismissal, his vigor sounds forced.

Ivy remains silent, but I can almost feel her stewing. She's smart enough not to voice any of her concerns in front of the man who rules over us all, though.

The king pauses, his gaze focused on me. "You seem even grimmer than I'd expect given the progress we've made and the disaster averted, Stavros. Is there another problem I'm not aware of?"

The woman next to me stiffens just slightly.

This is my opening, the time to tell him what she is if I'm going to. To send her off to the gallows where all the riven belong.

If nothing else, don't I owe my king my honesty?

In the instant when I teeter in indecision, the memory of Kosmel's sigil glowing on Ivy's chest flashes through my mind. My previous sense of resolve hardens.

I can't serve both my king and my gods, and I know which holds the higher authority.

"No, Your Highness," I say. "I'm merely frustrated that we weren't able to arrest more of the conspirators despite the crimes they've already committed."

Konram lets out a low chuckle. "I trust you'll remedy that shortly."

His image vanishes from the mirror. Gathering myself, I beckon the others to follow me out of the room.

We hustle along the discreet hall and then out into the passage through the hedges that obscure our departure from view. We've almost reached the wall when a familiar giggle tinkles out into the air.

My legs stall of their own accord. My head swings around, my gaze finding a narrow gap between the bushes.

I only have a clear view for an instant before everything fogs over, but that's enough. Enough to make out Neela's face in the glow of lantern light from the carriage she's just stepped out of.

Enough to notice her hand clasped around that of the courtier whose arm she then tucks herself beneath with another giggle.

I wrench my gaze away, my jaw clenching. My voice comes out harsher than I intend it. "Let's move along. There's nothing for us here."

And I won't let myself make another catastrophic mistake.

THREE

Ivy

A s we pass through the college gate into the outer courtyard, a steady rumbling sound carries across the field. I flinch instinctively in the instant before I make out the figures gathered around the ruined corner of the Quadring.

Several workers who must have a gift to do with building or mending are sorting through the rubble. In the glow of their lanterns, I can see a chunk of stone they've just raised melding back into place. More workers must be helping inside, handling the interior structure.

Julita speaks up for the first time in a while, though her voice is still more subdued than I'm used to. *They started the repairs quickly.*

Benedikt lets out a light chuckle. "In a couple of days, it'll be good as new. Like nothing ever happened."

A shiver runs down my spine. "Unless the scourge sorcerers rile up the daimon again."

"Konram's clerics should help with that," Stavros says in the brusque tone that's all I get from him now.

The college's yards and hallways are empty other than the workers and a few soldiers standing guard. How many students fled during the chaos, and how many were simply ushered back to their rooms once the daimon settled down?

The quiet niggles at my nerves. It feels too much like the prelude to a larger storm.

Once we've stepped into the Domi, Stavros gives Benedikt a quick clap on the shoulder. "You should get to your room and sleep. We'll all need our wits about us in the coming days."

Benedikt's gaze flicks between us, probably wondering why we're not heading up the same stairs as him. The staff quarters are just above the floors that hold the student dorms.

But he doesn't question Stavros. The bastard's bastard seems to have deflated a little since I first spotted him at the top of the tower.

The way his half-uncle spoke to him raised my hackles on his behalf—but I'd be a real idiot if I told off the king. Frankly, there are about a dozen other things I'd like to tell the king off for after our conversation, if I happened to be feeling idiotic.

A few locks of my pale hair have drifted out from beneath my hood. Benedikt reaches to give one a teasing tug, a trace of his usual smirk returning. "Until tomorrow then, Knives. Try not to get into any more trouble without me."

He heads into the stairwell, and Stavros nudges me forward in ominous silence. Past the dining hall and the main library doors, down the dimmer hallway with its old tapestries hanging on the wall.

When we stop and the former general grasps the sconce to activate the conjured secret passage, my gaze lingers on the tapestry of Signy beside us. She stands at the top of her hill with that heroic golden glow around her, her sword aloft and her stance full of determination to push back the mass of soldiers below.

I've thought about the Veldunian hero who freed her country a lot since I took up this mission. About how she faced an entire imperial army while I'm struggling just to tackle a college conspiracy.

At least she had three men at her side who did everything they could to support her. Who weren't contemplating hauling her to an executioner if she so much as blinked wrong.

When the thicker shadow that's not really a shadow spills down the wall in front of us, Stavros glances at me with a twist of his mouth, as if he's not sure whether he wants me ahead of him where he can see me or behind him where he can shield his comrades from me. With a rough sound, he prods me to go first.

As I step into the passage, a faint hiss tells me he's drawn his sword. Its tip grazes the scars on my back through my cloak.

He's getting ready in case he feels it's necessary to stab me.

The lump that rises in my throat nearly chokes me. My magic flares alongside it, yanking at my ribs, demanding I let it at him.

Good plan. Defend myself from stabbing by giving him a reason to stab me.

My magic might be potent, but it's not especially wise.

Thankfully, launching my power at Wendos seems to have appeased the worst of its resentment at being ignored. A prickling sensation creeps through my innards at my refusal, but nothing like the vicious searing that's brought me to my knees in the past.

I force myself to walk steadily down the hidden steps. The former general follows right behind.

When we emerge into the small archive room where we've held the meetings for our investigation, the two men waiting for us straighten up on either side of the desk.

Casimir's face lights up with what might be relief— because I haven't slaughtered Stavros with my riven magic so far?

Alek's posture stays stiff, his hand resting on the belt that holds the sheath for the royal sword now lying on the desk. Stavros sent him off with it and the belt when we parted ways, I guess so he didn't have to explain to the king how it ended up in my possession.

Looking at the sheath, an echo of the sense of solidarity that filled me in this room just this afternoon passes through me. My fingers itch as if I could reach out and snatch it back.

Any comradery I shared with these men was always fake; it was always based on a lie. But losing it makes my chest ache anyway.

"What did the king say?" Casimir asks.

Stavros grimaces. "At least until Wendos can speak, he wants us to continue our investigation. Ster. Torstem appears to be the cornerstone. We need to find out who else he's roped into this madness."

Alek glances at me before turning his gaze to Stavros. "How did you explain… everything?"

It's obvious what specific part of "everything" he means.

Stavros's grimace only deepens. "The thief spun a story about Wendos's accomplices turning on him." He taps my arm with the flat of his sword. "Was any of that true?"

I step to the side and lean against one of the shelves that holds heaps of books and loose records the librarians don't consider important enough to include in the main collection upstairs. Having something solid at my back helps ground me against the impending interrogation.

"There really were three people with Wendos," I say. "They were missing their hair, their eyes, their ears, their arms—at least one of them part of a leg. One of the women came from the brothel—that's where Wendos threatened he'd have Torstem take her back to. Her name was Fyrinth."

The tick of Stavros's jaw tells me he recognizes the name too. He's smart enough to put the pieces together like I did. "Torstem kept the children from the orphanage after they made their sacrifices and sent others to the temple in their place."

I nod. "Prostitutes' kids, I think."

A shudder runs through Alek's lean frame. "So they aren't having dedicates *die* in sacrifice… just asking them to give up everything they can *without* dying?"

"It seems that way." Acid sours the back of my mouth at the memory. "But they did die. Just not to stop Wendos. After I threw my knife at him, he couldn't concentrate quite as well through the pain. He wanted more power. So he told them to provide it, and they all threw themselves off the tower in a final sacrifice."

"That's why you called on your own power," Casimir says quietly.

I brace myself. "Yes. Whatever magic he and the other sorcerers were imposing on the daimon, it was working. I couldn't even move with the ones he had in the tower restraining me. I could hear buildings falling below. I didn't know how far behind you might still be. It was the only chance I had left."

Stavros adjusts his stance, his sword at his side but still in his grasp. "I think you'd better start from the beginning. Where you really came from. What you've done with your powers before. All of it. No feints, no lies. If you can manage that."

I can't stop myself from glaring at him for a second before I rein in my temper.

I have been lying to them all along, if mostly by omission. And somehow the truth might be the only thing that keeps them from murdering me right now.

It's not only them I've lied to.

Julita stirs in the back of my head. *I'd like to hear this too.*

I drag in a breath. "You've wondered about my upbringing. My parents run a printing press. Nothing fancy —they mostly handle posters and pamphlets—but I wouldn't be surprised if a few of the newer books up there came from their shop." I motion toward the main room of the library overhead.

Alek leans against the edge of the desk. "That's why you're such a reader."

I shrug. "It's a family calling."

Stavros's eyes have narrowed. "And they hid you—"

I shake my head adamantly to cut him off. "Not really. Not like that. I—"

My voice catches in my throat. I look down at my hands, which have twisted together in front of me.

I've never told anyone this before. Never talked about it out loud.

Dredging up the words sends the pain of the memory lancing through me even sharper than usual. "It was my parents and me and my little sister Linzi. When I was seven and Linzi was five, our mother got sick. One of the wasting fevers. It ate at her for two weeks until she could barely roll over in bed, she was so weak. She wouldn't eat, coughed up any water she tried to drink… The medics my father brought around couldn't do much, it was too far spread through her body."

Casimir's mouth slants at a sympathetic angle. "Even the palace medics can't combat certain types of illness."

"I know." I gird myself and hurtle onward. "One afternoon, my father was in the shop handling an order—he didn't like to leave my mother like that, but we needed money for the medics. Linzi and I were with her. And all at once, her breath got so thin and creaky, like she could hardly draw it, and her body went limp—I knew she was dying right that moment. And just as I realized that, I also realized I could save her."

I halt, my own lungs constricting with the images washing over me. Stavros motions with his sword for me to continue.

"I could just feel it." I press my hand to my sternum, where my magic fizzes faintly now. "The power welled up inside me, and I could already picture her happy and well again, so I reached out and let the magic flow into her. It worked. Her breath evened out—the color came back into her face. But—"

My throat closes up completely. My hand rises to touch Linzi's ribbon through the sleeve of my dress.

"But what?" Stavros demands.

I propel the words from my throat. They come out hoarse. "The energy I put into her had to come from somewhere. My sister... She collapsed. She was only three steps away, but by the time I reached her, she was already gone."

My head droops. All the anguish from that moment thirteen years past sweeps through me again, pricking at the backs of my eyes.

Oh, Ivy, Julita says softly.

I push onward. "My parents didn't know what happened. Not for sure. My mother was too far gone when I used my magic to realize, and my father wasn't there... I was so scared and confused, I just kept quiet. They said Linzi must have had the same sickness but it hit her all at once because she was so little. I don't know how much they believed that, though. They didn't know for sure what I was, but my mother definitely suspected."

Alek's jaw tightens. "You said she'd beat you."

"She took the belt to me anytime she got frustrated, which was a lot, and she didn't feel I deserved much in the way of food, and most of the time she couldn't stand to even look at me." I form a tense smile. "She said I brought a curse on the family. And her attitude rubbed off on Da. He loved Linzi so much, and losing her suddenly shook him hard."

I spent so many nights huddled in the corner trying to sleep, my stomach pinching from hunger and my back throbbing from the lashes of Ma's belt.

But none of it hurt more than the ache of loss and guilt that never left me.

Stavros's eyes are fierce with accusation beneath the fall of his dark red hair. "*You* knew what you were."

"I figured it out," I acknowledge. "We'd been to see a riven execution the year before, but I didn't totally understand… The next time one was caught, I heard some of the older kids in the neighborhood talking about the kind of magic they work, and I made the connection. But I knew my power wasn't a good thing even before then. It would tug at me, telling me other things I could do, but I just wanted it to go away."

The former general snorts. "At seven, you had the self-control not to give in to a magic that would provide you with anything you could possibly want?"

My back goes rigid. "I killed my little sister. That's what this fucking magic is to me. It can't give me Linzi back, and there's nothing I'd have wanted more. Nothing *terrified* me more than wondering what else I might lose."

Stavros's expression hardens, but it takes him a few seconds before he replies. "And you're trying to tell us that you never used it again until tonight?"

"No," I say, unable to stop an edge from creeping into my voice. "You haven't let me finish. Unless you'd like to tell the story for me, since you're apparently so sure of how it all happened?"

It might not be the wisest move to snap at the man most likely to send me to the gallows, but my nerves have frayed too much for me to care.

Stavros holds my gaze for several unsteady beats of my heart, with a tick of his head as he adjusts his vision. Then he waves his prosthetic hand. "By all means, continue."

I gather myself. "Even if I didn't use my magic again, what I'd already done with it was obviously horrible. So I didn't want the gods noticing me. The morning of my twelfth birthday, when my parents would have taken me to a temple out of obligation to have me dedicated, I ran away. I got by on the streets by stealing and begging and finding shelter wherever I could."

"And no magic."

I ignore Stavros's skeptical tone. "And no magic. Until a little more than a year later, a man cornered me in the abandoned house where I'd holed up and pushed me down and—"

My mouth presses flat before I can go on. "I'm sure you can imagine what he meant to do. I was too small and weak to fight him off, so I panicked, and I threw him off me with my magic. I wasn't *trying* to kill him, just stop him, but I wasn't exactly thinking clearly…"

That memory is doubly sickening. The revulsion of the man's hands pawing at my tattered clothes congeals with the horror of seeing his lifeless body, knowing I'd done it again.

At least you wouldn't have killed anyone to kill him, Julita says in an apparent attempt at optimism.

A choked laugh hitches out of me. "That wasn't even all of it. Ending his life made more life to balance it out, but I couldn't control that either. All these bugs came streaming out of the walls of the house—they swarmed the whole street, got into people's food, their gardens—people who barely had enough as it was…"

I hug myself. "I never wanted to feel like I had to use my power again. So from that point on, I did everything I could to prepare myself for whatever I might face the way I was living."

"You learned to fight," Casimir suggests.

"Yeah. I found a dueler who was willing to teach me in exchange for stealing various things. He trained me here and there for a few years. And I hoarded information on all kinds of subjects from listening in on conversations, reading every book I could get my hands on, studying and observing… It worked, well enough. Since that day when I was thirteen, I hadn't given in to the magic again until yesterday when I was dying. And not for lack of it badgering me, you can be sure."

Alek shifts forward on his perch against the desk. "You asked me about techniques for magical suppression, but you never brought it up again. That was actually for you, not stopping the scourge sorcerers, wasn't it?"

I shouldn't be surprised the scholar would be so quick to put those pieces together.

I meet his penetrating gaze with a half-smile. "I mean, I wouldn't have minded if it'd been useful against them too. But I did have an ulterior motive. My power has gotten… increasingly more insistent over the past year or so. I didn't want it distracting me. But I found the pipe fleece—it didn't do any good that I could see."

Julita hums to herself. *Ah. A lot of things make quite a bit more sense now.*

She doesn't sound all that upset with me. But then, she's been inside me all this time, aware of everything I'm doing. She knows I haven't been secretly going around carrying out malicious magic behind the men's backs.

With my confession over, I slump against the shelves. "So, what now? That's all of it."

"All of it?" Stavros guffaws. "Other than the fact that you could ruin more here with a snap of your fingers than the scourge sorcerers have managed to in months."

I scowl at him. "If I *wanted* to hurt any of you, don't you think I would have already? If it'd been up to me, I'd never have ended up in this situation to begin with. But I did, and I don't want someone else's toxic magic wrecking this city any more than I want my own to, so I stuck around and did what I could to help. Even though that meant being surrounded by the people most likely to have me hanged if I slipped up."

Stavros glowers back at me, but it's Casimir who speaks next, in a careful but gentle tone. "Why did you agree to take the risk, Ivy? You could have walked away, even with Julita's spirit in you."

I rub my forehead, abruptly embarrassed by the answer. "I did want to help. I wanted to protect the city. But it wasn't totally selfless. I—I had the stupid idea that maybe if I played a large enough role in stopping the scourge sorcerers, the godlen would forgive what I've done before. Maybe they could heal my soul so it wouldn't be riven anymore."

I can't quite bring myself to look at any of the men after my admission. Their silence seems to confirm how idiotic that idea was.

Riven sorcerers don't get forgiven. Our whole reason for existence is to remind the rest of society of humanity's past wrongdoings.

To show that limitless power is a curse more than a gift, and that no one should strive for it the way the scourge sorcerers did before.

Julita speaks up in a more spirited tone. *They* should *pardon you. It would only be fair, after everything you've done. You must have saved more lives than you hurt already!*

I don't know about that.

I wet my lips. "I'd like to keep helping. I know that by law you should consign me to execution—but I *have* kept my powers under control. You can see I'm nowhere near insane. I still want to stop the scourge sorcerers. Whatever happens after… I'll be happier knowing I did one really good thing no matter how my life ends."

"Ivy," Casimir says, with a rasp that makes me glance up. The compassion that made me fall for him gleams in his eyes before he looks at Stavros. "I think we should give her that chance. She hasn't done anything wrong the whole time she's been here."

Stavros glowers at both of us. "As far as we know."

I let out a huff of breath. "If you still don't believe *me*, you could check with Julita. She's been along for the ride every moment."

Stavros raises his eyebrows. "And how exactly am I supposed to ask her when she only talks through you?"

I think back to the first time I told them about Julita's ghost. "Ask a question only she could answer, about something you're sure she wouldn't have randomly told me about before. If she thinks I'm lying to you and doesn't want you to trust me, she won't tell me what to say. Simple enough."

Yes, Julita says. *Of course I'll speak for you.*

The former general pauses, his eyes going distant as he contemplates his test. Then he motions to me. "At the last ball—the last one she was alive for—what did she spill on herself?"

Julita's presence shifts restlessly. *Spill? I didn't spill anything on— Oh.*

I avert my gaze so the men won't think I'm talking to them. "Oh *what*?"

Her tone turns abashed. *It wasn't exactly "spilling." I was trying to be stealthy and sneak closer to Wendos to overhear what he said to the people around him. I was just slipping past the refreshments table when someone backed up right into me. I lost my balance and dunked my elbow in a bowl of crackleberry pudding.* She pauses. *I didn't realize Stavros even noticed.*

"Well?" Stavros says.

I focus back on him. "She says she didn't spill anything—someone bumped into her and her elbow landed in crackleberry pudding."

His mouth flattens, as if he's not happy that I've answered right. Was he trying to trip me up with his phrasing, thinking of another spill she might have mentioned already that I'd try to con him with?

Let him be disappointed. I proved my point.

"Kosmel himself gave her a vote of confidence," Alek points out. There's no hint of how he might feel about that fact in his flat voice. "We all saw it. And she has been a lot of help. It's not as if she poses any danger to the rest of the school right now."

Stavros scoffs. "The riven are *always* dangerous." But then he sighs and rocks on his heels with a resigned expression. "How exactly do you propose you're going to help next?"

Is he seriously giving me the chance?

I lift my head, trying to look more confident than I feel. "We know that Ster. Torstem is playing a major role in orchestrating the conspiracy. He has an inner circle of associates who are conducting scourge sorcery with him. The only campus organization he leads that Wendos was involved in is the entomology club—I even heard Wendos using bug talk as a cover to discuss the daimon attack at the ball. At least a few of the other members must be part of the conspiracy. We should focus on them."

"They're not going to admit to conspiring with illicit magic if you simply ask."

Alek appears to perk up. "I can dig into the records and come up with a list of current members for Ivy to spy on. They've got to slip up somewhere."

Stavros still doesn't look convinced. "They managed to conceal their activities so well that it's taken us all this time to be sure of *anyone* who's involved, even with Julita keeping a close eye on Wendos."

An idea sparks in my head, bringing a hint of a smile to my lips. "Maybe I need to do more to draw them out, then. I'm new at the college—no one will be totally sure of my goals and beliefs yet. I heard how Wendos talked. I can drop a few comments along similar lines near the bug club members and see how they react. Thinking a sympathetic party is around might loosen their tongues."

Alek pauses. "Won't they know to be wary of you? If Wendos realized that Julita suspected him, and you've told people you were friends with her…"

I shake my head. "Wendos bragged to me about how he took care of Julita all by himself without the other conspirators needing to know. I think he didn't want to reveal that his childhood experiments might be what exposed the rest of them. If he kept quiet about her, he wouldn't have told them about me either. And his accomplices who saw me in the tower are dead."

"We've been careful to keep our investigations secret," Casimir says. "Barely any of the king's soldiers saw Ivy even tonight. It sounds like a reasonable plan to me. And Julita would have ideas about how Ivy should behave. She must have heard plenty of scourge sorcerer attitude from her brother. If she's willing to draw on that."

I'm not going to abandon the cause, Julita says tartly. *You're the one taking the real risk.*

"She's contributed every way she can since I got here." I hesitate, realizing I owe her more than that. "And you should know—what I said here yesterday, when I was upset... It wasn't a lie, but it wasn't the whole truth. I think she's made herself sound more callous than she actually felt at the time, trying to distance herself from everything she's lost to deal with... with having lost it. I know you all mattered to her as more than just a means to an end. She gets worried when you're in danger. She appreciated how you stood by her. I'm sorry I made it sound as if she didn't."

Ivy, Julita murmurs. *You didn't need to—you had every right to say what you did. My mistakes are mine.*

Casimir offers me a soft smile. "You *were* upset. And you weren't the only one." He aims a pointed look at his companions.

Alek shuffles his feet. "Thank you. It's good to know that."

Stavros doesn't give any sign of being affected either way, his chiseled features hard as ever. "Then we've made our decision, and there's nothing more we can do tonight. Let's get some rest before we resume our investigations. But first —" He jerks his sword toward me. "Give Casimir back his locket."

Right. They wouldn't want to leave me with the ability to summon the rest of them on a whim.

I draw out the locket that can send a magical signal to those the rest of them carry and hand it over as swiftly as I can. I don't want the brush of Casimir's skin to dredge up my memories of the much greater intimacies we've shared.

How queasy does it make him to remember what he did with a woman who's really a monster?

The courtesan's fingers close around the locket, and he shoots Stavros another firm look. "We should get another one made for Ivy. If she's going to be associating more with the scourge sorcerers, she might need help quickly."

Stavros lets out a hum that sounds more like a growl. "We'll see."

The thought of our whole group stirs up another question. "What are we going to tell Benedikt?"

Another silence falls over the room. The men exchange a glance.

Casimir exhales softly. "I don't like keeping secrets from him when we've had a policy of sharing everything we discover. But he wasn't there—he didn't see any of it… I'm not sure he'd approach the situation with the proper understanding."

"He might think Ivy's bewitched us and report her to the king," Alek says with a wince.

After seeing how eagerly Benedikt sought his half-uncle's acknowledgment, the same worry winds around my gut. "He might."

I don't say how I feel about that possibility, but it shouldn't be difficult to guess. I like Benedikt, as much as I've gotten to know him in the past few weeks, but I can't say I'd gamble my life on his good will.

Julita appears to share our apprehension. *Benny can be a little… capricious. I don't know how he'd react.*

Casimir turns to Stavros. "The information doesn't really have anything to do with the investigation. Not having it won't stop him from pitching in as much as usual. It's not as if Ivy's ever likely to be around him without at least one of us there too."

I can't tell how much that's his own justification and how

much it's what he thinks Stavros would respond best to, but the former general makes a brief gesture of acceptance. "Fine. Let's not make this a bigger mess than it already is. That decision can be re-evaluated at a later date."

His last words come with a ring of finality. He picks the royal sword off the desk and slings the belt with its sheath over his shoulder.

The thought of him escorting me back to his quarters, radiating skeptical hostility the whole way, makes my skin crawl. I can't help thinking of the other unknown scourge sorcerers who were out there in the city tonight—the ones Wendos was trying to combine his magic with.

And the sooner I prove just how committed I am to this mission, the better.

"There is something else we can do tonight," I say. "Something I can do, anyway. Ster. Torstem and the other conspirators will need to regroup. They're still in the city… If they're going to discuss how their plans fell apart and their next moves, they'll want to be somewhere familiar."

Stavros frowns. "And you think you know where that is?"

I glance around at all of the men. "Does anyone know what room the bug club meets in?"

FOUR

Ivy

Even after Alek has unfurled a blueprint scroll and pointed out the entomology club's dedicated room on the third floor of the Quadring, Stavros keeps scowling.

"And how exactly are you planning to get in?" he asks me in an acidic tone. "With your magic?"

I bristle before I can catch my reaction. "No. I'm a thief, as you so enjoy reminding me. There are plenty of non-magical methods of breaking and entering. If anyone's there, I'll see what I can overhear. If they're not, I'll search for evidence. It's worth a shot."

It's better than waiting around to see if he'll decide to send me to the hangman after all. And I can hope that the more he sees me working toward the same cause he believes in, the less murderously inclined he'll be.

Casimir speaks up in his usual mild way. "If we're going to let Ivy stay a part of our investigations, we have to *really* let her be a part. In every way she can."

Alek finishes re-rolling the blueprint and hesitates for a second before adding his own understated vote of support. "She's never hurt anyone at the school before."

Stavros considers both of them, his jaw working. He knows I have hurt one person here—but only in self-defense. The rest of their points he can't argue at all.

"Fine," he bites out, pinning me with his gaze. "You see what you can make of the bug club's headquarters, and then you come straight back to my quarters. If I get the slightest hint that you're deceiving us about anything…"

He doesn't need to finish that sentence.

I nod in acknowledgment, and he moves toward the wall that holds the secret passage. As Stavros steps into the shadows, Alek ducks through the doorway that leads to the rest of the archives.

Casimir aims a soft smile at me. "We'll work this out."

I'm sure we will. I'm just not yet convinced it won't be worked out with a noose around my neck.

The courtesan vanishes after Stavros, and then I'm alone. I should give the men at least a couple of minutes to leave the area around the library before I come waltzing out too.

Well, I'm alone other than my uninvited ghostly friend.

Thank you, Julita says. *For what you said about me… You really didn't need to do that.*

I shrug. "I felt like I did. It was true."

She doesn't confirm or deny that point.

In her silence, I realize there's a little more I should probably say to her. I flop into one of the chairs near the desk. "Are you sure that *you're* okay working with me? Hanging out in the closest possible proximity to a riven soul? Now that you know."

Julita guffaws. *Ivy, I have been with you through everything. If more of the souls around here were like you, we'd have a much smaller mess on our hands. I don't know what it'll mean for you in the future, whether the power will start to control you, but right now, I'm not worried.*

More relief than I expected washes over me. I start to push myself upright, but Julita speaks again.

Are you sure you want me *hanging on?*

I knit my brow. "As opposed to…?"

You've already been stuck with me for longer than either of us expected. I know it can't be easy having your head invaded. I could try to leave, to pass on, however exactly that works.

I didn't ask to have another woman's soul lodged inside me. I've wished my life were entirely my own again more times than I can count.

But hearing her extend the offer makes my heart lurch.

It'd be like asking her to kill herself. No one knows exactly what happens when your soul moves beyond this plane of existence into the embrace of the gods—how much you'll remember, how much you'll be aware of.

The thought of Julita's determined spirit fading away just feels… wrong.

I keep my tone dry. "You dragged me into this mess. You can't leave me to fend for myself now. And Alek's right—your knowledge of how your brother and Wendos talked and acted should come in handy."

Julita sounds a little relieved herself. *Well, if you put it that way… I would like to see this through, as much as I can.*

"Then it's settled."

I peel myself off the chair and touch the books in the right pattern to re-open the secret passage. In the stillness of the night, I pad quietly through the darkened halls.

Staying far beyond the reach of the lanterns around the outside of the Domi and out of sight of the workers in the distant corner, I cross the inner courtyard swiftly and slink into the Quadring.

The square ring of a building that surrounds the Domi

feels even more vacant. No one's likely to venture over here until classes start up again in the morning.

No one other than, I can hope, at least a couple of disgruntled scourge sorcerers.

Holding the image of the blueprint in my mind, I dart up the stairs to the third floor and ease down the hallway to the right spot. Only the faintest moonlight seeps through a broad window at the far end of the hall.

I stop by the door I'm sure is the right one. Leaning my head close to the tiny gap between the door and the frame, I strain my ears.

No sound reaches me. But a quiver of magical energy wriggles through my nerves.

I pull back with a shudder.

What's the matter? Julita asks.

I answer in a murmur. "There's some kind of spell cast on the doorway."

Here in the teaching building, where hundreds of students might be coming and going from any given room during the course of a day, the college administration hasn't bothered with the fancy magical locks that guard the dorms and the staff quarters. This one merely has a regular keyhole below the knob. But someone's added an extra layer of protection.

Julita gives an ominous hum. *Ster. Torstem must have wanted to keep the club's space especially secure.*

"I guess that makes sense." No one who isn't riven would even notice the magical precaution if they weren't specifically looking for it. My broken soul automatically resonates with supernatural energy.

My power twitches in my chest. It could dissolve this spell in the blink of an eye. It could open the door as smooth as butter.

I did manage to take down Wendos without causing any unwanted destruction...

The second the thoughts pass through my head, I could slap myself. For fuck's sake, I told the men that I had my magic under control just minutes ago.

I deserve the noose if I'd make that promise a lie the first time I face a tiny bit of trouble.

I only made it through the confrontation in the tower because Kosmel answered my desperate call. My current problem hardly qualifies as desperate.

The moment I let down my guard with my magic, it'll screw me over. I can *never* trust its nagging call.

With guilt pooling in my stomach, I step back. I can't get access to the room by picking the lock without setting off some kind of alarm.

But the doorway won't be the only access point.

I pad down the hall to the neighboring room. That door gives off no impression of magic.

With a faint smile, I retrieve my one remaining knife from the sheath at my thigh.

The blade is thin enough that I can fit it into most keyholes, including this one. I wiggle it until I feel the right point of tension, and then I twist—and the lock clicks over.

I don't know what the room on the other side is used for, but whatever that is, it involves a lot of clothes. Racks of gowns, tunics, and jackets line the walls amid full-length mirrors. The odor of heavy perfume hangs in the air.

I hustle over to the window and ease open the hinged lower pane. The cool night air brings a welcome clarity.

The bug club's window awaits farther down the wall. A narrow ridge, about as wide as one of my feet, runs along the stone wall just below the window ledge.

That's all I need.

Julita lets out a soft laugh of approval as she must

recognize my plan, but she doesn't speak. Maybe wanting to avoid distracting me from this precarious maneuver.

Thankfully, no tremors are shaking the campus like they were this afternoon. The daimon the scourge sorcerers riled up around the college have gone quiet just like they did in the temple's tower.

I peer farther across the outer courtyard. A few distant figures shift in their guard posts atop the college wall. Lanterns cast a muted glow on the grass of the courtyard, but none close enough to highlight my perch.

I tug my dark brown cloak closer around me and knot the loose corners at the base in front of my ankles to ensure it covers my pale green dress. If all goes well, I'll blend into the shadows.

After one last scan of the courtyard, I clamber out the window. My toes jar against the ridge, which barely holds them and the balls of my feet inside my boots.

It's fine. I've made more difficult scrambles before.

I don't want to be visible on the wall for any longer than necessary. Sliding my hands along the gritty blocks, I glide my feet after them.

One sideways step, two, three. I lean so close to the building, the rough stone bumps my cheek.

I don't let myself think about what would happen if I tipped just a tiny bit backward and lost my balance.

My extended fingers bump the window frame. With a flash of gratitude, I feel along the glass for the movable pane and pop it open.

With one more furtive scramble, I'm swinging over the window ledge into the dark room.

All at once, I find myself missing the cloying perfume I left behind. The entomology club's headquarters holds a mossy scent that isn't entirely off-putting, but woven into it are hints of acrid smoke and an unpleasant tang I can't place at all.

Ugh, Julita says in apparent agreement.

At a rustle from my right, I freeze in place. But as my eyes adjust to the room, I realize I have nothing to fear from its current inhabitants.

Which are, naturally, bugs.

The entomology club can justify its dedicated room with the rows of tanks and jars that seem to cover every piece of furniture in the space. Beetles clamber over bits of bark and twigs; winged creatures flit along glass walls; jointed worms wriggle through murky water.

"Ugh," I mutter, echoing Julita's reaction.

I can think of few places it'd be creepier to sneak around in the darkness. Fortunately, I have no need to lurk in any of those places.

I do, however, have a job to do here.

Aiming to be methodical, I pick a direction and begin a careful circuit of the room. As I weave between the stands and shelving units, I scan every available surface for anything that might hint at intentions beyond the buggy.

I duck low to check under the containers I can lift, which was how I found the vague evidence Wendos left behind in his dorm bedroom. I even sweep my fingers under any furniture with a raised bottom, bracing in case I touch something unnerving.

All I find are labels with the names of bugs and instructions for things like feeding. A few scraps that look like pages from school reports that were tossed aside as unsuitable. Nothing that so much as hints at a conspiracy.

At the far end of the room, I determine that not quite every surface is covered in insect enclosures. A calendar hangs on the wall, with a couple of days marked off that I commit to memory.

Beneath the calendar stands a broad desk that's stacked with books, writing supplies, and a few loose papers, but no bugs.

The drawers on the desk hold tons more papers. I sink into the leather chair by the wall and go through them one by one.

Squinting in the dimness, I can't make out every word. But all the words I can make out seem to have to do with bugs: supplies and environments and behavioral studies.

If there's any hidden meaning to the records, I can't make it out. And I don't want to risk bringing any of these papers with me when I'm not sure they'll help our investigation.

It wouldn't do to tip Torstem off that we're on to him and his club.

I've stared at enough pages that my head is starting to ache when something taps against the door.

My pulse stutters. I nudge the drawer closed and dive under the desk just as the lock rasps over.

Where I'm huddled in the thickest shadows, I can't see anything of the people who enter. But multiple sets of footsteps scrape across the floor.

The first voice to speak, hushed even in the privacy of this space, I recognize as Ster. Torstem's. "We'll regroup. We took a gamble and it failed. There are plenty of other prizes to try for."

It definitely doesn't sound like he's just talking about rare insect specimens. I scoot a little closer beneath the desk, my heart thumping with both anxiety and eagerness.

A woman speaks next, no one I can identify just by her speech. "Do you know exactly what went wrong?"

"We lost some of the bugs, and there weren't enough left for our purpose. I think we'll get farther with the other enclosures. It's time to focus on more refined tactics."

I frown. I'm guessing that by "bugs" he means the

daimon, speaking in code to be safe. But what other enclosures? What would that word stand for in terms of their real plans?

A third figure, a younger man I also don't know, interjects with a short chuckle. "That seems like another kind of gamble."

Torstem makes a dismissive sound. "They allow for easier control. We've built up quite a supply already, and I've already sent someone on to speed up construction."

Well, that definitely doesn't sound good, Julita remarks with a sense of a grimace.

No, it does not.

"We'll need more people to exert that control, won't we?" the younger man goes on. "With Wendos—"

Torstem cuts him off with a chiding sound. Obviously the law professor is awfully careful about what he says even in here.

"Our club could always use more members with the right perspective," he says in a measured voice. "If you notice any likely candidates with appropriate interests, pass their names on to me."

There's a warble of fabric as he retrieves something. He must hand it to the woman, because she thanks him. Then they head back out into the hall.

With the click of the door shutting, I slump against the underside of the desk. My head is spinning.

The scourge sorcerers have some new plan—which may or may not involve the daimon, but if it does, it's using different tactics from before.

I don't really want to know how awful their new efforts are going to end up being.

But our investigations won't be finished until I do. And Ster. Torstem is looking to recruit even more students into his sick cabal...

I pause, lingering on that discovery. An uneasy flutter passes through my chest, solidifying into a ball of resolve in my gut.

That might be our answer right there.

As I slip back through the neighboring window and make my way to the Domi, I keep turning the idea over in my head. With each prod and poke, my certainty grows.

I ease open the door to Stavros's quarters to find him sitting at his desk, watching me with an expression like he's considering ramming a sword through my middle.

As the door swings shut behind me, he stands up. "Good. You kept your word once."

I swallow down the ache at the memory of past conversations we had in this room, when he looked at me like more than a criminal. "I found out something we can use. Something that could get us everything we need to take them all down."

The former general's eyebrows arch despite himself. "And what's that?"

My lips form a crooked smile. "I'm not just going to make friendly with a few students. I need to convince Ster. Torstem to recruit me into his conspiracy."

FIVE

Ivy

"And that," Stavros says from his lectern at the front of the classroom, "is why you should always check your boots before shoving your feet in them."

He offers a wry grin to his students as laughter ripples through the class. I set the quills I just collected in the storage case and resist the urge to fidget.

Seeing him banter with his pupils in his usual confident way only drives home how much his demeanor has changed with me. In the last day and a half, I've barely gotten more than grunts and brusque remarks—when he bothers to acknowledge my presence at all.

Of course, the alternative would be meeting the hangman, so I can't really complain.

The ringing of the palace bell—the smaller substitute while a proper new one is being constructed to replace the one the daimon broke—marks the turn of the hour and the end of the Field Strategy lecture. As the students get to their

feet, Stavros catches my eye. His expression tenses just slightly, but he gives me a small nod.

He informed me of the afternoon's schedule—curtly and coldly—this morning. He's off to check with the king's people about their progress in their own investigations, and I'm speaking with Alek to get the low-down on the bug club before our usual larger meeting.

It took about a half hour of arguing the other night before Stavros conceded that my plan to infiltrate the conspiracy is a good one. For all the same reasons I could have cajoled the bug club members into thinking I might be a kindred soul, I'm the only one of us who's unknown enough at the school that Ster. Torstem might believe I'd go all in on the scourge sorcery thing.

He's telling his followers to watch for ideal candidates. So I need to find out whose attention I should be catching.

I follow the stream of students into the hall. Their chatter is more subdued than usual, many gazes darting nervously at a rasp from down the hall that turns out to merely be another professor adjusting the position of his desk.

The daimon haven't stirred up any more trouble since my confrontation with Wendos. When I step out into the early afternoon light in the inner courtyard, the corner of the Quadring I watched fall to pieces two days ago looks startlingly solid. You'd almost think it never fell.

But we all know it did. And most of the students don't even understand why.

I assume everyone else is somewhat comforted by the greater number of soldiers now patrolling the campus, sometimes with a cleric in tow. The sight of the blue uniforms makes my skin crawl.

No one's come for me yet. No one's realized I lied about what happened in the All-Giver's tower.

I'm safe as long as the three men who do know my secret

keep believing they're better off with the riven monster alive than dead.

Entering the Domi, I smooth my hands down my skirt. It's hard to take any pleasure in the feel of the turquoise silk, even though I've come to think of this as my favorite gown. Wearing it now feels even more like a charade than when I first laced it up.

But it's perfectly designed for my needs, thanks to Casimir's thoughtfulness. The layers of fabric that rustle around my legs overlap to conceal slits at the sides of my thighs, allowing quick access to the knives strapped over the divided underskirt beneath.

I left my favorite knife behind in the tower. I'm not even sure where it ended up after Wendos yanked it out of his shoulder. Stavros didn't give me a chance to poke around the scene of my crime.

Students are coming and going from the main library entrance with a couple of soldiers watching over them. I stride by with the best haughty noble air I can summon, as if my nerves aren't jangling with apprehension.

A couple with their arms twined hustles past me from the corridor of tapestries, their faces flushed in a way that makes me suspect they were using the quiet passage for a hasty tryst. As long as they're not in my way, I'm not going to judge.

When I'm sure no one's in sight, I slip down the conjured stairs into the archive room.

I'm not at all surprised to find Alek already sitting at the desk, scrawling on a piece of paper with a quill. The scholar is ever dedicated to his work—whether his studies or our investigations together.

He glances up, and his stance tenses for an instant at my arrival. Then he forces a quick smile. "I've made a lot of progress with the entomology club. You should be well-informed about Ster. Torstem's people when we're done here."

"Perfect." I walk over, pretending I haven't noticed his discomfort at my presence. But when I grasp the back of one of the chairs to pull it over beside him, his posture stiffens again.

My fingers curl around the carved wood as a thread of loss coils around my stomach. Just days ago, Alek was grinning through our schemes together and gathering me in his arms when he thought I was wounded.

I swallow thickly. "If you'd feel better about it, I can sit on the other side of the desk. Keep my distance."

Julita lets out a huff. *He'd better not be an ass about it. Stavros is bad enough.*

Alek blinks at me. His mask conceals most of his reaction, but his mouth slants as if he's chagrined. "I—no, it's fine. It'll be easier for us to go over the information together if I'm not constantly having to flip the pages around."

I don't move. "You don't have to act as if you're okay with… with me. I can understand why you'd feel uneasy."

It's the first time we've been alone together since he found out what I am. Alek spoke up for including me because he believes at least one of the godlen approves and because I've been useful, but that doesn't mean he loves the idea of having a riven sorcerer hanging around.

I'm still alive, I remind myself. I have that. Just that is more than I should have hoped for.

Alek looks at the papers in front of him and then at me again. "You said you haven't used any magic in years—not until Esmae attacked you," he says abruptly. "Are you sure nothing ever slipped through, maybe without you even meaning it to?"

Is he worried I worked my riven power on him in some way?

I smile awkwardly and sink into the chair even though it's still a couple of paces from the desk. "I've had a lot of practice at keeping my power under control. I swear to you, no matter how much it hurt, I kept my grip on it."

I can tell Alek's eyebrows have drawn together just above the holes in his mask. "It hurt, stopping yourself from using it?"

A startled laugh spills from my lips before I can catch it. He hasn't put *those* pieces together.

"Yes, it hurt," I say. "Starting about a year ago, I started feeling as if the magic was lashing out at me from the inside when I refused it. More and more, the more I resisted. You're the one who found me when I collapsed in the library—you saw how I was after King Konram's visit to the college. I wouldn't have put myself through that agony only to let a little sorcery slip out some other time."

Oh. I always wondered— Julita shudders. *Gods above, Ivy, that power of yours really is a monster. It was vicious even to you.*

I suppress a wince at the thought of all the times I lied to her about the pain I was in.

Alek's mouth has dropped open, but it's a moment before he manages to speak. "That—that wasn't an attack from Anya or anyone else? That was your own magic hurting you?"

I guess I didn't make that aspect clear with my explanation before.

I find myself yanking my gaze away from the shock in his bright brown eyes. "Yeah. The power acts up worse when I'm in danger but shut it down anyway. And I've felt more in danger here than I did in my old life. In the library—I was scared of the guard, that he'd realize what I am. And then having the king right in front of me... I saw him just a few weeks ago talking about how wonderful it was that so many riven had been executed."

"And your magic thought you should strike out at him first?"

I shrug. "It thought I should do *something*. Shove them away, run for cover, disguise myself—anything to stop them from seeing me at all, from having any chance of arresting me."

"But you didn't. So your magic—" Alek's voice roughens. "Ivy, you were coughing up blood. It was literally tearing into you."

I aim a tight smile at him. "I know. But that was better than letting it hurt someone else."

For a few seconds, he simply stares at me. Then he scoots forward on his chair so he can reach my hand where it's clenched on my knee.

Alek's slim fingers slide around my own with a reassuring squeeze. The tenderness of the gesture makes my breath catch.

"I always knew you were strong," he says quietly. "But you're so much stronger than I even saw. I'm sorry I wasn't giving you credit for that."

My innards have completely tangled. "You didn't know. I'm sorry I lied to you about it, though I imagine you can see why. And I'm sure you had plenty of your own concerns to focus on."

Alek lets out a wry scoffing sound. "I once thought I had it hard being a devoted scholar in a family of weapons mongers and soldiers. I'd take all the derision and disappointment ten times over before trading it for what you've had to deal with your whole life."

I cock my head. "You said you were the son of a merchant."

"A merchant whose specialty was all things warfare, including when it came to his two other children. The idea of someone preferring to spend their time with books rather than swords was absolutely ridiculous to all of them."

My next smile comes a little easier. "Well, I'm glad you pursued your passion anyway—that you're here to help us tackle the scourge sorcerers. And fill me in on all the things I need to know. And—thank you for keeping my secret. I know it's a lot to ask."

Something shifts in Alek's penetrating gaze that I don't know how to read. "It isn't. It shouldn't have been at all." His grip on my hand tightens. "Is it still hurting you—your magic?"

I think of the other night when Stavros had his sword pointed at me. "Nowhere near as badly as before. I think the fact that I released it in the tower has mollified it for the moment."

"If it gets serious again, you have to tell us. *Before* you get to the point where you're writhing in agony. All right?"

Yes, Julita pipes up. *Listen to Alek. He always knows what he's talking about.*

I don't see that there's anything we could do to fix the problem, but if anyone could figure it out, I suppose it's Alek. And it doesn't cost me anything to agree. "All right."

He hesitates as if he might say something more. Then he gives himself a little shake and turns back to the desk, his hand slipping from mine with a beckoning gesture. "Come right over. We should get through all of this material before the others show up."

As I tug my chair next to his, Alek fans out a sheaf of papers. "I dug up everything I could on the entomology club's membership and activities. There are currently sixteen active members by the most recent record. It seems that for their off-campus excursions, they split up the group. So as not to be too intrusive on the wildlife, supposedly. Half of the members go sometimes, the other half the rest of the time."

Julita hums. *I'd be keeping an eye on whoever Wendos was associating with.*

I was just thinking the same thing. I motion to the papers. "Do we know who was in the group that Wendos was usually traveling with?"

Alek's mouth curves with a smile that's a little sly. "I was able to piece together a pretty good idea. These are the seven members who appear to have always gone along on the excursions he was a part of. There are a couple of others who bounced back and forth between groups, but I'm guessing they're not quite as involved."

I expect a series of names with a few notes jotted for each. Instead, the first page he shows me has a sketch at the top. Simple, sparing in detail, but keenly drawn enough that I'm sure I've seen that man in the dining hall a few times.

Alek's smile turns sheepish. "I thought it'd help if you had a visual so you can recognize them on sight. As much as my limited skill can allow that."

My gaze jerks back to him. "You drew this? It's very good."

He chuckles awkwardly. "I mean, no one's going to frame it."

"No, but it does what it's meant to do. You captured the shape of his features accurately." I risk extending a teasing bump of my elbow. "You didn't tell me you were an artist."

Alek holds up his hands. "I'm really not. I just—I do try to get down the information I want to convey as clearly as possible. And sometimes a quick sketch can accomplish that better than any number of words could. I've mostly created diagrams and the like."

Whatever amount of experience he has, he obviously has

an eye for lines and shading. The scholar has a lot of surprises up his sleeve.

"Well, it *is* good, and much appreciated," I insist.

Alek walks me through each of our main suspects—names, areas of study, godlen they dedicated to, gift if he was able to determine one, classes, clubs, and known habits. Not all of the faces in his sketches are familiar, but there's a guy who's been in some of Stavros's classes, a woman I think I noticed when I went on a hunt with some leadership division students, and two others I have a vague sense that I've seen but can't place.

I commit the images and facts to my memory as quickly as I can. Carrying Alek's carefully constructed profiles around with me is too risky.

It's amazing that he managed to compile all this information so quickly.

After going over the last of them, I brush my hands together. "All right. I'm prepared to put on a show of being morally degenerate. It shouldn't be too hard—Stavros thought I was right from the start."

Alek brings his hand to his mouth to cover a snort. As he eases the pages back into a canvas wrapper, his expression turns more serious. "I'm glad I could contribute something useful. We know how far these brutes are willing to go… I wish you didn't have to take on all the risk of getting their attention. If it would work for me to put myself out there—"

A different sort of ache passes through my chest. He really means what he's saying, even now.

He doesn't know even half the risk I'm planning to take on yet.

I touch his shoulder to stop him, doing my best to tamp down on the tingle of warmth at our closeness. "It wouldn't work. It makes much more sense for me to shoulder this challenge than it would for any of the rest of you—and I'm okay with that."

And you'll hardly be alone in it, Julita puts in.

I glance back at the profiles. "What about the former bug club members who'll have graduated? We know Torstem's been roping in orphans for a while."

Alek's gaze goes distant with thought. "I did check the older membership records. The trouble is, it's impossible to know which graduates were just bug enthusiasts. I'm following some threads to check for suspicious behavior after they left the college. The graduates I've looked at from particularly prominent families are still under one or both parents' shadows, though, so they're not in a position to enact new policies or anything like that yet."

I give a rough laugh. "That's a little good news. Of course, even if Ster. Torstem only started funding the orphanage fifteen years ago, I guess we don't know whether he already had allies then or if that was the start of the conspiracy."

"I think we can reasonably hope it doesn't go much farther back than that. They would have needed sacrificial accomplices to practice any kind of scourge sorcery." The scholar snaps his fingers. "But that reminds me! I also thought I should look into Torstem's gift, so you can be prepared if he tried to use it on you."

I should have thought of that myself. "Is it in the school records?"

Alek grins. "No, but he conducted trials before he came on as a law professor. The courts require all staff to disclose their gifts, and I was able to get access to those files. He's dedicated to Creaden, unsurprisingly, and his gift on record is the ability to quell anger. Possibly other agitated emotions as well, given the flexibility most gifts have."

The ability to quell agitated emotions. My jaw clenches.

"How very convenient for persuading kids to be at peace with the idea of carving themselves up for his use."

Alek's smile falters. "Yes, I think it's likely he applied his gift for that purpose."

"All the more reason we need to bring that asshole down before he ropes in any more orphans."

"I'll keep digging up all the information I can. And like I said, if there's anything specific you'd want me to look into, don't hesitate to tell me."

The offer stirs up the uncomfortable questions that've lingered in my head since the night in the tower.

I pause and then prod myself to speak. "I have actually been wondering—and if anyone would have come across information on this, I'd wager it'd be you... Have you read any accounts of the gods outright talking to people before? It wasn't something I thought generally happened."

Even in the fables I've read, the godlen make their desires known with glowing symbols and meaningful dreams. Not so much direct conversation.

If Kosmel ever decides to get chatty again, it'd be kind of nice to know what that means for me.

"Oh! Of course you'd be interested in that subject." Alek taps his mouth, his gaze going distant with thought. "It's certainly never happened to me or anyone I've spoken to. Although I suppose Estera probably wouldn't be inclined to say much to someone who didn't even offer a sacrifice anyway." His hand rises to his chest where his godlen brand lies beneath his tunic.

I can't hold back a guffaw. "I didn't even dedicate myself."

Alek shoots me a crooked grin. "Well, Kosmel is known for taking on difficult causes. I've definitely come across written accounts from clerics of their 'interactions' with the gods in various ways... I think I can find a couple of old journals that could give you some insight, and I'll do more research in that area after today."

He motions for me to follow him into the larger archive room next door. After several minutes of stalking along the cluttered shelves, he's handed over two small leather-bound books to me, one stained with dribbles of wax, the other with splotches that give off a sour smell that makes me think they're wine.

"Those should make a good start," Alek says.

I laugh as I tuck the books under my arm. "You really do know how to find out everything about everything, huh? We're lucky we have you on our side."

The scholar ducks his head with a hint of awkwardness at the praise. "I'm not sure just how helpful they'll be. One thing I've seen from reading anything to do with theology is there are all kinds of contradictory theories and observations... I'm not sure it's something we mortals can fully pin down."

"Even partly pinning it down would be a relief. Thank you."

We return to the smaller meeting room to find Benedikt lounging at the desk with his feet propped up on its edge. At our arrival, he tilts his head at a jaunty angle. "The both of you are down here already getting to work. What are you up to now?"

I don't know how to begin telling him about my new interest in the divine without revealing more than I'd like to. "Alek was just filling me in on the key members of the bug club."

"Ah, we're going to start poking at them like the bugs they are, hmm?"

Benedikt chuckles at his own joke, and it occurs to me that no one has filled him in on even the initial plans we made without him two nights ago.

"I, ah—Stavros and I decided that I should try to make myself look like an appealing new recruit to the scourge sorcerers," I say. "It'll be easier if I know whose notice I'm trying to catch."

Alek's head jerks toward me at the news.

One of Benedikt's eyebrows lifts. "You and Stavros decided, and Alek already knew to pull the information together?"

"I didn't know," Alek says, a little tightly, his gaze still fixed on me. "Not the recruiting part anyway. It was obvious we'd want to focus on the people most closely associated with both Ster. Torstem and Wendos. The medics still haven't been able to draw Wendos out of his coma. It seemed urgent that we get started."

"Yes. Urgent." Benedikt spins a quill he's picked up between his fingers. Can he tell that we're leaving out part of the story? "Those accomplices of his really messed him up good with their final sacrifice."

Or rather, I did. I don't know what my magic did to Wendos that the medics haven't been able to heal.

Before the moment can become truly strained, Casimir arrives through the conjured passage. He bobs his head in greeting to all of us, his gaze lingering on me with one of his gentle smiles. "Good to see you. Have you been getting on all right, Ivy?"

His concern sets off a flutter of warmth in me that I have no right to feel. I make myself smile back. "I always do."

Benedikt sits up straighter, his gaze darting between us. "Why wouldn't Ivy be all right? Has that bitch Anya been after her again?"

My stomach flips over. "No, no, I'm totally fine."

Casimir is better than me at smoothing things over. "I only thought she might be a little out of sorts after everything she went through the other night."

Then the wall wavers again, and I'm unexpectedly relieved to see Stavros's red-topped head ducking from the secret passage. Now the meeting can get going without any more questions I'd rather not try to answer.

As the former general glances around at us, he holds up a leather sack. "King Konram was good to his word. We'll have a new meeting place after today, and the means to enter it directly from wherever we happen to be."

A much more understandable sense of relief fills me. "That's great."

Stavros fixes me with a glower, his voice coming out in the sardonic drawl I like least. "I should have said, most of us will have the means. I'll be holding on to yours, Thief."

Benedikt waves his hand as if to redirect Stavros to what he believes is a more important subject. "What's all this about Ivy getting herself recruited by the scourge sorcerers?"

Casimir's eyes widen. "What?"

Apparently the former general has no more patience for that subject than he does for me in general. His voice turns terse but firm. "She thinks diving right into the villainy is the best way to unravel it. Her arguments sounded reasonable. If she's so eager to put her neck on the line, I don't see why we should stop her."

He glances around at the other men as if daring them to argue. I hold my chin high to show my commitment to the plan, even if I don't love the way he phrased his approval.

Casimir catches my eye with a questioning expression, and I give him a smile I hope looks confident.

At the lack of overt protests, Stavros claps his hands together with a thump of flesh against wood. "Now let's get on with determining how she can present herself as one of the villains."

SIX

Ivy

"What blasted book are you reading now?" Stavros demands as he strides into his quarters, back from another briefing with his contacts in the Crown's Watch.

I bite back a snarky remark about how he should be glad I'm reading rather than tossing my illicit magic around. Somehow I don't think the joke would go over well.

I tuck the book's ribbon between the pages to save my spot. "It's a journal written by a cleric who ran one of Prospira's temples under Darium rule. She claims that Prospira chatted with her from time to time. I'm trying to figure out how true that is and if it could tell me anything about what Kosmel wants with me."

Stavros pauses at the chest by the window. He retrieves his preferred prosthetic for the combat class he's about to teach—the broader hooked metal loop—and screws it into the harness around his handless forearm. "And has it been at

all enlightening? I certainly can't comprehend his interest in you."

I'm used to his acidic comments now. This one doesn't even sting.

Well, it barely does.

"I don't know," I admit. "Her overall grasp on reality seems pretty shaky. And the things she mentions Prospira saying to her so far are, like, what to have the temple cooks bake for breakfast. It's hard to believe a godlen would care."

After reading her account, I'd almost be convinced I hallucinated the voice *I* heard… except that would mean the man glowering at me and two of our colleagues hallucinated Kosmel's sigil too.

"Better dictating the breakfast menu than encouraging one of the riven," Stavros mutters under his breath.

I narrow my eyes at him. I might not be reckless enough to throw my unwanted power in his face, but I don't have to sit silently while he lambasts me.

I get to my feet. "I noticed you have quite a few novels in your bedroom. Maybe you're only harassing me about my reading material because you can't do much reading yourself these days. My offer to assist with that still stands, you know."

I say it mildly so he can't accuse me of mocking him. An honest gesture of generosity from the monster he's housing will irritate him more than if I returned his insults.

Ivy, Julita says warningly. *You know how grouchy he gets about his sight.*

But Stavros simply lets out a sound that's half huff, half growl. He doesn't dignify my comment with an answer.

I'm going to count that as a win.

And I need all the wins I can get. Because the truth is, when the former general marches over to join me, looming more than a foot both taller and broader than my gawky frame, every nerve in my body peals out in alarm.

And, okay, there might be a tiny bit of attraction still tangled up in there too. The man does cut an impressive figure.

But he isn't simply putting on a show of being intimidating. The tension coiled through all that brawn is very real, and very much directed at the threat he considers me to be.

Isn't it wonderful that our current plan requires me to go out into the hall and shout at him?

"Any interesting news from the Crown's Watch?" I ask, possibly holding on to the slight hope that they've rooted out all the major conspirators without me needing to do anything further.

The sound Stavros makes in answer is definitely a growl this time. "Nothing at the brothel they inspected last night. And no suspicious activity around the orphanage. Now that Wendos is in custody, the scourge sorcerers must be taking extra precautions. Whatever other sacrificial victims they have in the city, they may have moved them to a new type of hiding place."

Wonderful. Then as far as we know, our chances of uncovering the rest of the villains depend entirely on my fledgling plan.

I rub my arms to stop the creeping of my skin. "We'd better put on a good show, then. Are you ready?"

Stavros's glower returns. "Your performance is the one that really matters here, Thief. But we already know how good you are at lying."

My fingers curl into my palms. I simultaneously picture slamming my fist into his arrogant face and have a minor panic attack imagining the consequences of doing so.

I drop my hands to my sides instead and jerk my head toward the door. "Let's get out there."

Stavros pushes past me without another remark, leaving me to trot obediently at his heels like a good little assistant. I plaster a serene expression on my face as we head out of the Domi.

I'm dressed in a thin shirt and trousers this morning, because supposedly I'm going to be helping him with his combat lessons. But with the thick leather vest strapped over the shirt, it doesn't feel that much more comfortable than my frothy dresses do.

A pang of homesickness for my old tunic and breeches, for my old life without the judgmental stares and sneers, reverberates through my chest. I was never exactly *safe* roaming the streets, stealing from corrupt merchants and leaving coins for the needy... but it was definitely simpler than my current situation.

I don't even know if I'll be able to go back to being just the Hand of Kosmel after we've taken down the scourge sorcerers. Not now that my secret is out.

One problem at a time.

We hustle into the Quadring and up the stairs to the professors' offices. In theory, we're grabbing a piece of equipment from Stavros's office before the class.

Actually, we happen to know that Ster. Torstem finishes up his own office hours right around this time.

As we emerge from the stairwell, Stavros drops his voice so no one other than me will make out his voice. "Just up ahead. Third door on the right."

I nod. "Got it. Five paces past it?"

"That sounds reasonable. Then you'd better talk fast."

"I think I can manage that."

Our hushed conversation will sound terse even if no one who notices it can distinguish the words. Which is perfect, because five paces past the door to Torstem's office, I raise my voice as if getting caught up in an argument we've already been having. "You can't really think they're handling this problem properly."

Stavros spins around to face me. I jar to a stop with a flash of very genuine discomfort at the fierceness of his expression. "And you think *you* know better than the royal family?"

My magic stirs at the hostility vibrating through the air. I clamp down on it, reminding it that this is just pretend.

We're speaking loudly enough that our voices should travel through Torstem's door now. I think I catch the creak of the floor on the other side.

Just in case, I add a little more rancor to my words. "They're stuck doing the same old thing. It's obvious the gods aren't happy with them."

"So you'd prefer for the royal family to let the city collapse around our ears?"

I set my hands on my hips, restraining a shiver at rephrasing the words Wendos said to me in the tower. "Sometimes a few things need to get knocked down so we can build something better. Even the All-Giver thought so."

Julita shudders inside me. *And may the Great One have smote the first guy who said that.*

Stavros steps closer—for the benefit of anyone who happens to peek out, but I can't help suspecting he's enjoying looming over me. Letting me feel his frustration with this whole situation.

"You'd better watch what you say out loud," he says. "You'd better watch what you're *thinking*."

"I'm only saying the truth!"

He scoffs harshly. "Then you're a bigger idiot than I thought. Get out of my face until you've had a chance to get your head on straight."

That's my cue to take off. Tamping down the racing of my pulse, I give an exasperated sigh and storm off down the hall.

My heart isn't thundering so loud I miss the squeak of hinges behind me. Or Ster. Torstem's voice, low and even, just before I round the bend. "Having a little friction with your new assistant?"

A flicker of triumph cuts through my unsettled thoughts. He's taken the bait.

Now Stavros can vent to Torstem a little about my ridiculous attitudes—attitudes we know the law professor will secretly approve of.

That did seem to go smoothly, Julita says. It's hard to tell from her tone whether she's actually happy about that fact.

She has more experience with scourge sorcery than any of us, having been subjected to her brother and Wendos's experiments as a child. While she hasn't openly balked at our plan, I can't imagine she loves the idea of getting closer to people who bolster their own power through others' pain— or hearing me spout off their philosophies.

I round the corner—and find myself face to face with Romild, the leadership student who had designs on the position as Stavros's assistant. My self-appointed rival lets her lips curl into a sneer.

She probably heard at least part of our argument. She's thinking about how Stavros must be regretting giving the position to me now and no doubt hoping she'll get another shot at it.

The sense of her judgment shouldn't rankle me the way it does. Although Stavros is definitely regretting working with me, just not for the reasons she thinks.

I simply glower at her and stalk on to the stairwell.

I keep a peeved expression on my way out of the building. At the sight of a blue-uniformed figure who's appeared by the Domi's side entrance, my pulse kicks up a notch.

I'd veer off toward a different doorway, but these days I'm as likely to find two soldiers someplace else as none. So I stride ahead as if my mind is focused on some matter too important for me to acknowledge the man standing guard.

He doesn't stir from his post a couple of paces from the entryway. But as I walk past him, a faint tingle of drifting magic quivers through my riven soul.

My stomach lurches. Did he just cast a gift toward me?

What will it have told him?

I continue on into the building, but rather than heading upstairs to Stavros's quarters, I turn down the hall. At this time in the morning, students with later starts to their school day are still trickling in and out of the dining hall, but I don't pay them any mind.

I slip out through the front entrance, past two other soldiers who don't give me any impression of magic at all, and ease around the outside of the building.

Not for the first time, I'm grateful for the grand statues the college's administration erected around the grounds. A looming marble figure of some famous cleric hides me behind his sweeping stone robes.

Propping myself against the base of the statue, I peer toward the guard who used his gift.

What's the matter? Julita asks.

I pitch my voice low. "I caught a whiff of magic when I passed that soldier. As if he was working a gift on me."

It doesn't appear that the effort gave him any reason for concern, though. The man, who looks young enough to pass for one of the college's students, is still standing tall and stiff in the same spot next to the doorway.

I study him for a few minutes longer. Several students

and a professor meander through the doorway, and he doesn't so much as twitch in reaction.

If he's casting magic toward them too, it's slight enough that I can't pick it up from this far away.

It can't be unusual for soldiers to have at least some small gift they claimed with a dedication sacrifice. Even among the poor of the outer wards, I knew at least as many people who'd given up a piece of themselves for a little power as not.

I don't see any obvious markers of a sacrifice on the man. No missing fingers or bits of facial features. But there are plenty of possibilities I wouldn't be able to easily notice.

Casimir gave up several of his back teeth, replacing them with gems in the typical courtesan fashion. Julita told me she sacrificed her lowest two ribs.

There's only so long I can keep watching the soldier without it looking odd to anyone who starts watching *me*. I commit what I can see of his face to memory, so I'll recognize him if we cross paths again.

Short chocolate-brown curls that gleam under the morning sun. A strong but elegant nose. Creamy, unblemished skin.

Gods above, if he ever decides soldiering isn't to his tastes anymore, I'd bet the companionship division would welcome *him* as a courtesan. He sure as shit doesn't look as if he's seen a whole lot of combat.

What if it's for his magic rather than his fighting skills that the Crown's Watch recruited him?

I pull myself away from the statue with a knot I can't shake in my gut.

If the king is using gifts to seek out sorcerers… who's to say they won't pick up on the sorcery *I'm* trying so hard to suppress?

SEVEN

Casimir

As she leans back in the chair, the Elox dedicat who stopped by the companionship division's daily massage clinic lets out a rush of breath.

Even medics need someone to take care of them from time to time.

I dig my thumbs just a little deeper into her shoulders, finding the points of tension in the muscles. There's a special delight to be found in making someone's day better with just fifteen minutes and the press of your fingers.

But my current client also gives me the opportunity to support a greater cause.

I keep my tone light. "You're all knotted up. Stressful week?"

Her next breath comes with a soft sputter of agreement. "You could say that. I'm working on a case like nothing I've ever seen."

She's one of the medics assigned to heal Wendos from whatever exactly Ivy's chaotic magic did to knock him out. I don't hear any alarm in her voice, so I doubt they have any suspicions of the actual cause.

I work my thumbs farther down her spine through the thin fabric of her tunic. Patrons who stop by for the chair massages don't bother undressing. "I can tell you're devoted to your work. I'm sure you've already made progress."

"It doesn't seem that way. But we haven't made the situation *worse* either, so that's something, I suppose."

She's conscientious too, carefully not revealing any details of the circumstances or her patient. I can read between the lines well enough, though.

Wendos hasn't even begun to rouse from his coma, and the medics don't know how to mend what's wrong. But he isn't getting sicker.

We can still hope he'll recover and reveal his co-conspirators, but we can't count on it. Which means Ivy will have to continue courting the scourge sorcerers' favor for gods know how long.

A knot of my own forms in my stomach.

I'm careful not to let my uneasiness sour my voice or harden my touch, switching to asking the medic if she tried the particularly excellent sweet loaf the college's cooking staff served with today's lunch. A courtesan should show concern but not pry.

A courtesan is meant to distract patrons from their worries, not heighten them.

I happen to think there's more to learn when following those tenets than if one tries to circumvent them. I hear an awful lot in my daily work without any forceful questioning.

All the same, I was lucky the medic came in when she did. She's my last patron of the hour-long shift I pick up in the massage clinic once a week.

At the end of the brief session, I send her off with a relaxed smile and add her coins in compensation to the pouch on my belt. As I head down the hall, my gaze slides to the arched windows along this floor of the Quadring.

Late afternoon has darkened into evening while I worked. The shadows stretch long across the outer courtyard amid the streaks of light from the wavering lanterns.

A lithe figure moves through those shadows, aiming for the stables.

A hooded cloak covers most of the woman's form, but I recognize the determined stride. And it isn't hard to imagine the woman it belongs to deciding to slip out to the stables in the quiet of dusk.

It doesn't look as though much of anyone else is around. I amble down the stairs as if I simply felt like taking a stroll and wander over to the stables myself.

Only a faint glow seeps through the stable windows into the building, leaving the interior hazy. The scents of hay, leather, and horse wash over me, bringing a smile to my lips.

I really should venture out here more often, if only to say hello to my favorite animals. Being around them settles my nerves.

Walking down the aisle, I cluck my tongue at one gelding and rub the nose of an eager mare. I find Ivy exactly where I expected I would, leaning over the door of a stall at the end of the next aisle over.

"Oh, don't be grouchy," she says to Toast, the terror of a stallion whose jaw she's scratching. The obstinate animal snorts and stomps one hoof, but I notice he doesn't pull his head away.

He's met his match in this woman—and it looks as if she's won him over despite himself. As I watch them, affection swells in my chest.

For a second, I try to picture the woman whose soul Ivy is carrying inside her. From the way Ivy spoke up for Julita the other day, they've forged their own unusual understanding.

Behind all her charm, Julita always struck me as being a little lost… maybe lonely. But she held me at a distance even when she was being flirty. I never got to know her much beyond the coyly confident front she put forward.

I wish she'd had the chance to find the friendship she seems to have with Ivy while she was alive. At least she's been able to form that kind of bond before she's passed away completely.

With just a couple more steps, Ivy notices me approaching. Her head snaps around, her hood sliding back over her pale amber hair.

When she's looking right at me, it's impossible for me to see anyone but the woman in front of me. The woman who's captured so much of my attention she lingers in my mind even when she isn't around.

Ivy's expression softens a little when she sees it's me, but tension lingers in the set of her mouth. Over the past few weeks, I'd mostly won *my* way past the instinctive wariness in her bright blue eyes, but the incident in the tower has brought it back.

I stop a few stalls away and reach to give my favorite mare, Pepper, a pat in welcome. "Taming that horse might be your greatest accomplishment."

Ivy relaxes more at my teasing tone. She gives Toast one more scratch under his chin and steps back. "I don't think anyone really gave him a chance before."

I can't help thinking of how much that remark could apply to her own situation.

The urge runs through my body to walk right up to her, wrap my arms around her, and tell her that she's still got me on her side. That she never needed to earn a chance to begin with, in my opinion.

I hold myself where I am instead. I'm not sure she'd welcome the embrace, let alone believe me, and I can hardly blame her for that.

It isn't as if I was free of doubts when we first came around the top of the All-Giver's tower and saw her summoning vines at her feet. I make a career out of seeing the best in people—I'm aware that my judgment isn't infallible.

But with every word she's said since, every emotion that's played across her face and colored her voice, it's become increasingly clear that she's still the woman I found myself drawn to from the start. Still just as sharp and bold and kind as ever.

Of course, she might not want my affection regardless of whether she believes in it. Some part of me thought—some part of me *hoped*—that the deeper fondness kindling inside me had sparked inside her too.

From the way she reacted after our last intimate moment, though, it was nothing more than casual pleasure to her. Which was all I'd offered anyway.

All I'm meant to offer.

I allow myself to take a single step closer, studying the interplay of reactions I receive. A faint flush colors her cheeks, but her posture goes slightly rigid as if she's bracing herself to flee.

She's grappling with some conflict within herself, and I can't say what it even is. Do I stir up feelings in her that she's feeling awkward about? Is she afraid I'm going to push for more than she actually wants?

Another impulse itches at me—to tap into my gift, to find out how I could make Ivy happiest—but I quash it. It feels like too much of an invasion of her privacy now.

And just because something would make her happy in

the moment, that doesn't mean it's what she'd actually appreciate in the long run.

So I stay where I am, but I dig into the pocket of my trousers. I can give her one thing I expect she'll enjoy.

I retrieve the item I've been carrying around waiting for a moment like this and hold out the knife to her grip-first, my fingers around the slim hilt. "I managed to pick this up in the tower while we were leaving. It's been cleaned... I thought you might want it back."

The way Ivy's eyes light up makes my heart skip a beat. She steps forward and plucks the knife out of my hand as if she's afraid it might be a trap.

As she gazes down at it, a grin stretches across her face. "It's my favorite one. I thought it was gone for good."

She lifts her gaze to meet mine again, the wariness still there but faded. "Thank you."

I return her grin. "I would have given it back earlier, but I wasn't sure how Stavros would react if I attempted it in front of him."

Ivy gives a dry laugh. "Yes, he wouldn't want me getting even more dangerous."

She bends down to slide the knife into one of the boots she's wearing, mostly hidden beneath the rippling skirt of her dress.

When she straightens up again, her voice turns tentative. "Can I ask you kind of a strange question? There aren't a whole lot of people around here I *can* ask."

The fact that she's willing to turn to me for any help at all brings a glow of warmth into my chest.

I spread my arms. "Be my guest. Indulge your curiosity."

Ivy glances around the stable, confirming that we're alone here. There's no sound but the shifting of the horses in their stalls.

All the same, she drops her voice low and keeps her

question vague. "You seem pretty… close with your godlen. Does Ardone reach out to you in different ways, let you know how she feels about what you're doing or what else she might like you to do?"

I don't need to ask why Ivy's curious. She looked confused and a little terrified when she talked about Kosmel's divine voice speaking to her.

My thoughts dart back to the night of the incident in the tower, after Ivy made her full confession.

That night, I knelt at my small shrine to Ardone in my dorm bedroom and asked my godlen to show me if my heart was being led astray. If I needed to beware the woman who's unknowingly claimed so much of it.

I answer Ivy in the same subdued tone. "Not the way you've experienced it, from what you've said. But I've felt Ardone's presence regularly in smaller, subtler ways. Every now and then I have a dream I can tell she's touched, but mostly it's simply sensing my attention being drawn to specific objects or images, like a symbolic sort of message."

Like that night after I made my appeal, my gaze drifted up through the flickering candlelight to see a shadow like a butterfly's wings fluttering by. Flying free without a care.

My godlen might as well have spoken to me in that moment, saying, *Follow the path to your joy unhindered.*

Ivy's brow furrows. "I haven't noticed any smaller messages. It's like he comes out of the blue, and then he vanishes."

I cock my head. "You haven't exactly been open to accepting his presence—or any other godlen's—have you? The connection between mortal and divine has always felt like a matter of meeting halfway to me, rather than having someone else's will imposed on me. They guide rather than command. And you can't guide someone who's shutting you out."

"I guess I can't argue with that reasoning." Ivy lets out a huff of breath. "I don't know if I *want* to let any divinity in."

"It's up to you. You could always see if you're comfortable opening the door just a little. Nothing's stopping you from slamming it shut again if you're unhappy with the outcome."

Ivy snorts. "Assuming I'm in a position to do anything at all once he's done with me. Listening to him has already gotten me into more trouble than I ever did on my own."

I have a flash of an image of Ivy slumped on the hangman's platform, and my stomach lurches. My hand instinctively flicks down my front—tapping my fingers to forehead, heart, and gut, and then a fist to my sternum over my godlen brand—as if I can ward off that horrific potential future.

Ivy's mouth twists at my gesture. I take another step toward her. "Kosmel protected you with Stavros—with all three of us—when he needed to. I'm sure he will again if it's necessary. And… in case it wasn't clear… he *wouldn't* need to with me. Stavros may be having trouble coming to grips with your magic, but I know you're still our Kindness."

A look that's almost haunted comes over Ivy's face. Before I can panic that I've disturbed her somehow, she lets out a laugh—if a bit of a stiff one. "You've always been kinder to *me* than I probably deserve. Thank you, for now and before. I'd better get back to the Domi before the former general thinks I've gone rogue."

She pats Toast's head and ducks past me without waiting for me to answer.

I reach over the stall door to stroke Pepper's neck, grappling with the tangle of emotion inside me.

I gave Ivy a little comfort, a little happiness. As much as I probably could. I should be grateful for that.

Once I've given Ivy the distance she appeared to want, I

head back to the Domi myself. On the third floor, I find a different woman waiting outside my dorm.

As I approach, taking in her features, her name rises up from my memory: Agata. The second daughter of one of the court Barons, a student in the scholarship division. A couple of months ago, she hired me for a night on the town and a private interlude afterward.

At the time, I suspected she'd become a returning patron. The tangle inside me knots tighter with the knowledge that I'm about to be proven right.

I stop a couple of paces from her and smile. "Hello, Agata. It's good to see you. How have you been?"

She twists a strand of her sleek auburn hair around her finger. "Pretty well. But I was feeling that there's a little something missing. When are you free for another evening? We could have a similar outing to last time."

From the suggestive note that's crept into her voice, I have no doubt that she intends a similar ending as well.

It's the work I do. Sex is a celebration of the godlen I dedicated myself to, an act of both worship and joy.

But not a single part of me feels joyful at the idea of carrying out that particularly intimate work right now.

I manage to hold my smile in place. The words slip out before I can totally think them through. "I'm not. Free, that is. I'm sorry. I'm on a short hiatus from taking private patrons."

At least, as of this moment I am.

"Oh!" Agata giggles. "I suppose you must have schoolwork and so on to keep you busy like the rest of us do. Let me know when you're in business again, then. I'll be looking forward to it."

As she saunters away, a lump of guilt forms in my gut. I've never turned down a potential patron before.

What in the realms am I here for if not to serve? To pay back everything that was given so I could be here at all?

I clamp down on my roiling emotions and press my college bracelet to the door to disengage the lock.

I'm serving Ivy. I'm serving the royal family.

What greater purpose could there be than tackling a menace that threatens the entire continent? Our mission deserves all our focus.

I won't entertain any thoughts of the other reasons I might be making this call—or what they'll mean for *my* future.

EIGHT

Ivy

I bob and dodge, blocking a punch and narrowly avoiding a knee to my gut.

My sparring partner swivels, and I see a brief opening where I could whip a jabbing thumb into her eye. That's what I'd do if this were an actual life-or-death fight, but I don't think my employer would approve of street tactics in his combat class.

And the noblewoman I'm sparring with doesn't deserve it anyway.

I rein in my defensive instincts and shoot out my fist more loosely, giving her the opportunity to block. The point of this drill is for the students to get a feel for constantly moving on their feet while in face-to-face conflict, not to destroy my opponent.

I'm grateful Stavros is allowing me to participate in the lesson at all. It'd be terribly boring standing on the sidelines handing out water and patching up minor scrapes.

No doubt he's studying my every movement, watching for an excuse to declare that I really am an irredeemable menace after all. He might even be hoping he gets one.

The former general's voice rings out from across the field. "All right, people! Switch partners again. Every enemy you go up against will have a slightly different approach. If you're on the ground in a battle, you need to be prepared to adapt in an instant, or you'll find yourself underfoot rather than on your feet."

A few of the students around me chuckle at his dry tone. I turn away from the woman I was up against, wiping at the sweat that's formed on the back of my neck, and look for the guy I particularly wanted to have some face time with.

My gaze catches that of the male student I was searching for, several paces away. When I make a gesture of invitation, he strolls over to take the position across from me.

Even though I prompted this face-off, my pulse gives a brief hitch alongside a tiny defensive flare of my magic. The man approaching me is one of the bug club members from Alek's homemade dossiers. The scholar's simple sketch captured the bulky guy's broad nose and boxy jawline perfectly.

Julita must recognize both him and my intentions. *Better be careful with this one, Ivy.*

As the possible scourge sorcerer comes to a stop in front of me, I dip my head in acknowledgement of both our intention to spar and Julita's point. The sparse facts Alek pulled together whirl through my thoughts.

This is Olari Igorek, second son of Provint Igor of Yersi, who governs that province. Dedicated to Sabrelle, in his third year at the college.

A family as prominent as his would normally see any children going into military service becoming majors, if not generals, right out of the gate. Olari has shown a preference for more hands-on field tactics rather than broader strategy, in line with settling for captain.

He'd rather be bossing around the infantry and engaging in regular skirmishes than worrying about the larger issues of a conflict, apparently.

Other than the entomology club, he's a member of the fencing club and the darts league. Obvious competitive streak. He received an award in a dueling contest last year.

None of that tells me whether he definitely enjoys the idea of using others' pain to fuel whatever gifts he came by through his own sacrifice. Although I see what sacrifice he made when his lips draw back in a grin of challenge.

His upper front four teeth have been replaced with steel replicas.

If we ever get into a real fight, I'll have to make sure he's never in a position to bite me.

Olari makes the first lunge without waiting for any additional signal that I'm ready to begin. His fist sweeps over my ducked head.

I spring to the side. Thank all that's holy I spent most of the past several years honing my speed as well as my strength.

"You're pretty skilled for your size," my opponent remarks as we circle each other. "I can see why Stavros hired you."

Is he trying to lower my guard with compliments?

I can't complain, because he's giving me my opportunity to drop a hint of my supposedly deviant attitudes in case he'll pass the information on to Ster. Torstem. "I don't believe we should be limited by what we were born with. I've always striven to become more."

Olari hums approvingly, and our conversation falls off into a series of blows and blocks as he tries to land a strike. I keep my silence patiently, waiting for another good opening to throw in a telling remark, not wanting to come on suspiciously strong.

As we circle each other, Olari eases slightly back. "You've arrived in the middle of a rather chaotic time here at the college. You mustn't have been expecting to deal with daimon crashing balls and toppling buildings."

Interesting that he's bringing that subject up. I shrug, debating my answer.

The scourge sorcerers were obviously in favor of chaos, but Wendos didn't make it clear exactly why. Only that he thought somehow it'd set the world "right."

Julita pipes up with a hushed suggestion, as if she's afraid Olari might overhear. *My brother and Wendos sometimes talked about how violence and pain are just the natural order of things.*

That does sound like the sort of sentiment scourge sorcerers would appreciate—to justify the pain *they* inflict.

I pick my words carefully. "There's so much chaos in the rest of the world, I guess it's more surprising that the spirit-creatures don't act out more often themselves. Although I'm sure that's not much comfort to those who were harmed."

Olari lets out a faint snort. "Indeed."

He swipes at my jaw and then my ribs, managing to knock my side just slightly before I dart away. I answer with a sweep of my foot against his calf that would have sent him stumbling if he wasn't so sturdy.

Maybe I can pick his brain for a hint about what the scourge sorcerers' current plans are, if he's involved with them. "The daimon have settled down quite a bit since the day they broke the Quadring. The clerics the king sent in must be very skilled."

Will the remark sting his pride and prompt an

insinuation about other reasons the spirit-creatures seem to have backed off?

Olari chuckles, his breath only a little rough with exertion. "I suppose we'll see." He attempts another strike. "There's been a lot of speculation going around about why the daimon were so agitated to begin with."

He leaves that open-ended comment hanging. Apprehension prickles through my nerves with a deeper certainty.

He didn't give any clues with his vague statement about the daimon's current behavior, but I'm increasingly sure this guy is on Torstem's side. He's adding chatter to our sparring match specifically so he can evaluate what I say on topics of particular interest to the conspirators.

It was two days ago that Stavros and I staged our argument for the law professor's benefit. Plenty of time for him to order an underling to feel me out further.

I don't need Julita's help to figure out the best response this time. Wendos obviously wasn't happy with the way things are being run in Silana, and most of the running is done by the king.

I wouldn't be surprised if the scourge sorcerers started the rumor I'm about to repeat.

"Some people are saying the daimon must be upset with the royal family. That's the only real theory I've heard." I rub my hand across my mouth as if nervous about saying too much. "I don't know what exactly they're upset about, though."

Torstem wouldn't want to recruit someone foolhardy enough to shoot her mouth off without concern for the consequences. I can give the impression that I think the theory is plausible without openly supporting it.

As I throw another punch, Olari laughs. "I've heard that

claim too. Although sometimes I think maybe they're just tired of getting stuck with nothing but bits of cast-off food for offerings and they're rallying for something more."

I'm not sure the remark would sound so ominous if I didn't see the obvious parallel to the scourge sorcerers' bid for power. As it is, my skin crawls.

"I suppose we all can't help wanting more than we have from time to time," I say mildly, just as the bell for the hour starts ringing.

Stavros motions to his students, his metal prosthetic flashing in the sunlight. "You know what that means. Off to the showers, the lot of you. I won't be held responsible for any sweat-stink in your next classes."

I restrain myself from rolling my eyes at the tongue-in-cheek order and turn to find an unexpected gaze on me.

The woman who's watching me from several paces away isn't even part of the military division. Petra was one of Julita's frequent classmates over on the leadership side. But she's dropped in on occasional combat and strategy classes before.

My ghostly passenger informed me that she's a distant relative of the queen's. She definitely looks more like Queen Ishild's side of the family than the king's, with olive-toned skin and features more elegantly proportioned than the imposing nose and jutting chin of the Melchiorek line.

Her dark gaze flicks from me to Olari with unsettling intensity. Then she pivots on her heel with a swish of her straight black hair.

What's Petra in a stew about? Julita mutters.

A hollow forms in the pit of my stomach. I can make a few educated guesses.

Did Petra overhear some of what I said? She's seemed bothered in the past when people repeated the rumor about the daimon being upset with the country's rulership.

King Konram knows I'm investigating the scourge sorcerers on his behalf, but we purposefully kept that fact quiet from everyone else in court.

Which means I have to worry about making new enemies just as much as turning my existing foes into friends.

NINE

Ivy

I'm shoved around in the dark, blinded by scratchy fabric wrapped across my face. It's suffocating me.

I can't draw a breath through it. I can't tell where I am.

What in the realms is happening?

I have to get out of this. I have to tear free. I—

My feet thud onto a raised surface. Wooden boards. Something creaks overhead.

More footsteps thunder after me, as if on all sides. Their impact reverberates through the boards and into my legs.

I try to suck in air and only drown in the coarse fabric. I can't feel my hands.

My throat strains with an attempt to cry for help, but my lungs are burning for breath. With another shove, I stumble to the side.

Then someone wrenches the fabric from my face.

It's still dark—night all around me, glowing with distant lanterns. Voices murmur, maybe hundreds of them, but all I

can do is stare at the man whose shadowed face looms over mine.

"You couldn't keep hiding," Stavros grates out, and lifts his hands.

All at once, he's gripping a loop of rope. He jerks it down over my head, his metal prosthetic scraping my cheek.

"No," I murmur. "No. I swear, I never…"

Never what? Never killed? Never hurt innocent people?

"We both know that's a lie," Stavros sneers as if he read my thoughts.

We do.

I always knew I'd end up here.

But my heart thuds madly as Stavros tightens the rope around my neck. The heavy cord digs into my throat.

I start to twist my head, but he catches it between his hand of flesh and his hand of metal. His voice is the darkest growl.

"You're not going anywhere. Stay and take what monsters like you deserve."

There's nothing but ice in his eyes and his tone. It chills me right through to my veins.

He takes a step back and lifts his right hand to give the signal, his lips curling into a triumphant—

"Ivy!"

My body jolts, and my eyes open to more darkness. Darkness that's also tangled with fabric, although this material is thin and silky, draped across my torso and legs.

I jerk upright, my hand flying to my thigh instinctively, but I've woken up here often enough that some part of me already recognizes what happened.

I'm in the outer room of Stavros's quarters, on the sofa where I always sleep. It was only a dream.

My gaze finds the man who haunted me in that dream standing a few paces away, his arms crossed over his chest, his expression set in a glower. "You were mumbling and thrashing around. It was getting disturbing."

My mouth tightens. "Sorry I disrupted your sleep."

The other time the former general woke me from a nightmare, he leaned right in to shake my shoulder. He seemed mostly amused when I nearly sliced open his throat before I realized who he was.

He trusted that I wouldn't actually hurt him then. He doesn't now.

He knows how easily I could.

Not a single bit of magic squirms in my chest, though. There's nothing about this situation it can fix, as even it is apparently aware.

Stavros shrugs, and a different part of my brain kicks in, noting that he's only wearing an undershirt and drawers. The sculpted brawn of his arms and legs is on full display, his biceps flexing with the movement. "I'm sure my sleep is very high on your list of concerns. I'll be fine now."

I expect him to stalk away, but he pauses with just a slight shift of his feet. "What was terrifying you this time? Ster. Torstem and his cronies?"

My gut twists at the memory. An honest answer tumbles out before I can think better of it. "The hangman's noose."

Stavros's stance goes absolutely still. He stares at me for a moment, all trace of the glower gone.

We also both know who's most likely to lead me to that noose.

Does he have any idea how nervous I've been of him all along? Has it even occurred to him how much courage it took to stay here night after night, knowing how badly things could go wrong if *he* of all people discovered my secret?

Even when he'd warmed to me, even when he was being *nice*, I was still a little bit terrified of him.

It's all out on the table now, though. I don't have to hold

back anything I'd want to say out of fear of what he'd realize if he reads between the lines.

Maybe it would help me re-earn his trust if he could see that I've considered his side too.

I swallow against the dryness of my mouth. "I understand, you know. Why you consider me a threat. Why you see riven as monsters. I don't trust my magic either. Why do you think I've tried so hard not to use it?"

A little of the bite comes back into Stavros's voice. "Why not turn yourself in, then?"

I grimace at him. "Because I haven't been using it. I've kept it under control. If I really thought I was on the verge of being a danger to the people around me…"

"It doesn't seem as if most riven think of themselves that way."

"Most riven go insane," I mutter, and hesitate. I've barely admitted what I'm going to say even to myself before.

But it's true.

My fingers curl into the sheet puddled around my waist. "I assume the insanity comes from using the power. So as long as I restrain myself, my head shouldn't get muddled like that. Sometimes… sometimes I think it's a good thing the first time I realized what I could do, I killed my sister. If it'd been a smaller act with smaller consequences, I'd probably have kept going. I'd have hurt so many more people. This way the damage was mostly contained."

Julita speaks up from the back of my skull. *Ivy… you can't think any of it was right. You shouldn't have had to deal with this mad power at all.*

And yet I do have to deal with it. I can't say my pain is worse than what I could have inflicted on hundreds of others combined.

Stavros's jaw clenches. For a second, I think he's either going to shout at me or laugh.

But when he speaks again, his tone is milder. "Is that why you took up your calling as the Hand of Kosmel? You said you had things you wanted to set right. You decided it was some kind of penance?"

"Something like that." I look down at my hands. "I was born with a broken soul. I know that makes me a monster. But for as long as I'm able to... I'd like to be other things too."

My body tenses, braced for the blow I'm expecting to come, whether verbal or physical.

Stavros props himself against the side of a nearby armchair, no longer looking as if he's holding himself back from storming away. His arms come down, the one that ends in a stump resting on his thigh. He doesn't wear a prosthetic to bed, of course.

He swipes the hand he still has across his mouth. "I suppose there are worse reasons."

"So glad you think so," I can't stop myself from muttering and then snap my mouth shut.

I peer up at him tentatively through the darkness of the room. He's looking at me with the little twitch of his head that tells me he's refocusing his vision. Studying me rather than accusing me with his gaze. His red hair and his eyes with their blue-and-brown-ringed irises both look nearly black in the dimness.

"You still don't have any idea what Kosmel wants with you?" he asks.

I shake my head. "He hasn't spoken to me since that night in the All-Giver's tower."

"Perhaps you should try to speak to him. He's got a shrine right in that temple."

My body balks instinctively. It was unsettling enough entering the Temple of the Crown, the largest building of worship in the country, when I knew the entire city was on the line.

To simply go in to try to chat with one of the godlen who should theoretically hate what I am, even if this particular godlen doesn't seem to mind at the moment…

"Maybe," I say. "I'll see. He didn't tell me anything all that useful the two times he did talk to me anyway."

"Sounds like typical theology to me."

Stavros straightens up again, presumably planning to finish the sleep I interrupted. The tentative peace between us feels as if it might shatter the second he walks out of this room.

I open my mouth, and the other topic I've been afraid to bring up leaps onto my tongue.

"I'm sorry about your friend too. I—I never wanted to remind you of any horrible part of your past. Was it the riven sorcerer you tracked down two years ago who was responsible?"

The first day I stayed in this room, the former general told me one of the riven had "butchered" his best friend. He has a more personal reason than most to hate me for what I am beyond all the atrocities the riven have inflicted on broader society.

Stavros stiffens. "No," he says shortly. "It was—we were teenagers when it happened."

Anywhere from ten to fifteen years ago, then, if he's in his late twenties like he looks. A grief he's being carrying about as long as I've mourned my sister.

"What happened?" I venture.

He takes a step back from me, his expression hardening. "I was living with my mother as I told you I usually did. He was one of her supporting officers' sons. We had the idea we'd make an adventure of having a ramble through various towns in the area. And we ended up in the wrong place at the wrong time. We were stupid and careless, and I didn't realize until it was too late—"

Stavros cuts himself off. His voice goes totally flat. "We were stupid, and we crossed paths with a monster. That's all there is to it. You don't need to know the details to ensure you don't end up doing the same."

He prowls off into his bedroom without another word.

It'll be okay, Julita says, her voice a little too quavery to be totally convincing. *He'll come around. He's got to see you're not like the other riven.*

Does he? I don't know about that.

I thought we'd made a little progress, but I might have dashed it to bits with my curiosity.

Exhaustion from my own interrupted sleep drags at my eyelids. I force myself to lie back down on the sofa and tug the blanket up to my chin, trying not to think about the conversations I've had with Stavros in this room that ended on much better terms.

Trying not to ache with the knowledge that he may never speak with me like an equal again, and I'm not sure that's even unfair.

TEN

Ivy

I didn't realize how much I appreciated having a friend to sit with in the dining hall until that friend was gone.

Granted, Esmae was only pretending her friendliness. She murdered Julita and tried to do the same to me.

But she was good company before all that came to light.

Gripping the breakfast plate I've picked up from one of the room's many counters, I scan the tables. The first familiar face I spot is Anya's.

My former nemesis has her blond hair piled on top of her head in her preferred style and a sharp smile curving her lips. I disarmed her by pretending to be *her* friend shortly before my confrontation with Wendos in the All-Giver's tower, but I have no desire to cozy up to the bully beyond that. I'm just glad my gambit worked well enough that she hasn't resumed her harassment.

A few tables over, there's Romild, who probably thinks

even less of me now than she did when she insinuated that I'd fucked my way into the assistant position. It's become clear that Wendos used her as a diversion to lead my investigations astray and that she isn't actually involved in any illicit sorcery, but it's been equally clear that she'd sooner spit in my face than have a genial conversation with me.

My gaze snags for a moment on a tawny head I've come to know well. Casimir is seated with his back mostly to me, but there are only a few other students sitting at his table.

It wouldn't look *that* odd for me to grab a chair at the other end, would it? I don't even have to talk to him—simply being in his presence would make me feel less alone.

But just as I start to take a step toward him, a noblewoman with ebony ringlets sashays to his side and rests her hand on his shoulder as she leans in to speak. It's the woman I saw him dancing with at the ball.

He told me he uses the balls to let possible patrons "sample" his skills as a courtesan. Is she looking to hire him now?

My stomach twists, and I yank my gaze away.

It's his job. I've got no right to feel queasy over him embracing his calling.

I don't really want to witness a transaction in progress, though. It's safer for him if I keep my distance anyway.

Really, it was selfish of me to consider going over there when I could be putting him in danger.

That thought helps me focus on my larger mission. Are there any bug club members around I could contrive to sit near?

I don't want to be blatant about seeking them out, but even being able to listen in while they talk with other students might reveal something useful.

I meander between the tables, casting my gaze about as if I'm looking for an ideal seat.

While I can fake the airs of a noblewoman reasonably well, I've always stuck out a little among this upper crust crowd. No one meets my eyes other than once, briefly, followed by a disdainful curl of a lip.

I've only made it past a few tables when a clear, even voice speaks up from behind me. "Ivy, isn't it? You could join me over here."

I swivel to find distantly-royal Petra aiming a subdued smile at me. She motions to a few empty chairs at a nearby table.

My legs lock, just for a second. I don't have any reason to believe that the queen's niece-twice-removed—or whatever exactly she is—would see me as an ideal dining companion.

What's she really up to?

Will it be more of a mistake to accept her invitation or to refuse her?

Go on, Julita murmurs. *Let's find out what she wants. It's not as if you couldn't take her in a fight.*

I restrain a snort at that sentiment and make myself return Petra's smile. "Thank you. I'll do that."

As we walk to the chairs and take our places, I surreptitiously study the other woman.

Julita is probably right in her assessment of our fighting capabilities. Petra has a few inches on my short frame, but her arms look soft in contrast with my wiry muscle. Her figure is more curvy than combat-hardened.

I have to assume she drops in on Stavros's classes to try to develop skills she's lacking rather than to hone an established talent. I definitely haven't seen any impressive moves from her during sparring sessions.

She is a little hard to pin down, though. Her dress is fine, with delicate embroidery across the bodice and down the skirt—eye-catching but not entirely fitting the typical styles around the college. She must have enough interest in fashion to appreciate impressive work without caring whether anyone else is impressed by the same.

Like the other times I've seen her, she's let her black hair spill loose over her shoulders, only a small portion braided back from her tan brow. I've looped my own hair into an updo so I can fit in with most of my schoolmates, but apparently Petra doesn't care about that either.

I guess when you're related to the royal family, even if only by marriage, you're a little above those concerns. She does always seem to keep a subtle distance from the other students.

But not with me, not right now.

I glance around to confirm no one I'm keeping an eye on from the bug club is nearby. The kinds of things I'd want them to overhear and the kinds of things I'd be comfortable saying directly to Petra have very little overlap.

As I lift my fork, my nerves buzz with apprehension. Thankfully, Petra speaks before I have to decide how to start a conversation with her.

She flicks her hand in a graceful motion toward the room at large. "You've only been at Sovereign College for a few weeks, haven't you?"

I nod and stick to my standard cover story. "I only meant to come for a visit, but I ended up meeting Ster. Stavros at just the right time and found myself with a job."

"I've seen that not everyone has been all that welcoming, but hopefully you haven't regretted staying."

I can't suppress a laugh. She has no idea how much I have to regret.

But I can still truthfully say, "No, I like having the chance to accomplish more than I could back home."

Petra gives a light laugh in return and tears the crescent roll on her plate in two. She has to hold it carefully in her right hand, where her little and ring finger are both missing —her dedication sacrifice, I assume.

Giving part of her dominant hand would have earned her a greater gift. I don't sense her working any magic on me now, but some divine talents are more passive while still useful.

"You've found a few things to like, then," she says. "Ster. Stavros hasn't been too difficult an employer?"

Oh, that's a topic and a half. I turn my answer over in my mind, deciding on the best way to word it. Last night's tense conversation stands out starkly in my memory.

"He has high standards," I say. "And he demands a certain amount of deference. But he isn't unreasonable. I don't mind having to work hard if the situation is fair."

I wouldn't say he's been all that fair to you lately, Julita puts in.

Petra tips her head thoughtfully as she chews. "I haven't attended many of his classes, but he does seem to have a good balance between being supportive and firm."

A little of my own curiosity bubbles up. "You're in the leadership division, aren't you? Why have you joined any of the military classes?"

The corner of Petra's mouth kicks upward in a crooked smile that looks a little odd on her otherwise dignified face. "My parents have always maintained that it's important for us all to be able to defend ourselves and what we care about if need be. You never know when you might end up under threat with no one with more expertise to call on for help. And everyone says Ster. Stavros is the best to learn from."

The smile gives her a more youthful appearance than before. I assumed she was late in her schooling, a couple of years older than me, but suddenly I'm not so sure.

"How long have *you* been taking classes here?" I find myself asking.

"A little over a year now," she says, which means if she started at the college at eighteen like most nobles do, she won't be more than nineteen now. I'm actually her senior, though not by much. "Also, I honestly enjoy the physical exertion of the sparring. Haven't you found activities here that you enjoy even though they're not part of your official focus?"

I shrug. "Of course. I appreciate the chance to go riding when I get it. And there are a lot more books in the library than I had access to at home—I'm certainly not reading about warfare all day long. But having fists thrown at you isn't most people's idea of a good time."

"I suppose not." Petra keeps smiling at me, though I still get the sense she's studying me as much as I am her. "But it's appeared that you're not all that concerned about being like 'most people' either. That's one of the reasons I thought it might be nice to talk."

One of the reasons. Gods only know what the others are.

Julita hums as if in agreement. *There's definitely more to this overture than she's letting on.*

"Well, thank you," I say awkwardly, not sure how else to answer her.

We eat in silence for a few minutes while I wonder if I'm giving away something uncouth in my gestures or expressions. What does she believe she's learned about me so far?

Does she think I might be acting against her family? What will she do if she decides I am?

Petra pops one last piece of roll into her mouth and leans back in her chair as she swallows. "You became friendly with Esmae very quickly. It must be difficult, her leaving so abruptly."

It sounds like an off-hand remark, but I have to stop my

spine from stiffening. Stavros told me that the king decided to put out an official story that Esmae returned home rather than reveal her death and all the complicated circumstances around it.

After a week or two without her turning up, people will start to assume she was waylaid on her journey and murdered. I'm not sure if her family will find that more comforting than the idea that she'd become a murderer herself, but it's not up to me anyway.

Good riddance, Julita mutters.

As much as I can't regret my act of self-defense, a lump rises in my throat with the memories of the meals I shared here with Esmae when I thought we were friends. It's a particularly uncomfortable sort of loss, missing a person while also feeling ashamed that they managed to deceive you so thoroughly.

My smile probably looks a bit rigid, but surely I'm allowed to show a little of my emotions even if I'm pretending it's a less permanent loss. "It seems as though people come and go pretty often here. But it has been a bit lonely without her."

And with most of the men I'd counted on before eyeing me with varying degrees of suspicion.

Petra gives my hand a light pat. "You should join us for another hunt sometime. That'll give you an excuse to ride."

She gets up to carry her plate to the counter. I chew the last of my bacon, but my stomach stays clenched tight.

She definitely had some other agenda. Now I've got to make sure I'm playing this game right to keep out of trouble with her too.

If Esmae taught me anything, it's that I can't underestimate just how much damage one student might do.

As I drop off my own plate, I notice Casimir and the

ringleted woman heading out. When I reach the doorway, they're ambling toward the main staircase, her hand grazing his shoulder while she lets out a bell-like laugh.

Julita stirs in the back of my head. *The patrons don't matter all that much to him, Ivy.*

Maybe that's true, but it doesn't mean I want to watch them canoodling the whole way up to my room.

I veer in the other direction and just keep walking—past the games rooms and other leisure venues I haven't investigated, all the way around to the narrow hall at the back of the Domi's first floor.

The sight of the stone columns along the walls makes my lungs constrict. It was farther down this hallway, at the other end near the row of tapestries, where Esmae stabbed a knife into my back.

I stride on into the dank, cramped stairwell barely anyone bothers to use back here. No need to worry about running into prying eyes on my way to the fourth floor.

I emerge amid the staff quarters a few minutes' walk from Stavros's rooms. A couple of other teaching assistants are just wandering around the corner ahead of me.

Ducking my head and itching for the anonymity of my cloak, I meander slowly after them so I won't catch up and have to navigate either sneers or awkward small talk. My gaze slides along the rug that runs the length of the hall—and snags on a small, gray-furred body that's just wiggling out of a crack between the stones at the base of the wall.

A rat. It freezes against the wall, maybe noting my presence.

There's nothing so strange about a creature like that scurrying through a building like this. Even nobles have to fend off vermin from time to time, especially when there's food around.

But as I come up on the animal, a quiver of magic jitters through my nerves.

It's not just a rat. Someone's used their gift on it, somehow or other.

And then left it to sneak around on the staff floor. I can't think of many good reasons to do that.

In my hesitation, the creature darts forward along the wall. I don't think, just leap after it.

My fingers snatch at the rat's tail, firm enough to stop it in its tracks.

I expected it to squeal or freeze in terror. Instead, it whips around with its teeth bared to chomp at my thumb.

"Shit," I hiss, smacking the rat's head away with my other hand.

It only flails more wildly, its jaws and tiny claws raking at every bit of my flesh it thinks it might be able to reach. I fumble to try to get a grip on it that would restrain its body, and it sinks its teeth into the base of my palm.

My hand jerks instinctively, slamming the rodent into the wall. It hits the plaster surface headfirst with a crunch of its skull.

Before I can even curse that I couldn't capture it alive, the creature's limp form turns hard and heavier in my grasp. I'm so startled by the sudden change that I drop it.

The thing that was once a living rat hits the floor and cracks into a few jagged pieces. Jagged pieces of what looks like fired clay.

What in the world is that? Julita demands.

I don't know. Totally bewildered, I hunch down to take a careful look.

The chunks of clay would form a sculpture of a rat if I nudged them back together. Fine lines of fur are even carved into the reddish-brown surface.

But it had actual fur when I grabbed it. It felt like a real rat—it moved like one.

It bit like one, as the blood dribbling over my hand can attest.

A chill seeps through my body. Something is very wrong here, and I've never seen anything like it.

ELEVEN

Ivy

As he lays the cord in a loop on the floor, Stavros shoots a wary look at the small canvas bag I'm clutching. "What exactly is your big surprise?"

My fingers curl tightly around the bag's neck. "I think it'd be better if we all discuss it together."

The former general is going to find my story hard enough to believe without me needing to tell it twice.

He grimaces but lays out the second circle of cord without remark. His is red. Mine is black.

The cords are the key to the new meeting room King Konram set up for us before he left on his courtly tour. We each got a different color.

The other men have kept their own cords, of course. Stavros hasn't budged about holding on to mine as well as his own, so I can't use it unless I have his permission.

Who knows what horrible riven things he thinks I'd get up to on my own in a room full of books and maps?

It doesn't matter anyway, since I'm not likely to be attending meetings without him present. I manage not to roll my eyes at him when he steps back from my loop and gestures toward it as if to say, "Go ahead."

As I step toward the ring of cord, my chest tightens just a little. I *can* thank my wretched magic for the fact that using this enchantment sends a wriggling sensation right down the middle of my soul.

The cords must have been blessed by Jurnus, the godlen concerned with travel as well as communication and weather, through the gift of a dedicat who made a particularly hefty sacrifice.

Girding myself, I step into the center of the loop—

And with a thud of my heart and a shudder through my veins, I'm standing in a matching loop positioned between a set of bookshelves and a gilded wooden desk.

I step out of my cord and nudge it off to the side just as Stavros's massive form pops into being next to me, as if out of thin air. He doesn't look remotely disturbed by our means of arrival.

We're the first to arrive. I take a moment to survey the space, which we've only used once before.

According to Stavros, this room is somewhere within the palace, next door to the college. The king told him the cords' power wouldn't extend much farther than that, as incredible as it already is.

I can't say whether we really are inside the palace and not just some secluded room on the campus, because the room hasn't got any windows. The only illumination gleams from a chandelier overhead, with candles I have to assume light up magically when there's movement below and snuff themselves out when we're gone.

It's hard to imagine King Konram assigning one of his

staff to stop by on a daily basis just to replace those that have burned out. The thick wooden door next to one of the bookcases is secured by three different locks that even we don't know how to open.

We can't go out into the palace... but presumably no one can get in either.

The desk is certainly fit for a king: broad, heavy, and glinting with gold detailing. Four leather-padded chairs stand around it, as if he decided there'd never be any need for all five of us to sit down at the same time.

Set against the walls on either side, the massive bookcases rise all the way to the ceiling. One is packed with books of history and theology, the other with scrolls on the same subjects as well as various maps.

A narrow doorway leads to a smaller supply room with blank paper, ink pots and quills, and more recent records from the college and around the city. Everything King Konram thought we might need for our pursuit of the scourge sorcerers.

I'm not anywhere near as well-versed in the college library's materials as Alek is, but he swooned when he saw some of the volumes that'd been hidden away in the royal collection. It was almost too bad when Stavros hauled him over to begin the actual meeting.

Only almost. I don't need to become any fonder of the eager glint that can light up the scholar's bright brown eyes than I already am.

The space is like a fancier version of our old archive room —an archive befitting a king. Including an additional feature I'm not sure how to feel about.

Hanging on the wall by the supply room door is an ornate mirror about half the size as the one we used to speak to King Konram more than a week ago. I'm guessing this one could be used for the same purpose, unless he thought fixing our hair would be vital to the cause.

Does he expect to be let in on our discussions here when he returns to Florian?

Pushing aside that uneasy thought, I set my bag carefully on the tabletop. A waxy scent laces the air, telling me that the bases of the candles are real rather than conjured. I breathe it in, but I can't take any comfort from the subtle sweetness.

This is going to be a difficult conversation no matter who's involved.

Casimir arrives next, his short waves faintly damp as if he's just toweled off from a bath. I yank my gaze back to the table before the heat that sparked between my legs at the sight can flare any hotter.

He notices the bag on the table at once. "What did you bring, Ivy?"

I have to meet his eyes then; have to smile because I don't want to be a jerk. Even though a twinge runs through my gut with the memory of seeing him with his patron this morning.

"I made an interesting discovery today," I say. "I thought we should discuss it."

Benedikt arrives with a typical jaunty grin. As he saunters over to me, he digs his hand into his pocket. "I have a little present for you."

He retrieves a locket dangling from a chain—just like the ones the men all carry. "I had my merchant echo the blessing on mine, so yours should work the same way. It seemed about time you had one."

My skin prickles with my sense of Stavros looming nearby. Benedikt wasn't around when the former general dismissed Casimir's suggestion that I needed a means to summon the rest of them.

"Oh," I say, reaching to take it carefully, a little

concerned that Stavros might swipe it out of my hand. "Thank you. Hopefully I won't need to use it again."

"Better safe than sorry," Benedikt replies cheerfully, and hesitates as his gaze slides to Stavros. "Did I beat you to the punch, Stav? If you were having one made too, it can't hurt to have a backup."

"It's fine," Stavros says, but Benedikt's brow knits at the edge in his voice.

He laughs it off a moment later and flops into one of the chairs with a return of his carefree air. Alek materializes a moment later, shooting a longing glance toward the bookshelves before joining us.

Stavros points his prosthetic hand toward me. "Ivy has something to share with us."

He manages to make it sound like a punishment.

Ignoring his mood, I tug open the mouth of the bag. "This is going to sound crazy, but I promise you, I know what I saw."

I saw it too, Julita pipes up. *I mean, it was insane, but it was also real.*

I slide the broken pieces of the clay rat out onto the tabletop. As I nudge them into an approximation of their correct form, all four of the men lean closer.

"Is that a sculpture of a *rat*?" Benedikt asks in an amused tone. "What, did you pilfer it from a shrine of Kosmel to try to catch his attention again?"

Rats are one of the godlen of trickery's symbolic animals, but I don't think my divine acquaintance had anything to do with this one.

I shake my head. "I saw a rat nosing around on the fourth floor of the Domi. Something seemed… off about it." Benedikt doesn't know about my magical sensibilities because he doesn't know about my actual magic, but hopefully the others can guess what I mean. "I tried to catch it so we could examine it, and it attacked me. I killed it accidentally—and it turned into this."

I motion to the clay figure.

No one speaks for a few seconds. Alek's lips part, but it takes another beat before he gets any words out. "You're saying an actual rat turned into clay?"

"Yes," I say. "The second it died. Which makes me think it was *always* clay, just someone magicked it into looking and acting alive."

Stavros clears his throat. When I look at him, his gaze burns into mine. "That's an incredible feat. You're suggesting the scourge sorcerers were responsible? Not anyone else?"

Benedikt's forehead furrows in confusion. "Why would we think it's anyone else?"

I know exactly what the former general means. He's suggesting my fathomless magic was responsible somehow.

I glower right back at him. "I can't think of anyone else who'd have an interest in doing something like that." Including myself.

Casimir rubs his chin. "There are a lot of purposes a scheme like that could serve, aren't there? The conspirators could be using small animals totally under their control to spy on staff or retrieve items or create some kind of effect. But I've never heard of anyone with a gift that could bring inanimate material believably to life."

We all look toward Alek.

The scholar leans forward to snag his fingers around one of the chunks of clay. Frowning, he examines it.

Then he lifts his eyes to meet mine. "You're absolutely sure it transformed? It wasn't just a trick of the light that made you mistake it for real?"

"Yes," I say quietly. "I was holding its tail—I could feel the skin and its fur brushing my fingers. And its teeth when they bit open my hand." I hold up said hand where a faint mark lingers after a medic's healing efforts. "I heard its skull break when I smacked it against the wall."

Alek's mouth twists. "I've heard of people who could animate figures like puppets before—still *looking* like the constructed object, made of wood or clay or what have you. But even in those cases, they had to stay close by to direct them. It's possible the scourge sorcerers have combined gifts to be able to conduct that kind of magic from more of a distance... But to turn it from clay into a creature of flesh..."

"People have tried," Benedikt says in a flippant tone. "It's one of those horror stories they like to tell, at least in the kind of childhood I had. Mothers who went seeking someone who could bring their infant back to life out of a doll. Parents who tried to recreate a beloved pet for their grieving children."

Julita shivers. *One of our maids told me that one about the baby.*

Alek is nodding. "Right. They're horror stories rather than histories because it doesn't *work*. No human being has ever been able to use magic to create life itself."

He taps his fingers down his front in the gesture of the divinities. "It's said that the All-Giver brought life into being by combining breath, blood, and flesh—sky, sea, and earth— as well as divine will. A *person's* will isn't enough. All you get is a body that looks real but remains totally lifeless. Not a rat that could scamper down a hall and fight being captured."

I sink down onto the arm of one of the chairs, hugging myself. "We didn't think the scourge sorcerers should be able to control daimon either, but it turned out they'd found a way. I heard Torstem saying they needed to switch tactics."

Stavros scowls as if he's displeased that he has to agree with me even a little. "You said he mentioned something about construction, didn't you?"

"Yes." I stare down at the remnants of the clay rat. "He could have meant figures like this."

Even Benedikt looks startled out of his normal breezy attitude. His face has gone paler than usual. "Gods above, if they can create life itself…"

Julita lets out a discomforted sound. *How can the villains be getting even* worse *than they already were?*

"We don't know exactly what's going on," Casimir points out in his gentle tone. "It could have been a very elaborate, very convincing illusion over a puppet-like figure. Or some other trick we haven't thought of."

The former general draws his brawny body even taller. "Still, it's nothing good. They're pulling together a new plan. We need to be more prepared this time. I'll pass on word to the king and let him decide whether he wants to put his staff on guard for vermin. It's a delicate balance between defense and tipping the conspirators off before we can take them down."

"*We* can all keep an eye out," I say. "For any animals—it may not be only vermin. If you see a bird hanging around the school more avidly than is normal, or even a stray cat or dog that comes out of nowhere… We should try to catch it. Then we can examine it properly and get a better idea of what the magic is."

Benedikt chuckles. "Don't use your strategy, you mean."

I make a face at him. "Killing it was an accident."

"We don't need to rely on Ivy anyway," Stavros breaks in. "We can handle a few things ourselves."

The bastard's bastard flicks his attention to the former general with another furrowing of his brow. He's got to be picking up on the new tensions that've formed between us—and he won't have any idea what could have caused them.

My skin itches with that knowledge.

I gather together the clay pieces and set them on an

empty section of shelf as the start of a collection of evidence. "We should all get on with it. My attempt at drawing Ster. Torstem's interest hasn't born any fruit yet. The daimon haven't caused any more trouble—the scourge sorcerers have to be up to *something* else."

"And the Crown's Watch hasn't turned up any further evidence of their activities," Stavros admits grimly. "The medics appear to have made a little progress with Wendos, but they still can't rouse him."

Alek dips his head with a jerk. "I'll see what I can find out about this sort of magic. We don't know how long we have before they make another major move."

He pushes away from the table but pauses to glance my way once more. "Be careful."

Before I have time to wonder why he aimed that concern only at me, he's stepped into his loop and vanished.

"I'll see what new rumors I can hear around the card tables as well," Benedikt offers, and hops into his own makeshift portal.

I straighten up, and Stavros motions me brusquely toward our adjacent rings of cord.

Casimir takes a hasty step toward us. "Stav—if I could talk to Ivy, just the two of us, for a minute?"

Stavros's scowl comes back, but he lowers his hand. "Fine. But I'm waiting for her here."

He stalks over to the doorway to the supply room to give us a little more space, though I can feel his gaze on me. I go over to join Casimir, pretending my heart doesn't wrench at his bright smile.

The courtesan lowers his voice so it's just for me. "Are you still coping with everything all right?"

I shrug as if rats made out of living clay are just another typical day. "Same as usual. Wishing we were making progress faster."

He pauses, his gaze flicking to the floor and up again. "You were in the cafeteria this morning—you might have seen me with—"

A flush sears up my neck. I interrupt before he needs to barrel any farther into whatever unnecessary explanation he's going to make. "It's fine. I know what we did the other day was just a little fun. I'm not going to get offended."

Is my heart aching like it's been stabbed through? Absolutely. But that's not Casimir's fault.

He wets his lips, the movement of his tongue only provoking more heat I wish I could will away. "With all the commotion afterward, we never really talked about our tryst. If anything about it left you out of sorts, I'd want to know."

The flush creeps up to my cheeks. Great God filet and fry me, has he been able to tell that I've fallen for him?

Have I been mooning over him despite my best efforts, and he's trying to get me to admit it so he can let me down easy?

I force my tone to stay as cool and steady as possible. "There isn't really anything to talk about. We both enjoyed ourselves, which was the whole idea, wasn't it? I haven't regretted it, if you're worried about that."

Gods smite me, has *he* had regrets?

Before I need to grapple with that awful thought for more than a second, Casimir offers me a softer smile that sends a flutter I can't suppress through my chest. "Good. Neither have I."

He draws in a breath as if to say more, but I don't know how long I can keep up my impression of nonchalance with him just a pace away, looking at me with those compassionate eyes in that gorgeous face.

"Then all's well," I say briskly. "I'd better not leave Stavros waiting any longer, or he might explode, and that would be quite a mess."

I say the last bit loud enough that the man in question hears it and lets out a derisive snort. With a bob of my head farewell, I hurry back to the former general's side.

Julita makes a puzzled sound. *Ivy, you have to know Cas would never do anything to hurt you. He really is concerned.*

I know he is. But with who we are and how I can't help feeling, his kindness hurts almost as much as cruelty would.

Twelve

Ivy

The hum of the Temple of the Crown's magic wraps around me as I gaze up at the immense marble building. I restrain a shiver at the sensation.

The gold spires of the four towers—three at the corners and the one in the middle that looms twice as high—shine as impressively as always. There's no sign that a week ago, a sorcerer of the most reviled sort of magic attempted to carry out a horrific purpose from that central tower.

If I'd had any doubt that the All-Giver abandoned our continent after punishing the first rise of scourge sorcery with fiery retribution, the scene before me would erase it. How could the One who is all things be here and *not* have noticed a mortal carrying out such horrific work in one of the grandest temples on the continent, in the tower dedicated to the highest of all divine powers?

I'd wonder why the lesser gods the All-Giver created haven't noticed either, but clearly at least one of them has.

Kosmel helped me direct the backlash of my unpredictable magic while I knocked down Wendos.

Why haven't the godlen intervened further? Is Kosmel up to something, and he's hidden what's happened from the others?

Are they all waiting, giving us mortals a chance to set things right on our own? Poised to rain down more punishment if we can't prevent the scourge sorcerers from going too far?

I don't know where they might draw the line. We could be teetering on the edge of a second Great Retribution right now.

Which doesn't make me feel any keener to step inside those pale marble walls devoted to all nine of the godlen as well as their creator. But I've got my part to play in the whole mission to set things right.

Benedikt passed on word through Stavros that a couple of the bug club members from Wendos's group played a few hands in the cards room last night... and mentioned that they were planning to make appeals to their godlen at the grand temple this morning.

Stavros decided we would spend *our* morning strolling the outer field near the main entrance marking out spots for future strategic exercises. At least, until I spotted the two students I was watching for making their way out of the college.

I followed them at a careful distance, only stepping into view of the temple's broad front steps just as the two of them vanished through the huge arched door at the top. They're inside now, asking for a blessing or insight from the godlen they're dedicated to.

It doesn't matter what they want. What's important is that they see and hear me.

I square my shoulders and stride over to the steps.

Climbing them today in the bright autumn sunlight isn't quite as unnerving as my first trip up these stairs through the thickening twilight. Not knowing if I'd be struck down the second I set foot inside. Not knowing what deviant magic was being carried out up in the tower.

I survived my initial venture, and as far as I know, no one's trying to destroy the city right at this moment.

My boots tap across the smooth marble of the entrance hall. I've taken to wearing them with my dresses even though slippers are more the fashion.

I'd rather not end up anywhere without every knife I can have on me. You can't conceal much weaponry in a slipper.

I could walk silently, but I want the worshippers inside to hear my approach. It seems as if Ster. Torstem has already mentioned me to at least one of his followers. I can hope these two will be curious about what I have to say to the gods.

A few other figures pass me on my way to the vast worship room. When I enter the space beneath the vast arching ceiling with its panes of stained glass, I see several people kneeling at the godlen's alcoves or simply strolling through the room in silent contemplation.

Thankfully, Kosmel's alcove is currently empty—other than the tall statue of the godlen himself.

I march over, letting my boots hit the floor a little harder than is strictly necessary. From the corner of my eye, I see one of the two bug club members—who's crouched before Inganne, godlen of the arts and play, in the next alcove over —glance my way.

Good.

I sink to my knees by the base of the statue and look up at the marble-cloaked figure of the trickster godlen with his sly smile. The sight of the carved rat on his shoulder makes me want to grimace.

What does my self-appointed divine overseer make of the scourge sorcerers co-opting one of his symbols for their use? He's been awfully quiet the past several days.

Casimir suggested that I should come here and open myself up to Kosmel, see if he'd offer more of his inscrutable commentary. Even here, with the multicolored light shining down on me from the painted glass above and an aura of divine power quivering through my nerves, my body balks at the idea.

The first time the godlen addressed me, I was nearly dead with my defenses crumbled. The second time, I invited him in out of pure desperation.

I'm not dying or desperate right now. I'm not sure there are any other circumstances where I'd welcome that imposing presence into my head.

It's plenty crowded as it is.

What are you going to say? Julita whispers. *You can't mention anything too unsettling with all these other worshippers around.*

As if I need to be reminded. But I've had time to contemplate my tactics while waiting for the chance to act.

I bow my head and pitch my voice so that it sounds low but still carries beyond the alcove. As if I'm trying to stay quiet but my emotion is getting the better of me.

I'm hardly yelling, but if anyone nearby pays attention, they'll be able to make out my words.

"Kosmel, please guide me. How do I make them see that sometimes change is necessary? I know that's what you'd want too."

I lapse into a brief silence. No divine voice resonates through my bones, but if there's a door inside me I'd need to crack open, I'm definitely holding it tightly shut.

I'd rather the godlen realizes I'm *not* actually asking him these questions genuinely.

Maybe this is the last time I'll have to put on a show. Stavros passed on word yesterday that Wendos was showing more improvement. Maybe he'll wake up within the day and spill everything he knows, and the conspiracy will fall just like that.

Until that moment comes, I have to continue as if it won't.

After a few moments, I speak up again. "Give me the fortitude to hold my ground when so much around me is wrong. Let them see how it could be better. Let us not cower in fear of the risks worth taking."

Julita hums with an uneasy sort of amusement. *Those do sound like the sort of sentiments Wendos would have approved of. And my brother would have whole-heartedly agreed with your point about risks worth taking.*

I can hope I've earned a few points with any eavesdropping scourge sorcerers, then.

My gaze settles on the dice scattered around the feet of the statue. Gambling falls under Kosmel's purview, and his dedicats often make their appeals or ask their questions with a roll that may convey his answer.

A tumbling die feels a lot less intimidating than a divine voice ringing through my skull.

I pick one up and squeeze it against my palm, thinking as loud as I can at the stone figure before me. *Am I on the right path? You want me to take down the scourge sorcerers—is infiltrating their conspiracy a sound strategy?*

Then I flick the dotted cube across the marble base.

It taps against one of Kosmel's boots and rattles a short distance to the side, landing on a three.

The standard interpretation is that odds are yes and evens are no, higher numbers indicating a more emphatic response. If I believe the godlen had any hand in how the die fell, I could take a little comfort from that result.

If I believed it. Sometimes I still have trouble believing I haven't hallucinated Kosmel's interference with my life altogether.

I stand up, giving one last addition to my performance. "Thank you for watching over me and all others who don't quite fit expectations."

Without glancing around, I head out of the temple.

My stance doesn't start to relax until I've left the last marble step behind. I meander across the cobblestone courtyard, taking a few moments to simply breathe before I barge back into the equally judgmental atmosphere of the college.

An urge niggles at me to rove farther into the city—to slip into Crow's Close and find out the latest shady street gossip, to check in on the outer-warder families who haven't been visited by the Hand of Kosmel in weeks now. To snoop around the brothel where Torstem hid some of his accomplices or the orphanage he plucked them from in case the Crown's Watch has missed something.

But I don't know how closely the conspirators might be watching me. I can't do anything that could suggest I have other, suspect motives for acting like a good scourge sorcerer candidate.

As I amble into the lane around the side of the temple that leads to the college, raised voices catch my ears. I pick up my pace and spot several guards milling about outside the palace wall farther down the lane.

My magic quivers in my chest with a hitch of my pulse. What's going on?

I slow down to give me time to study the guards as I continue toward the college gate, and a well-built figure falls into step beside me. I have to suppress a twitch of surprise at Benedikt's boldness, approaching me here in public.

"Don't worry," the bastard's bastard says from the corner

of his mouth, strolling along at a matching pace with his hands slung carelessly in the pockets of his embroidered trousers. "I'm using my gift of distraction to divert curious eyes."

It can't be that strong a gift when his dedication sacrifice was nothing more than the lobes of his ears. But there isn't much traffic coming in and out of the college along this road anyway, and the guards now hustling into the palace grounds aren't paying us any mind.

"What was so urgent you had to see me right away?" I ask, keeping my gaze ahead as if I'm walking on my own.

Benedikt pauses. His jaunty tone turns strained. "Those guards have a lot to answer for. Wendos is dead."

I flinch before I can rein in my reaction. Julita lets out a cry of frustration in my head.

With a deep inhalation, I regather my composure. "What? I thought he was recovering."

"From what I've heard, he seemed to be. He was starting to move, to murmur—more like he was in a dream than unconscious. The medics left him for the night—supposedly guarded, of course—and this morning they found his spirit had... departed."

The scourge sorcerers murdered their own to cover their tracks, Julita mutters. *No surprise at all.*

The same thought had occurred to me. My jaw tightens.

I drop my voice to the faintest murmur. "It must have been his 'friends.' They realized he might talk."

"Agreed." Benedikt lets out a rough laugh. "Although how they breached the security of the palace prison... Well, I suppose if they have even rats on their side, we're doomed."

Not doomed. Just out of hope that we can count on anyone other than ourselves.

Anyone other than me and my precarious plan.

As my stomach knots, Benedikt risks a glance over at me. He seems to hesitate again.

"Ivy… Did something more happen up in the temple's tower than what you all have shared with me?"

Shit. It takes all my self-control not to let my gaze jerk to his face. What has he figured out?

"I can't think of anything," I say cautiously. "Why?"

At the edge of my vision, I see Benedikt's mouth slant at a discomforted angle. "I've simply gotten the sense that our lovely group dynamic has been thrown off since that night in a way that doesn't fit what I do know. Stavros in particular has been acting rather oddly when it comes to you."

I'm going to have to lay into the former general about how poorly he's been hiding his hostility. My mind scrambles for an excuse.

"I think he's a little sore that I tackled the threat without him," I improvise. "The man does have quite the ego."

Benedikt chuckles, but he doesn't sound quite convinced. "You know, if there was anything else going on—we've been on this mission together from the start. We've looked out for each other. I hope I've never given you any reason to feel I couldn't pull my weight."

I swallow thickly. I don't think Benedikt has fumbled the investigation. He's been a valuable ally… Sometimes almost a friend.

When he kissed me that one time, mainly to give me cover, I could have imagined us being even more.

But he's also the half-nephew, bastard or not, of a king dedicated to ridding the country of the riven. A king I've seen him yearning to impress, as much as Benedikt tries to pretend he doesn't care much about anything.

I have no idea how he'd react if he found out the truth about me. And taking that gamble would put not just my life but our one current hope of destroying the scourge sorcerers in jeopardy.

"Of course not," I say firmly. "Although I might start questioning your judgment if you insist on accompanying me right into the college for all to see."

I give the second part a teasing lilt, but it serves its purpose. Benedikt winces and gives another chuckle that doesn't manage to hold much humor.

"Point taken, Knives. I've got matters to attend to elsewhere anyway."

He tips his head and veers off to make for the palace rather than the college.

Guilt sits leaden in my gut as I flash my bracelet to the gargoyle at the entrance and navigate the conjured maze to the directions embedded in this week's absurd password. *Flaming roaches lurch for righteous lust.* I'm not feeling any better when I step out into the courtyard.

Julita makes a sound as if clearing her throat. *I wouldn't tell him either. He didn't see Kosmel's mark on you—that's what's kept Stavros from going overboard. And Benny can be a little erratic. This isn't a matter where we'd want any more excitement than we've already had.*

Her confirmation takes the edge off my guilt but doesn't dissolve it completely.

I force myself to duck into the dining hall, because I'm supposed to be assisting with classes for most of the afternoon. Stavros will be incredibly unimpressed if I faint from hunger.

All through the hallways and between the tables inside the vast room, I sweep my gaze in search of furtive creatures sneaking about. I don't see anything except the usual haughty nobles.

I'm making for the classrooms in the Quadring after my

hasty lunch when a prickling sensation spreads across my left palm. I jerk my hand open in front of me.

The prickles soften into an unnerving tingle that seems to crawl across my palm alongside spindly lines even paler than my sallow skin. Spindly lines that form letters before my eyes.

You want more from this world. Tonight at the single bell. 50 paces into the woods. Come alone.

As the conjured writing fades away, my mouth goes dry.

I've been summoned.

Thirteen

Ivy

Like with the rat, I wait until the last of the men emerges from his loop of cord in the palace meeting room. Although unlike the rat, Stavros already knows what I need to say, which is how I convinced him that we needed this impromptu meeting.

As Casimir glances around at us with a worried expression, Benedikt sets a plate of pastries in the middle of the table. "Confiscated from the dining hall. I thought we all might need a little refreshment at this time in the evening."

I guess we know what he was doing when he felt the tug to come. Naturally he'd bring dessert.

The rest of us eye the assortment without making a move to grab one. I know my stomach is clenched too tight for the idea of eating anything to be appealing.

Benedikt plucks up a tart and sprawls into one of the chairs. "Well, let's hear the urgent news. I interrupted an excellent dinner for this."

The former general shoots him a disgruntled look. We weren't supposed to meet again until tomorrow, but I signaled the others with their lockets.

"Ivy received an invitation," he says before I can speak. "Presumably from the scourge sorcerers."

Alek's shoulders stiffen as he stares at me. "What? Already? Who delivered it?"

I glance down at my hand. "I don't know. Conjured writing appeared on my palm and then vanished again. They obviously don't want me having any proof of the summons."

"What did they tell you to do?" Casimir asks quietly.

"I'm supposed to go into the campus woods—at least, I assume that's the woods they meant—at the first bell after midnight tonight, alone. That's all I know so far."

Benedikt has paused halfway through his tart. He licks a stray drop of berry filling from his thumb. "The woods. That seems rather ominous."

I shrug as if I'm not all tangled up with apprehension inside. "We know they've conducted rituals out there. Julita pointed out evidence of it before. And it'd be away from prying eyes."

Alek frowns. "Which means they could do anything to you and no one would see to help."

I tap my thigh where one of my knives lies beneath the skirt of my gown. "I am reasonably good at defending myself."

"But you don't know how many of them will be waiting for you. Or what magic they might be ready to wield."

All of that is true, which is the reason for my tangled apprehension.

I force a smile. "I'll cross that bridge when I come to it. If they simply wanted to kill me, I'd imagine there are easier ways to arrange that."

Stavros pulls one of the scrolls off the shelves and spreads it on the table. It's a map of the college and its grounds. "I may be able to obtain something that'll help conceal my presence. The king is supporting us, and he has plenty of resources. If I enter the woods from a different angle—"

I tug at the edge of the map to interrupt him. "No. The message emphasized the *alone* part—and Alek's right. We don't know what magic they can bring to bear. They managed to murder Wendos while he was under palace guard! You can be sure that whatever they're doing, confirming that no one's going to spy on their activities will be at the top of the list."

Stavros's cocky voice takes on the edge of a growl. "You can't go waltzing off into the woods in the middle of the night to meet a group of murderous psychopaths totally on your own."

I set my hands on my hips. "That's been the plan all along, hasn't it? What did you think would happen if I caught Ster. Torstem's notice—he'd invite me to tea to discuss the possibilities for overthrowing the royal family? Anyway, I won't really be on my own. Julita will be there with me, and she knows what these people are like better than any of you."

You'd think I'd get a little credit from this bunch, Julita says with light-hearted offense, but she can't totally hide the tension in her tone. *I'll get you through it as well as I can. I don't know exactly what you'll be facing. I never saw Borys and Wendos initiate anyone into their practices.*

I can't imagine she's looking forward to potentially reliving aspects of her childhood trauma. But she hasn't said a word against me continuing with this plan, no matter how much danger it puts her continued survival in too.

Of course, it isn't the danger *I'm* in that Stavros is worried about so much as the danger I might pose everyone else.

The former general narrows his eyes at me. "It'll be an unnerving situation, and they *could* mean to harm you. It'd be easy for you to get careless in how exactly you defend yourself."

I might slip and unleash my magic, he means.

Benedikt raises an eyebrow. "Does it really matter how 'careless' she gets with blades when it'll be these pricks getting cut by them? I say Ivy can stick it to them any way she likes."

I fix Stavros with a firm look that hopefully he catches at least a glimpse of with his faulty vision. I warned him just an hour ago that the fourth member of our group was catching on that we were hiding something from him. "I'm sure I won't be flinging my knives so far that they hit anyone who doesn't deserve it. Although if you decide to lurk in the woods and jeopardize whatever trust I've gained with them, I'd count you among the deserving."

Benedikt stifles a snort of laughter.

Stavros glowers back at me, but he seems to relax his stance with concentrated effort. "I'll keep my distance, then, but I'll be on watch."

"Fine."

Alek sets his hands on the table, the bronze-brown skin of his knuckles paling. "You may have their trust now, but what if they're looking for something from you that you can't give them or don't realize? Once you've interacted with them at all... they're not likely to give you the chance to report anything back to the authorities."

I've already thought about that too. "I'm good at thinking on my feet. This is our best shot. What other options do we have now that they've killed Wendos?" I glance at Stavros again. "The surveillance of the brothels and the orphanage still hasn't turned up any leads, has it?"

He grimaces. "Not so far."

"I just—" Alek's hands clench against the tabletop. He drops his gaze to them before meeting mine again, his bright eyes so intense my pulse skips a beat. "You've already risked so much for this investigation. I don't even know if we could get justice for you if they murder *you*."

"Alek," I start, not even sure what I'm going to say to reassure him, but he shakes his head as if he already knows.

"I've seen records—there've been a couple of members of the entomology club who disappeared at different times. One body turned up looking like he'd been mugged. Another was set up to look as if she'd gone boating on the river and drowned. I'd guess they saw something they shouldn't have... and Ster. Torstem's people know how to remove 'problems' without it even looking like murder."

So if I die tonight—or later—at the hands of the scourge sorcerers, even my death might be for nothing. My stomach knots tighter in response to the agitation Alek's failing to hide.

"We'll know," Casimir says in his gentle way. "Ivy has all of us on her side. The scourge sorcerers don't realize that. No matter what happens, we'll see through their lies."

Alek still looks so miserable even with his expression concealed by his mask that my heart wrenches. He opens his mouth and closes it again in a tight line, as if there's something he wants to say but doesn't feel he can.

Has he found out something else that he doesn't want Benedikt—or Stavros, for that matter—hearing about?

A chill ripples down my spine.

I make myself pick up one of the glazed puffs from the plate of desserts and take a nibble. The sweetness laces my tongue without providing any comfort.

"Well," I say with a wave of the pastry, "it seems like that's all there is to talk about. I'll go into the woods tonight and not get murdered and find out what the scourge sorcerers are up to. The rest of you can go back to your dinners or what have you. I'll signal you through the lockets in the morning so you know I'm back at Stavros's quarters safe and sound."

Benedikt gets up, though I think the look he aims at the rest of us is a little wary. "I may have to indulge in a second dinner to make up for the first that'll have gone cold before I could finish," he announces jauntily, and steps toward his makeshift portal.

Casimir aims a soft smile at me. "I know you're stronger than them." He pauses until Benedikt has vanished and then adds, "They might ask about your magic—the magic they'll assume you have from your dedication."

I glance down at my right hand with its missing fingertip —what the men around me assumed was a sacrificial offering at first. "I can make up a story. They won't expect anything major with this small a 'sacrifice.'"

I'd sooner kiss Stavros's boots than tip the scourge sorcerers off that I'm godless, let alone what other magic I can wield despite that fact.

"We don't know what lengths they'll go to in order to confirm your story." The courtesan tips his head toward Stavros. "I can use makeup to imprint a believable godlen brand on her chest. I'll come by a couple of hours before they're expecting her?"

The former general gives a begrudging grunt. "We should be prepared for every possibility."

I hadn't even considered that one. My hand closes against the unmarked spot between my breasts. "Thank you for thinking of it."

Casimir's smile comes back. "Even if we can't go into the woods with you, you'll have our support."

Alek clears his throat with an urgent note. "Shouldn't Ivy be able to support herself in every way she can? If she has to prove something to the scourge sorcerers, or if she needs to defend herself, or there's a chance to find out more… Her riven magic would allow her to—"

"No." Stavros cuts in with a tone so dark and harsh it makes my pulse jump. "We're not adding more horrors to the mix. If Ivy's looked after herself so well for all these years without her magic, she can continue to do so."

"But—"

"We are *not* unleashing riven sorcery within a stone's throw of the capital palace," Stavros snaps.

I hold up my hand, catching Alek's gaze. "It's all right. I agree with him. I don't want to be throwing my power around either—I don't know what the consequences could be."

We stand in silence for a few tense moments before the scholar lowers his head in acceptance. I can't quite believe he'd approve of me bringing out my magic to begin with.

Just how worried is he about what will happen tonight?

"I know you can handle yourself," Casimir says with a brief touch of my arm. He vanishes through his ring of enchanted cord.

Stavros shifts as if he expects the rest of the meeting to break up, but Alek is still hesitating by the table. If there's something more he knows, he doesn't want to reveal it in front of the former general.

I motion to the dessert plate. "Why don't you have one, Alek? Take a moment to savor a little treat and remember how far we've already gotten."

He studies me for a few seconds and then reaches to pick up a tart.

I take another delicate nibble of my puff and raise an

eyebrow at Stavros, who's standing stubbornly there waiting for me to trot back to his quarters at his heels. "I could use a moment too, without you glaring daggers at me. You're about to let me wander off into the woods on my lonesome tonight—how much trouble do you think I can get up to in a locked room?"

Stavros attempts to glower me into submission, but he hasn't drawn his sword, so I feel reasonably secure it's a bluff.

After a moment, he sighs. "If you insist. I'm going to finally get *my* dinner and negotiate field time with the other military division professors. I should be back at my quarters by tenth bell—I expect to see you then too."

I bob into a mock curtsy that's probably less respectful than doing nothing at all. He shakes his head and strides over to his cord.

When he's gone, Alek sinks into one of the chairs. "You didn't need to stay with me."

"I figured dessert is more enjoyable with company," I say. "And I really do need a break from that oaf."

The corner of the scholar's mouth twitches, but the impression of gloom around him doesn't shift. All the same, I can't help tracking the movements of his full lips as they close around the edge of the tart.

All of these men are too ridiculously handsome for their own good. Or for *my* own good, is more like it.

Yanking my eyes away, I pop the rest of the puff into my mouth while I consider my words.

Propping myself against the table near his chair, I motion toward him. "What are you really worried about? You seem more concerned than everyone else combined. Did you find out something you didn't want to tell the whole group?"

Alek looks startled enough that I believe his denial. "What? No. It's only…"

He frowns and glances away. When he fixes his attention on me again, it's with an air of determination. "You're going in there with Julita. How much is she supporting what *you* think is the best plan, and how much is she pushing you to do what *she* thinks is?"

My hackles come up automatically, even as Julita makes a chagrinned noise. "I'm perfectly capable of coming up with good plans on my own."

Alek holds up his hands. "I'm aware of that. That's not what I was implying. I—I remember what you told us about how she persuaded the four of us to start investigating, and you said she'd used a similar strategy with you. Now you're diving into this mission that could very well be fatal. I know how much it mattered to her to stop the scourge sorcerers."

Oh, Julita murmurs. *Well. I suppose that's fair.*

It isn't, though.

I shake my head. "I also told you afterward that I blew the situation out of proportion. She's been a good friend to me, on the whole—as good as she can be, the way things are. It's a messy situation. But I didn't survive for eight years on the streets by letting other people badger me into doing things I thought were a bad idea. And this idea I came up with myself, whether you think it's bad or not."

Alek winces. "It's not so much that I think it's bad. It's just so risky, putting yourself in the scourge sorcerers' hands. And we'd lose both of you just like that."

Is that really the crux of it? He doesn't trust Julita whole-heartedly anymore, but he's also afraid that what little life she's clung to will be snuffed out? And maybe he's conflicted about wanting her and yet feeling he shouldn't both at once.

He always did seem to be the most devoted to her out of the four men.

An unexpected melancholy descends over me. I can gaze

at his handsome face and admire his incisive mind, and he once told me he wouldn't think I was an idiot for making a pass at him, but the scholar is just as out of reach to me as the courtesan is.

I can't give him what he really wants, because what he really wants is a woman who's only a ghost. Who maybe didn't even totally exist the way he saw her when she was alive.

But he still cared enough to make sure I wasn't being shoved into dangers I wasn't totally okay with. He trusts *me* despite the reams of research I'm sure he's done on the riven.

I want to give him something that means as much as that back, so badly my chest burns with the urge.

If he could just hear from Julita in her own words...

My stance goes abruptly still. Ah. But he *can.*

The mere thought sets my pulse thumping anxiously fast. I wet my lips and shoot him a hasty smile. "Can you just... wait here for a minute? I think I might be able to show you something that'll settle your mind at least a little."

Alek eyes me with obvious curiosity but nods in answer. I push off the table and slip between the shelves to the adjoining supply room.

What are you thinking, Ivy? Julita asks. *Did you stash something in here that I didn't notice?*

"No," I whisper, low enough that Alek shouldn't be able to hear. "I was just thinking—"

I halt with a jolt of apprehension that shoots from my gut to my throat. Am I really going to put this proposition out there, even tentatively?

I said she'd been a good friend, didn't I? I've told her I trust her, and I do.

This would be as much a thank you to her for all the ways she's helped me navigate this world as it is to Alek.

It's some kind of miracle that I can offer her anything at

all after the awfulness she's been through, including her own brutal murder.

I take a couple of steadying breaths to solidify my resolve. It still takes concentrated effort to form the words. "I thought we could make a deal. If I... relaxed and let you come forward, the way you've tried to before—the way you did when you made me let Alek and Benedikt into Stavros's quarters... you could talk to Alek. Reassure him about how you really feel. Explain things. Show him you're all right, or as well as can be expected. Just for a few minutes, and then you'd pull back. I wouldn't—"

Ivy, Julita breaks in, her voice a little shaky with shock. *Are you sure? I'd never have asked—*

"I know. That's the only reason I feel okay offering." I swallow down the nausea that's pooled in my stomach and square my shoulders. "You—you deserve to have at least one more glimpse of actual life while you're still here."

Julita lets out a raw laugh. *I wish I could hug you right now. You have no idea how honored I am that you'd give me this chance. You just let me know when you're ready. And if you change your mind, I won't be upset.*

I inhale and exhale one more time and lean against the wall. "Let's get it over with. Ready when you are."

I will my mind to wander as if in a daydream. My heart thuds on, but it feels more distant in my detached state.

Then the tingle of Julita's presence at the back of my skull ripples through my awareness.

My nerves jump with the instinct to block her way. I manage to rein myself in, floating on those ripples rather than fighting them.

My sense of my body turns fuzzy, as if I'm slightly numb from head to toe. My limbs move—my arms nudging me off the wall, my feet stepping across the floor—without any direction from me at all.

It is like floating. Drifting along inside a body I no longer control, all sensations clouded.

Is this how Julita feels all the rest of the time, when she's the one towed along by my decisions?

She saunters into the main meeting room but jerks to a stop when Alek glances around at her.

At us.

Her mouth stretches with a smile. "Gods above. Alek— it's so good to properly see you again. I don't even know where to begin."

Her voice sounds strange to my ears even though it's technically my own. I'm not sure if it's only because of my warped perspective or because she actually has a different cadence until Alek stiffens in his chair.

He can clearly tell something's changed.

"What's going on?" he says. "Ivy—"

Julita lets out a giggle that's definitely not a sound I'd normally emit. "She gave me a chance to speak to you properly. She really is a much more spectacular human being than any of you give her credit for."

Alek's posture stays rigid, but his jaw slackens. "Julita?" he croaks.

"In the flesh! Well, Ivy's generously lent flesh." She walks toward him, sliding her hand along the edge of the table as if reveling in the sensation. "I'm so sorry everything's become such a mess. I—"

Alek springs to his feet when she's still a couple of paces away from him.

"No," he interrupts, his voice taut. "Stop. Bring Ivy back."

Julita freezes, and I go still inside her.

Why's he so upset? I thought he'd be happy to get this chance.

"She suggested this, Alek," Julita says quietly. "She

offered. I promise you I'd never have—"

A tremor runs through Alek's tensed frame. "It doesn't matter. This is *wrong*. You've already— Bring her back, *now*."

Julita seems to flinch, and then her presence is slamming straight through my mind like a sprung arrow. I jolt back into full awareness with a stumble and a gasped breath.

The impression of my ghostly passenger whips into her usual place at the back of my head and dwindles away. She's not just retreated but pulled right in on herself the way she has a few times in the past—into the distant, darkened state where she's told me she can't sense anything at all.

"Julita?" I venture, but as I expect, there's no response. Not even a quiver of acknowledgment.

Alek is staring at me. He wavers on his feet as if he's not sure whether to step closer or not.

His voice comes out rough. "Ivy?"

I yank my attention back to him. "Yes. Why— I was trying to help. I didn't mean to upset you."

He still looks upset. His mouth forms a series of only partly familiar sounds that I recognize with my rudimentary Woudish. "*Do you know the hour?*"

"*A little past eight,*" I answer automatically in the same tongue, and understand why when Alek all but lunges forward to grasp my arm.

Julita didn't know a word of Woudish. Hardly anyone at the college does.

He was making sure it really was me, not Julita just pretending to have left.

I'm vaguely offended on her behalf, but Alek speaks before I can defend her, the slide of his fingers sending a distracting tingle up my forearm. "Don't ever do that again. She had her life. This is yours."

I frown at him. "Well, she's completely withdrawn now —tucked away so deep she won't even be hearing this conversation. You were worried about her. It was the only way I could give you a chance to talk to her directly."

He steps closer, his bright eyes piercing mine. "I don't need to talk to her. Not like that. You're worth more than that. I was mostly worried about *you*. You've already given up a piece of your mind and a heap of freedom and everything you were doing before you were dragged into this place."

"It was my own choice to come. I decided—"

"You decided what your conscience could bear, not what you'd find easiest." Alek lifts his other hand to touch my cheek. "She's right, you know. You're the most spectacular person I've ever known, and I don't want to watch you whittle even a little of that away to make yourself less for someone else."

Warmth blooms in my skin at his tentative caress, making it harder to think. But I'm nothing if not stubborn. "It was only temporary. I wasn't giving anything up."

"You weren't *you*," Alek says. "It matters. It matters to me. I—"

He cuts himself off with a choked sound, and then he's dipping his head to press his lips to mine.

My mind blanks in shock and a blaze of heat. I barely manage to do more than stutter a breath before Alek is yanking himself away.

"I'm sorry," he mutters, pressing the heel of his hand to his temple. "I'm sorry. Of course you don't— I'll go."

He spins toward the loops of cord. Through my reeling thoughts, it hits me that he thinks *I* couldn't possibly want *him*.

Gods smite us all, how did we end up so muddled?

I throw myself after him before he can reach his ring and catch his hand. "Alek—"

I don't know what else to say. I ache with all the things I

want and the possibility that this stunning, brilliant man might never realize it.

Maybe this surge of emotion matches what he felt just moments ago.

So when he turns back toward me at my tug, I let the flood carry me. I slip my hand around his neck, bob up on my toes, and meld my mouth to his.

FOURTEEN

Alek

I'm kissing Ivy.

Ivy is kissing *me*.

I haven't kissed anyone at all in a long time, but I think the moment would feel miraculous regardless.

So much about this woman is tough and unyielding, but her lips are perfectly soft against mine, sweet from the pastry she just ate. The heat of her floods me from the meeting of our lips and her hand at my neck all the way down my body.

I want to drown in the sensation.

My pulse races madly with the giddying thrill of the embrace. How is this even possible?

I don't know, but all I can do is kiss her back and slide my arms around her slim frame. Pull her closer against me.

Through the heady rush, the memory rises up of seeing her emerging into the archive room with Casimir at her heels. Of the jolt of a different hot emotion that shot through me at the sight of their flushed faces and her rumpled dress.

A stab of jealousy, a searing impulse to protest that she was *mine*, and a dull burn beneath that tempered the other two reactions with the knowledge that of course she wouldn't want me that way.

But she does. By some miracle, she came to me. For at least the space of this kiss, she's mine after all.

Her fingers tease up my neck to my jaw, her thumb brushing the lower edge of my mask, and reality comes crashing in with a lurch of my gut.

She isn't really mine, not in any way that counts. I can't say she's picked me when she doesn't even know who I am.

Imagining the recrimination that would appear on her face makes me recoil. I pull back even though it feels like a piece of me breaks putting that distance between us.

Ivy stares at me, her cheeks flushed for me now, with the same ruddy tint that laces her hair. Her lips part, and then something shifts in her sky-blue eyes. Her body starts to tense.

As if she's bracing herself. I've seen that reaction before.

I know *her* well enough now to recognize what it means. Buried deep inside the fierce, resourceful woman who captivates me is the girl whose mother starved and beat her, who fled to the streets of the outer wards rather than risk catching the attention of the gods.

And I'm catching a glimpse of that wounded girl in those doubtful eyes.

"No," I say hastily, grasping her shoulder. Trying not to let the soft warmth of the skin at the edge of her neckline divert me from my purpose. "I'm not stopping because of you. Gods help me, there isn't a single thing about you that I don't want."

She lets out a rough laugh. "Not a single thing? Somehow that's a little hard to believe. There are at least a few things about me *I* don't even want."

I swallow thickly. I don't know how to tell her in a way she'll accept that her being riven has only made me more sure of how incredible she is.

Maybe once she knows what I really am, it'll make sense to her. Even if that means she wants nothing at all to do with me.

I keep my voice as even as I can. "That might be so, but I know what those things are. I know what you've done and who you are. But you... you have no idea how much I have to be ashamed of."

Ivy's forehead furrows. "You don't need to give me a list of all your wrongdoings. Everyone's made mistakes."

My chuckle sounds hollow even to me. "Not like mine. I —I can't feel right about this unless we're on level ground, aware of exactly who we're both welcoming." Whether she will still welcome my embrace afterward or not.

I pause. "Unless you'd rather end things here without—"

"No," Ivy interrupts, soft but firm.

Her gaze searches mine. She lifts her hand to rest it over mine on her shoulder, giving my fingers a quick squeeze that just about unravels me. "If you feel like you have to tell me, you can tell me."

All at once, my stomach is churning. But I asked for this —I practically demanded it.

I've tried so hard to only look forward. To plaster over every bit of my past failings so nothing matters but what I've done since.

But if there's even the slightest chance she'd kiss me again even after she knows, dredging up my shame is worth it.

I glance over at the gilded table. "You might want to sit down. It's a bit of a long story."

As I let go of her shoulder, Ivy follows my gaze. She walks back to the table, but rather than take one of the chairs, she hops up to perch on the edge of the tabletop itself.

Somehow she looks more comfortable there with one leg tucked under her skirt and the other dangling casually, her hands set by her hips as she leans slightly back on them.

I've started to treasure moments like this—glimpses of the real Ivy who isn't pretending noble airs and manners. The way she should always get to be.

It was so obvious from my very first glance when it wasn't her moving her body at all, when Julita was molding Ivy's shorter and wirier figure to the flirty poise that came so naturally to her in her own frame. It was like watching a contortionist manipulating someone else's limbs, twisting them into shapes they weren't meant to form, almost more horrifying for how subtle the shifts were.

Ivy let Julita's ghost play with her body like it was a puppet for *me*. Because I bungled things so badly she thought I'd want that—that I cared more about getting time with Julita than having Ivy be Ivy.

It doesn't matter whether she wants to kiss me again. If I can at least convince her of how much she matters to me—as she is, without needing to bend herself to anyone else's whims—that will be more than enough.

I rest my hands on the top of one of the chairs. My fingers curl around the ornately carved wood, grounding me.

Where to start but at the beginning?

"I've told you a little about how I grew up," I say.

Ivy nods. "Weapons merchant parents, brothers who joined the army, none of them appreciating how smart you are."

The corner of my mouth kicks up at a bittersweet angle. "You might revise your opinion of my intelligence once I'm done." I run one hand back through my hair, gathering myself. "I suppose you're aware of the provincial schools some temples run?"

"You started your education at one of those?"

"Yes." I suck in a breath. "There's a temple of Estera that has a school a couple of towns over from where I grew up. When I turned thirteen—that's the youngest they'll let you enroll—I convinced my parents to let me travel there to apply for entrance. I think by that point they were glad to have me out of sight and out of mind. When I was accepted and came back to gather my things, they barely bothered with good-byes."

"Better off without them," Ivy mutters.

I can't argue with her there.

"I thrived at the school," I continue. "I quickly started earning top marks, and that only made me more eager to continue my success. The fact that I could achieve so much without any gift seemed to impress people even more. My teachers offered me exclusive opportunities, my classmates wanted to collaborate with me. I even had a few brief flirtations, as far as those ever go at that age."

Ivy gives me a smile soft enough to tug at my heart. "You must have been pretty happy."

I wish I could remember the happiness in all the vividness it must have had at the time. Every bright moment I think back on is soured by what came after.

I look down at the chair I'm still clutching. "I was. But then, about a year and a half after I began my education, a boy and his twin sister enrolled. They were late arrivals, around the same age as me, but right from the start, the teachers started fawning over him—they graded his work even higher than mine, let him in on the same opportunities."

"It makes sense that you'd find that hard," Ivy says.

"In some ways, maybe, but..." I grimace. "A lot of my frustration was pure prejudice. They were from a lower-class family—pig farmers, I think. At least a few steps down from most of us there and several from me. He'd made a dedication sacrifice, and it rankled me that he might only be besting me because of his gift. And he barely even seemed to *try*. He was always going off to play sports or cards or what have you rather than studying. Over the course of a few months, I convinced myself more and more that it simply wasn't fair."

Ivy is sharp enough to recognize where my story is going. Her voice comes out quiet. "What did you do?"

I push myself away from the chair, too restless in my discomfort to stand still. But pacing to the bookshelves and back doesn't make me feel any better. It only reminds me of the long nights I spent poring over books on subjects that had nothing to do with my usual areas of scholarship, my eyes burning from concentration and my shoulders twinging from hours spent hunched.

"I told myself it was only right that I leveled the playing field. The strategy I came up with was to dose him with a botanical chemical that's considered a 'berserker' drug—in a few countries in the past, it's been used by warriors to fuel their ferocity and stamina in battle. At the proper quantity, it lowers your inhibitions and sparks your aggressive urges for a few hours. I thought he'd act out a little, insult some teachers and get in trouble, and people would stop seeing him as such a shining star."

"I'm guessing it didn't work out that way."

"No." A lump clogs my throat. "Neither botany nor chemistry are areas I've spent much time delving into, and less so then than now. I don't know... Either there was something about him that altered the effect, an extra sensitivity, or I gave him too high a dose. He went on a violent rampage, stabbed a classmate, punched a few teachers who tried to subdue him... and he never fully recovered. His temper remained frayed; he couldn't concentrate on schoolwork. They had to expel him. I ruined his entire life."

My voice has gotten rough by the end. Ivy sits silently, absorbing my words.

I keep going before she feels the need to comment. "Obviously I felt horrible. But not horrible enough to confess what I'd done, because I felt even more horrible about the idea of getting expelled myself. Still so fucking selfish… But my rival's sister did have an interest in chemistry and suspected what I'd done. She brewed a potion meant to test my guilt—it would only burn a person's skin if they were guilty of whatever the person applying it accused them of."

Somehow, after everything I've told her, Ivy still winces in apparent sympathy as the implications must sink in. "She threw it in your face?"

At the memory of the searing pain and the acrid smell that flooded my lungs, I have to suppress a shudder. "Yes. In the middle of the dining hall at lunch time, yelling what she thought I'd done so everyone would see and hear. And the proof showed plainly. I'm lucky I flinched to the side and jerked up my arm, or the stuff would have splattered my eyes and *every* bit of my face."

"Couldn't the medics do anything about it?"

"I don't know," I admit. "The staff had the one on staff look at me, but I'm not sure how inclined they were to absolve me of my crime. She claimed the damage was set too deep for her gift to alter."

Ivy's jaw tightens. "So you were expelled after all."

I incline my head. "The temple school obviously didn't want to keep me. The only reason I'm here at the college is because one of the teachers saw particular value in my work. I've been most interested in finding traces of the parts of the continent's history that the Darium empire tried to destroy during their reign, piecing together fragments from journals and asides from treatises on other subjects… I'd managed to uncover quite a bit even back then. He took me under his wing privately and oversaw my continued work, and he recommended me to the scholarship division when I was old enough."

"It's been several years since your expulsion, then?" Ivy asks gently.

I can't bear the compassion in her voice. "Six. But that's no excuse. I was nearly fifteen. You knew better than to risk harming someone for personal gain by the time you were that age, even though you could have done it so much more easily."

Ivy's stance tenses. "I just made my mistakes earlier."

I sweep my hand through the air dismissively. "Because you were trying to save your mother's life and then your own. That's the most defensible excuse there is. I destroyed a classmate's entire future because of wretched *jealousy*. If either of us is a monster, it's obviously me. I even look the part."

"Alek…" Ivy scoots along the table, closer to me. "You're not a monster. You acted badly, but you saw how wrong it was, and you've made up for it. You've dedicated yourself to your work; you've been helping expose the scourge sorcerers. And I assume you've never been tempted to repeat the same mistake—you're not spending every day holding yourself back from making another spiteful attack."

"I'm not. But that doesn't change who *you* are. You can't help having the magic, but you've refused it, over and over."

"All right. Maybe I can believe that you don't think I'm a monster. Can you believe that I don't see *you* as one?"

My throat constricts even tighter. I make myself meet her gaze. "You've never really seen me."

The words hang between us for a few seconds. Then Ivy reaches out with a beckoning gesture. "Then let me see. Take off the mask, and you'll know for sure what I make of you."

Every particle of my body resists the idea. I haven't let anyone see my scars in years.

The last was one of the college medics when I first arrived. Her shiver of revulsion told me plenty.

But if I say no, then what? What has this whole confession been for if I'm going to refuse to expose the clearest evidence of my transgressions?

My shoulders have stiffened. I inhale sharply, and Ivy's eyes widen.

"You don't have to. I shouldn't have asked—"

"No," I break in. "You're right. We may as well settle this."

And let the cards fall as they may.

I take a step toward the table and reach for my mask.

FIFTEEN

Ivy

Alek sets his fingers against the edge of his mask as if he's looping a noose around his neck. I brace myself against the urge to leap in and stop him—not for my sake, but because he looks so conflicted.

Maybe taking this step will be better for him. But I don't know exactly what he's about to reveal.

He undoes a snap that attaches the mask's strap around his head and eases the molded leather away from his face. His head starts to droop so his dark hair falls forward, as if he wants to hide himself as much as he can still, but he catches himself and lifts his chin.

When he lowers the mask, he turns his face so the most damaged side is angled toward me. So the full impact of the chemical burn is obvious.

Across his forehead and nose other than a strip over his eyes where he shielded them, down his right cheek to the edge of his jaw, streaks of mottled scars discolor his bronze-

brown skin. Ruddy patches mingle with darker brown ridges, crossed through here and there by marks of deep gray.

In that first glimpse, my heart lurches, but only in shock. I hadn't pictured the damage looking quite like this.

But as I steady myself, gazing at him, it doesn't take long for my mind to adjust. There's nothing gory or frightening about the face before me. It's simply… different.

The swathes of different hues make me think of the impressionistic paintings I've seen—portraits and landscapes conveyed in broad strokes of paint that don't appear realistic up close but merge together into a cohesive image when you take in the bigger picture.

It's a style favored more by poorer artists who can't always take the time to match every tiny detail for pure realism, but I've always appreciated the vision that goes into them.

Alek shifts his gaze to meet mine, his bright eyes part of that varied canvas now rather than standing out starkly amid an even plane, but no less penetrating for it. His stance is so taut I'm almost afraid to speak.

He needs to see that I'm not afraid of *him*.

I slip off the table and raise my hand. "Does it still hurt?"

"No," Alek says quietly, with a hint of a rasp. "Not since the first few weeks."

I rest my fingertips gingerly against the right side of his face. Alek somehow tenses even more, but he doesn't pull away.

Ever so cautiously, I trace the erratic, overlapping streaks of color. The ridged lines are only slightly raised, the texture rough to my touch but not unpleasantly so. Even in the smooth areas between them, the scarred flesh feels thicker, denser, like scales more than skin.

But still just as warm as the other parts of his body I was pressed up against minutes ago.

"You know," I say lightly, "I think I like it. It's as if an artist decided to experiment with his techniques on your face. You're art. There aren't many people who can say that."

Alek sputters a laugh. "You don't have to pretend it isn't bad. I have a mirror. I know how it looks."

"You know how it looks to you. With the weight of all your regrets, with the knowledge of how all the haughty assholes around here would talk about it." The corner of my mouth quirks slightly upward. "You know, the same assholes who'd assume I must be a monster because of the crack in my soul."

"It isn't the same. You—"

"*You*," I interrupt, resting my palm flat against his mottled cheek, "are a pretty incredible person too. You don't have to let your past mistakes and the judgment of idiots define you. If a riven sorcerer can make a go of being a hero, then gods be sure you can decide what you're going to be now. I don't see how anyone can stop you."

Alek grimaces. "I don't think simply deciding is going to absolve me of my crimes."

"What about everything you've done since then?" My mind trips back over all my memories of our times together, my heart squeezing. "I don't think I've ever thanked you for how much you've been here for me. You tried to get me help when you could tell I was hurting, even though I was pushing you away so you wouldn't realize why. You listened to me. You kept an open mind in spite of the awful circumstances that brought me into your life. Even when you weren't sure you could trust me, you answered all my questions, you brought me all the information I asked for and more."

At the thought of all the reasons he's had to distrust me, my gaze drifts away, but Alek tugs it back with the grasp of my other hand in his. "I never thought you were a bad person, Ivy. Maybe I didn't know what to make of you at every moment, but I could tell you were doing the best you could with this mess."

A small but ever so real smile crosses my lips. "I'm glad I've had you and your brilliant scholarly mind on my side."

Still cupping his scarred check, I guide him to me so I can claim another kiss.

My mouth brushes Alek's tentatively, and his breath stutters hot over my lips. But then he presses closer and kisses me back.

It's not the hasty rush of our first coming together. More a careful feeling each other out, meeting halfway, testing just how far we can take this tenderness.

I run my fingers up into his thick hair, reveling in the texture that's a mix of soft and coarse. Alek lets out a rough sound of approval.

His arm slides around me, his hand on the small of my back beneath the worst of my own scars, but I can still feel tension in his stance. A trace of hesitation, as if he's nervous about giving himself over to the moment completely.

I ease back just an inch, teasing my thumb along his jaw. "You know, I thought you were breathtakingly handsome from the very first time we met."

Alek lets out a light guffaw. He tips his head so his nose grazes mine. "Did you?"

"Oh, yes." I tap those full lips that caught my attention even while he was interrogating me on our second meeting. "And now I know you're also clever and caring and brave... and just as stubborn as me."

He brings both of his hands to my face, framing it between them. "I can't keep my eyes off you when you're nearby. You *glow*, in so much color, like the sun shining through one of the stained-glass windows in the temple out there. And yes, you're stubborn, but about things that matter —and if we're talking cleverness, who manages to teach *themselves* Woudish—and the dedication you've shown to this mission that wasn't even yours…"

Alek pauses. For a second, I think he's going to kiss me again, which I'd fully approve of. But his voice dips lower.

"I'm not the only one who's noticed how fantastic you are. You and Casimir—I'm sorry I went off on you when I saw you two together—"

I grasp the front of his shirt with a firm tug to emphasize my point. "You've already apologized. I understand."

"I shouldn't have taken my jealousy out on you."

I draw back far enough that I can meet his eyes directly again. "You don't need to be jealous. Casimir made it clear from the start that what happened between us was only casual for him. He's been sweet to me, but that's how he is with everyone. I don't know if he even *can* see 'companionship' as something exclusive."

Alek studies me with his incisive gaze that picks up on so much. "But you would have wanted him to."

My throat constricts. I've had enough of lying to this man.

"I have… feelings for Casimir that I'm still sorting out," I say. "But that doesn't mean that I want you any less. It simply means that I've had a *lot* of feelings since coming here that don't seem to know how to make up their minds."

"And if Casimir showed that he was interested in something more committed…?"

I can tell the scholar is trying to sound detached about the subject, but his voice has gone a bit raw all the same.

I turn my head to press a kiss to his palm before I lock eyes with him again. "I wouldn't use you to pass the time while waiting to see if he comes around. I… I don't think that would be good for either of us, would it? If we're doing this, I'm choosing you. For however long it lasts, however it all plays out. And I'll be nothing but happy with that choice. I'll feel like the luckiest woman alive that I got to make it."

My voice drops to a whisper with that last sentence as it hits me just how true it is. A few weeks ago, I could barely imagine risking another no-strings-attached roll-about, let alone having an actual partner who wanted to stick around. Who I could trust with everything I am.

Alek gives a strained laugh, but his face has lit up. He leans closer again to speak in a murmur. "And what exactly are we doing here?"

Elation sweeps through me at the promise in his question. At the sense that we're teetering on the edge of crossing a line we'll never come back from... but that I wouldn't want to back away from anyway.

A wider smile curves my lips. "Well, I'm about to go on a deadly mission with an uncertain outcome. And—"

The ding of the palace bell, somewhere overhead, interrupts. Nine resonant peals.

I raise my eyebrows at Alek. "And we still have an hour before Stavros gets peeved. That's plenty of time. Why shouldn't we make the most of it?"

Alek beams back at me. "I think that's the most brilliant idea I've ever heard."

Then he's kissing me again, and it really is nothing short of brilliant.

Our mouths collide over and over, my desire flaring hotter until I have to gasp for breath. Alek takes advantage of the moment to grasp me by my hips and lift me back onto the edge of the table so I no longer have to stand on my toes to reach his lips.

I'm not sure what thrills me more—the strength I always forget he's hiding in those slim arms or the greater access he's given both of us.

Alek steals another kiss, tracing his fingers along the

neckline of my gown. "You know, maybe you shouldn't have to choose. From that poetry book you gave me, it's obvious women taking multiple partners like Signy did is pretty common in Woudish culture."

A breathless giggle slips out of me. "Or at least the culture of Woudish erotic poets."

He hums in shared amusement. "Whatever the case, it was kind of... exhilarating to read about."

"Oh? Did you get a lot of enjoyment other than scholarly out of my present?"

I think Alek has blushed beneath his dark skin at my teasing. He pauses. "I don't have very much practical experience to draw on with all of this. In case that wasn't obvious. I—there was barely anything with the girls I knew before my time at the temple school ended, and here... In my first year, there was a woman who pursued me, but I found out right afterward that she just thought it'd be exciting to fuck a freak."

I bristle around a rush of sympathy. "You're not a freak. Who was it? If I—"

Alek nuzzles my cheek. "It's all right. I don't need you to defend my honor. I just don't want you to expect more than I can offer."

"Hey." I angle his face to catch his gaze. "So we're clear, I can count the number of roll-abouts I've had on my fingers, without needing all of them. And half of those I didn't even really get off, which is why it stopped seeming worth the risk. You don't have anything to prove to me."

"I still want it to be good for you," he mutters. "I *have* done plenty of reading—poetry and otherwise. Scholarship can come in handy in all sorts of ways."

"I'd imagine it can."

He tilts his head next to mine, his lips brushing the shell of my ear. "You have no idea how many fantasies I've indulged in where I offer to help you expand your Woudish by reading that poetry book, and while we're going through it you turn to me and suggest we try bringing the verses to life…"

A giddy shiver races through my veins. But even more potent is a swell of affection so fierce my heart aches with it.

I hug him to me, absorbing the warmth of his lean frame. "That sounds like a lovely way to spend a day. But right now I'm happy to keep it simple. We *do* have less than an hour."

"Hmm. Better stop talking then."

He claims my mouth and slides his hand down the front of my bodice. His fingers chart the slopes of one breast, gradually working their way to the peak.

When his thumb travels over my nipple through the fabric with a sharper flare of pleasure, my breath catches. Alek grins against my mouth and repeats the gesture with a firmer pressure.

The delight his touch provokes builds with each iteration. I arch into him, urging him on.

In every caress, I can feel Alek gaining confidence. With a pleased hum, he gives my hair a light tug to tip my head to the side and applies his mouth to my neck.

His breath and his lips brand the sensitive skin from my jaw down to the crook of my shoulder. I sway in his embrace, a gasp slipping out of me at a tentative nip of his teeth.

"I want to kiss every part of you," he murmurs, "just to find out which get me the best reaction."

I let out a little huff of amusement. "If you're going to study me, then I want to study you too."

I give the collar of his tunic a yank. Rather than simply helping me, Alek pulls back just far enough to peel the shirt off himself.

Apparently he's a lot less shy about his body than his face. And there's nothing to be shy about.

My fingers reach out, drawn by the softly defined planes of muscle that cover his slim but toned torso. His godlen brand, Estera's sigil that's both looping and pointed, reminds me of his usual purpose in life. "I'm guessing you don't spend *every* spare moment with your head in a book."

Alek chuckles with a trace of sheepishness. "Exercise helps keep your mind honed. It's actually part of the scholarship regimen, to ensure we don't turn into sickly lay-abouts."

"Well, I approve."

I trail my hands right down his front, stopping just above the waist of his trousers. On an impulse, I tip forward to kiss his smooth skin just above his own nipples.

The cool, citrusy tang of him fills my lungs. His chest hitches, and then he's bowing into my explorations, fondling my chest in turn with one hand while the other slips around me.

With a few deft jerks, he loosens the lacing on the back of my gown. It only takes him a second to delve his hand beneath both my bodice and my undershirt.

The feel of his hot palm right against my breast brings a whimper to my throat. I mark a path of kisses up his chest and neck before our mouths crash into each other again.

Alek tugs my bodice a little lower and then slides both of his hands under the layers of fabric. He cups my breasts in unison, working me over with eager precision as he discovers exactly what sorts of movements spark enough bliss to shock more sounds from my lips.

A burning heat has formed between my legs—and I'm far too aware of the time ticking away before we might be interrupted. Nothing would put a damper on this interlude faster than Stavros barging into the room with his judgmental scowl.

I scoot forward on the tabletop so I can run my fingers right down Alek's abdomen to the bulge behind his trousers.

A guttural sound tumbles out of him. "Fuck, Ivy. I—"

He seems to decide taking action is better than talking. As I curl my fingers around his erection through the fabric, he shoves the mass of my skirt upward.

I squirm to make it easier to push the layers of silk aside, but my legs are still mostly covered by the divided underskirt that's like billowy pants underneath. The underskirt with knives strapped around my thighs overtop of it.

Alek lets out another chuckle at the sight of my weaponry, with no sign of being put off. With a shaky inhalation, he rocks into my grasp and fingers the overlapping folds of cloth between my legs to find the gap between.

Just the brush of his hand at the apex of my thighs sets off a sharp enough flare of pleasure to have me moaning. I give his cock another squeeze, delighting in the groan I achieve in return, but this partial closeness doesn't feel quite satisfying.

"Let me..." I unclip the straps that hold my knife sheaths and then wriggle right out of my underskirt and drawers in one go.

My intention couldn't be more obvious. Alek's breath quickens. He jerks at his trousers, and I help him yank them down.

Then I wrap my knees around his hips and grasp his shoulders. With a heady pressure that sends tingles all the way to my fingertips, he enters me.

The slickness of my sex can't leave any doubt about how eager for this moment I am, but Alek guides his cock in slowly, his breath turning even more ragged. When we're fully joined, he stops, just holding on to me and panting into my hair.

"You have no idea how good you feel, Ivy," he mumbles.

I try to push toward him, to encourage him onward. Alek grips my bare ass beneath my skirt to hold me in place.

"Wait. I don't know—I don't want this to be over too quickly. I need to last long enough that you get to feel just as good."

I brush my fingers over his hair, exerting all my self-control not to buck against him. "I already feel pretty fantastic." As I pause, the larger truth of the matter rolls over me with a sudden catch in my throat.

It takes a moment before I can speak again, my voice gone rough. "You know, this is the first time I've ever been with someone who knew all of me. I don't have any more experience with that than you do. But I can't imagine anything feeling better than I do right now."

Alek exhales in a rush and tips my head to capture my lips. He kisses me until my head is spinning with the passion emanating off him.

As his tongue flicks out to tease over mine, he tucks his hand between us and sets it low on my belly. His thumb strokes downward until it hits the spot just above where we're connected. A jolt of bliss shoots through my core.

His lips travel across the edge of my jaw. "Right there?"

His thumb pulses against my clit, and I whimper before I can answer. "Right there. So fucking good, Alek."

He works his thumb over me until so much pleasure is racing through my body that I start to shake—and only then does he finally move his hips. First in careful, shallow strokes while dappling kisses across my face and neck.

I grind into him with a needy sound, and a raw chuckle reverberates from his chest. He picks up the pace, thrusting into me faster, harder. Setting me alight from the inside while his thumb keeps conjuring more bliss against my clit.

Even with Casimir, the expert on all things carnal pleasure, it never felt quite like this. Maybe because even with him, I had to keep some part of me distant. I had to close myself off.

But Alek has already embraced every terrible part of me. He wants me as I am.

I have nothing left to hide here. I can simply be.

And oh, it's wondrous being me at this moment. My nerves sing with the pleasure thrumming through my body.

Alek's fingers dig into my ass with a firmness that only heightens the sensations. He holds me in place as he slams even deeper into me.

Our mouths crash together with messy kisses between hoarse breaths. The swell of ecstasy inside me builds and expands until I'm barely aware of anything except my hands clutching Alek's shoulders, his cock plunging into me, and the magic he's creating with his thumb.

The muscles in his hips tense against my thighs. "Ivy," he mutters. "I can't—"

But it doesn't matter, because just as he starts to spill himself inside me, the wave that was rising washes through me. I hug him even tighter to me, quaking and crying out with the force of my release.

Alek groans and wraps his arms around me just as firmly. He buries his face in my hair as his panting subsides.

For a minute or two, we simply rest there against each other, sweaty and spent but ever so sated. Alek stirs first, seeking out another kiss.

Then he freezes up. "We didn't take any precautions. I should have thought—"

I rest my hand against the scarred side of his face. "It's all right. At this time of the month, it's not much of a risk for me anyway. But just to be safe, I could take mirewort. I got the impression it's not too hard to come by here at the college."

Alek nods. "I can request some. Since we won't want anyone wondering who you're seeing if you ask about it."

I hadn't even thought of that. Trust Alek to consider every possible threat—and mitigate them for me. "It's effective as long as it's taken within a couple of days. You can give it to me at our meeting tomorrow. Which I will definitely be making it to, perfectly safe and sound."

A tinge of anguish crosses Alek's face as he gazes back at me.

"You'd better," he says with sudden fierceness. "Or I don't care what the king's orders are—I'll kill Ster. Torstem myself."

Sixteen

Ivy

"It may create a prickling sensation," Casimir says as he dabs a thin brush into the little pot of burgundy paste he brought with him. "But it shouldn't actually hurt. If it does, let me know, and we'll wash it right off."

When he brings the brush to my chest, I hold myself perfectly still. The touch of the paste does set off a faint and not uncomfortable burn—but the more prominent sensation is my heated awareness of how close we are, our bodies just inches apart.

With his courtesan training, can he tell what I was getting up to with Alek an hour ago? I had just enough time to dunk myself in one of the bathing rooms before I met Stavros back in his quarters, but a renewed flush ripples under my skin every time my mind slips back to my interlude with the scholar.

It doesn't help that I'm half-naked for this task. The

typical spot where a godlen sigil is branded lies well below the necklines of any of my clothes, so Casimir brought me a thin towel to drape across my shoulders and over my breasts for some kind of modesty.

It's not as if he hasn't seen those breasts bared before. But he isn't the only one in the room with me.

While Casimir paints the shape of Kosmel's sigil on my lower sternum, Stavros paces from his desk to the sofa and back again. "You're sure this technique will pass for an actual dedication brand? They'll be far more suspicious if she shows up with a fake one than none at all."

Casimir adds the thin horn-like points to the top of the sigil with a delicacy that has me suppressing a heady shiver. "I brought some rouge to make sure the details are just right. But the mark this paste will leave behind is pretty convincing all on its own. I have a colleague who uses it sometimes when he's working with a patron who might object to godlessness. So far, no one's called him out as a fraud."

"We don't even know if the scourge sorcerers will want to check who I'm dedicated to," I point out.

Stavros grimaces at me. "You'll be in a much bigger fix if they do and you're not prepared than if you're more ready than you need to be."

Well, he isn't wrong about that.

Casimir steps back, and my next breath comes a little easier.

I meant what I said to Alek—he's more than enough. I wouldn't pursue anyone else. But that doesn't mean the feelings that already existed have vanished.

"We leave the paste on for ten minutes," the courtesan says, rinsing the brush in a bowl of water. "Then we wipe it off, and I'll touch it up as much as it appears to need. The imprint should last at least a few days, but if you get called to another secret meeting in the woods after that, we'll want to repeat this process."

I nod. "Hopefully it won't take too many late-night wanderings to find out everything we need to know. Thank you for helping."

Casimir gives me one of the warm smiles that still makes my pulse flutter. "Of course. I'm sending you out there with all the armor I can provide."

Stavros clears his throat. "On the subject of combat equipment... We don't know how thoroughly they'll examine you in general. I'm not sure what they'll make of a noblewoman carrying a whole arsenal of knives. I'd rather send you with as many blades as you can carry, but..."

"That might be more dangerous than going relatively unarmed," I fill in. "Fine."

I reach between the folds of my dress to detach the thigh-strapped sheaths. "I'll keep one in my boot. It's not unreasonable for a noblewoman to be a *little* concerned with self-defense. That's my favorite knife anyway."

Stavros rolls his eyes skyward. "Of course you have a favorite."

I raise my eyebrows at him. "Don't you have a favorite sword?"

His silent glower is answer enough.

Casimir goes to the latrine to wet a cloth at the sink, but when he returns, he simply holds it in his hands, considering me.

"If you get a bad feeling about the situation," he says. "Worse than you'd expect, I mean—there's no reason you shouldn't retreat. You don't know anything about them yet. They shouldn't see you as a threat at this point. You could walk away if you need to."

I smile tightly in return. "I suppose we'll see."

He doesn't know that for sure. And it doesn't really

matter anyway.

I have to do this. The king is counting on us to take down the scourge sorcerers. I need to prove to Stavros that I can keep control over my magic.

What am I even here for if I back down now? I might as well flee straight back to the outer wards.

I might have to flee the whole city if Stavros decides I'm a traitor to this mission.

No. I've spent most of my life in hiding. I've finally found not just a purpose big enough that it might balance out the harm I've done but at least a couple of people who accept all of what I am.

I can't give that up. I have to be worthy of this chance.

When Casimir removes the paste, the pinkish-brown mark that remains on my sallow skin does look an awful lot like the brands I've seen. As the courtesan gives it a tad more depth with his rouge, my lips curve crookedly.

"I hope the gods don't see the imitation as outright blasphemy. I guess if any godlen would approve of this kind of trickery, it'd be Kosmel."

Casimir chuckles. "He has given you his show of support before." He touches my cheek with a graze of his fingertips. "Make it back safe, Ivy."

My throat constricts. "That's my plan."

As Casimir gathers his supplies, Stavros steps toward the loop of cord the courtesan arrived here through. "After you've returned to your room, I'll bring this back to its usual place. We'll see you at tomorrow's meeting."

Casimir bobs his head in acknowledgment and farewell, aims one more gentle smile my way, and then vanishes through the cord's magic.

While Stavros is sorting out the cords, I quickly don my chemise and pull up the front of my gown. I'm nearly done with the laces by the time the former general returns.

He eyes me with one of his inscrutable expressions and a brief twitch of his head, and an uneasier heat tickles over my skin. I have the sudden, misguided urge to ask him to come over and help me finish tying the laces.

As if he'd agree. As if I should even care whether he does.

I give them a few final tugs myself and smooth my hands down the skirt of my dress. Across the courtyards, the palace bell starts to ring out its longest series of peals.

Midnight. One hour to go.

I fold my arms over my chest and give Stavros a pointed look. "You know, you should probably at least make a show of going to bed. It's not going to look like I snuck off on you if anyone notices the light's still glowing in your window when I'm leaving."

Stavros sighs, but he knows I'm right. He makes a vague motion toward me. "You have everything you need?"

A dry laugh hitches out of me. "As far as I know. It's a bit difficult to be fully prepared for illicit meetings with mysterious figures."

He balks for a moment longer, as if he thinks he can intimidate my power into staying under wraps with his frown, and then he stalks away into his bedroom. The door thumps shut behind him, but I don't exactly feel alone.

I douse the lantern in the main room and sit down on the sofa. The darkness wraps around me, the quiet of the night feeling unusually ominous.

A tingle stirs in the back of my skull. *Ivy?* Julita whispers.

She's returned from wherever exactly she goes when she withdraws from my awareness. I was starting to wonder if she'd end up missing our first foray among the scourge sorcerers.

She might not have minded if she did. I can't imagine what horrific memories tonight will stir up for her.

I open my mouth and close it again, settling for simply

tipping my head in response. I don't think there's much chance Stavros actually *has* gone to sleep, and I feel strange talking to her where he could easily eavesdrop.

Maybe I should get a bit of a head start on the whole sneaking out thing.

I pull my hooded cloak over my dress and hair before slipping out into the hall. The lanterns there have all been snuffed out for the night.

From around the nearest corner, I can hear someone stumbling between drunken giggles and someone else doing their best to shush them. Otherwise the staff halls are empty.

I turn in the other direction, toward the narrow hallway at the very back of the school that's too cramped and dreary for the nobles to venture into unless they're feeling particularly secretive.

As I walk, I veer from one side of the hallway to the other, keeping my senses alert for any unexpected quivers of magic. I don't know how many enchanted creatures the conspirators might have created, but if they could use one to spy on me now, it seems likely they would.

Nothing catches my notice. I duck into the stairwell and pad down the spiraling steps halfway to the third floor. Then I sit down against the cool stone wall.

"Are you okay?" I ask Julita in a murmur. "I'm sorry—I didn't know Alek would react that way."

How awful must she have felt to finally have a moment to speak to him again only for him to shove her away?

Julita lets out a soft laugh. *How could you have known when I had no idea either? Obviously... obviously he's become even more attached to you than I realized.*

Is there a bittersweet note in her voice? My ghostly passenger has made a good show of not caring about the men she assembled beyond their usefulness in tackling the scourge sorcerers, but I've noticed cracks in her façade.

She might not have believed it'd be a good idea to pursue anything deeper with them, might even have convinced herself that none of them would truly care about *her* beyond the unflappable, charming front she presented, but they mattered to her. She was abused by her brother and his friend as a child, had no one around she trusted enough to turn to for help—that'd mess up anyone's mindset.

Probably the only reason she trusts *me* is she doesn't have much choice.

"I wasn't expecting him to care that much about me either," I say.

I trust he was able to forgive you for letting me take charge. I told you before, Ivy—you should have your happiness where you can take it. Why shouldn't it be with Alek? She pauses. *Did he say whether he forgives* me?

I actually can't remember if Alek said anything at all about Julita after she returned my body to me, other than to confirm it really was me he was talking to. "He didn't mention it, but he didn't appear to be angry with you. I made sure he knew it'd been my idea."

Ah. Well, I suppose all's well that ends well.

She doesn't ask what happened between Alek and me afterward. I don't know whether she can guess or she doesn't want to know or she's allowing me my privacy.

Possibly it's all of those reasons at once.

There's still time before I need to enter the woods. I continue down the stairs and make a brief detour to the stables to apologize to Toast that I haven't taken him out in a while. Then I meander toward the back of the outer courtyard where the tree line looms.

When the palace bell lets out its single peal, I venture down the main path into the woods.

I count off the paces silently. Fifty would lead to a fair bit of variation depending on the length of the legs doing the walking, but I guess it'll get me to the right general area.

The glow of the school buildings' external lanterns falls away behind me. The branches overhead block out most of the moonlight. By the time I reach fifty, I'm finding my way by squinting at the dim columns of tree trunks to avoid walking into them.

I stop and glance around, but I can't make out anything at all except the nearest, incredibly vague shapes of the trees in the darkness. Leaves rustle overhead, and an insect buzzes by somewhere to my left. The cool breeze licks under my cloak, rippling the fabric.

My magic tugs at me, offering to sharpen my sight and form shapes out of the darkness. I clench my jaw in refusal.

What I said to my men was true. Even if my power could make this task easier, I don't trust it. It'd probably turn someone blind to give me greater vision.

Kosmel helped direct the consequences before, but I have no idea if he's listening now. If he'd think it worth extending his divine power just to spare me from the darkness.

I have no idea how quickly the madness might start to creep through my mind if I embraced my broken soul.

It's safer for everyone, including me, if I continue turning to my magic only as a last resort.

The seconds tick by with the thud of my heart. Nothing happens.

This is rather anti-climactic, Julita murmurs.

Did I already make a misstep, and the conspirators have decided not to bother with me? Did I misread the message that appeared on my palm?

I adjust my weight, restraining the urge to pull my knife from my boot so it's closer at hand.

How long should I wait?

This could be part of the test. Evaluate how committed I

am, whether I'm intrigued enough to hang around rather than giving up and leaving.

They're probably also keeping watch to ensure I've actually come alone.

I have no idea how long it's been already. Wetting my lips, I keep my breaths steady and my ears pricked.

Something slides across the ground to my right. Tensing, I glance down.

My eyes have adjusted enough to the traces of moonlight that I catch the curve of a sinewy form winding into the grass at the edge of the path. A snake.

My nerves jitter with a sense of magic. Was that creature conjured from clay like the rat?

Or am I getting so bored I'm imagining things?

Two peals of the palace bell resonate through the night. I lift my head—and all at once a more potent wave of magic sweeps around me, setting the hairs on my arms on end.

"Welcome, Ivy Euridya of Nikodi," a voice warbles, thin and yet seeming to reach me from several directions at once.

The magic I sensed must be carrying it—disguising the speaker and the direction they're standing in. I don't recognize the voice at all.

I'm supposed to be playing the part of a disgruntled but idealistic noblewoman. I draw myself up straighter. "I came as you asked. What did you mean about wanting more from the world?"

The words continue to drift around me as if carried on the breeze. "You can sense that something isn't quite right, can't you? The way the kingdom is run, the way we honor our gods."

I shrug as if I'm being careful about sharing my opinions. "The daimon definitely seemed to feel there's a problem. I don't think anyone could argue about that."

"And would you want to heal the damage that's been

done if you could? If you had the chance to change all of Silana—all of the continent—for the better, would you take it, even if the way was hard?"

Julita lets out a scoffing sound in my head. We know what ways these people have been turning to—and that they've been cajoling kids into taking on the real hard parts.

I remain cagey. "I suppose that would depend on what kind of hard you mean. Of course I'd want to serve the godlen as well as I can."

Wendos thought that what he and his associates were doing was somehow honoring the gods. I'm going to assume that's a common line of thinking among the conspirators.

They have to justify the horrors they're committing somehow.

"There are many who'd stand in the way of rebuilding what was lost," the voice says. "You would need to work against them and risk punishment if you're found out."

My brother never trusted anyone—except maybe Wendos, Julita says. *I don't know if you can even dabble in scourge sorcery without getting paranoid. They'll be suspicious if you give in too easily.*

I can believe that.

I cock my head to the side. "Why should I accept that *you* know what's right when you won't even show yourself? I have no idea who you are."

"We must be cautious if we're going to succeed. The fate of the world rests on our shoulders. Any indiscretion jeopardizes that goal."

These murderous psychopaths do think awfully highly of themselves, don't they?

"How am I supposed to fit in, then?" I demand. "If you're not going to tell me anything specific, I don't see how I could help even if I wanted to."

"Once you've earned our trust, we can reveal more. We

will give you simple tasks, and if we're satisfied with the result, you'll earn more responsibility. Trust can flow both ways."

How very poetic.

I restrain myself from wrinkling my nose. "I'll admit I'm intrigued. What do I have to do first to get you to tell me more?"

I guess I shouldn't be surprised by the request that follows, knowing what I do.

"Show that you're willing to give of yourself. There's a dagger on the ground a few steps ahead of you. Find it, cut your palm, and offer your blood to the All-Giver with whatever prayer feels most fitting to you."

To the All-Giver, not to the unknown speaker and their fellow conspirators.

I don't see how that act can hurt anything—other than my hand. "I can do that."

I feel along the ground until my fingers brush the hilt of the dagger. It's a small one, the grip barely long enough for me to wrap my whole hand around it.

As I straighten up, I cautiously arch my eyebrow in a silent question. What does Julita think these people would consider an appropriate prayer?

When my invisible companion speaks, her tone is more subdued than usual. *Borys and Wendos mostly talked about their own personal power. But sometimes they'd add in something about how they'd use that power to honor the gods.*

That gives me a little more material to work with beyond what I heard from Wendos in the tower.

I bring the blade to my right palm, half expecting Julita's presence to withdraw before she has to experience the pain of blood-letting again. But she remains, the tingle of her presence twitchier than usual but still with me.

Go ahead, she says. *I'll be all right. This is all so we can defeat them in the end.*

I drag in a breath and dig the edge of the blade into my skin.

Pain stings along the line I've cut down the middle of my palm. I kept it shallow but pierced far enough that several drops of blood streak across my hand and patter to the dirt below.

I tilt my head back toward the sky. "All-Giver, Great God, the One who made all that exists around me, I give of myself to you. See me, show me the way that is right, and I will carry out whatever purpose you put me to. Whatever strength you give to me, I'll use it to better this world."

My nerves jitter with the words, but it's actually less frightening calling out to the All-Giver than any of the godlen. After all, the Great God abandoned the realms of the continent centuries ago... after razing the first scourge sorcerers from existence.

Really, we have the same goals.

I doubt my voice can reach wherever the All-Giver has gone. And I mean what I'm saying anyway, even if not in the way I intend the conspirators to think.

But making a plea to the highest power I know of is still a little intimidating.

No godly voice answers in my head. Only the unknown watcher from wherever they're poised amid the trees. "You could do great things with an attitude like that, Ivy of Nikodi. You could be one of the few to truly serve the All-Giver as the Great God deserves."

Ah, so now they're buttering me up, making me feel special in the hopes that I'll want to chase that feeling. I've watched so many con artists using similar tactics on the streets of the outer wards.

"If I can, I will," I say more earnestly than is truthful.

"Put the dagger down and bind your cut with the cloth

that was lying next to it. We have one more matter to discuss tonight."

As I wrap the strip of fabric around my palm, the pain of the cut dulls with a quiver of magic. The bandage is Elox-blessed.

"What's the other 'matter'?" I ask.

"There's a small package we'd like you to deliver for us. You'll be able to carry it in a pocket unnoticed. We ask that you bring it to the Temple of the Crown tomorrow night and leave it behind Prospira's statue."

I knit my brow. "What *is* this thing I'm going to be carrying around?"

"All you need to know is that it's heavily enchanted, and the magic must not be disturbed. Opening the pouch it's enclosed in could ruin its potency."

My skin crawls. The question I think anyone else would most likely ask first is, "It won't hurt me, will it?"

The voice chuckles. "Oh, no. Especially not if you leave it be and carry out your task as requested."

"What's the point of bringing it to the temple anyway? What's it going to be used for?"

"The powers that be stand in our way, but our work needs to be done. We do what we can to thin their numbers."

I stiffen against a very honest hitch of my pulse and let more concern seep into my voice than I would have if I didn't want to sound normal. "You mean it's going to hurt someone *else*? Someone important?"

"I didn't say that. And nothing at all will happen while you're nearby."

The implications are there, though. This is the real test—seeing if I've bought into the speaker's grand talk enough to risk being party to treason.

What else can I do? If I refuse, the road ends here. I might not even survive the walk out of the woods.

"This is your first opportunity to serve the All-Giver as you said," the voice goes on at my hesitation. "If you would prefer to return to your previous life of following orders and bowing to those who haven't earned it—"

"No," I say quickly, with feigned urgency. "I'll do it. Where's the package?"

"At the base of the tree directly to your left. Take it, and leave the woods. And remember to keep the pouch closed."

"I know."

I approach the tree I can only vaguely see and kneel down. My heart is thudding in anticipation, my body braced for the magic I expect to feel radiating from my new cargo.

My hands find a leather pouch no wider than my smallest finger. I can't imagine it's holding anything much bigger than a ring.

I take it into my grasp…

And there's nothing.

Not even a tiny quiver of magic wafts off the pouch and its contents. As far as my riven soul can tell, there's no power attached to it at all.

Suppressing my confusion, I stand up and tuck the pouch into the pocket at my hip. Were the conspirators somehow mistaken about an artifact they got their hands on? Or—

The answer comes to me like a flaming arrow out of the night.

It's all a trick. A gambit to test me in all sorts of ways.

They wouldn't trust me with a blessed object when I've barely started proving myself. They simply want to know whether I'll do as they say. Whether I'll alert the authorities to their supposedly violent scheme.

This time.

When I carry out their task, gods only know what they'll ask of me next.

SEVENTEEN

Ivy

A n even thicker silence hangs over the school when I
return to the Domi. Even the drunkards have
found their way to their beds.

I slink through the halls with every sense on the alert.
The small weight grazing my hip with the sway of my skirt
keeps me tensed even though it appears to be a decoy.

I bring my bracelet to the right spot on Stavros's door
and ease it open at the click of the lock. To my surprise, the
former general hasn't prowled out so he can glower at me
immediately on my return.

As I shut the door behind me, a grunt reaches my ears
from the bedroom. Then a violent rustle of fabric.

My pulse lurches. Has someone broken into the rooms
and attacked him?

I dash to the bedroom door and yank it open.

In the thin moonlight, it's immediately clear that Stavros
is alone on his expansive bed. He's sprawled on top of the
covers, his vest discarded on a nearby chair but his massive

frame still clothed in the same dress shirt and trousers he was wearing when I left.

That and the prosthetic hand still attached to his wrist prove he didn't plan to fall asleep. It looks as if he propped himself up on a pillow leaning against the headboard and then sagged to the side when he drifted off accidentally.

I have been gone for a while.

The chiseled planes of his face have softened in this state, but somehow that makes him look both younger and wearier. I can't help remembering the way he talked the first time he woke *me* up from a nightmare, when he let his cocky assurance drop for long enough that I could see how much the loss of his gift and his military career weighed on him.

He's carrying plenty of burdens of his own. Which must be why his sleep is anything but peaceful.

As I take in the scene, his arm jerks against the covers with another rasp of fabric. His brow furrows, and he sucks in a hitched breath.

"No," he mutters. "Michas, watch— Stop!"

The last words come out so raw I can't bear to walk away. I dart to the edge of the bed and grasp his ankle.

"Stavros," I say, low but forceful, giving his leg a quick shake. "Wake—"

He jolts upright before I can even finish the command. His hand whips toward me as if to grab me, and I throw myself backward.

My shoulder jars against the side of the doorframe. My magic flares with a defensive lash, but I grit my teeth and tamp it down.

Prickles spread through my chest in response, like a dozen needles scraping their points over my innards. It's still a mild enough pain that I can stand against it, but a chill quivers through me.

My power is getting more restless. How long until it starts ripping open my lungs and whatever else again?

The former general glares at me, both his hair and his eyes fathomlessly dark in the dimness, his entire body rigid. "What do you think you're doing?"

The cutting tone, somehow even more hostile than what he usually aims at me these days, kindles my temper and burns away every shred of sympathy. As if I'm not already dealing with enough without him becoming an even bigger jerk.

I stay where I am, crossing my arms and glaring right back at him. "Waking you up from what sounded like a pretty unpleasant dream. You're welcome."

His lips draw back from his teeth. "I don't need *you* fighting any battles for me. Worry about yourself. What happened in the woods?"

"I didn't cause any disasters," I shoot back. "And I think I played the part well enough that I'll get deeper into the conspiracy. They're too cautious to give away much at the beginning, of course."

"So you've got nothing useful after all that fuss."

I swallow a hiss of exasperation. "Nothing that'll take down the scourge sorcerers right this minute, but I'm on the right track."

"Wonderful. If you haven't set the school falling down around our ears, get out of my bedroom and I'll hear about the rest with the others."

The dismissal stings, which maybe is why I let my curiosity get the better of me as I scoot into the doorway. "Who's Michas?"

The snarl in Stavros's voice confirms just how unwise a question that was. "You're the last person who should be bringing up that name. Get the fuck out!"

With a wince, I scramble over the threshold and yank the door shut behind me.

I've never heard him talk about anyone named Michas before, Julita murmurs. *What under the gods' gaze is the matter with Stav tonight?*

Stavros's parting words have made me abruptly sure of the answer, with a sour taste that's crept up the back of my throat.

Who would enter one of his nightmares that he'd be particularly offended by me talking about? What are the chances it's *not* the one person close to him who was murdered by a riven sorcerer like me?

And if he came out of a dream about monstrous magic only to see the most recent person he's witnessed working it... I can't say I forgive him for his animosity, but I can understand it.

Even if I can explain his reaction to myself, that doesn't make the atmosphere in his quarters any more comfortable. I drift over to the sofa, but my skin is itching, my heart beating at an anxious pace.

I'm not getting any sleep like this. How can I drift off with just a door between me and a man who's looking like he wants to murder *me*?

My head feels heavy with fatigue after the late night and the stress of everything I've been through, but with every second I stand within these walls, my nerves twitch with more agitation.

My magic will act up even more if I'm in a panic. I need to walk it off. Clear my head, give Stavros time to simmer down.

Maybe by the third bell, I'll feel like I can take a little rest.

Julita stays silent as I slip back into the hall. She's been with me through enough turmoil to know my usual habits for dealing with fraught situations.

I don't want to roam around inside the building where I might disturb the other inhabitants. So I descend the back stairwell again and step out into the cool night air.

My feet carry me of their own accord across the courtyard. I tip my head back and take in the vast stretch of stars in the clear sky above me.

A pang like homesickness runs through my chest. The tops of the buildings on either side of me cut off a lot of my view, though.

I sneak through one of the Quadring's side halls to the broader fields of the outer courtyard. There's a gazebo a short distance behind the stables, where I often see students gathered to gossip and flirt during the day.

At night, it's just an empty shell. An empty shell with a conveniently placed railing for my purposes.

I hang back at the edge of the entranceway while a soldier on patrol marches past. When he's disappeared around the front of the Quadring, I steal across the field to the gazebo.

Clambering up the side isn't quite as easy in a gown and cloak as it would have been in my typical outer-wards tunic and breeches, but I manage with a minimum of fumbling. My sliced palm doesn't even sting in its bandage of healing fabric.

I haul myself onto the slanted roof and lie back on the smooth boards with the sky spread above me.

"Now that's a view," I whisper.

I've never paid much attention to the stars, Julita admits. *I suppose if I was up after dark, it was usually at a dance or a pub, not out in the open.*

When I was little, Linzi and I occasionally snuck out at night to the small park near our house. We'd huddle together on the grass, suppressing giggles, and I'd point out the constellations I'd learned to her.

Back when the world seemed like a relatively safe place, with not much more to worry about than tripping on a loose cobblestone or getting ink on a favorite dress.

Melancholy swells up inside me. I push it away with a lift of my hand toward the stars.

"That line there they call Elox's Staff. You see it makes kind of a curve at the top like a shepherd's crook?"

So we're supposed to think Elox is lounging about up there in the sky?

My lips twitch in amusement. "It's more of a poetic thing. But I guess he could be. Aren't the godlen supposed to be everywhere all at once?"

Julita chuckles. *It's a wonder they ever pay attention to anything at all down here when they're spread that thin. We should be glad Kosmel, at least, noticed enough to get involved.*

I'm not sure I love the results of the trickster godlen's involvement, but I keep that to myself and point to a different part of the sky. "That diamond-ish cluster is supposed to be Inganne's greatest kite."

Hmm, I can almost see that one. I think she'd appreciate a sparkly accessory.

Having been to one of the joyfully chaotic temples dedicated to the godlen of creativity and play, I can agree with that.

I squint at the twinkling specks of light to see what else I can pick out. "That bright line there with a triangle at the end is Sabrelle's Spear. And the clump over there gets called Prospira's Basket, but no one seems to be able to agree whether it's full of fruit or bread or coins."

Julita lets out a soft snort. *Somehow I'm suspecting it depends a lot on the interests of the person making the claim. It just looks like a big jumble to me.*

A smile crosses my lips. "Yeah, I've always thought that one is kind of a stretch."

An unexpected sense of peace has settled over me as we've talked, as if Elox has cast a blanket of serenity down over me with his starry staff. The tension in my chest has loosened.

I'm not alone, no matter where I go. Sometimes that's frustrating and unnerving… but sometimes it's kind of wonderful.

I push myself up on my elbows to study the horizon. "I think right over there you can see Estera's Tome, that square-ish shape with—"

A hard but level voice cuts through the night. "What are you doing?"

I flinch in surprise and brace my hands against the boards on either side of me to hold my balance. I've kept my voice so quiet I hadn't thought anyone would notice, and I didn't hear footsteps approaching.

Pulse thudding, I tilt forward to peer over the edge of the gazebo's roof.

A man in the deep blue uniform of the Crown's Watch stands just below me. His pale face with its topping of chocolate-brown curls is tipped to fix me with a stare as hard as his voice.

Even if my nerves didn't shiver with the traces of magic wafting off him, I'd instantly recognize those stunning looks. It's the guard who's made me uneasy before.

Despite the darkness, his striking blue-green eyes seem to hold a light of their own. An alertness that's piercing me right now.

Fortunately, as far as I'm aware, nothing I'm doing at the moment is any sort of crime. The soldiers who've been assigned to monitor the college must be getting used to the random habits of rich young nobles.

"I'm stargazing," I say honestly.

A small furrow forms in the middle of the guard's smooth brow. He really is far too pretty for his job. "Watching the stars? What for? They aren't doing anything."

He might be pretty, but apparently he's also a stick in the mud.

I can't stop a dry edge from creeping into my tone. "Because they're spectacular to look at? Because they inspire all kinds of stories?"

The expression on the guard's face suggests he'd question what stories are for too. Instead, he shifts his focus. "Who were you talking to?"

If the magic vibes he's giving off have anything to do with judging my honesty, I can still say this and not really be lying. "My sister."

Her memory has been hovering alongside Julita and me since I climbed up here, after all.

The guard frowns. "There's no one up there with you."

"I know. She's dead."

I probably shouldn't let myself get a perverse pleasure out of seeing my interrogator's face turn even more perplexed, but he's kind of asking for it. Surely it didn't look as if I was actually causing any harm sitting up here, but he had to interrupt me anyway.

"Why would you talk to someone who isn't alive?" he asks.

I shrug. "Sometimes they still have meaningful things to say, even if only inside your head. If you don't believe there's anything more to the world than what you can see right in front of you, you're going to miss a lot."

I can't tell what the guard makes of that comment. He pauses for a second and then motions to the school buildings behind him. "You should be inside. Everyone's sleeping now."

"*You* aren't," I point out pedantically, but I scoot to the edge of the roof and drop to the ground with a soft thump of my feet. "I'm going now. You can be reassured that the world is set back into order."

I stride toward the Quadring without a backward glance, but I can feel the guard's gaze on me the whole way.

Do you think we need to be worried about him? Julita asks.

I can only grimace in answer.

I don't know. But I sure hope not, because it's not as if I've got a shortage of worries as it is.

EIGHTEEN

Ivy

After he's laid out the rings of cord, Stavros points to mine. "You go first."

Like usual. Like he thinks I'm going to inflict something terrible on his quarters if he leaves while I'm still here—as if I don't have access all day long anyway.

He's been even surlier and more prone to glowers all morning, though he hasn't said much. I'm not sure if he's forgotten our strained conversation after I woke him up last night or if he's simply pretending it never happened.

I don't particularly want to dwell on the way he snapped at me—the way he *looked* at me, like I'd just eviscerated someone—either. I'll take avoidance over a repeat.

"Ladies first, after all," I say with wry primness, and step into the ring.

Even after several rounds of practice, the sudden lurch of magical transportation makes my pulse stutter. I step out of the matching ring in the palace meeting room with a slight wobble in my step.

Alek is already there, waiting right by my looped cord. At my arrival, his face brightens so visibly even with his mask back in place that I can't stop myself from smiling giddily in return.

What happened between us last night was real. Right here in this room, he cherished me like I was one of the noble ladies he should be looking to for a match.

No, he cherished me like he'd rather have a thief from Slaughterwell than any kind of lady.

Alek grasps my hand, both to give it an affectionate squeeze and to pass on a small packet. "I thought I should get this to you right away."

The mirewort. I'll chew on a leaf when I have a little more privacy.

Because before I've even had a chance to tuck the packet away, Stavros is emerging from his ring, eyeing the two of us with a puzzled frown.

I'm not sure I want to deal with the former general's reaction to our newfound closeness. But I don't want to pull away from Alek as if in rejection.

Thankfully, the scholar seems to have a similar sense of discretion. He bobs his head to Stavros in greeting while stroking his thumb over my knuckles in one small caress and then eases back. "It's wonderful that Ivy returned to us unharmed, isn't it?"

As if he'd only approached me in friendly welcome.

Stavros appears to take the comment in stride, although he doesn't stop frowning. "There certainly could have been worse outcomes."

I restrain myself from rolling my eyes and surreptitiously slip the packet into my pocket. "I should check the room for any roaming magical vermin."

Just as I finish my circuit of the space, Casimir and Benedikt arrive within seconds of each other. Both men brighten in their own ways when they see me: the courtesan with one of his soft smiles and the bastard's bastard with a typical smirk.

I set off a signal through my locket this morning as planned, so they knew I'd returned, but I can imagine they were a little worried all the same.

"You survived the start of your scourge sorcery initiation," Benedikt says in a teasing tone, sprawling in the chair at the foot of the table. "Soon you'll be a fully-fledged menace."

I manage to laugh, but Stavros stiffens—enough that I see Benedikt mark his response with a furrow in his brow.

Casimir slides a box across the table to interrupt the awkward moment. "Since Benedikt set the precedent yesterday, I thought I'd bring a treat to celebrate Ivy's initial success. One of my dormmates who's on the culinary track had a batch of chocolates to sell."

The sight of the glossy brown orbs laid out in the box has my mouth watering. I lean over to snatch one up. "That was a fantastic idea. Thank you."

He passes paper-thin linen napkins around the table, and even Stavros concedes to taking a chocolate. The former general holds it in his hand without taking a bite and fixes his stare back on me. "Are you going to tell us what happened during your 'victory,' Ivy?"

I sink my teeth into the bonbon and pause for a moment to let the richly sweet flavor with its edge of bitterness lace my mouth. There's nothing wrong with using a treat to bolster my spirits.

"I'm not sure it was much of an initiation yet," I say. "It felt like they were merely feeling me out. They were obviously trying not to give much away. I couldn't even tell how many people were watching or where they were—the one who spoke to me stayed hidden and used some kind of magic to project their voice from different directions."

The eager gleam in Alek's eyes dims. "So you wouldn't be able to identify any other conspirators yet?"

I shake my head. "I guess it makes sense. They don't know if they can trust *me* yet, so why would they risk showing themselves?"

"It isn't surprising," Casimir agrees. "What did they say to you?"

Julita gives a little shudder in the back of my skull. *Rather a lot of madness.*

I rub my mouth, thinking back to the conversation. "They talked a lot about the All-Giver. I got the impression that they think they're doing things the Great God would approve of, or that they can make an appeal even though it's been ages since the All-Giver abandoned us. And they're obviously dissatisfied with the current ruling powers, although they were careful not to come right out and say they want to overthrow the Melchioreks."

Benedikt lets out a rough guffaw. "I suppose that confirms who's been encouraging the rumors that the daimon were acting out to spite the royal family."

I nod. "Undermining King Konram's rule might have been the main purpose of their plans all along. Create as much turmoil as possible and blame it on how things are being run at the palace."

Stavros finally pops the chocolate into his mouth and manages to look angry about the fact that he's chewing it. "What exactly makes them so upset with our current ruler?"

I spread my hands. "I've got no idea. They didn't bother to mention that part. I think they're waiting to see if I prove loyal before getting into any detail."

Alek tenses where he's standing next to me. "How are they testing your loyalty?"

"Well, first they had me spill a little blood to honor the All-Giver." I hold up my hand, where the Elox-blessed bandage I've since discarded left me with just a pale scar. "And they gave me some secret object I'm supposed to leave at the Temple of the Crown tonight."

Stavros's eyes narrow. "What sort of object?"

"I don't know. One of their conditions is that I'm not supposed to open the pouch it's in. They must have some way of telling if I do. But I think it's a sham anyway. They made a big deal about the powerful magic it's supposedly imbued with, but I can't—"

I cut myself off, remembering at the last second that Benedikt doesn't know I can sense magic. He doesn't have any reason to think I should be capable of doing so without my revealing the cracks in my soul.

Stavros, of course, has no concern for my need for caution. Although he might not realize what I was going to say. "You can't what?"

I choose my next words carefully. "I can't see how it's likely they'd give anything all that powerful to a candidate they've barely talked to. It's got to be a decoy so they can see how I'll handle it without overplaying their hand. Having held it, I just have a feeling that there isn't much to it."

I aim a pointed look at the former general with those last words, willing him to remember that the part of me he hates also means my "feeling" on this matter should be trusted.

He scowls. "And what are we risking by going by your gut?"

"They hinted that the object would be used to hurt the ruling powers somehow. Very vaguely, for plausible deniability, but it seemed clear they *wanted* me to think that. I'd imagine they'll be watching closely to confirm that I follow their instructions and that no unexpected contingent of guards shows up at the temple to arrest whoever comes to retrieve it."

Casimir hums to himself. "They want to know that you'll go along with their plans rather than turning them in once actual harm might be done."

"I think so."

Benedikt looks unusually pensive. "We can't be sure, though. Before we potentially put a weapon in our enemies' hands, we should ensure it won't do any significant damage."

"If Ivy says this is the safest way, we should trust her," Alek says, a little too quickly. When Benedikt casts a puzzled gaze his way, maybe wondering why the man who's normally the most cautious of us all is advocating for jumping in feet-first, the scholar recovers as well as he can. "She's the one who spoke to them. She has a much better idea of the situation than any of us."

Benedikt glances at Stavros next, probably thinking the former general will back him up, but Stavros simply grimaces in resignation. "The thief does also have plenty of experience with trickery. If we give the sorcerers any indication that she's tipped someone off, our whole stratagem falls apart."

The furrow in Benedikt's forehead deepens. "There must be some subtle way we can—"

"She follows through with the orders, and we keep our eyes open as we have all along," Stavros interrupts brusquely. "Don't *you* go tattling to anyone at the palace, unless you want to go to the king with total failure of the mission he assigned to us next."

Benedikt shuts his mouth. The bewilderment in his eyes wrenches at me, but I don't know how to reassure him.

I'm going to have to share my secret with him eventually, aren't I? How long can we keep going like this?

But just imagining confessing to him makes me queasy.

"I won't jeopardize the mission," Benedikt says quietly

after a moment, with a tip of his head to me that's almost apologetic. He squares his shoulders. "I'll do whatever I can to help without getting in your way."

I offer him a grateful, guilty smile. "Thank you."

"Did the conspirators give any indication of when they'd reach out to you again?" Alek asks.

I drag in a breath. "No. I'm assuming they want to wait until they see what happens in the next couple of days, and then I may receive another invitation."

Or another knife in my back, depending on how they evaluate my performance.

Stavros claps his hands. "All right. That aspect is settled. Has anyone else made even a sliver of progress toward unraveling this conspiracy?"

Each of the men has a little to say about gossip overheard or purchases of supplies, but nothing that gives us solid evidence. Always more threads to follow up on, which seem to wind onward and onward without ever reaching a useful end.

Maybe once I've found out more information directly from the scourge sorcerers, we'll be able to stitch all those scraps together into a clearer picture.

Stavros declares the meeting is over with a thump of his boots as he steps back from the table. "It sounds as if we've covered everything. You all have lives to get back to. Well, for the most part." His gaze flicks to me.

All at once, I balk at the thought of trudging back into his quarters and then spending the rest of the day tagging along at his classes while he offers more warm congeniality to his students in a minute than he has to me in weeks.

The words slip out before I've totally thought them through. "There's a book of records in the storage room that I wanted to consult with Alek about. I'll catch up with you in a few minutes."

Stavros's jaw clenches, but after he left me and the scholar alone for hours last night, he must feel he'd look more odd arguing than not. "I'll need you for my cavalry class at the next bell. Make sure you're not late."

"I would never miss a chance to commune with the horses," I inform him tartly, and usher Alek over to the side room.

The scholar comes along obligingly and turns to scan the shelves of supplies once we're through the doorway. "What book did you find in here? I didn't think—"

I tug him farther out of view. "There's no book. I just wanted to do this without an audience."

I tease my fingers into his thick hair and bob up to claim a kiss.

Alek makes a soft, urgent sound in his throat that makes me quiver in delight and kisses me back. One of his hands comes to rest on my hip while the other cups my cheek.

For a few moments, nothing matters but the heat of his mouth and the lean strength of his body aligned with mine. I want to stay right here, wrapped up in the heady pleasure of his affection, where no conspiracy or sneering nobles can reach me.

Unfortunately, I can't escape my responsibilities for very long. I settle for hugging him tightly to me through one more lingering kiss before easing back.

We did have one bit of audience I couldn't remove us from. Julita makes an awkward coughing sound. *Ah, if this is going to continue, I suppose I should...*

I give my head a subtle shake to tell her there's no need for her to vanish herself and smile up at Alek. He's gazing down at me with so much delight of his own that an uncharacteristic giggle bubbles up from my chest.

"Very sneaky," he says.

I give his hair a teasing tug, remembering how

exhilarated he got when we contrived to steal Ster. Torstem's financial records a few weeks ago. "And you love it."

Alek bows his head closer to mine. "Yes, I do."

It's strange seeing him in his mask now that I know what he looks like beneath it. I trace my fingers along the edge of it at his jaw. "I didn't want to leave without doing that first. I hope that soon we'll have enough time for me to see all of you again."

He chuckles and leans in to brush a kiss to my cheek. "There's a lot of you I'd like to see," he murmurs by my ear. "Gods, I wish we could spend time together on anything other than meetings. If you didn't have to be so careful with Ster. Torstem's people watching you…"

"We can hope that won't be for long."

I don't want to think about where we'll end up when there is no more conspiracy to tackle. Will I be able to stay at the college? How would we get on if I have to return to my old haunts?

Those are problems for another day.

"We should get back," I say, but I can't resist gripping the front of his shirt and stealing one more quick kiss.

Right as Casimir steps past the doorway.

"There are a few chocolates left, if either of you—" he's saying, but his warm voice falters as Alek and I jerk apart.

I grab the scholar's hand before he can get too far, abruptly afraid he'll take my startled reaction as shame. As I squeeze Alek's fingers, Casimir's gaze flicks between us.

I wait for him to laugh or make a playful remark about our subterfuge. It isn't as if I'd expect the courtesan of all people to be offended by anyone indulging in a brief moment of bliss, even someone he's done the same with himself.

But just for a second, the light fades from Casimir's

gorgeous face. In that moment, he looks so lost I forget how to breathe.

He recovers quickly with a straightening of his posture and a hasty smile that doesn't totally cover the awkwardness of the moment. "I— Well, never mind. I apologize for accidentally interrupting."

He retreats with a brisk bob of his head. I stare after him through a few thumps of my pulse, an ache expanding through my chest.

Was he actually *sad* to see me with another man? Why would it even matter to him, unless—

I shake myself out of my daze and turn back to Alek... who's watching me with a wistful but not accusing expression.

"You should go after him," he says. "Tell him how you feel."

My fingers tighten around his where I'm still clutching his hand. "No. I don't— It doesn't change anything about how I feel about *you*. I told you—"

"I know. And I told you I wasn't sure you should have to choose." He steps closer and tips his head to press a kiss to my forehead. "I'm sure now that you *shouldn't*. Signy managed to juggle three lovers. I think you're nimble enough to handle two."

I sputter a laugh. "I'm hardly another Signy."

"I don't know. I think someday they'll be weaving tapestries and singing songs about you too." Alek nudges me toward the door. "I want to see how happy you can look when you're getting all the devotion you deserve. Go on, or *I'll* have to confess on your behalf."

I can't say whether it's the tenderness of his words or the panic that he might carry out his final threat that propels me back into the main meeting room.

Stavros and Benedikt have already departed, thank all

that's holy. Casimir is just gathering the napkins that were scattered on the table.

As I hurry over to him, he sets them on the box of chocolates and spins toward his ring of cord.

"Casimir," I say. "I—"

"It's all right," he breaks in swiftly, with a much more convincing smile now that he's had more time to gather himself. "I'm happy for you both. I was only surprised I hadn't realized sooner. I'll leave you to—"

"Wait." I grasp his elbow.

Casimir turns back toward me to meet my gaze. Staring into his deep blue eyes, I find my thoughts have scrambled.

How am I supposed to "confess" in any way that doesn't sound ridiculous? What if I mistook his reaction just now and he really was simply surprised?

Through the whirl of my thoughts, it occurs to me that there's one way both of us can know exactly what we mean to each other.

My voice comes out quiet. "Use your gift on me."

Casimir blinks. "What?"

"Use your gift. See what you could do that would make me happiest right now."

It wouldn't make me happy for him to lie. I'd rather he let me down easy if that's what he needs to do.

The courtesan knits his brow for just a second before his stance relaxes. His eyes go a bit distant, and a quiver of magic passes through my nerves.

All at once, he's tossing the chocolate box onto the table and wrapping his arms around me in the warmest of embraces.

"Oh, Kindness," Casimir murmurs with a catch in his throat, his head lowered so his cheek rests against my temple. "Do you really not already know how much I adore you?"

I choke up a little too. "I mean, you seem to think a lot

about *everyone's* happiness—I didn't realize I mattered that much more. I'm sorry I acted like I didn't care. I was trying not to make a fool of myself."

Casimir makes a rough noise and strokes his fingers over my hair. "My fault. I was worried about overwhelming you, and instead— I've been falling for you since the first day we met. You're woven into me now. I get an ache in the pit of my stomach when we're apart and a glow around my heart when you're nearby."

He glances up, still holding me close, toward where Alek is ambling over to join us. "Not that I would try to claim you all for myself if you're finding joy other places as well."

I glance over at the scholar, my cheeks heating with a flutter of my nerves.

To my relief, Alek's crooked smile is all fond amusement. "She doesn't believe me when I tell her she's going to become the next Signy." He trails his fingers down the back of my arm. "I'm not sure how much more proof she needs."

"I'd rather not have to face off against an entire imperial army any time soon," I protest.

Casimir just chuckles. He ducks his head to seek out my lips.

As the courtesan's kiss floods me with tingling warmth, Alek slips his arm around my waist from behind and presses his mouth to the side of my neck. My heart skips a beat.

It is overwhelming, being caught up between these two men, but only in the best possible way. I can barely believe *this* moment is actually happening while I'm in the middle of it.

Casimir draws back just an inch, his breath still caressing my lips when he speaks. "I'm not taking patrons now—not that kind. I wanted to be sure of where I stood with you first."

I hesitate. "I saw you with that woman in the dining hall..."

He gives his head an emphatic shake. "She hired me to play music at a party she's hosting. Nothing more intimate than that."

"Oh." I let out a shaky laugh and lean into Alek, looping my arm around his to show him how much I welcome his embrace too. "But—I mean, it's your calling; it's what you always meant to do..."

I can't ask him to give something that important up, even if the thought of him caressing another woman—or man— makes my gut twist.

"I don't know how I'll handle things in the future," Casimir says. "But for right now... I don't think it'd be good for me to muddy the waters."

I guess I can accept that. If he starts to seem miserable trying to hem himself in, I'll have to speak up, however painful it might be for me.

It can't be more painful than thinking I barely meant anything more than the women who pay him for his affections.

I lift my head toward Alek to aim a peck at his jaw. I wouldn't have found out any of this if the scholar hadn't pushed me. "Thank you."

Alek's arm tightens around me. His voice comes out a bit rough. "I think you've spent too long thinking you were barely worth anything at all, Ivy." A wry note creeps in. "Now I'll have some help convincing you otherwise."

I'd like to linger here and find out how they'd continue their convincing, but my awareness of the impending class niggles at me. With a regretful sigh, I ease away from both of the men.

"If I'm not ready for class in time, Stavros will probably come for all our heads."

"We'll see you again soon." Casimir gives my shoulder a quick squeeze, his eyes shining with so much affection it wraps around me like another embrace. "Stay safe, and know our thoughts are with you."

As I reluctantly step toward my circle of cord, Julita finally speaks up again. *Well. Capturing hearts all around, aren't you?*

She lets out a giggle that I can't help thinking sounds a bit forced. I swallow thickly as I step into the ring.

Julita has always urged me on when it comes to pursuing her men... but she might not ever have expected more than one of them would return my interest.

She might not have been prepared to think about all the experiences she can now never hope to have for herself.

I don't know how many of those experiences *I'll* even get to have if I continue down the path I'm on.

I've found so much more here at Sovereign College than I could have predicted. And that means I have so much more to lose if this all goes wrong.

NINETEEN

Ivy

I'm heading to one of the Quadring's side entrances after another afternoon class when I cross paths with Anya and a couple of her friends.

The vindictive noblewoman who spent most of my early weeks at the college heckling and harassing me pauses for just an instant, a flicker of apprehension flitting across her face. I don't think she knows what to make of me after I disarmed her with supposed friendliness.

The fact that I also threatened to let Stavros have her arrested for treason probably plays into her wariness as well.

She settles for a stiff smile and a primp of her hair and sashays on past me while her friends shoot me curious looks.

Ha, Julita says with a triumphant air. *You knocked her feet right out from under her without needing to land a single blow.*

My body has tensed up in anticipation of some kind of spat. It feels strange to be able to simply relax and walk on.

For all the turmoil I've been through with my men and our investigation in the past couple of weeks, my regular life

as a supposed assistant has been relatively tame. I guess I should be thankful that the snobbish nobles have decided I don't make an ideal target in their jockeying for dominance, settling for disdainful looks if they pay attention to me at all.

I've got much bigger enemies to contend with.

Enemies who may be lurking closer than I'd prefer. As I step out of the doorway, a faint prickle of a magic catches my attention.

My head jerks around in the direction it seemed to be coming from—just in time to spot a lithe, scaled form slithering through the grass toward a gap in the wall's mortar.

It's a smaller snake than the one I noticed in the forest three nights ago, as slim as my thumb and only as long as my forearm—the perfect size to slip into the school's walls. And do gods know what inside the Quadring.

As I spring after it, my mind spins with a torrent of urgent thoughts. The rat lashed out at me violently—I have to assume the snake will too. But I only have a matter of moments before it's glided out of reach.

I want to take this one alive.

My magic flickers up eagerly, offering its services, but I ignore its pull. My hand darts between the overlapping fabric of my skirt and retrieves one of my tiny stashed knives. I yank it through one of the strips of silk and return the blade to its sheath in the space of a heartbeat.

Grasping the swath of fabric I've cut off, I pounce on the snake.

It flings its tail like a whip and snaps its head around with fangs bared, just as I expected. But I slam the fabric down over it and clutch it through the layer of cloth.

Be careful! Julita cries, as if I'm not already trying to be.

As I flip the snake over and knot the fabric around it into a bundle, it flails against its silky prison. A seething hiss filters through the cloth.

Once the makeshift pouch is fully closed and secure, the creature squirms for several more seconds and then goes still as if giving up. Or biding its time until it senses a better opportunity for escape.

Julita's presence shivers. *I wonder what they're trying to find out with all these horrible spies.*

"A very good question," I mutter under my breath.

I push upright from my hunched position by the wall and glance around cautiously. Several students are meandering around the field, but no one's all that close to me.

I catch one raised eyebrow aimed my way from a nobleman I don't recognize, too far away for him to have realized what I was doing. I aim a prim smile at him and stride off toward the Domi as if I have nothing to feel awkward about.

Everyone already thought I was a little strange anyway.

My hand remains clamped around the top of the bundle of silk, keeping a firm grip on my captive. I need to summon the men as quickly as possible in case this creature vanishes into dust or a poof of smoke if it's restrained for too long.

Who knows how the scourge sorcerers worked their illicit magic on the thing?

I can't go straight to our new meeting room, because Stavros in his infinite wisdom is still holding my enchanted cord hostage. Gods forbid I have free access to an entirely locked and secure room we can't even tell is within the palace.

But we still have our original meeting spot, even if the archive room seems dreary and cramped by comparison.

I march through the Domi's main entrance and head past the library doors. It's just a short distance to the hall of tapestries—

"Ivy! Where are you off to in such a hurry this morning?"

Petra's clear, melodic voice rings out from the library doorway. I jar to a stop with a silent curse.

Her question was casual enough, but it'll look awfully suspicious if I charge on by without acknowledging her. And the lesser royal has already shown more interest in me than I'd like.

I tuck my strange parcel close to my gown as I turn to face her. Since it's the same fabric the skirt is made of, it should blend in.

I don't trust my knots quite enough to risk stuffing the snake in my pocket.

Petra steps out of the library. Her smile is friendly enough, but her dark eyes look pensive.

"Oh, I'm simply on an errand for Ster. Stavros," I say with a light laugh. "He doesn't like to be kept waiting, you know."

Petra echoes my laugh. "I suppose in his past line of work, most tasks were much more urgent. I hope he isn't putting you under too much stress."

"No, not at all. But I'd better get on with it."

I dip my head to her, praying that she doesn't try to stall me any further. Her voice doesn't follow me down the hall, but my old scars itch with the sense of her studying my retreating back.

Why is she *so interested in you all of a sudden?* Julita murmurs.

I wait until I've turned the corner into the hall of tapestries and confirmed that no one else is around before replying. "Do you think King Konram might have asked her to keep an eye on me—back when he first heard from Stavros that I was helping the investigation? I'm new to the school, after all."

It'd make sense for the king to be concerned that I'm so

involved in delving into a conspiracy that could have dire consequences for his family.

Julita lets out an uncertain hum. *I'd have thought he'd trust Stavros's judgment more than that. And he didn't even want to inform his closest staff—I can't see him revealing all this trouble to a girl who's only distantly related to his wife. The success of our mission depends on its secrecy.*

Maybe the king picked up on Stavros's recent apprehensions about me. It's not as if the former general has been all that great at hiding them.

On the other hand, after what happened with Esmae, I'm hesitant to assume anyone who strikes a sudden interest in me has good intentions. Better to treat Petra as a hazard until I have irrefutable evidence that she's not one.

While I tweak the sconce with my free hand, I spare a glance at the tapestry of Signy. At the three men gathered around her on the hill.

Did she find herself totally bewildered when she realized more than one of them returned her feelings—and was willing to stand with the others at her side?

The stories never give much detail about their romance, making it sound as if her magnificence made it inevitable that she'd win their hearts. I'd like to think someone selfless enough to take on an entire empire to free her country would have a little more humility than to take anyone's affections for granted, but who really knows?

The much-celebrated hero of Velduny died before I was even born.

The moment I've descended the conjured shadowy staircase into the small archive room, I grope for my locket, flick it open single-handed, and press my thumb to the inside. The signal will tell the men where to find me.

I peer around the room with an odd waft of nostalgia,

though it's only been a couple of weeks since I last came down here. As if sensing my momentary distraction, the snake makes another attempt at thrashing its way free from the bundle of silk. I clench my fingers around the gathered edges of the fabric.

If the creature is acting as some kind of spy, we shouldn't have an unguarded conversation about it. What might the men give away when they rush in to answer my call?

A jolt of anxiety sends me to the desk. I paw through the drawers one-handed and dig out a piece of parchment, a quill, and a bottle of ink that's still half full.

I have to pull the stopper out with my teeth while I'm holding the snake's silk prison, but I manage to wet the quill and scrawl a quick message across the parchment. *STAY SILENT.*

I've just pushed the stopper back into the ink bottle when Benedikt emerges from the wall. "What's the—"

In an urgent motion, I jerk up the paper with my command. He snaps his mouth shut, his eyebrows arching.

With a shrug, I hope I convey that I realize how ridiculous the situation might seem. Then Alek comes hurtling in through the door from the larger archives, and I whirl toward him with my message raised.

He's only sucked in a breath when he sees it, his voice catching before he's released a single word. As he frowns at me in concern, I offer an apologetic smile and swing back around to aim the message at Casimir, who's come down the hidden staircase a minute behind Benedikt.

It takes another few minutes of awkward quiet before Stavros finally makes his appearance. He glances around at all of us, taking in our expressions and my demand, and folds his arms over his chest with a pointed look.

I set down the paper and motion to my silk bundle. The snake has gone still, so they won't have any idea what's going on.

Bracing myself, I feel along the creature's body through the fabric. It wriggles, but I manage to grasp it between my thumb and forefinger just behind its head.

Keeping the snake secured like that, I loosen the folds of cloth and delve in with my other hand. Gingerly, I ease the green-and-brown-scaled serpent from my trap.

It flings around its tail some more, but it's short enough that I can easily hold it away from my body. The position of my hand prevents it from taking any bites out of me.

Alek's eyes widen with a light of understanding. He makes a creeping motion with his hand and mouths, "The rat?"

I nod.

He eases closer, and after a moment, the other men follow suit. It should be obvious to all of them that the animal in my hand is no more clay-like than I am.

Stavros taps the top of its head as if he needs to feel its scales to be sure. Then he draws the sword he always carries on his belt and motions for me to lower the snake to the desk.

I hold it there as still as I can between my hands. The former general braces himself and chops the edge of the blade downward like a chef's knife, just an inch from my clutching fingers at the creature's neck.

The snake's body squirms away from its head—and stiffens. The surface against my fingertips turns harder and rougher.

I lift my hands away from the two clay pieces now lying on the desk.

The unpolished reddish-brown surface has been etched with faint lines to indicate scales and two dots for eyes. It's not a particularly realistic replica other than in shape.

Alek's eyes widen. His hand flicks down his chest in a three-fingered tap to the gods.

All sense of the magic in the snake has vanished. I exhale in a rush. "I think we can talk now."

"You're just guessing?" Stavros says darkly.

I glower at him, and Alek jumps in with a suitable explanation that doesn't reveal my magic-detecting ability to Benedikt. "The enchantment on it has obviously been broken. The sorcerers wouldn't want anyone to be able to test the magic once it's been discovered."

Casimir runs his fingers over the clay body. "That's incredible. It really did look and move exactly like a living animal."

I wipe my fingers against my skirt, the sensation of writhing scales clinging to them. "None of you have ever encountered or even heard of a gift that could accomplish this?"

Alek shakes his head. "I'd imagine it has to be multiple gifts combined, or some kind of temporary magic gained through sacrifice."

With that last word, he looks a bit sick.

What kind of sacrifice would it take to bring a lump of clay into something so close to life?

Benedikt leans back against one of the shelving units, tapping his lips. "I've kept an eye out for anyone handling clay objects around the campus and the palace. Haven't noticed anything unusual so far. Pottery isn't exactly a common conversational topic at the cards table."

"I couldn't find any connections between Ster. Torstem and a place where he might be sourcing or working with the clay," Alek says. "He must be keeping his distance from that part of the conspiracy's operations. I'll extend my search and see what else I can find—I'll make it my main priority."

I catch Stavros's gaze. "You should warn the king that it's not just rats. Maybe the clerics who've been watching for more daimon antics would be able to pick up the magic in these creatures and 'discover' them on their own."

Stavros's mouth tightens as if he doesn't love taking a suggestion from me, but he can obviously recognize it's a decent one. "I'll pass on word to him as soon as I can."

Casimir frowns, picking up the snake's clay head and examining it. "What real purpose would these serve? Who would the scourge sorcerers want to be spying on? It seems like a totally different tactic than what they were attempting with the daimon."

It does, which unnerves me more than I'd like to admit. "Maybe they feel they need to use a more subtle approach after how things turned out before."

"At least we know," Benedikt points out. "That keeps us one step ahead of them."

I'm not sure we're ahead so much as not as far behind as we could be. But before I can decide whether to put that depressing thought into words, a creeping sensation spreads across my palm.

I jerk my hand toward me in time to see the words flicker across my skin. *Tonight, same place and time. Alone.*

"What?" Stavros demands, taking in my reaction.

I let out a raw chuckle. "It looks like I'm going to get another chance to dig into the scourge sorcerers' plans directly—tonight."

TWENTY

Ivy

This time, I don't have to remind Stavros to head to his bedroom and turn off the lights. After Casimir finishes touching up the false godlen brand I haven't needed to show off yet, the former general simply casts his gaze toward me and says, "Be careful."

From his tone, it's obvious what he's actually saying is, "Don't you dare burn the school to the ground with your crazy riven magic."

"Good night to you too," I call after him, and flop onto the sofa to wait until it seems like a reasonable time to head out.

Julita gives a resigned sigh. *I didn't think it'd take him this long to come around. It's not as if you're a different person from who you were before he found out.*

I grimace. "In his mind, I am."

He's got to see that you have a handle on your magic eventually… I suppose being stubborn was an ideal quality in a general.

I chuckle under my breath. "Good thing I'm awfully stubborn too."

I pause for a moment, debating how much of a conversation I want to get into even with my voice low when Stavros is in the next room. But what I want to ask Julita about isn't anything I'd dare saying out loud anywhere else on campus.

"Is there anything else you can remember from your brother and Wendos's rituals that I should be prepared for? There's the blood-letting and the appeals for power, but we've already covered those."

Julita is silent for a moment before she answers—long enough that I wish my current mission didn't require that she dredge up those awful childhood memories.

That was most of it, she says. *There were things like drawing symbols with different materials like the dartling eggshell powder, and odd chants similar to the things Wendos was saying in the tower—but not quite the same. I don't think they had the full picture. Which doesn't mean this bunch of scourge sorcerers does either, but they seem to know more.*

"And they want more. Your brother never said anything about undermining the royal family, did he?"

I have the impression of Julita shaking her head. *Nothing on that large a scale. I mean, they were barely teenagers while I was involved. Stupid boys, dabbling with magic they didn't understand, hoping they'd get some extra power that'd make them feel special. I never got the impression they even thought all that much about politics or religious ideals.*

"Nothing along those lines came up around the family dinner table?" I can't help asking.

Julita snorts. *My parents didn't—don't—care much about what goes on beyond our county either. Frankly, I wouldn't have if I could have gone back to Nikodi and simply focused on running things smoothly there. You know, all the territory we managed from our estate only contained about a quarter of the people who live just in this city. When you spend all your time in a place like that, the world feels… smaller.*

"That makes sense." I doubt many intrepid merchants or travelers bothered to linger within Nikodi's far-flung borders either.

I might have spent most of my life struggling to keep food in my belly and find any sense of home, but my world was far larger than Julita's until she came to the college.

"Is there anything you'd like to see?" I say abruptly. "I mean, when we're done here—you've missed out on a lot of things—and *I* wouldn't mind taking in more of Silana or even farther abroad. The king's got to offer a good enough reward that we could do a little traveling with plenty left over."

Before she moves on for good, that is. My stomach knots when I consider saying that part.

Julita's voice goes quiet. *That's very kind of you to offer. I'll have to think about it. Mostly I wanted to be such a good countess my parents couldn't possibly wish Borys had stuck around instead.* She lets out a dry laugh.

The apprehension about the unknown tasks ahead is starting to get to me. I pace the room a little, taking in the twelve rings of the midnight bell, and wander out to the stable again.

I'm tempted to take Toast out for a ride into the woods —the conspirators never said the fifty paces had to be human —but I'm not sure I want to find out what might happen to him if they object.

I rub his neck and call him a good boy, and drink in the comforting stable scents until my restlessness drives me onward.

I can't stay out in the open in the outer courtyard without the patrolling guards noticing me, so I duck into the shadows at the edge of the hunting woods. Setting my feet carefully so I don't make any noise, I slink between the trees off the path.

I don't come across any trace of the scourge sorcerers' presence. How far ahead of me do they come into the woods themselves?

Or do they have some magical means of arriving here, the way we can use the enchanted cords to jump between the college and the palace?

A niggling tug of my own magic reminds me that *it* could expose any figures lurking in the shadows if I let it. I grimace at the sensation.

At the single peal marking the first hour of the morning, I square my shoulders and set off toward the fifty-pace meeting spot.

Like before, I'm met with silence. I stand still and calm, taking in the breeze and the warble of swaying leaves, on the alert for any sign of supernatural power.

The conspirators can't know about my sensitivity to other people's magic any more than Benedikt does. I do have a few aspects of my unwanted abilities that I can draw on without doing any harm.

Abruptly, the voice—which may or may not be the same voice as last time—wavers around me again. "Ivy of Nikodi, you fulfilled your first task. All of us who are committed to a better world thank you."

"I thank you for the opportunity to work toward that better world too," I say, the false gratitude sour on my tongue. "Is there more that I can help with?"

If they could get on with the part where they fill me in on their plans, I'd be truly grateful.

But we wouldn't be in this predicament if the scourge sorcerers were that carefree.

"There will be more opportunities," the voice says. "Tonight, we want to see how much restoring the All-Giver to these realms means to you."

So they aren't delusional enough to believe the All-Giver never left. They just think they can bring the Great God back?

I guess that's some kind of delusion too.

I give a slight bow. "I can't think of much I wouldn't do." As long as the All-Giver dispatches all the sorcerers and their sick tactics without harming the rest of us. Which, granted, isn't a sure thing, so we'd better be able to take these psychopaths down ourselves first.

The voice shifts as if changing direction in its rippling path around me. "We must return to the old ways from when the Great God watched over us. We've distanced ourselves too much from where we came from. Can you tap into the roots of humanity, Ivy?"

A shiver travels up my spine. "I'm not sure what you mean."

"We're all animals at heart. We're born wild, meant to revel in sky, sea, and earth by immersing ourselves in them, not holding ourselves apart. Too many have forgotten the essence of our nature."

Born wild. What was it Wendos talked about? He mentioned "the Order of the Wild" as if that was the name of the group he was allied with.

Julita hums. *This does remind me a little of some of the things Borys used to say. Mingling blood with the earth because it all comes from the same place and things along that line.*

I nod as if I agree with what the speaker said. "We've cut ourselves off from our origins. I can see what you mean.

Everyone's so concerned with making rules and keeping peace."

"Good. Then you understand. Now embrace that thought. Get down on your hands and knees."

My muscles tense against the command, but I force myself to kneel, my skirt fanned beneath me. As I set my hands on the hard-packed dirt of the riding path, I wish I'd changed into my combat training clothes for this secret rendezvous.

The scent of the earth fills my nose, pungent and loamy. There is something a little exhilarating about getting down in the dirt, shedding expectations of proper posture and noble elegance.

"Now run," the voice says.

My head jerks around—aimlessly, since I have no idea where the speaker is. "What?"

"*Run*. Like the animal you are. Follow the wildness within."

I feel more uncomfortable than wild in that moment, but I can't let the evaluating sorcerers notice me hesitate.

With a jerk, I untie the cloak from my neck to let it fall on the path so it won't tangle with my limbs. Then I push myself forward, scuttling in my crouched position along the packed dirt.

After a short distance, I decide it'll feel better if my legs are squatting rather than kneeling, my feet propelling me instead of my knees.

As I adjust my stance, the voice hollers after me. "Deeper into the woods. Away from all the restrictions they've tried to place on us!"

I spring between the trees, wincing as broken twigs and sharp pebbles bite at my palms. The toe of my boot snags on a jutting root, and I sprawl forward, scraping my chin before I'm scrambling back up again.

Pain stings along my jaw as I hurtle onward, but I tune it out. I focus on the brush of the vegetation against my skin, on the hiss of my skirts against the ground.

The silk catches on a broken branch and tears. A strange sense of satisfaction passes through me at the rasp of sound, followed by a swell of horror.

I can't be buying into this madness. I shouldn't be enjoying anything about this moment.

But the conspiracy wouldn't be growing if their ideals didn't have a certain appeal. Maybe in some ways I *am* the sort of person they'd have wanted to recruit.

I scramble on through the darkness, my torn gown flapping around my legs, my fingernails digging into the dirt. I don't know how long they expect me to keep this up.

Should I throw back my head and howl at the moon like a wolf, or would that be too much?

The idea kind of amuses me, which makes me uneasy all over again.

As I swerve around a tree trunk, fern fronds swiping across my cheek, my magic unfurls through my chest again. If I don't want to be here, I can wipe out every other person in this forest, just like that.

I can force them to leave me alone. I can end this wretched madness.

I grit my teeth against it.

No. I'm fine. No one's hurting me.

No one except my own wretched power. When I clamp down on it, it thrashes against my hold harder than before. Claws of pain rake across my ribs and down to my gut.

I swallow a gasp and dash onward, hoping whoever's watching will attribute my stumbles to the uneven ground. As the pain digs in deeper, tears burn behind my eyes.

Even my broken soul knows that this bizarre display is

wrong. But I can't lash out the way it wants when I still know so little about our enemy.

With every thump of my feet, I will my roiling power to calm down. I can keep up this act for as long as I need. There's no real threat here.

Then I stumble into a glade, and a pale gray rabbit leaps in front of me.

"Kill it!" the voice says, bouncing between the trees. "Tear it apart with your hands and offer up its life to the one who made us all!"

My heart lurches, and I lunge forward. My panic that I might fail the trial cuts through my nausea at the task.

I catch the softly furred body in my arms. My hands grope toward its neck.

I've killed rodents before—when I was desperate, when both my stomach and my power were gnawing at me to act.

Normally I'd have used a knife, but I know how to feel for the knobs of the spine—

Crack.

The body goes limp in my grasp. As I hold up its body to the thin beams of moonlight, the voice calls out again.

"Spill its blood. Dedicate it to the All-Giver!"

My stomach churns with another wave of queasiness as I squeeze my hands. My magic reverberates through my limbs, offering its service—I can't give in. I have to do this myself too.

I wrench and heave, and flesh tears. Fur and skin part; blood spurts onto the ground.

"For the All-Giver!" I rasp. "I run wild and show the animal I am for the All-Giver."

The scourge sorcerers aren't done yet. The voice echoes through the woods around me—or is it multiple voices now —in an emphatic chant?

"The right rulers should rise, and the wrong should fall!"

"The right rulers should rise, and the wrong should fall!" I repeat, restraining a shiver of horror. How exactly do they mean to see the "wrong" rulers removed?

And who do they think the right ones are? Does Ster. Torstem expect to take the throne?

I don't know. I'm smeared with dirt and blood, and all I can do is play along.

Play along until I've tumbled far enough into this rabbit hole to see my way out again.

TWENTY-ONE

Stavros

Ivy is stealthy, but I haven't lost any of the hearing I honed in sparring rings and on battlefields. At the ever-so-faint click of the door to my quarters closing, my head snaps up.

I learned my lesson from last time. So my mind would stay alert, I sat myself in my bedroom's armchair rather than on the bed and forced myself to track the periodic patrols of guards and the few students arriving late to the dorms.

I shouldn't have fallen asleep before regardless. The tension coiled in my gut gives off constant pangs of uneasy adrenaline.

The problem is that tension I'm carrying hasn't subsided since the moment I found out what our thief really is. For the past two weeks, I've only been sleeping in brief fragments, made even less restful by the nightmares I haven't managed to shake.

The problem is I'm fucking exhausted.

But I've survived on stints of little sleep plenty of times in

the midst of an ongoing skirmish or siege. I can hold myself and my blasted temper together.

I have to, because the chaotic and unnerving conflict I've found myself in the middle of is the closest thing to a war I'll ever fight again. If I can't defend my country from even that…

Rather than following the uncomfortable thought to its conclusion, I push myself from my chair and stalk over to the outer room.

Ivy is standing by the sofa, peeling off her cloak. Her hair falls loose across her shoulders, many of the strands clinging damply to her skin.

Did she stop at the bathing rooms on her way back?

Gods smite the flare of heat that idea sends to my groin.

She startles just slightly at my entrance. Something about the tensing of her stance, more nervous than boldly defensive, has me striding closer with a tick of my gaze to refocus it.

As I round the sofa and get a full look at her dress, my feet stall beneath me. I stare, with another twitch of my head and a lurch of my stomach.

Dark streaks stain the pewter gray silk of her gown all down the skirt. The bottom hem is tattered as if she ran it through a thresher. And a few of the stains, including a couple higher up on the bodice, have a ruddy hue I can make out even in the hazy light that creeps through the window.

I'm striding straight to her in the instant before I catch myself. I halt just a couple of paces away, my right hand clenching at my side.

My voice comes out harsher than I like. The idea that she might be injured *torments* me more than I like. "Did they make you cut yourself again?"

Ivy lets out a laugh, ragged enough to pierce my heart. "No. Not me. Just a poor little bunny. Sorry I'm a mess. I kept my cloak over my gown on the way back and washed up as well as I could."

Hearing her apologize sets me even more off-balance. How shaken is she that she'd act as though she needs to justify herself rather than brush me off with her usual banter?

"They asked you to kill a rabbit?"

She glances down. "With my bare hands. After I raced around the forest on all fours like a wild creature. These scourge sorcerers have very strange ideas about what the All-Giver would want."

Her voice has lightened, but it doesn't reassure me. She still sounds unnervingly detached.

I know that tone. Soldiers often get it after their first intense battle—when they've had to kill in ways they never imagined, when they've seen too many comrades slain in front of them.

Two chilling thoughts cut through me in quick succession.

The scourge sorcerers' tactics are rattling Ivy more than anything I've ever seen.

How is she going to control her riven magic if they keep breaking her down?

"You shouldn't go back," I say before I've thought the comment through.

Ivy blinks at me, and a little of her usual keenness comes back into her gaze. It'd reassure me more if her next words weren't, "Of course I should. I'm gaining their trust. I've got a better idea of how they think than I did before, and they'll keep revealing more."

"That only works if they leave you in one piece," I retort.

She makes a scoffing sound that also sounds more like her usual self and swipes her hair back from her face. "I'm all right. It was just very weird. They've already told me I'm supposed to come back tomorrow night—we might get something concrete on their plans then."

She's putting herself in their grasp again that soon?

My pulse stutters. "Ivy—"

She holds up her hand. "We made *our* plan, and I'm following it as well as I can. Have I screwed anything up so far?"

I scowl at her. "No, but—"

"Then let me do what I came here for. At some point you've got to believe I'm on your side and not the villains'." She brushes her hands over her dress. "Now I'm going to get out of this ruined thing and get some sleep."

She marches past me to the latrine to change. I hesitate in the middle of the room, but she's obviously recovered from her initial shock.

What am I going to do, stand sentinel over her all night to confirm her magic doesn't slip out of her in her sleep?

Some part of me wants to. Gods help me, some part of me longs to gather her slight but strong frame in my arms and let my own strength shield her from the horrors she's experiencing.

But what happens tomorrow when the insane conspirators might put her through even worse? How long will it take before their madness starts rubbing off on her?

I retreat to my bedroom, but I can't walk away from the qualms that are nibbling at the edges of my mind even more insistently than before.

How far can I really let her mission go?

If I judge the situation wrong, if I extend more trust than I should, the resulting disaster could be even worse than if the scourge sorcerers go unchecked. One of the riven unleashing her magic right outside the palace gates? Right in the same *building* as the royal family during our meetings?

I can't count on our companions to notice the warning

signs. Even with my faulty sight, I've seen the way Aleksi and Casimir look at her.

It isn't as if I don't understand the attraction. The sly humor that can shine in her stunning eyes, the confident might in every movement of her lithe body—

But *I'm* keeping those compulsions reined in. The two of them appear to have welcomed her back into their trust—and who knows what else—whole-heartedly.

The security of the entire kingdom rests on my shoulders.

I slump onto the bed and close my eyes to try to get some rest, but it takes ages before I drift off. And then the images of Michas sear up from my unconscious.

Flashes of real memory: the riven sorcerer's snarl, Michas's face blanching in panic, the way the unharnessed magic wrenched through his body, tearing it limb from limb...

And in the dreams, Ivy stands here too. She echoes the snarl of the man from my memory.

She waves her hand, and another slash rips through Michas with a gush of blood.

I wake up in a sweat with my heart racing. Pressing my arm to my forehead, I tip my head back against my pillow.

I can't go on like this. *I'm* fraying at least as much as Ivy is.

An idea wavers up through my fatigue like a lantern in the fog.

Maybe there's a way I can be sure of my choice. A way to test the control she claims will never falter.

If she's going to unleash her magic, it'll be better if it's when I'm prepared for it than off in the woods in the middle of the night.

The test won't even take that much.

💀

The hardest part is deciding which of my students will shoulder the responsibility—far more responsibility than they even know.

In true fairness, I should take the risk… but if Ivy lashes out at me, I won't be around to put her down. That would undermine all the reasons I'm carrying out the test at all.

I have to be alive to protect everyone else from her magic.

If it's not me, it has to be a student. I can't turn to my fellow staff or the guards of the Crown's Watch. They'd ask too many questions—they'd talk with their colleagues.

The students know Ivy. They're used to seeing me as a teacher, to participating in combat scenarios I set up purely so they can learn.

I stew on the question for most of the morning, the guilt that I have to ask it at all digging deeper into my gut with every passing hour.

Finally, at the end of my senior strategy class, I motion for Ivy to take her leave and gather a cluster of my most dedicated students. The ones I expect to recommend for positions as higher officers at the end of the school year.

"I may have a mission I need to send a few people on," I tell them. "It'll be dangerous—I can't promise you'd come out of it safely or even alive—but it'd be for the protection of the country. I won't order anyone to take it up while you're still in the middle of your studies. But if any of you feel prepared to tackle that kind of task, I can accept potential volunteers."

Bartos, the second son of one of the counts who rules not far from Florian, speaks up without hesitation. "I'll go, if you need me. That's what all this studying has been for."

The others add their own voices in agreement. I've obviously judged their devotion to their country well.

Bartos wasn't just the fastest to leap at the chance, he's

also the strongest physically. For my actual mission, I need someone who'll pose an obvious threat.

As the others leave, I keep him back for a minute longer. "I appreciate your enthusiasm. There's a smaller task I could use some help with right here at the school today, if you don't mind lending a hand there as well."

Bartos simply smiles. "I'd be honored to assist."

"Good. Go get yourself some lunch and meet me by the storage rooms right after."

I can't tell him that the smaller task and the dangerous mission are one and the same. At least I've gotten my confirmation that he's willing to put his life on the line for a cause like this.

By the time Bartos arrives at the building where the college keeps most of its military training equipment, I've already worked out the most viable strategy. I meet him with a length of sturdy rope in my hands, willing down my nausea at the hiss of its corded surface sliding against my metal prosthetic.

If Ivy really isn't a threat to us, then I'm ensuring she never has to meet the fate I'm going to stage.

I've worked out my story as well. As I wave Bartos into the hall between the supply rooms, I keep my tone casual.

"I've been working with Ivy one on one to judge her aptitude for a promotion to an officer role or taking up teaching herself. I'd like to get a clear view of how she'll respond to a perceived attack. You'll need to be convincing, but I'll step in as soon as I'm sure of her reaction—before you'd do any real damage, if she can't fend you off."

My guilt only digs in deeper at Bartos's unquestioning nod. "I can do that."

"She can't realize you're one of my students, or she'll know it's just a test," I go on, handing him the rope. "You'll need to come at her from behind and get this around her neck. Fast enough to startle her. She'll be coming in to start setting up for our afternoon class at the second bell. You can wait here and catch her right after she arrives."

I have him stand in the shadows just beyond the doorway Ivy will pass on her way to the leather figures she's sometimes complained about hauling around. I position myself on the other side of the hallway, where I'll be able to see the struggle without Ivy noticing my presence.

When the palace bell starts to peal, I draw my sword and hold it ready at my side.

If Bartos shows any sign of being under magical attack, I don't know if I'll be able to charge in fast enough to save his life. But I can ensure no one else gets hurt by her chaotic power.

And if Ivy can fight her way out of this test without drawing on her power, maybe I can stop worrying about the stress the scourge sorcerers are putting her through.

If she can't… then there's too much chance of her control slipping during so many other dire situations she could find herself in.

My throat constricts, but I tighten my grip on my sword. I'll do what I have to do. What maybe a stronger man would have done to begin with, glowing godlen sigils be damned.

Ivy might mutter about the work sometimes, but she shows up promptly. She casts a slim shadow across the floor from the open doorway, changed into a short tunic, breeches, and leathers for the combat exercises to come.

She's got one knife on a belt at her hip, but Bartos can see that for himself. I've no doubt there are two more hidden in her boots, but if he plays his part properly, she won't have the chance to reach for them.

She strides into the hallway with a brief glance around and what looks like a suppressed yawn. I can't help wondering if this test wouldn't be fairer after *she's* gotten a proper night's sleep.

But life is hardly fair. The scourge sorcerers don't care how well-rested she is.

My body tenses in anticipation.

The second Ivy steps past Bartos's doorway, he launches himself at her.

As he whips the rope around her neck, he lets out a brief roar. Apparently he's going all in on the role I gave him.

He snaps the rope against Ivy's throat and wrenches upward, towering a full foot over her short body. I flinch at the sight, even though I'm the one who brought it about.

I can't afford that kind of weakness. I can't... I can't trust my own judgment when it comes to this woman.

But I feel strangled myself as I watch Ivy's frame go rigid. Her eyes widen, blown out with panic, and my stomach lurches in anticipation of how she'll retaliate.

Bartos yanks her back against him, hauling her high enough that she's left stumbling on tiptoe. Her arms flail out, but in the first few seconds they're jerky and imprecise.

Great God help me, is she picturing the noose from her nightmares right now?

I lift my sword with a twitch of my head to clear my vision. If only I could focus my blasted eyes for long enough for my gift to take hold, to witness her next moves before she makes them...

In the middle of my anguished thought, Ivy regains her wherewithal enough to grope for her knife. Bartos slaps her hand away.

I brace myself for her to defend herself the easiest and possibly the only way she can.

Her boots scrape frantically against the floor. Her arms fling out again—but all at once something in her posture shifts.

Her muscles coil, her focus sharpening.

She manages to swing her body to the left, heedless of the rope, and slams her heel upward. It jars against Bartos's kneecap.

He sways just slightly, but he's already a little off-balance from her squirming. He bats away a fist she aims backward at his jaw only to take an elbow in the middle of his gut.

Ivy strikes him hard enough to knock the breath out of him. My student pitches backward, Ivy snatches at her knife again—and without any divine gift necessary, I see how the blade will stab straight into his heart.

"Stop!" I burst out from my doorway, dropping my sword with a clatter.

I snag the hooked end of my prosthetic around Ivy's wrist just inches from the knife piercing Bartos's flesh.

Bartos drops the rope and staggers out of range. Ivy's feet jolt all the way to the ground. She stands there, panting and staring at me as if she doesn't recognize me. Wisps of her red-blond hair have stuck to her temple with sweat.

"Good work," I say in the easy-going drawl I normally use with my students. I don't want Bartos realizing I lied about my motivations. "You got your fear under control and found a way to turn the tables. A pass with flying colors."

She didn't use a single trace of magic. She mastered herself more than Bartos could realize.

Relief floods my fatigued mind so swiftly it's dizzying.

I wasn't wrong to guard her secret after all. I didn't misjudge her control or her determination.

She's still the woman I believed in.

I lift my gaze and nod at my student. "Thank you for your help. You can get on with the rest of the day—I trust your knee is all right?"

Bartos gives a rough chuckle. "Oh, I'm sure I'll recover quickly enough. You did pick quite a tenacious assistant."

He bobs his head to both of us and ambles out—with a hint of a limp, I can't help noticing.

"You," Ivy mutters under her breath. "You *asked* him to — You were testing me?"

The last word is broken by a hiss. She wraps her arm around her belly and reels backward to brace herself against the wall.

Any relief that was buoying me washes out of my body. I dash forward to grab her elbow. "Ivy—are you hurt?"

"Fuck you," she spits out in a strained voice, all pretense of a noble lady dropped.

Her legs wobble. She stiffens them for a second before they buckle completely.

My fingers clamp around her arm to slow her collapse. I sink down with her, my pulse suddenly thundering.

"Where are you wounded?" I demand. "You have to let me—"

Her words spill out between hitches of breath. "I don't. Have to. Do. *Anything*. For an asshole. Like you."

Her head bows forward to rest against her upraised knees. Her whole body shudders, a whine seeping from her lips.

The sound is so agonized it guts me.

I did this to her. My wretched test has left her more injured than the scourge sorcerers ever have.

My hand slides up her arm to her shoulder. I tip my head close to hers. "I'm sorry. I had to know—I had to be sure that even under duress— He wasn't supposed to really harm you."

Ivy manages to emit a derisive snort. "Wasn't Bartos. Stupid power. Gets mad. When I won't. Use it."

She raises her head shakily, pain etched across her pale features, so her bright gaze can burn into mine. "But I didn't. I never want to. I'm not. A fucking. Monster."

Understanding jars into place in my head with a sharper swell of regret.

Did she tell us that much before and I didn't heed it? I know she indicated that it was hard for her to resist her magic, but I didn't quite make the connection—

That time Aleksi called us all to the archives because Ivy had supposedly been attacked. And later, when Benedikt raced into my classroom to tell me I needed to hurry to my quarters, that she'd collapsed and was coughing up blood…

Those incidents weren't caused by spite from the idiots at this school. That was her magic lashing out at her. Because it wanted to take action and she refused it?

I never saw her in the worst grips of either of those fits. She was already recovering when I reached her the first time, and the second she appeared perfectly fine once we tracked her down.

I had no idea she experienced anything like this just to restrain her power.

How many times has she put herself through this agony since coming here, with all the threats and animosity she's faced? Not least of all from me.

Gods above, she could have run back to the streets of Slaughterwell any time.

But she stayed. She stayed to fight the scourge sorcerers with us and protect so many people who'd have sent her to the gallows—even though she knew how I felt about the riven, even though the constant danger of staying in this place might have been killing her from the inside out.

She's proven the truth again and again. Since the horrors of her childhood, she's never used her magic except when the consequences of not using it were worse.

Have I ever really wished she'd let Wendos tear apart the city instead of stopping him?

She'd allow the power to destroy *her* before she inflicted

even a fraction of the damage she's capable of on this world, wouldn't she? Curse it all, seeing her like this, I can't imagine her doing anything other than falling on one of her own knives if she thought she'd truly lost control.

And I just egged on the magic I've hated so much. I made it bring her to her knees.

I've encouraged it to torment this woman who's shown more honor than I can imagine ever achieving myself, despite all my doubts.

In that moment, I want to stab myself, but that won't help either of us. Instead, I hug Ivy closer, swallowing the lump in my throat.

From what she's been saying to me, she probably doesn't find my embrace all that comforting, but I don't know how else to show how sorry I am.

I knew how resilient she is. I knew how far she's gone to help the people who needed it most.

I let the fact of her magic blind me to everything else she'd already shown me.

I'd tell me to fuck off too.

My voice comes out hoarse. "I'm sorry. I didn't realize it would do this to you. I shouldn't have been such an ass about it anyway. Is there anything I can do to help you through the pain?"

Ivy expels a rough breath. "It's starting to… ease up."

I rest my right hand against her cheek, resisting the urge to bury my face in her hair. To soak up everything I've found wondrous about this woman that I buried under anger and fear.

"I can get by in my afternoon classes on my own. I'll help you to the infirmary, and then you should go back to my quarters. You might need all the rest you can get before tonight."

Ivy peers at me. "You're not going to order me to stay out of the woods? Claim I'm too much of a liability?"

My shamed laugh sears up my throat. "Ivy, if it's possible to stop those fiends, I wouldn't put my money on anyone but you."

Twenty-Two

Ivy

When Stavros returns to his quarters just after the tenth bell, it's with a plate holding three of the flaky, custard-filled pastries the nobles call "moon rolls." I glance up from the sofa and have to pretend my mouth doesn't water at the sight of them.

As he stops across from the sofa, looking at me, my silence starts to feel awkward. "Needed a late-night snack?" I ask.

His gaze drops to the plate. I'm not sure I've ever seen the former general act hesitant before.

It's a little unnerving.

"They're meant to be for you," he says, in the careful, faintly beseeching tone he's taken with me ever since he sicced one of his students on me this afternoon.

Oh. I stare at him. "I was just in the dining hall a couple of hours ago. I ate plenty of food."

"I'm sure. But you like these, don't you? I saw there were

a few left and thought you might want to fortify yourself for whatever's coming tonight."

Julita shifts within my skull. *Did you* break *Stavros? This morning he couldn't glower at you enough, now he's tripping over his feet to cater to you. I've never seen him so rattled.*

So it's not just me unnerved by the change.

Of course, if Stavros is broken, I don't know what she'd call what's happened to me. He rushed me to the infirmary as soon as my magic had finished lashing out at me and claimed the red mark around my neck was the result of a training mishap, but my throat still stings faintly when I swallow.

The medic repaired the encroaching bruise, but the damage went deeper than that. Possibly not just in my neck but various internal organs as well, thanks to my magic's frustration.

I take the plate and simply hold it, not sure what to do with it. My taste buds might be eager, but my stomach is clenched tight both in anticipation of yet another trial with the scourge sorcerers tonight... and however the former general might react to me next.

Will he take a rejection of his generosity as a sign of malicious intent? Should I choke down one of the rolls to prove I appreciate the gesture?

His mood has shifted so much in the course of the day that I have no idea what to expect.

"I'm quite full," I say tentatively. "But it might be nice to have them to come back to, after everything."

I set the plate on the small table by the arm of the sofa. Stavros's gaze follows its descent with an odd air of sadness.

Well, he's not shouting accusations at me, so I guess I'll call that a win.

It was horrible, what he did today, Julita says. *He shouldn't have gone that far—he shouldn't have felt he needed to. I wouldn't forgive him just yet, but I don't think he really wanted to hurt you, Ivy.*

Does it matter what he wanted? He was willing to hurt me anyway to get whatever proof he needed, since apparently he judged that I wasn't offering enough evidence of my loyalties on my own.

Who knows what else he might feel he needs to do?

Stavros's head ticks as he studies my face. "Is there anything else that might help you prepare for your meeting with the scourge sorcerers tonight?"

I splay my hands. "Hard to say when I don't know what that meeting will entail."

His presence in the room and the weight of what he put me through this afternoon is becoming increasingly suffocating. I turn away and reach for my cloak. "I was thinking I'd stop by the temple and see if Kosmel has anything else to say for himself."

"Ah. That seems worth trying." Stavros pauses. "Will you come back here before you're expected in the woods?"

I shrug as I fasten the cloak around my neck. Stavros tracks the movement of my hands, maybe thinking as I am of the rope that wrapped across the same spot just hours ago.

"I suppose that depends on how talkative the godlen is and whether I can find anything else to pass the time," I say. "But you shouldn't be waiting up anyway."

"Of course."

There's another pause, the silence so awkward I practically flee for the door.

Once I'm walking down the hall, the pressure lightens, if only a tad. I still have my impending foray into the woods to worry about, and that's no small thing.

I really don't have any idea what to expect from the scourge sorcerers either.

One of the guards by the college gate stops me briefly to

check where I'm headed at this late hour, but when I tell him, he waves me on. I hurry along the cobblestone road and slip through the temple's grand doorway.

In the thick of the night, the only illumination in the massive worship room flickers from sconces set above each of the godlen statues. The glow catches on swaths of red silk that've been fixed to several of the columns and two immense gold swords now crossing each other over the entrance to the central tower.

I've been so distracted it takes me a moment to remember the reason for the adjusted décor. Sabrellia, the festival for the warrior godlen, is coming in a couple of days.

Each of the godlen get one day a year when everyone celebrates their contributions to our world. I can't say I'm looking forward to honoring the violent divinity Stavros dedicated himself to, though.

I doubt I'll be in a festive mood.

A couple of devouts pass through the worship room with subtle dips of their head toward me. The temple is open at all hours—they must be used to worshippers arriving at random.

I approach Kosmel's alcove with a sense of trepidation. The godlen of luck and trickery insisted I stay alive. He must have some purpose for me.

It'd be nice to get a clearer idea of what that is.

But the thought of hearing his divinely overwhelming voice in my head again makes every part of my body tense up.

The one thing both of the clerics whose journals I read agreed on is that you can't dictate when or how you'll receive messages from the gods. You have to extend your question into the universe and watch for some indication it's been heard.

Kosmel probably loves keeping us mortals on our toes.

I kneel before his statue, ignoring the dice this time. A simple *yes* or *no* doesn't feel like enough to satisfy all the uncertainty inside me.

I'm doing the best I can, I think at him. *Is there anything I'm missing? Do you have any advice at all? I want to take down the scourge sorcerers soon—I don't know what else they're going to ask of me.*

I close my eyes, thinking maybe images will float up from my mind the way the cleric of the Temple of Fruitful Abundance sometimes described. When all I get is an ache forming in my knees from the hard floor, I glance upward at the statue.

At the same moment, the sconce above Kosmel flares. The shadows on his marble form shift—and I swear I catch a shape like a gowned figure leaping headfirst into a thicker clump of darkness.

A chill settles over me. Maybe I only imagined that.

But even Casimir said that's how he feels Ardone guides him sometimes—drawing his attention to meaningful details in the world around him.

I raise my eyebrows at the smirking godlen. "Just dive farther in?" I murmur.

He doesn't say anything, naturally. In frustration, I pick up a die and toss it by his feet.

It lands five up. The most emphatic yes.

Swallowing thickly, I pull myself to my feet. My innards feel all jumbled up.

Until the last few weeks, I've avoided the notice of the gods. I don't really like the sensation of one of them dabbling in my life.

Is that really *better* than being left to my own devices?

My skin creeping, I stride out of the temple. There's nothing more for me in there at the moment.

The apparent message nags at me all the way back to the

college. I pause in the outer courtyard, marking the eleven peals of the bell, and veer around the Quadring to make for the woods.

Isn't it awfully early? Julita asks.

I let out my voice in the barest mutter. "He wants me to dive in; I'm diving in. They can ignore me until one o'clock if they want."

Or maybe we can get the next trial over with, and I can take a break from the precarious balancing act I've been performing for a day or two.

I count out my fifty paces into the woods and sit down on the forest path, settling in for what might be a long wait. The warble of the breeze through the leaves and the periodic buzz and chirp of forest life are becoming familiar.

There's nothing in this darkness I really need to fear except the human beings venturing into it alongside me.

I breathe in and out at a regular pace, absorbing the sounds around me, the shifts in the cooling air. I might even drift into the sort of meditative state the clerics sometimes talk about, though I can't say any great insight comes with it.

Apparently Julita can't do the same. She stirs restlessly within my head. *Of course they'd have to pick the creepiest time and place to conduct their initiation tests. I'm sure they simply want you to be as off-balance as possible.*

As if to prove her point, a voice abruptly breaks through the quiet. It's distorted by the same magical effect as usual, but this once I have a definite impression of it coming from somewhere ahead of me and a bit to the right.

"Why are you here already, Ivy of Nikodi?"

Interesting. So there are probably at least two conspirators who've been conducting these trials, only one of whom is able to project their voice widely.

Determining that fact doesn't get me any closer to knowing who those people are, though.

I consider what sort of answer the scourge sorcerers would most want to hear from a potential recruit. "What's been happening out here feels much more important than anything I could be doing in the college. I thought I'd see if I can get more in tune with the All-Giver."

Julita gives a chuckle of approval. *Buttering them up. Very nice.*

I can't hear any hint of movement in the forest. Either the speaker has been standing wherever they are for a long time without moving, they're propelling their voice from quite far away, or they're incredibly stealthy.

They don't bother to answer, maybe waiting for companions to join them. I go back to my sort-of meditation, but I keep my ears even more pricked than before.

Sometime after the midnight hour has been rung in, a voice breaks the quiet again, surrounding me in the more usual fashion. "The All-Giver would appreciate your commitment, Ivy. We'd like to know what else you can do for the Great God."

I ease myself carefully to my feet. "Did you have anything in particular in mind?"

"You made a small sacrifice of your finger, it appears. What godlen are you dedicated to, and what is your gift?"

My heart stutters for an instant before I remember Casimir's gentle touch as he re-imprinted my false dedication brand yesterday night. When I looked at it this evening, the pink-toned mark between my breasts still looked completely believable.

How much can the conspirators even see in this darkness if they demand a peek?

"I'm dedicated to Kosmel," I say, bringing out the answer I prepared. "I asked for a talent for forgery. There've always been things I wanted to do that my parents wouldn't approve of. It's helped... clear the way."

I do have a talent for forgery, but it's one I developed entirely without divine intervention. And the scourge sorcerers might see some use for it, sooner rather than later.

If I can get them to hand over any physical evidence of their plans—documents related to their schemes that they need false signatures on or adjusted duplicates of—that might be enough to bring the whole conspiracy down.

There's a brief silence that makes me think the sorcerers are consulting with each other. Then one speaks up again. "Have you ever tried to create a forgery on a larger scale? An illusionary copy of a real object, for example?"

A shiver runs down my spine. Are they thinking I might be able to help with their clay creatures?

That wasn't the kind of job I had in mind.

Well, I can answer honestly. "No. I'll admit it's a fairly small gift since it was a fairly small sacrifice. I was more cautious at twelve than I've become since."

"Then if you could increase your power with a new sacrifice now, you would do it?"

My uneasiness grows, but there's only one way I can answer that question that keeps me in the game. "Of course, if it's for a good purpose."

"This time, it'll be for the purpose of showing us how committed you are to challenging what's wrong in this world."

I dip my head. "I can understand why you'd want to confirm that. But how would a new sacrifice work?"

"We wouldn't ask it of you often," the voice says. "Much can be gained by combining the gifts we already have. But what you can do on your own matters too. Come to the edge of the woods, and we'll see what fits the moment."

I don't like the sound of this, Julita mutters as I tramp back the way I came.

Neither do I, but I don't see how there's anything she or I can do about it. At least I'm not having to kill living creatures with my bare hands tonight.

I stop in the shadows of the trees at the edge of the patch of forest. Moonlight streams down over the field between me and the back of the Quadring.

"We have decided," the voice says as if from right behind me.

I suppress a flinch and glance backward, but no one's in view. I will my muscles to relax. "What did you decide?"

"The Crown's Watch carries out orders without concern for their legitimacy. They only care about their own power, not what pleases the gods. You've seen that, haven't you?"

I let out a light guffaw. "Oh, yes."

At least, I've seen them abuse their authority. I can't say I'm sure of what pleases any of the gods.

"You could put a couple of them in their places. Remind them that there are greater powers at work in the universe."

My gaze darts across the campus. The first figure it catches on has a pale face topped by glossy brown curls—the gifted guard who hassled me when I was stargazing. He's walking next to the Quadring's back wall.

Can I use any magic on *him* without his gift reacting? Do the scourge sorcerers even realize he's got magic he uses regularly?

How deep a pile of shit are they going to throw me into?

"How should I do that?" I ask tentatively.

"On the eastern wall," the voice says. "Do you see the two soldiers stationed there who are speaking to each other?"

My attention jerks to the outer wall with a jolt of relief. Not that I know for sure the two figures I spot atop the stone barrier *don't* have gifts of their own.

I nod. At least one of the conspirators must be close enough to see me, because the gesture seems to be answer enough.

"You will ask Kosmel to expand your power so that you can 'forge' an object of your choice out of the air. You will use it to startle the guards. If you can start a fight between them, we'll be even more impressed."

I wet my lips. "I don't think Kosmel will grant my request just because I ask nicely."

"That's why you'll do more than ask. You'll show how committed you are to the task with an offering."

A figure shrouded completely in black steps out of the trees to approach me. I can't tell whether they're male or female, young or old. Even their face has been covered by a swath of black fabric that hangs from the edge of their hood, though it must be thin enough to allow them to see through.

The scourge sorcerer lifts their hand, and a knife glints in the filtered moonlight. My magic wakes up at the sight, squirming in my chest.

Julita shivers. *I don't know... I think this might be deep enough right here, Ivy. You could make a run for the college buildings—you're fast.*

And then what? The scourge sorcerers will want me dead for what I already know.

"What would you have me give?" I ask, managing to keep my voice steady.

The figure in black motions with the knife, but the voice that speaks comes from elsewhere, farther off in the forest. "You will give up your full forefinger from your left hand, with a plea to bolster your gift for tonight. We will not numb it and seal it immediately as the shirking clerics do. The blood and the pain show the depth of your sacrifice. The All-Giver wants us to *feel*."

My breath catches in my throat. Not at the thought of the pain—I've experienced worse just this afternoon.

But if I give up my entire forefinger on my dominant hand... I'm not sure how long it'll take me to learn how to handle a knife without it. Whether I'll ever be able to effectively fight or steal again.

So many of the skills I counted on for survival in my old life—so many that have helped me survive even at the college—

Do they even realize how much they're truly asking from me?

Ivy, no, you shouldn't have to go this far, Julita is saying, at the same time as the voice from the woods demands, "Are you willing?"

I swallow a broken laugh. My power twitches in my chest, begging to thrash the sorcerers for even asking to harm me, but I clamp down on it tight.

Kosmel indicated I should go deeper—I should throw myself straight in. I did commit to this course, even if not for the reasons the scourge sorcerers think.

How much of a life will I have left if I refuse?

I extend my hand. "Absolutely. Thank you for the opportunity."

Every word scrapes up my throat like a jagged stone, but I must have answered quickly and convincingly enough. I can almost hear the speaker's smile. "You're most welcome."

It all happens so quickly I barely have time to second-guess my decision. The figure with the knife grasps my wrist, presses my other fingers and thumb close to my palm, and jams my hand against the nearest tree trunk.

Before I've so much as sucked in a breath, they swing the knife.

Gods help me, the blade is sharp. It chops straight through flesh and bone with a burst of pain.

As I clench my jaw against a whimper, blood streaks down the bark and across my hand. I keep just enough wherewithal to remember the plea I'm supposed to make.

My voice tumbles ragged over my lips. "Kosmel, All-Giver, whoever hears me: Give me the power tonight to forge so much more than I could before."

I swing toward the guards on the wall, stretching out my bleeding hand.

I just want to get the trial over with. My head is whirling with pain and horror and a twinge of regret; I want to scream at someone for dragging me into this place.

I don't have a normal gift anyway. I'll try, and it won't work, and the scourge sorcerers will make of it what they will. Or maybe Kosmel will step in and conjure up an illusion on my behalf.

But that's not what happens at all.

My riven power surges inside me alongside the stream of blood pattering onto the forest floor. My head spins—and all at once I can't contain the churning energy inside me.

I can't plug all the holes. I can't smother every shred of the magic jangling through my nerves.

A punch of the errant magic slips my hold. It flings through the air toward the guards, latching on to the intention I claimed to have, the image the conspirators put in my head.

I don't know what illusion it forms. All I see is one guard lurching toward the other.

No, no, not like this. I hug my other arm around my gut, desperately scrambling to rein my magic in without giving away what I'm grappling with.

The ground bucks under me. I can't tell if that's scourge sorcery or the backlash of my own power, but it knocks me to my knees.

My magic flails out of me in one last attempt to carry out my will, whether I like it or not.

The guards stumble again—and one of them smacks into the low crenelation along the top of the wall with so much force she flips right over it.

The thud of her body hitting the ground carries through the night straight to my ears.

I gulp for air and shove my power down as far as I can go, fighting to keep my horror off my face so the conspirators won't see my distress. My unwounded hand braces against the damp earth to steady me.

My magic tries to lash out again, but I clamp it tight. Its frustration reverberates through my bones.

I grit my teeth against it. No more.

Gods above, what did I do to her? Has she even survived the fall?

I never meant to—

The black-robed figure crouches in front of me. A voice rings out with obvious satisfaction from the woods beyond us. "An impressive performance. The gods look kindly on you. You don't have to worry. For your service, we'll see you made whole again."

I don't understand. I'm too scattered to even realize what's happening until the figure who wielded the knife presses the finger they chopped off against the bleeding stump, and a hot tingling spreads through my flesh.

She has a healing gift. She's melding my hand back together.

It shouldn't surprise me. How would the conspirators expect me to explain away the sudden loss of my finger once I returned to school?

Healing me is for their benefit at least as much as my own.

But as the sinews and bones bind back together, my gaze

returns to the wall. To the guard shouting for help from where he's still poised at the top, peering down at his fallen companion.

The scourge sorcerers didn't realize the true source of my magic or how little I wanted to let it loose. But I know.

I lost control, just for a matter of seconds, and this is what I've done.

Maybe Stavros has been right all along. Maybe I can't be anything other than a monster.

Twenty-Three

Ivy

T he whole city is draped in red.

Scarlet banners hang above storefronts and stretch high across the streets. Crimson streamers dangle from windows. Ruby ribbons festoon every cart and carriage.

And the people only add to the cacophony of red. Every noble and inner-warder milling around the courtyard outside the Temple of the Crown wears silk, satin, or finely woven wool dyed in some shade of that hue.

Even in the outer wards, where few can afford full outfits in every divine color, people will be tying red sashes and scarves around their bodies to join in the celebration.

Casimir didn't fail me in his self-assigned role as my official costumer. Airy silk wraps across my chest and tumbles over my legs in a deep wine-red that somehow makes my sallow complexion look creamy rather than sickly.

The assault of color that meets my eyes everywhere I look makes me *feel* a little sick, though. At the edge of the square

where Stavros and I have halted to survey the festivities, I shift my weight and reach to adjust the lace that shades my eyes.

Along with Sabrelle's color, everyone in the inner ward has donned helmet-inspired headdresses to honor the godlen of war. For women, that means a light metal cap with silver-toned filigree meant to mimic chainmail, which flows over my hair and down my face to the tip of my nose.

Nobles do love an excuse to be semi-anonymous while they revel.

Thankfully the face covering includes eye holes, so my vision isn't too obscured. I'm not here to revel myself, but to keep watch.

Beside me, Stavros frowns at the crowd from beneath his own helm. The men wear a less dainty version, with silver plates over the nose and cheeks.

"Our performance for the military division isn't until the seventh bell," he says. "You'll have lots of time to circulate. From what I saw of the planned layout, the entomology club has their demonstration of sorts set up in the northeast corner of the square. You should be able to get a look at most of the members there so you can keep track of them."

I nod. "I already spotted Ster. Torstem. He's got golden stags embroidered on his jacket."

"I doubt *he'll* make any concerning moves." Stavros sighs. "I'm not sure any of them would risk revealing their intentions with so many witnesses around. But they did strike at Prince Jacos in the middle of the college. With the royal family making an appearance, we can't be too careful."

A blare of a trumpet brings my head around. "And here they come now."

The crowd parts around the front of the temple to make way for the royal procession. No doubt as aware of the threat as we are, the king has brought a dozen members of his personal guard, their usual uniforms swapped for a striking garnet-red.

King Konram and several other figures walk in their midst. He, Queen Ishild, and their two living children—Princess Klaudia and Prince Jacos—wave to the revelers, who raise their voices in eager cheers.

They only just returned from their tour of the provinces last night. Not a bad welcome, coming home to a massive party.

I'm not familiar with their companions. A stately woman in a belted dress that looks more like a cleric's robes than a noble gown strides along behind them, one of her eyes covered by a patch that reminds me of Esmae's. At her left trots a spindly, ivory-haired man whose uneven gait could indicate the stiffness of old age or a leg-related sacrifice.

And behind them—

My breath hitches at the sight of the third man's misshapen form. He holds his substantial frame tall and haughty, but neither his posture nor his thick cloak can disguise how lopsided his body is.

He's missing one arm, all the way to the shoulder.

Gods above, what kind of gift will he have gotten for *that* sacrifice?

"Who are those three with the royal family?" I murmur.

Stavros dips his head lower so he can match my quiet tone. "I suggested to the king that he might have his magic advisors join him for this excursion. I don't think he's mentioned specific concerns to any of them except his chief sorcerer, Hessild Korinya there, but any of them are likely to pick up on unusual magical activity around them. The two men are Tinom Akorek, the smaller one, who specializes in illusions and ephemeral blessings, and Lothar Riosemek, who's a master of herbal and chemical concoctions."

I can't help raising an eyebrow. "He gave up an entire arm just to mix potions?"

One corner of Stavros's mouth crooks upward. "I'm not sure exactly what his gift is, only that he dedicated himself to Creaden. I'd imagine it allows for more than just smooth mixing."

"But not impressive enough for the king to make *him* chief sorcerer."

The former general shrugs. "I believe Hessild has a powerful gift in her own right. An eye isn't a minor thing. And there's a family history. Her mother and grandfather both served as chief sorcerer before her."

Julita lets out a huff in my head. *You'd think between three royal sorcerers, they could keep this scourge menace in check themselves.*

Stavros pauses, and his hand slips around mine as if to emphasize his next words. "Be particularly careful if you cross paths with Lothar. He's been more vocal than the king himself in encouraging the hunts for the riven and the public executions. I get the impression he has a personal vendetta."

A lump fills my throat. "I wasn't planning on—"

"I know." Stavros runs his thumb over the base of my forefinger—over the tiny scar that's the only evidence of my temporary sacrifice two days ago. "Just… be careful."

He lets go of me, but the ghost of his touch lingers on my skin with an unwelcome warmth. My gut knots with the memory of my confession yesterday morning.

I knew he'd find out about the fallen guard. He'd be suspicious about when and where it happened. If I'd tried to lie, I'm not sure he'd have believed me.

And maybe a part of me thought I'd get some kind of confirmation out of it. That if I told him, the man who's reviled my magic from the moment he discovered it, his reaction would give me whatever punishment I truly deserved.

Somehow, he didn't run me through or drag me to the gallows. When he growled a few curses, they were directed at the scourge sorcerers rather than me. Then he stormed off and returned simply to inform me that the guard had lived.

She's still in the infirmary, undergoing additional care from the medics. Her skull cracked with the fall. But apparently they expect her to fully recover, given enough time.

Neither of those facts has loosened the guilt still tangled up inside me. I think I might actually feel more reassured if Stavros *had* dragged me off to be executed.

I lost my grip on my riven power. Only for a few seconds, and with consequences that weren't absolutely dire —but we don't know what the scourge sorcerers will demand of me next.

How can I promise it'll never be worse?

A couple of days ago, I was angry with him for not trusting me. Now I'm not sure I deserve the trust he's decided to offer.

Stavros shifts forward. "I'm going to stay close to the king until it's time for the performance. But it looks as though you'll have some company while you keep an eye on the rest of the festivities."

I glance around to see two men weaving through the crowd toward us.

I'd recognize Casimir's graceful stride anywhere, regardless of the helmet covering most of his face. His soft smile brings an answering one to my lips despite the tangle inside me.

I can't say military gear suits him, but he manages to look stunning in his crimson-and-gold tunic even with the lump of metal on his head.

Alek's lean form follows right behind the courtesan. He's wearing a festival helm that extends all the way to his jaw, hiding his mask completely. His red tunic is edged with embroidery in a bronze tone, and his breaches are more fitted than Casimir's fashionable billowy ones, but he cuts just as striking a figure.

We can explore the celebration together at least for a little while, with our identities concealed to anyone who doesn't know us quite so well.

Stavros nods to them discreetly and heads off toward the royal procession.

Casimir slips his hand around my elbow. "How are you doing, Kindness?"

The tenderness of his tone tells me he's not just asking if I'm enjoying the festival. Stavros was able to alert him and Alek to meet us early yesterday so I could tell them everything that happened without worrying about revealing my secret to Benedikt. The courtesan stuck close to me for the whole rest of the meeting, as if he could tell how unsteady I'm feeling.

"Wishing I was back in my room with a book," I say with a light laugh. "But I suppose we'd better celebrate Sabrelle properly."

Alek comes to a stop in front of me, his expression solemn. He spent several minutes yesterday arguing with both Stavros and me about whether we should call off my plan to infiltrate the conspiracy.

Not because he's worried about what I might do. Because he's worried about how it's affecting me.

"Sounds like a better way to spend an evening than this," he says. "We could go do that right now."

I wag a finger at him to try to show I'm all right. "We've got work to do here. I should probably see if I can enjoy myself too. I've never spent very long at any festival but Signy's."

It never seemed like a good idea to strut around when everyone's trying to draw one or another godlen's attention in every way possible—not when I was trying to *avoid* the gods' notice. Unless there was an item it was an ideal time to steal or a con I needed to pull, I stayed off the streets during festivals.

Casimir's thumb strokes my arm through the sleeve of my gown. He can probably guess at my reasons. "Does that mean you've never tried bloodfruit pudding?"

I give him a skeptical look. "It does. I wouldn't have thought that was a great loss." How good can any dessert made from a favorite field snack of soldiers be?

The courtesan chuckles and tugs me with him into the throng. "You'll be surprised then. I don't care for the stuff dried as army rations, but it's got a lot to recommend about it when cooked fresh."

We squeeze through the crowded square to a stall selling small paper cones filled with the jelly-like pudding, designed to be eaten straight out of the disposable dish. I lap up a little with my tongue, and my eyes widen at the tartly sweet flavor with a tang that's almost spicy.

"Okay, you've proven me wrong. What other delights have I been missing out on?"

Alek's smile turns a bit sly in that way that makes my chest flutter. "All the best weapons-smiths have their goods on display. I saw some skillfully crafted throwing knives for sale."

Casimir guides me onward. "And you won't want to miss the cavalry show."

I release my first real laugh in days. "All right, all right. Apparently you know me better than I know myself."

They've gone all sappy, Julita remarks, in a tone almost as tart as the bloodfruit. *We do have a job to do here too. I hope they won't forget.*

She doesn't say anything about *me* forgetting it, but I immediately feel a pang of guilt. As we continue on through the courtyard, I keep my eyes peeled for any other familiar forms.

I don't know the members of the bug club all that well. It's hard to recognize much of anyone beneath the helms.

Over by the smiths' stalls, a group of duelists and soldiers are putting on a series of sparring matches—some with each other with flashy moves, and others open to challengers from the crowd. While I allow myself to buy a particularly appealing little dagger that might give my current favorite a run for its money, one of the fighters plants his fists in another's face, making blood spurt from his opponent's nose to match his scarlet jacket.

Farther along, the hunter's guild shows off a rack of skins from various slain animals. Illusionary images of deer and hare romp in the air above their stall, periodically crumpling with the strike of a conjured spear.

They've set up a compact archery range for revelers to try their luck at shooting one of the very real pigeons whose wings they've clipped. A little girl squeals in victory when her arrow hits its mark with a thud of the feathered body.

This is a celebration dedicated to the godlen who presides over sports and hunting as well as warfare. But taking it all in, my stomach sinks.

Are the scourge sorcerers totally wrong? The ones who've spoken to me have claimed that the gods want us animalistic and wild, not bound by strict standards of behavior.

It certainly appears that at least one of the godlen would rather see us bloody and squabbling than maintaining lawful peace.

Why would the All-Giver have created a godlen like Sabrelle at all if he didn't approve?

Why haven't the lesser gods intervened more forcefully if they're unhappy about what the scourge sorcerers are doing? If Kosmel knows, surely others have noticed the conspiracy too.

The trickster godlen seems to want me to interfere, but I don't really know why. Or what ultimate outcome he's looking for.

I'm drawn out of those uneasy thoughts at the sight of the bug club's demonstration up ahead. Alek lets out a disgusted sound, but we all go over together.

The scholar hasn't forgotten our purpose, no matter what snarky remarks Julita makes.

Several bug club members stand around a semi-circle of small terrariums, with a large glass tank in the middle of their assigned area. As we approach, two of the students are just dropping a couple of beetles nearly as large as their palms into the central tank.

The hulking insects lumber toward each other, and Julita's presence cringes in my head. Then I'm suppressing a cringe of my own as one of the beetles hurls itself at the other and wrenches off a jointed leg.

Ah. So this is how the entomology club celebrates Sabrelle—by staging bug fighting matches. Lovely.

It does fit the general theme of the celebration.

I jerk my gaze away from the battle of bugs and scan the figures staging the fight.

One of them grins, and I identify him as Olari from the gleam of steel teeth between his lips. His decorative helm has a little red tassel, and he's wearing a dark gray belt with red stitching over his tunic. That should help me recognize him if he roams into the crowd later.

With a couple of the others, I catch enough of a glimpse

of their features to connect them to students I've observed on campus. The rest I'm not sure of—they could be from the second group that Alek suspects isn't involved in the illicit magic part of the club's practices.

I commit the most distinctive details of their clothing to memory and then turn away. "I think I've had enough of that."

Casimir tucks his arm around my waist. "Let's find those horses. It's amazing what the top trainers can coax them to do."

It's obvious that he and Alek are committed to making the event as enjoyable as possible for me, no matter what else I have on my mind. We watch a parade of horses prance by and perform several feats of agility and strength with their riders. Then Alek pulls me over to a stall serving freshly steamed dumplings that I happily devour a handful of.

The scholar points out the scrolls unfurled by a bookshop's storefront, missives from old historical battles that I can tell he's itching to carry back to the library.

I give him a teasing nudge with my elbow. "I could probably arrange for a few of those to end up in your possession."

Alek looks vaguely horrified, but on my behalf rather than at the suggestion. "I wouldn't ask you to take that risk—"

"Oh, it'd barely be any." I pause. "But I suppose I should stay on my best behavior in all things not strictly necessary, given everything else I've been getting up to."

Before my uneasy melancholy can settle over me again, Casimir waves us on toward a dog breeder's tent. "It looks like the royal houndsman has a new litter on offer. Who doesn't like puppies?"

I have to admit that the sight of the furballs tussling and tumbling does lift my spirits a little.

I want to sink into the strange sense of normalcy I'm tasting traces of, wandering around the festivities with two men who somehow want to be here with me. But every time I glance up, I need to be watching for the bug club members on the move. I'm always at least a little aware of the cluster of guards around the royal procession.

Finally, the peal of the bell tells me it's time to help out with the college's military performance. I hustle over to the space set aside for Stavros and the three other professors who organized the display and hand out the assigned weaponry to the participating students like a good little assistant.

As the professors and students launch into a re-enactment of one of the most famous historical battles, I take a step back from the ring.

A jaunty voice speaks softly by my shoulder. "You should be over there putting them all to shame with your skills, Knives."

I chuckle and glance over at Benedikt, who's come up behind me. Always a fan of luxury, he's gone with a gold-plated helm that I can't imagine any actual warrior wearing into battle, and his striped jacket is as much gold as red as well.

I can't say the look doesn't suit him.

"I don't think they'd appreciate me changing the course of history," I retort.

"Oh, I don't think anyone could fail to appreciate you once they witnessed those impressive skills." He pauses. "I saw you surveying the crowd earlier. You've been making the rounds with Casimir and Alek?"

There's a hint of tension in his voice that I know I'm not imagining, because Julita picks up on it too. *Why is he asking? Who else would he expect you to spend your time with?*

"We bumped into each other early on," I say. "You could have joined us."

"Oh, I was having plenty of fun with my dormmates. It was just a little odd—when I showed up for the meeting yesterday, it almost felt as if you all had been discussing things for quite a while already."

A prickle of apprehension runs down my back. "Just a little small talk while we waited for you to show up."

Benedikt's hum sounds skeptical. "You were awfully vague about that last trial our 'friends' put you through."

I didn't mention my actual last trial in front of him at all, only the one from the night before. But he doesn't know that.

I force my tone to stay dry. "They aren't exactly pleasant memories. I don't see how they're all that useful beyond the little bits of information I've been able to pick up."

"True, true. Our conspirators do have an interesting way of seeing the world, don't they?"

Again, his tone niggles at me—and not just me.

What's he getting at? Julita murmurs.

I shake my head ruefully. "If by 'interesting' you mean absolutely horrifying, then yes. Oh!"

I've just caught sight of Ster. Torstem, his embroidered stags glinting in the lantern-light that's glowing through the falling dusk. The stout man is shouldering through the crowd... directly toward the procession that includes the royal family.

Julita's voice sharpens. *And what is he aiming for?*

I'd better find out. Of course the law professor would approach the king while Stavros is occupied.

Benedikt follows my gaze. His tone turns bitter as it drops even lower. "Yes, let us all fawn before the great King Konram."

He's obviously in a sour mood in general.

"Maybe I'll cross paths with you later," I tell him hurriedly, and set off after Torstem.

The royal procession has come to a stop by a booth offering mulled wine, just beyond the houndsman's tent. Ster. Torstem sidles closer to them and dips his hand into his pocket.

What *is* he up to? He definitely doesn't look as if he has any legitimate reason to catch the king's attention.

And who knows if his illicit sorcery will allow him to launch some kind of surreptitious attack right through the host of guards around the royals?

We have to stop him, Julita frets. *But if he realizes you interfered, it'll ruin all the progress you've made with his sycophants.*

I grit my teeth, my gaze searching the crowd. How can I alert the guards to a potential threat when he doesn't look threatening at all—and without Torstem realizing I'm doing the alerting?

My magic lurches to the ready with a smack against my ribs, but I shove it right back down with a clench of my jaw. It's hurt enough people in the past few days.

My attention settles on the nearby tent. Maybe I simply need to provide a different "threat" to disrupt the guards' current complacency.

I slip around the back of the tent, drawing my new knife. No time like the present to break it in.

Listening carefully to make sure there's no one near that corner of the structure, I slit the ties holding two folds of fabric in place. Then I duck down and lean inside just long enough to sever the ropes securing a few of the larger hounds to their post.

With a silent apology to the animals, I pick up a sharp stone from the ground and flick it into one of the dog's haunches, right by his fellow beast's muzzle.

The first hound lunges around, sure he's been nipped. The second barks at the sudden hostility. In a matter of seconds, they're chasing each other and the third hound in their midst out of the tent, snapping and baying at each other.

The nearby crowd scatters. Torstem himself has to stumble to the side to avoid being bowled over.

The royal guards draw even closer around their charges. I catch one's comment to the king: "I believe we should move on from this commotion, Your Highness."

King Konram must decide he's had enough commotion in general, because the procession weaves its way back toward the palace, only stopping for a moment here and there for the royal family to give their greetings.

I lean back against the nearest building with a sigh of relief. Ster. Torstem can't follow them right into the palace.

But I don't even know what disaster I might have averted.

Twenty-Four

Ivy

My head spins in the darkness. Then hands grip the edges of the sack by my shoulders.

I already know what's coming, with a lurch of dread in my gut. I've been here too many times before.

The sack wrenches away from my head. I find myself staring into Stavros's searing gaze, his mouth curved into a vicious sneer.

He reaches for the hangman's noose—

And I manage to jerk myself out of the dream before I have to face the horror of the rope tightening around my neck.

I exhale raggedly into the dimness of the room I've woken up to. A faint stinging lingers at my throat—how much from the nightmare and how much from the memory of a very real rope that pressed against it a few days ago, I'm not sure.

Ever since Stavros's test in the equipment building, that

unnerving dream has come for me every night. No matter what he says or how much he apologizes, my mind doesn't totally believe him.

As I sit up on the sofa, trying to shake off the awful images, a hazy but urgent muttering filters through the bedroom door. It's followed by a harsh rustle of sheets.

It sounds like neither of you is sleeping well, Julita remarks.

I let out a rough laugh under my breath. "We make quite a pair, don't we? Giving each other nightmares while we're sharing the same quarters."

I'll bet Stavros never bargained on this development when he insisted I stay in his rooms.

A grunt reaches my ears, muffled but clearly uneasy. My fingers curl around the edge of my blanket.

My ghostly companion must be able to tell what I'm considering from the tensing of my body. *I wouldn't disturb him. He's survived worse than a bad dream or two. After the way he reacted last time... But I suppose I don't really know what to make of his behavior anymore.*

I grimace. "He obviously doesn't know what to make of me. I never meant for anyone to find out."

Of course you didn't. But better you did than let Wendos finish his wretched plans. If Alek and Cas can accept you, he should be able to too.

"I'm guessing they didn't lose anyone they cared about to someone like me."

Julita lets out a huff. *Whatever murderous villain killed Stavros's friend, they weren't like you at all. I've had to live with someone who was merely* trying *to become an evil sorcerer, and I can assure you, you're leagues better than even that.*

My mouth slants into a crooked smile. I wish I could appreciate Julita's reassurances more.

There's a soft thump, as if Stavros has struck the mattress. I wince.

It might not even be about you, Julita adds. *I can't begin to imagine how many horrifying things he must have seen during his days on the battlefield.*

That's true, but the next sound that filters through the door comes in perfectly distinct words. "Ivy. No."

My stomach lurches. Before I can think better of it, I've sprung to my feet.

As I stride to the bedroom door, Julita lapses into silence. She must be able to tell there's no point in arguing with me now.

I can't bear to just sit there knowing he's trapped in a dream with me doing who knows what despicable things.

I push open the door and hesitate on the threshold. Stavros is sprawled on his side on the bed, the sheets tangled across his torso and thighs, his face half buried in his pillow. His brow is furrowed, his hand clenched tight.

I don't think I want to get within striking range.

"Stavros," I say, carefully quiet. When he only hisses through his teeth, his eyes still squeezed shut, I raise my voice. "Stavros! Wake up!"

With a flinch, he rolls onto his back. He swipes at his face and stares at me blearily through the faint moonlight.

I'm abruptly aware of the fact that I've got nothing on but the chemise and drawers I normally sleep in. Not that Stavros hasn't seen me in a similar state of undress before.

The sheet has fallen far enough on his chest to reveal some of the sculpted muscles that fill out his massive frame. The brand of Sabrelle's sigil marks his light brown skin with a darker, ruddy shade low on his sternum.

I have the sudden, ridiculous urge to find out what those muscular planes would feel like under my fingers.

Heat trickles through my veins, but I clench my hand against the thought, resting the other on the doorframe. At least the former general isn't yelling at me.

So far.

He pushes himself into a sitting position, his arms tucked in front of him—his hand of flesh cupping over the stump left by his sacrifice.

"Did I wake you up?" he asks with a hint of a rasp in his voice.

I shake my head. "Already had my own nighttime terrors taking care of that."

His mouth sets in a grim line. "I'd say 'good,' but that isn't really good at all."

"It meant I was awake to disturb your sleep in a less discomforting way," I say with forced brightness. "I'll let you get more rest that's hopefully better."

As I start to turn, Stavros leans forward. "Ivy—wait."

I glance back at him. "What?"

Now that he has my attention, he looks as if he's groping for something to talk about. "You haven't had any further contact from the scourge sorcerers?"

"I'd have mentioned it if I had. Nothing since the last trial four days ago. But I suppose making me stew might be a trial in itself. There were a few days between their first and second tests anyway."

I pause with an uncomfortable pang through my chest. "Or maybe they realized something was odd about my magic that night after all, and they're deciding what to do about it."

Stavros gives a guffaw derisive enough to be weirdly comforting. "Whatever they might speculate, it won't be the truth. There's no way at all they'd imagine *I* could tolerate hiring a riven sorcerer or that you could have been in my presence so long without my realizing it. The riven generally avoid notice by staying away from anyone who'd want to execute them, not prancing around in plain sight."

I smile tightly. "Yes, it is pretty bizarre that I'm still here.

Although I suppose that might change, given that *you* do know what I did to that guard."

Stavros blinks at me. His next words come out careful but firm. "I don't think that had anything to do with you being riven."

It's my turn to stare. "What are you talking about? It was my blasted magic that knocked her off the wall."

"Yes. Your magic. Which probably would have done the exact same thing if it'd been the typical kind of magic that no one would think of hanging you for."

My arms come around to hug myself. "I'm not sure why you'd think that."

Stavros's tone turns a bit dry. "I'm not sure why you wouldn't. You told me yourself that they went as far as cutting off your finger to bolster your power. They've constantly talked about how people should give in to wildness and violence. Unless you've been misportraying the scourge sorcerers, it's sounded to me like what you did is exactly what they meant to happen if you'd had a regular gift."

I open my mouth and then close it again. I hadn't considered the situation that way.

You know, Julita murmurs, *he does have a point.*

Maybe so, but all the same— "It *was* riven magic, though, because that's the closest thing to a 'gift' I have."

Stavros lifts his shoulders in a subtle shrug. "Does the source of the magic matter if the end result was the same? If *any* person, including myself, would have trouble controlling our gift in the same situation, then I don't see how you can blame the riven part of you for it. Or really blame yourself at all. And even with all that going on, you mastered it the moment you realized someone had been hurt."

"Someone did get hurt all the same," I can't help saying.

"Ivy, I've seen trained soldiers with gifts stumble in the face of unexpected attacks more times than I can count. The fact that you regained control so quickly in a situation you'd never experienced is *impressive*, not anything I could call weakness."

I swallow thickly. I had no idea he was thinking about the situation this way.

I don't know if I can too.

My voice drops to a whisper. "I hate it. I hate that I did it. I hate that I lost control for even a few seconds."

A shadow crosses Stavros's face. "I know. I could see it when you told me. That's the other reason I didn't think I needed to be concerned. Unless *you're* concerned that it's gotten too much—if you want to put an end to this whole recruitment scheme—"

"No," I interrupt. "It's not as if I even could at this point."

He considers me with total seriousness—and a twitch of his head that tells me how intently he's studying my expression. "You could. As far as they know, you have no idea who any of them are, so they might leave you alone regardless. But even if we feared they wouldn't, we'd find a way to extricate you and keep you safe. If that's what you want."

He sounds so certain I believe him. But the idea of fleeing from this mess doesn't budge the resolve balled inside me.

"I want to know we don't have to worry about these psychopaths hurting anyone anymore. I'm getting closer—they're showing themselves to me more. I'm not abandoning ship now."

A small smile crosses Stavros's face. "That's exactly what I assumed you'd say, Lady Thief. I just wanted you to know you have the option. I mean it."

The emphatic words and the affectionate nickname he hasn't used since he found out what I am set me off-balance. I don't know what to say other than, "Thank you."

He snorts. "I should be the one thanking you. You're taking on the lion's share of the risk." He hesitates. "And I should *definitely* let you return to bed."

Something about the way he says it and the fact that he doesn't adjust his own position as if he's going to lie back down hold me in place. "Are you going to be able to get back to sleep all right?"

Stavros chuckles faintly and rubs his forehead. "Nights like this I'd normally read something light to settle my mind. But the reading is more of a stress than a comfort these days."

He glances toward the bookcase beyond his bed—the one I looked over when I found myself in this room a few weeks ago, after I was stabbed.

One corner of my mouth quirks upward. "Is that what your adventure stories are for? To put you to sleep? They mustn't be very thrilling ones."

The former general looks a bit sheepish. "There have been nights when the tactic backfired and instead I was up hours longer than I'd have preferred. But they're comforting in a way—all the action and excitement without the pain and the grit you'd have if it were real."

"And you hide those tales away in here because…"

He fixes me with a look that's only mock-stern. "Even a former general has certain appearances to keep up."

I can't restrain a laugh. And then, for reasons I couldn't totally explain if asked, I find myself saying, "I said before that I could read to you. If you won't take it as an insult, the offer still stands. It might help settle my thoughts too."

I tense automatically, half expecting him to snap at me like he did before. But Stavros simply goes still as if taking the suggestion in.

"All right," he says finally, his voice a bit stiff in a way I can't decipher. "Only for a chapter or two. Close the curtains so you can put on the light without being seen from the window. I'll pick out a decent story."

I keep behind the heavy folds of fabric as I drag the curtains across the high window. By the time I've lit the lantern by the chair in the corner, Stavros has set one of the slim leatherbound volumes on the corner of the bed.

I pick it up and settle into the chair, tucking my legs on the seat beside me. With the former general's gaze on me, I feel abruptly awkward.

Flipping the book open, I focus on the pages rather than the man across the room from me. "*Charlster's Journey: A heroic tale of the mountain kingdoms. Chapter One. It started with a fire in the stables.*"

I read on through a typically spirited beginning about an intrepid stablehand saving a countess's prized horses and being granted the responsibility of carrying an urgent message across the mountains to the realm's king. As my voice carries through the room, Stavros sinks down on the bed.

He doesn't interrupt. From the corner of my eye, I notice when his head starts to droop.

I pitch my voice gradually lower, not wanting to interrupt any impending slumber. Around the point when the stablehand encounters robbers on the mountain path, I glance up and see Stavros's eyes have closed. A slow breath rasps from his slightly parted lips.

An unexpected twinge of affection runs through me. I set down the book and douse the light.

The floor doesn't so much as creak beneath my stealthy feet as I creep back to my sofa. I've just bundled myself in my blanket when a prickling sensation digs into my palm, sharp enough that I think it'd have woken me if I *had* been sleeping.

I jerk my hand up. The words gleam briefly against my palm.

50 paces into the woods. Alone. Now.

TWENTY-FIVE

Ivy

I'm not sure what time it is until the bell rings three while I'm darting across the outer courtyard. The conspirators have never summoned me out to the woods this late before.

They've never summoned me with no advance notice before.

Well, this is a rotten trial, Julita grumbles, as if she's suffering from the lack of sleep too.

I give my tired eyes a brief swipe, allow myself a moment to long for the comfortable sofa I left behind, and then train all my attention on the task at hand.

Who knows what other tactics the scourge sorcerers might have up their sleeves tonight, designed to rattle me and betray any lack of commitment?

I have to stop by the far side of the equipment building when a patrolling guard swings into view around the corner of the Quadring. As soon as she's marched well past me, I sprint through the shadows with barely a rustle of the grass.

I take a little comfort in having exchanged my nightclothes for my linen combat shirt and breaches rather than a gown. Casimir chose my dresses well, but I can't move while smothered in layers of silk the same way I can when my limbs are unencumbered.

If the conspirators think there's anything odd about my choice in clothing, I'll simply tell them that I wanted to follow their instructions as swiftly as possible, and it takes much longer to lace up a gown than to pull on a shirt. I've worn these clothes around the school plenty of times, so the outfit shouldn't come as a total surprise.

My racing pulse only starts to slow once I'm swathed in the thicker darkness between the trees. I hurry along the path with my chin raised high, putting on my best noble airs alongside my haste.

Forty-eight, forty-nine, fifty.

I plant my feet on the path and peer into the blackness around me. You'd think after they dragged me out of bed, my evaluators would be prompt about greeting me.

There's a faint crinkle somewhere behind me to my right, like a foot stepping on a dried leaf. I can't tell whether it was a human foot or some animal passing by, though.

The hairs rise on the back of my neck.

The air stirs *right* behind me. I move to whip myself around when a sharp edge digs into my scarred back.

My muscles freeze instinctively. My breath halts in my throat.

"Turn left and walk into the forest," a magically-distorted voice says, no more than a pace behind me. I can't tell whether that's a sword, knife, or spear against my back, but any of those options would be equally fatal if rammed deeper. "Keep going until I tell you to stop."

Drawing more air into my lungs, I force myself to obey.

Twigs snap under my feet as I tramp onto the uneven ground off the side of the path. Leaves brush my arms.

My magic unfurls in my chest, tugging at me to let it bowl over the person who ambushed me. To melt the blade. To send it rampaging through the woods after every comrade who approved of this plan.

No. This is probably just another test, not an actual threat.

I will my power to stay coiled and quiet—not attacking them *or* me.

After letting it out to play a few nights ago, I find it easier to settle the restless energy. But the farther we walk in tense silence, the harder it gets to suppress my worries.

Gods smite me, have the scourge sorcerers figured out I'm a monster after all? Or maybe someone noticed my trick with the hounds during the festival.

But why would they have waited two more nights to do anything about it? It's not as if they could even have been sure I meant to interrupt Ster. Torstem rather than merely creating trouble for the royals, which would be a mission I'd expect this bunch to approve of.

Or this really could be just another trial. Make me *think* they're upset with me, see if I babble any excuses, reveal errors they didn't actually know about.

I guess I'll find out.

Ivy, Julita says, her presence contracted at the back of my skull, *this could be really bad. If you* need *to use your magic… I think you should.*

My mouth tightens. My automatic reaction is to refuse, with all possible vehemence, but I'm no longer completely sure that's the right answer.

Only as an absolute last resort. Only if it's clear there's no other way to escape—and that escape is worth the consequences.

The second I start treating these people like the enemies I know they are, everything I've put myself through to make it this far will be for nothing. We'll lose the one small foothold we've gained.

My power continues to roil within my ribcage, but it doesn't lash out too forcefully. It's waiting like the rest of me to see how this situation will play out.

Whether I'm facing actual danger or only a staging of it.

I step into a small clearing that might be the one where I tore up the rabbit or a totally different spot—it's all vague shapes in the night. The figure behind me says, "Enough."

I jar to a halt.

More forms move in the darkness between the trees, shrouded in black like the knife-wielding healer was before.

Most of them I only catch vague glimpses of. I think there are four or five people lingering at the outskirts of my limited sight.

Two of the figures step closer, to the edge of the clearing where they stand side by side with a narrow tree trunk between them.

"You accuse this woman?" says the figure on the left. His voice is distorted like the one behind me but deep enough to definitely be male.

The other new arrival wasn't given the same benefit of magical warbling. "I do," he says, in a gruff but clear voice that sends a quiver through my nerves.

I don't recognize it exactly… but I have the sense that it shouldn't sound that way. That there's something unnatural about its tone.

"Accuse me of what?" I demand, keeping my head high and peering at the unknown man through the darkness.

My nerves jitter with the sense of the presences around me forming a circle to pen me in. They're afraid I might run for it.

This definitely isn't good. But if it's an accusation from an outside source, I might be able to turn the tables on my opponent.

Who could know anything all that incriminating about me?

The first figure, directly in front of me, draws himself straighter with a pompous air. As I note the way the black fabric shifts against his broad frame, the suspicion tickles through my head that I might finally be face to face with Ster. Torstem in his scourge sorcerer guise.

When he speaks again, I listen hard for traces of the law professor's voice through the magical distortion. "Another of our number claims you're a traitor to our cause. That you have courted our favor not to serve the All-Giver and see the world returned to its former divine grace, but to undermine everything we've worked for."

A chill trickles through my veins. How could any of Torstem's people have guessed that much? Are they simply fishing to see if it's true without really believing it?

Presumably they don't actually *know*, or I'd already be dead.

Julita mumbles a string of curses and then speaks up in an urgent tone. *I know how to play this. Act all sweet and innocent, like you have no idea how anyone could think that of you. Like you're a naïve twit who's too brainless to have even considered that these fiends deserve to be undermined.*

I'm sure that's how she would have played it, but the idea of acting like an idiot doesn't sit right with me. It isn't as if it'll match what Torstem and his followers have seen from me before.

Innocence, though, I'm totally on board with.

I knit my brow. "Why would I want to undermine you? I've kept everything to myself, as you've asked."

"Lies," my accuser says in the gruff voice that feels even

more wrong with each word it speaks. "She's an excellent pretender. You can't believe anything that comes out of her mouth."

What rot. Go on and simper like you're shocked by his claims.

My body balks. I can't shake the sense that me simpering would come across just as fake as my opponent's gruffness.

There are other ways to show I have nothing to hide.

I set my hands on my hips and hold my voice steady. "Has my accuser brought any proof? As far as I can tell, *he's* the liar. He must think he has something to gain by turning you against me."

"I heard her," the shrouded figure insists. "I heard her plotting with that lout of a failed general she works for, talking about how they'd bring the Crown's Watch down on you all."

He flicks his hand beneath his concealing robe, and the fragments of recognition crash together with a sickening certainty.

His gruff tone faltered with the urgency of that last claim, more of his natural voice coming through. And something about his flippant phrasing, about the gesture he just made...

Is that *Benedikt* hiding beneath the shroud?

I try not to react, but I have to stiffen against the cold rush of nausea that floods my body.

What would he be doing out here? Why would he—?

The scourge sorcerers are waiting for my answer. Maybe I'm mistaken.

I wrench my scattered mind back to the most vital matter at hand and manage to let out a snort. "I can barely stand to discuss the weather with my employer, let alone get involved in some ridiculous scheme. I accepted your invitation to discover what more I could be in this world partly for a chance to get *away* from that man."

Ivy... I don't know... Julita squirms inside my skull, but she must realize I've decided to ignore her advice.

She's guided me well so far, but I'm the con artist between us. I've handled tricky situations with everyone from the lowest street rats to the highest nobility.

If I'm going to get through this mess, and without my magic tearing me and who knows what else apart, it has to be my way.

The figure who might be Ster. Torstem crosses his arms over his chest with a ripple of his shroud. "We *are* only going by hearsay."

He turns his head toward the man I don't want to believe is Benedikt. "And you did have a motive. You were trying to make up for your failure tonight."

His failure? At one of the initiation tasks?

Since when was Benedikt even aiming to get recruited? That was my job.

I want to think that means I was wrong, but with my accuser's next protest, even more of his familiar voice, taut with strain, shows through. "If I were making this all up, how would I have known she's been sneaking out here in the first place?"

My stomach has tied itself in a dozen knots, but I can put on an even better performance than he probably expects.

I roll my eyes skyward and let a sneer creep into my voice. "I can't imagine it'd be all that difficult if you know what to look for. What, were you watching the woods every night to see who'd sneak out here so you'd have someone to point a finger at if *your* loyalty was too shaky to keep up?"

Make the scourge sorcerers see him as the potential traitor. Take the heat off me and aim it back at him.

A sour tang of bile creeps up the back of my throat, but I don't know what else to do.

And if that's Benedikt, then he *is* a traitor. To me, to Stavros, to Julita—to everything we were supposed to be working toward.

"You question *my* loyalty," he starts to sputter, but I'm ready for him. Ready to fight.

I fix him with a glare. "I do. How selfish can you be to try to compensate for your own weaknesses by dragging someone else down with you? Someone who actually wants to see the All-Giver return and create a world the Great God would be proud of."

I sense a shifting in the circle of figures around me. I'm sowing doubt in their heads.

One thing Julita's made more than clear to me is how arrogant the scourge sorcerers are. They think they deserve greater power than anyone else; they think they have some special calling.

Like every upper class prick I've ever dealt with, the fastest way to win them over is to stoke their horrific egos.

I fix my attention back on the possible Torstem. "The nights I've spent out here, immersing myself in your teachings, are the most alive I've felt in my whole life. There's so much more I want to learn. So much I can tell I could accomplish with your guidance. If I've failed you in any way —if I've given you any reason to fault me—then I'm not worthy of this opportunity. I'll accept whatever judgment you'll give."

"Don't listen to—" Benedikt says.

The other man cuts him off with a jerk of his hand. I feel his gaze on me. "I have only your word too, Ivy of Nikodi."

I bob my head in a slight bow. "And whatever you've seen of my acts in service of your cause. But if that isn't enough…"

Julita breaks in with an urgent whisper. *I know! Borys and Wendos—when they couldn't agree on a course of action—they'd call on their powers to decide who was right.*

Hmm. I'm not going to invite my riven magic into the mix… but there is another, higher power I can appeal to.

My pulse stutters at the idea, but I don't have a better one. The words tumble out, no chance to fully think them through. "Why not let the godlen show their favor? Everything we're doing is to bring back their full glory and the world they'd want, isn't it? Test us together, and let the gods support the one whose heart they know is faithful."

Which would be me, wouldn't it? Seeing as I'm the one who's had a godlen talking to me, when he can be bothered to?

It'd better fucking well not turn out that Kosmel is playing a big prank and the lesser gods are all in favor of scourge sorcery after all.

Possible-Torstem is silent for several moments. When he speaks again, I think I can make out a pleased smile in his voice.

"That may be a reasonable suggestion. We'll need to discuss exactly how to proceed. Both of you, come along until we can settle this matter once and for all."

TWENTY-SIX

Ivy

The figure who prodded me through the woods strides along between me and Benedikt, a slim sword in their grasp. Whether they're protecting him from me or me from him, I can't tell.

Perhaps it's a little of both.

With every step we take through the night-draped forest, I'm surer of my earlier impressions. With every loping stride of the man across from me, more quivers of stomach-churning recognition race through me.

I don't understand, but somehow one of the men I counted as an ally has become my enemy.

He's accused Stavros too, in an indirect way—saying the former general was conspiring with me to double-cross the scourge sorcerers. If the fiends believe him, they'll attack Stavros without any warning.

But he's kept Alek's and Casimir's names out of it. Because he does have some kind of conscience still, or

because he didn't know how to explain they were helping me without revealing that *he* once was as well?

It takes all my concentration to keep my expression impassive and my own strides steady. If our interrogators realize that I've identified my accuser, that I feel betrayed... then they'll know I really did have secrets *to* betray.

The figure I think is Ster. Torstem marches between the trees ahead of us. I haven't seen enough of the law professor to confidently recognize him from his gait, but nothing about his movements contradicts my suspicion.

I'm still vaguely aware of a handful of others tramping in their loose ring around us. Guarding against any attempt to escape.

Where are they taking us? What are they going to do with us?

My magic slithers through my chest like the snake I caught by the Quadring. I can almost hear it hissing in frustration.

It would like to knock Benedikt's feet out from under him, to punch through his ribcage and wrench him apart. Even though I'm horrified by what's happened tonight, the images that flash through my mind sicken me too.

I need to know more. I'll be safer if I can play this cool and careful.

For now, I'm managing to convince my power of that. That the threat isn't significant enough for it to punish me for not letting it loose. No one has a rope around my neck so far.

I doubt I'd have kept it as well contained if it hadn't gotten that brief chance to exert itself a few nights ago. How much worse can this situation get before it sinks its claws into me, and the conspirators realize something's going wrong beyond a squabble between their recruits?

I push down that worry, keeping my hands loose and

relaxed at my sides. Mentally charting the distance to the knife in my boot, for the small comfort the thought provides.

Our strange procession draws to a halt at a looming stone barrier. We've reached the back end of the massive wall that surrounds the entire campus.

Guards will be patrolling all the way around it, but there mustn't be any within sight right now. The man I think is Torstem steps forward and presses his hands to the lichen-spotted stones.

I can't see what he does or make out any words from the faint murmur that leaves his lips. Then the stones seem to ripple as if the shadows are condensing in a thicker patch right in front of him.

It looks like the secret passage in the hall of tapestries. As our escort prods us onward, a chill seeps through my skin.

The scourge sorcerers have managed to alter the walls of the school itself during the time they've been active here. What other defenses have they managed to penetrate?

A deeper chill washes over me on my way through the conjured opening, and then I'm standing on the rocky bank of the Starsil River.

At this early hour, only a couple of spots of lantern light gleam among the middle-ward buildings on the other side of the coursing waters. No one stirs on the streets.

The man in charge leads us several paces along the bank to what looks like a bunch of scattered boards. When I'm close enough, the image shimmers with a tingle of magic, the boards melding into a small wooden boat.

An illusion—designed to conceal the watercraft they've stashed here.

There's nothing I can do but clamber onto the boat at the swordsman's gesture. Benedikt follows. The leader, the swordsman, and three other figures sit around us.

We cast off onto the water. No one brings out paddles,

and the craft has no sail, but somehow we glide along a fairly straight course along the river. The tingling sensation I felt before heightens—there's more magic guiding us on our path.

It takes us diagonally across the Starsil, avoiding the built-up banks within the city proper, gliding on toward the wilder stretch beyond the main walls.

I spot a few members of the Crown's Watch on guard on the city side, but the illusion must hide us well enough. Not a single shout goes up.

No one's patrolling in the sparse forest across from the main harbor. We disembark and trudge on, leaving the city behind.

None of the conspirators have spoken the whole time. I assume they don't want to risk discovery, but the silence gnaws at me.

How far are we going? Do I still have a chance at turning this situation around, or are they cutting their losses and marching both of us to our deaths?

The sound of the palace bell filters through the trees, marking the fourth hour. The forestland thickens around us, the ground starting to slope upward.

I'm not sure how much farther we've walked before the man who might be Torstem signals for us to stop.

We've reached a low cliff face, only about twice as tall as my scrawny frame. The swordsman directs us to a narrow crack that turns out to be the entrance to a cave.

"You'll wait here while we confer," the man in charge tells us.

He picks up a lantern from just beyond the cave entrance, lights it, and ushers us inside.

It's clear they've kept prisoners in this place before. The conspirators lead us down a short passage to a small cavern only about ten paces across... with several chains fixed to the walls, manacles attached to their ends.

As the swordsman pushes me to sit down next to a length of chain, Julita shudders in my head. I have to restrain a cringe of my own, letting the sorcerer clamp the manacle around my ankle.

At the other side of the cavern, the lead man grasps Benedikt's shroud. "This will only get in the way now. The accusations go both ways; you should be on equal ground."

He wrenches the fabric off Benedikt's head in one yank.

It *is* him. The jaunty bastard's bastard stares across the cave at me, his golden hair rumpled and his mouth clamped flat as if he's trying not to vomit.

My gut lurches at the confirmation. I manage to take him in with a slight furrow of my brow, as if I'm confused rather than shocked or horrified.

The conspirators will be watching my reaction, judging whether I have any connection to this man.

It's a good thing they can't hear Julita's yelp that rings through my head. *Benny—what in the realms—how the* fuck *could he—*

Apparently she didn't pick up on the same hints I did. Not surprising when her awareness of what I see and hear is dulled, if it's anything like what I experienced the one time I let her spirit take over.

She doesn't seem to know what else to say, lapsing into stunned silence.

Benedikt leans his well-built frame against the wall of the cave and accepts his own manacle. He's dressed for the occasion all in the same black as his shroud: black silk tunic, black trousers, black boots polished enough to gleam in the lantern light.

Queasiness fills my belly. I study him for any clue as to

why he's turned on me, but his betrayal doesn't make any more sense than it did before.

He focuses on the man who might be Torstem. "I await whatever test you'd conduct for us. I know the gods will be on my side."

He's trying to keep up his usual nonchalant tone, but I pick up a slight quaver he can't totally smooth out of his voice.

The scourge sorcerers stalk out of the cave. They take the lantern with them. The light wavers away, leaving us in total darkness.

I drag in a careful breath despite my rattled nerves, not wanting to show any emotion. I can't sense any magic lingering around us, can't hear anything other than the erratic thud of my own heart and the faint rustle of Benedikt's clothes as he adjusts his position, but there's still a chance the conspirators are monitoring us.

I'm so sorry, Julita says. *I never would have imagined he'd— I thought he'd do anything to support the king! I have no idea what's the matter with him.*

All I can do is raise my shoulders in a shrug to indicate my shared confusion.

For several minutes, we sit there in silence. The cool but stuffy air of the cave seems to congeal around me, thick with a moist, mineral scent. My head keeps whirling, my thoughts getting even harder to pull into order through my growing fatigue.

Benedikt shifts again with a clink of his chain. "I didn't mean for things to turn out this way."

His voice is low but abrupt, making my nerves jump in response. I peer toward him through the darkness but can't make out even the outline of his body.

It seems safest to stay silent, as much as my confusion gnaws at me.

"You have no idea what it's like," he goes on. "Nothing I've ever done has mattered to the people who are supposed to be my family. I got in the habit of acting like an idiot because that's all they see me as. That's not what I *wanted* to be."

Julita brings the snark I can't voice out loud. *And he thought turning on you would make him less of an idiot? If I had my hands to slap him with...*

"I thought I had a chance to do something real with Julita and... everything." Benedikt pauses, maybe as aware as I am that he shouldn't say anything too incriminating. "But what do I get? I'm dismissed over again. Treated like I'm useless. Two chances are better than one, aren't they? I went to see what I could find out on my own."

He set himself up to be recruited just like I had, presumably. Hoping he'd come up with answers before I did?

I guess it mightn't have been that hard to make Torstem's supporters believe the bastard's bastard didn't give a rat's ass about the royal family given how irreverent he's tended to act.

And he did it because he could tell the rest of us were keeping something from him? It isn't as if we totally shut him out.

If he had any clue why our group was starting to fracture...

Gods help me, it's a good thing I never trusted him enough to reveal my power.

"Fine," Benedikt says. "Keep ignoring me. But you know what? The more I've heard, the more I think these people have the right idea. What has the royal family done for anyone except the people who fawn and flatter them the best, really? Why should the exact circumstances of your birth dictate how you'll be treated for your entire life?"

My stomach sinks at the caustic note that's crept into his

voice. I had no idea Benedikt was concealing so much resentment behind his carefree attitude.

But then, I've only known him for a matter of weeks, barely talked with him outside of the business of our investigation. I saw him as a friend because of our shared cause, but we aren't much better than fleeting acquaintances, really.

"Everyone else does whatever they have to do to get ahead," he goes on. "Why shouldn't I? What have you ever done to earn *my* loyalty? If I hadn't—"

He cuts himself off and lapses into a heavy silence. My lungs tighten.

There's one subject I can bring up without giving any validity to his claims. "The people who brought us here said you failed a test. What makes you think you deserve *their* loyalty?"

The silence stretches a little longer. "I didn't know. I wasn't prepared. They said to carve my whole cheek off, and I only—I only *hesitated*. I never said no. I simply needed a moment to be sure..."

Carve his whole cheek off. I can't restrain a wince, echoed by Julita's presence within my skull.

They must guess at what sacrifice would be most difficult for each potential initiate. Benedikt is a flirt as well as a jokester.

He didn't know they'd heal him afterward any more than I did, and he was afraid to return to the world with a mangled face.

I'm not sure I can blame him for that. In a way, he has grounds to say it was partly my fault—because I never told him about how that trial went for me. If I had, he'd have known in advance it was only a temporary sacrifice.

For pointing his finger at me to save his own skin—I can assign plenty of blame just for that.

A wave of anger sears through my nausea, choking me. I gave up my entire life, the small bits of security I counted on, and the anonymity that protected me for so long to help this prick continue his mission. And the first time things got really hard, he decided I'd make a better sacrifice than any part of him.

I was good enough to sweet talk and kiss, but nothing he couldn't toss aside the second he needed to save his skin.

Fuck him and his semi-royal airs.

My voice hardens. "I was right then. You knew you couldn't hold your own, so you watched for someone to take the fall for you. Why would *anyone* want to count on an asshole like that?"

I turn my back on him, not that he can tell anyway, and sink onto the rough floor with my arm cushioning my head.

I'm not interested in hearing anything else Benedikt has to say. Maybe I can steal a little sleep while we're stuck in here for however long it takes the scourge sorcerers to deliberate.

Whatever comes next, I'll be able to face it better the sharper my mind is.

As I close my eyes, it occurs to me that the conspirators never searched us for weapons. My knife is still hidden in my boot.

I might be able to land a killing blow in the darkness, just judging by Benedikt's voice.

The idea makes me feel sick all over again. It feels so cowardly.

And that's how it'd look to our captors too, isn't it? Like I didn't think I could stand up to him in a fair trial.

No. I need to triumph over him on their terms to have any hope of keeping their trust.

Their terms... and maybe the gods'?

I think hard in my head the way I've prayed silently to

Kosmel before. *Guardian of tricksters, I could use a little luck down here right now. If you want me to survive to keep playing this awful game, you'd better have my back.*

No one answers. But a soft pressure comes to rest on my shoulder, like someone setting a reassuring hand there. Like a confirmation that I'm not alone.

Like my father's touch when I was lying in bed sick or shaken by a bad day. Back when he still cared to try to comfort me.

Unwelcome tears prick at the backs of my eyes. I squeeze the lids tighter closed and tuck my free arm across my chest.

And somehow, with the simultaneously unnerving and comforting impression of a god watching over me, my mind drifts off.

I wake at the scrape of footsteps over the uneven floor. My head jerks up as I blink to clear my bleary eyes.

A thin stream of light is seeping down the passage from the narrow cave opening. Day has arrived.

Hurrah.

As I push myself into a sitting position and swipe at the grit that's stuck to my face, I don't bother to glance Benedikt's way.

I don't want the shrouded figure approaching us to see any reaction I wouldn't be able to control, looking at the man who tossed me to the wolves.

In the faint daylight, the black shroud looks even more unsettling than at night. It's like a loose, hooded robe that falls all the way to the wearer's feet. I can now see there are slits for sight cut in the black cloth that falls from the top of the hood, but the face beyond them is too shadowed for me to make out even the glint of its eyes.

"Come and let the gods judge who should earn our trust," the man says in the voice that might be Torstem's.

Even though the strategy was my suggestion, an ominous hollow forms in the pit of my stomach.

I hold myself stoically still while one of the other shrouded figures unlocks the manacle from my ankle, but Benedikt can't restrain his restlessness. "What's the trial?"

"You'll see." The leader beckons for us to follow him.

I don't spot any of the other scourge sorcerers when we emerge from the cave, but I suspect they're somewhere nearby. Braced in case they need to intervene.

The possible Torstem points at two particularly expansive pine trees about twenty paces apart. "Stand by one of the trees marked with the All-Giver's sigil. You'll find what you need there."

Every nerve on edge, I head toward the tree that's slightly closer to me. As I come up on it, I make out the sigil of the All-Giver etched into its bark—upside down, like Julita mentioned she's seen it before.

The scourge sorcerers think they can call the Great God back to our level. What more ridiculous hubris could there be?

Any confidence *I'm* feeling drains out of me as I reach the base of the trunk and see the objects waiting for me.

A large wooden bow leans against the tree. A quiver with several arrows lies on the forest floor beside it.

Oh, fuck.

Julita's presence shifts with obvious agitation. *It could still be all right. I don't know that Benedikt is that wonderful a shot.*

He doesn't have to be wonderful to best me. I've only handled a bow once in my life, and that time I don't think I clipped a single target.

I pick up the bow, testing its weight, and finally look toward my betrayer. Benedikt is staring right back at me, his hand clenched around his own bow... and a trace of his usual smirk curving his lips.

He was there for the hunt when I showed off my ineptitude at archery. Great God smite him, he must be silently crowing over how easily he'll beat me.

"You have a minute to prepare yourselves," the lead man calls out in his magically warbled voice. "You will stay within reach of your tree. Once the trial begins, you will shoot at your opponent until one of you is too injured to continue. But if you *kill* them, your victory is forfeit. May the gods guide the one who deserves it."

As his voice fades from the crisp autumn air, my gut plummets all the way to my feet.

He wants us to destroy each other without killing. Like the mutilated accomplices who sacrifice so much for the scourge sorcerers' demented cause.

He's not just testing us against each other but evaluating our willingness to maim for our convictions as well.

My fingers tighten around the bow. I sling the quiver over my shoulder and slide out one of the arrows easily enough.

Across from me, through the mottled shadows cast by the leaves overhead, Benedikt's smirk has only grown. Curse it all, he doesn't look the slightest bit guilty about what he intends to do.

He'll tear me to pieces with his arrows until I'm slumped bleeding on the ground, and then he'll waltz back to the college to pretend he has no idea how I went missing. He'll learn all the king's plans for protection and feed them back to the scourge sorcerers.

Or I could tear him apart and leave him for the conspirators to murder.

Even after everything, I can't say that I want the man in front of me dead. He can't be *that* horrible, can he, after all the good things he tried to do before?

Just so incredibly misguided.

But faced with his triumphant smile, with the selfish excuses he gave me yesterday echoing in my ears, I can't say the idea of hurting him makes me feel all that guilty either.

It's a matter of survival. Me or him. And if he survives, a whole lot of people other than me could die because of it.

The choice should be simple, if not for the power roiling in my chest.

The only way I can win is to use my magic. I don't stand a chance of hitting him effectively unless it or some divine intervention guides my arrow. And Kosmel has never offered any physical assistance before.

I've sworn so many times to keep my riven soul under wraps. The only time I released it on purpose, the city was literally on the verge of crumbling.

What will the cost be this time?

How many times can I use it and still stay sane enough to rein it back in?

How many will die if *I* survive... and turn more into the monster every riven eventually becomes?

Benedikt notches his arrow. I have only a matter of seconds left to decide.

As I grip my bow, a swell of resolve rises up inside me. The same iron conviction that came over me when I lay dying in the Domi's back hallway.

I want to live. There's more I want to do.

Maybe, like then, I should let the gods decide just as I told the scourge sorcerers I would.

I position my arrow against the bow and open my mind to the trickster godlen with his wryly divine voice. *If I ask my magic to guide my arrow, will you see that I don't hurt anything I would regret?*

My pulse stutters with the overwhelming voice that resonates through my body for the first time in weeks. *I can*

guide the backlash, my wayward rogue. But you have to pull the
string. The choices you make here can only be yours.

I swallow against the dryness of my mouth.

Yes. It's my life. My choice.

I'm playing this game to win.

A mortal man's voice reverberates through the forest.
"Begin!"

My hand looses the arrow.

The bowstring twangs, and my power leaps with it. I
hone it onto the arrow, narrowing it to my target with all the
control I can summon.

Just this act. Just this once.

Land one shot so Benedikt can't shoot another.

I might not be much of an archer, but I know how to
deal an effective wound. Benedikt needs his arms to shoot.

So I simply have to disable them.

The power ripples through me, pulling the arrow on
course—and part of me senses a branch somewhere far off in
the woods cracking as it wrenches *away* from its natural
direction.

So much of my focus is on my magic that I barely
remember to jerk myself away from the arrow Benedikt
aimed at me. The vicious tip slices through the sleeve of my
tunic with a stinging line of pain and thuds into the trunk
behind me.

The break in my concentration jostles my magic. My
arrow plunges into Benedikt's shoulder—into the fleshy
outer muscle, not right at the center of the joint where I'd
have rendered his arm useless.

Benedikt sputters a curse and snatches at another arrow,
his bow wobbling in his damaged but not disabled grasp. I
whip another projectile of my own out of my quiver and
notch it as quickly as my hands can move.

Please, please, please. I don't want this to turn into the torture session the scourge sorcerers must be hoping for.

I don't risk allowing any magic to speed my movements. Even with his injury, Benedikt moves faster than my inexperienced fumbling.

A second arrow thrums through the forest. As I leap to the side, my bow sways in my grip.

I have to do this. I have to end this—*now*.

Gods help me, truly.

I yank back the string and release before Benedikt has a chance to position a third arrow. My second careens toward him, my heart aching with the power bleeding out of me, hurtling it straight to its mark—

He tries to dodge, but my magic either catches him or makes the arrow veer. It slams home, digging into the sinews that attach his arm to his torso.

An anguished groan bursts from Benedikt's lips. His arm sags, the bow slipping from his grasp.

He slumps back against his tree, blood coursing in a wet streak down his tunic. His fingers dangle limply. He gropes for the bow with his other hand, but there's clearly no way he can shoot one-armed.

"No!" he shouts. "No, I swear, I was telling the truth. I don't know how—"

A black-shrouded figure emerges from behind the tree and smacks a rod against the top of Benedikt's head. He topples over, limp as a sack of potatoes.

My stomach heaves. It's all I can do not to hurl the remains of last night's dinner onto the earth by my feet.

I did it. I won.

But every inch of my skin feels as clammy as if I'm about to die too.

My magic flails around me, desperate to deal out more

vengeance, and I clench my hands as I drag it back inside me.

A couple of broken branches. Not too horrific for payment.

As if that's the most awful thing about this situation.

The man who's probably Torstem steps toward me, his voice unnervingly warm. "An impressive showing, Ivy. The gods must smile on you. It's our honor to know your loyalties lie with us."

Twenty-Seven

Ivy

I don't know where the conspirators got the dress from. They must have felt it'd be too suspicious to send me back to the college in a dirty, torn set of training clothes.

They had me change by shoving a bundle of fabric into my hands and sending me into the cave to put it on. I swapped my shirt and trousers for the simple riding gown as quickly as possible, wanting to be out of the dank space.

Now, the silk skirt whispers across my legs as I stride back toward the river, the man who might be Ster. Torstem on one side and the swordsman on the other. The fabric is light, but it feels out of place in the wilderness around us. The brush snags on it, tugging it against my legs.

I pop the last bite of the cheese-stuffed roll they gave me into my mouth and force it down my throat. I didn't really want to eat anything these psychopaths provided, but it's late enough in the morning now that my stomach was gnawing on itself with hunger.

And if I'd refused, they'd have questioned my faith in them all over again.

I'm not sure how many of the other conspirators are following discreetly behind us and how many have hung back to deal with Benedikt. One of them—presumably the same woman who healed my finger the other night—approached me to seal the wound on my arm before I left.

I doubt they're giving the bastard's bastard the same courtesy.

As if he can guess the directions my thoughts have gone in, the possible Torstem glances over at me with a rustle of his shroud. "We didn't enjoy the process of judgment. With such a major accusation, the gods demand an equally intense trial."

The gods demanded it. Sure.

That's a heap of cow dung if I ever heard one, Julita mutters, and I'm inclined to agree. If there's one thing I know about the scourge sorcerers, it's that they encourage pain rather than shying away from it.

Does he think I've forgotten how they ordered me to rip apart a rabbit and provoke a fight between the guards?

Of course, he doesn't realize I already know the worst of their crimes: the immense sacrifices they demand of the children they con into joining their cause. Eyes, ears, hair, arms… Everything they can remove while remaining alive. Who knows what else on the inside?

Just remembering the sacrificial accomplices who'd crouched around Wendos in the tower makes my stomach turn.

I keep my revulsion off my face and concentrate on playing the role of devoted recruit. Even a loyal applicant would have a few questions about what just happened— especially one who isn't supposed to know as much about the Order of the Wild's practices as I do.

"What will happen to him?" I ask. "The man who accused me?" Better if they think I'm not even sure of his name.

The shrouded figure gives a shrug. "The gods will decide on the appropriate justice for his crime, and we will carry it out on their behalf. We can't let such a betrayal of our principles go unpunished, of course. Those of us who embrace the All-Giver's true will must support each other."

How convenient that the ones who have so little end up supporting the ones with plenty, and in much more drastic ways.

"You can be sure he won't threaten you again," the man says, as if he thinks my silence means I'm worrying about that.

He doesn't seem to be concerned about revealing that much to me, but then, he isn't explicitly saying that they're going to kill Benedikt. And even if he thought I might report a possible murder to the authorities, what could I tell the Crown's Watch at this point?

I don't even know for sure that the man next to me *is* Ster. Torstem, let alone who any of the other conspirators who participated in this charade of a trial are. I have no proof of anything, not even the tests I myself carried out.

I could point to a cave with shackles in the woods, if I could retrace my steps there, but I doubt the scourge sorcerers will leave any evidence of who used the chains.

Torstem doesn't need to be careful. In a way, this is all another trial. Will I turn on them after all, or will I accept the brutality I just participated in as reasonable?

The sun lifts higher, streaking warmth I can't appreciate through the trees. It feels as if we walk for ages longer than we did coming here, a fact that's confirmed when the trees thin and I can make out the landscape beyond them again.

We've come around the curve of the river to where it

starts to narrow. As my escorts stop there, a soft nicker reaches my ears.

I jerk around and spot Pepper, Casimir's favorite mare, saddled and bridled with her reins tied to a nearby tree. The horse whinnies and bobs her head as if beckoning me over.

"How…?"

The man next to me chuckles. "It'd look odd for you to return through the city on foot. We would have contrived to bring the steed we understand you've been most inclined to use in the past, but the stallion proved… difficult. This one seemed a reasonable alternative."

I can just imagine Toast's reaction to mysterious figures he hasn't warmed up to trying to drag him off in the middle of the night. I hope he bit one of them.

But now I understand why they brought me a riding dress. They really do think of everything to cover their tracks.

The scourge sorcerer points to the bridge farther along the river across the field of shrubs and grass. "You can cross there, and you'll be close to the college. Show the guards at the gate your bracelet, and they'll let you through without any trouble. You're clear on your story if your employer asks where you've been?"

"I got an urgent message from my uncle," I rehearse, not that I'm actually going to use the lie. Little do the conspirators know, the real Ivy doesn't even have an uncle. "I hurried over to help any way I can. I'll apologize profusely for not being able to leave word beforehand."

"Good. Go ahead, quickly. We'll call on you again when it's time."

Time for what? I want to ask, but I don't think he'll tell me. And he might not appreciate the prying.

I take Pepper's reins, clamber into the saddle, and set off across the field at a canter. As I sway with the horse's strides, Julita stirs in the back of my head.

Stavros will be having a fit. Gods only know what he's imagined you've gotten into. I hope he isn't too difficult to talk down.

My stomach knots. Whatever the former general is imagining, it might not even be totally untrue. I did tap into my riven magic today, on purpose.

As my escort suggested, the guards take one look at my college bracelet and silk dress and wave me through without comment. I set Pepper trotting through the streets at as fast a pace as seems appropriate for a noble and remove her tack quickly at the stable, though I do linger there for long enough to check on Toast and give him an apologetic chin scratch for whatever trouble the conspirators gave him.

Then I hustle the rest of the way to Stavros's quarters with my heart thudding at the base of my throat. As I slip inside, I brace myself.

No furious former general waits on the other side. I stall in my tracks, unsure what to do with myself, and notice the ring of cord stretched open on the floor near his desk.

He must have called a meeting with the other men.

Stavros still has my own portable portal—if he thinks I'm trustworthy enough to carry the cord myself now, he's forgotten to hand it over. But we've only separated them out for convenience's sake. Anyone can use any of the magical passages.

I hesitate for just a moment and then stride over to step into the corded circle.

The world around me flashes to darkness and then to the sconce-lit, windowless palace meeting room with a jolt of magic through my nerves. As I stumble to a halt one step past Stavros's cord, the three men poised around the table whirl toward me.

Casimir's face breaks into the most brilliant grin I've ever seen. Alek's breath rushes out of him in a whoosh of relief.

But Stavros moves fastest. The massive man crosses the floor in a matter of seconds and grasps my shoulders with his wooden prosthetic and his real hand, peering down at me.

His stormy expression makes my pulse hiccup, but the growl of his voice sounds more anguished than angry. "You're all right. Where have you been? It was the fucking scourge sorcerers again, wasn't it?"

My mouth opens, but it takes me a couple of seconds to find my words with his dark eyes searing into mine and the heat of his hand coursing over my skin. "Yes. They summoned me in the middle of the night—wanted me to arrive right away. I…"

I falter, the enormity of what I need to tell them hitting me like it hadn't quite before, and Stavros's grip on my shoulder tightens. "*Are* you all right? What did those vermin do to you?"

Well, Julita remarks with an awkward laugh. *I suppose Stav didn't get the wrong idea after all. You really have turned his head, haven't you?*

"That isn't one of your regular dresses," Casimir notes quietly.

Stavros bares his teeth. "If those assholes—"

"The dress barely matters," I interrupt. "And it wasn't—it wasn't exactly all the scourge sorcerers."

"What do you mean?"

"Stavros," Alek says, sounding as if he's keeping his usual even tone through sheer force of will, "why don't you give Ivy room to breathe so she can explain exactly what she's been through?"

The larger man stares at me as if it hadn't occurred to me that his presence might be just slightly imposing. He lets out a strangled sound and dips his head so low his forehead comes to rest against mine.

"I'm sorry," he says. "I thought—I thought they'd murdered you."

A lump fills my throat. I'm even more overwhelmed with him leaning so close. His smoky scent floods my lungs dizzyingly.

I can't claim the heady thump of my heart is only anxiety.

Was he really so worried about *me*? How much was he simply afraid that our plans to ensure his king's safety would fall apart?

Despite the questions whirling in my mind, I find myself resting my hand on the front of his shirt as if to give him additional confirmation of my words. "I'm here. Not murdered. Not even really hurt."

Stavros lets out a huff and places his hand over mine. He tips his head to the side, and I'm struck by the impression as I have once before that he might kiss me.

My heart lurches, torn between apprehension and a longing that's never quite died.

Like before, he doesn't follow through. He squeezes my fingers and steps back, his jaw flexing with continued agitation. "Go ahead. Tell us what happened."

From his tone, he might as well be saying, *Tell me who I need to kill.*

"Wait," I say. "Let me just—"

I stalk around the edges of the room, confirming that I can't sense any magically enhanced creatures lurking in the walls. By the time I return to my original spot, I feel a little steadier but no happier about the conversation ahead.

I drag in a breath to start. "The summons came around three in the morning..."

I give them the full account, from walking into the woods to being accused to my first suspicions of who my accuser was. When I say Benedikt's name, Alek's stance goes rigid.

Stavros outright bares his teeth. "What? What wretched game did the royal bastard think he was playing at?"

I swallow thickly. "I don't think he saw it as a game. He talked to me a little later—he'd been feeling like we were shutting him out, which we were, because we were hiding my magic from him—he thought he'd prove himself by getting information from the scourge sorcerers on his own, but they ended up swaying his loyalties. Convincing him that what they're doing is right."

Alek's jaw drops. "He's siding with *them*?"

His shock echoes my own. "I guess they're more persuasive than we gave them credit for."

Stavros slams his hand against his thigh. "The blasted idiot. He treated our mission like a joke half the time, and then he— I'll wring his fucking neck."

The former general shoves himself away from the table, but I hold up my hand to stop him. "I don't think you can do anything at all to him. I—I don't think you'd need to. The scourge sorcerers will be taking care of that now that they've decided they can't trust him."

The ominous silence that follows my statement tells me all three men know exactly what I'm implying.

Stavros's jaw works. "And he blathered about our entire investigation?"

I shake my head. "He hadn't given away anything about the rest of you. Well, other than trying to claim that he'd overheard me making plans with you, but I'd imagine the conspirators will dismiss that idea now that they've assumed it was all a lie. He didn't mention Casimir and Alek at all."

"That's the least of our concerns right now." Casimir shakes his head. "I suppose none of us were all that close with him. Meetings were all business, and we couldn't spend time together outside of them. But I still wouldn't have thought..."

"Neither would I," Alek says hoarsely. "It's his own *family* they're encouraging people to turn against."

I remember Benedikt's remarks over the past few weeks—and the way he looked when his half-uncle chided him. "I think that might have become a benefit rather than a problem."

We linger in our shared horror for a minute before Casimir ventures another question, his voice gentle. "How did you persuade them to trust you over Benedikt?"

More haltingly, I explain about the trial I suggested, the way the scourge sorcerers put it to us, and Kosmel's divine assistance. I tense up when I get into the part where I used my magic—used it to wound a man these three recently considered a friend—but Stavros only reacts with a rough exhalation when I mention the arrow that wounded me.

"They healed it," I say before he can reach for me again. "Like they did my finger."

What I can see of Alek's bronze-brown face has grayed beneath his mask. "Are you sure they completely believed you? If they wanted to eliminate any risk of betrayal, they could have gotten rid of both of you."

And they still could, he's obviously thinking.

I hug myself. "As far as I could tell, they were convinced. I'm sure they'll be watching me even more closely for the next few days, though."

Stavros starts to pace. "You can't go back. This is too much. They had you chained in a fucking cave."

I grimace. "If I don't go back, they'll definitely want me dead."

"I never should have let you start off on this reckless path to begin with."

My hands drop to my hips. "You didn't *let* me do

anything. I made my own decisions. And even with everything that's happened, this is still our best chance at taking the scourge sorcerers down."

Which Stavros well knows, because he can't even argue that point, only hiss through his teeth in frustration.

He stops, raking his hand through his ruddy hair. "I have to report to the king. Benedikt was part of his family, if not a totally legitimate part."

Casimir steps forward and touches my arm. "You do that. Alek and I can look after Ivy. I'm sure she could use some peace after what she's been through."

He pauses. "You have the cord she normally uses, don't you? Could you give that to me before you leave? We should be doubly careful about any arrangements we make from now on."

I'm not sure what the courtesan is thinking, so I doubt Stavros is either, but he digs into the pouch on his belt and hands over my cord without argument. He moves toward his own portal ring but turns toward me at the last second.

He lifts his hand to touch my cheek. "They are going to pay for this. All of it. I can't wait until that day."

Twenty-Eight

Casimir

I've spent many hours in the former General Stavros's presence. I noted the spark of interest that lit in his eyes when Julita turned on her charm. A couple of times, I observed him from afar with one of my carnal arts professors on his arm—a woman of unarguable beauty and sensuality.

In the course of our association, I've witnessed him pleased and angry, resolved and disheartened.

But I've never before seen the intensity that's come over him while he speaks to Ivy right now.

There's immense passion smoldering in his eyes as he gazes down at her, and I can tell with every emphatic word and gesture that the emotion goes much deeper than mere attraction.

From the moment his temper erupted at the sight of her with me after our interlude in the archives, I've suspected he has some kind of interest in her. Now... Now it's obvious and potent enough to stir up my own emotions: approval, compassion, and a dollop of jealousy I don't have any right to feel.

It's about time he removed his head from his ass when it comes to her. About time he started treating her like the awe-inspiring woman she is.

After what she's just been through, the betrayal she's just faced, she deserves nothing more than full commitment from the rest of us in every way we can offer it.

And I'm starting to think all three of us *can* offer our devotion in every conceivable way.

I'd encourage Stavros to explore all those ways right this moment, but I can't deny the urgency of alerting the king to the traitor within his own family, no matter what dire fate Benedikt may already have met. Who knows if the scourge sorcerers will find some final way to use the royal bastard before they're through with him?

The shock lingers like a knot in my gut. I was wrong about Benedikt. He put on such a carefree front during our short meetings that I got into the habit of not checking in on his emotional state that closely.

How long has a deeper resentment been simmering inside him without us even realizing—bitter enough that the scourge sorcerers were able to draw him in?

We may never know. Gods help us, I wish I'd paid more attention while I could.

Maybe I couldn't have changed his mind, but I might have been able to spare Ivy the trauma she endured at his bidding.

Stavros pulls himself away from Ivy with what looks like incredible effort. I can read his reluctance to leave her all through his stance as he turns toward the loop of cord that'll take him back to his quarters.

I offer him my most reassuring smile.

We'll take good care of her. We'll give her everything she could need until he's able to join us.

I turn Ivy's cord in my hands. "Leave your loop at the other end open so Ivy will be able to follow it back to your quarters once she's ready."

Stavros gives a quick nod and one final, anguished glance over his shoulder at Ivy before stepping into the circle of cord and vanishing.

Ivy stares after him, shock etched on her pale face. It's a crime how much trouble she's had accepting that any of us could truly care about her. In Stavros's case, it must be even more difficult after how harshly he treated her when he discovered her magic.

I slip my hand around her arm again, stroking my fingers from her shoulder to her elbow and back again. Maybe it'll help her believe if she knows I can see it too.

"If you're our Signy, I suppose you did need a third paramour."

Ivy's gaze jerks toward me. "What do you— He wouldn't really…"

She trails off, uncertainty mingling with the weariness in her expression. She's been through so much in the past day.

I brush her amber hair back from her face in a gentle caress. "I think Stav has been fighting with himself even more than he's fought with you. It's a relief to see that devotion finally won over fear."

A blush spreads across Ivy's cheeks. "He hasn't said anything. We haven't *done* anything."

I chuckle. "Oh, he's said enough. And you don't have to worry. I'm not complaining. You should get all the adulation we can offer you."

I glance toward Alek, who's been watching the whole interaction with a mix of concern and bemusement. At my silent prodding, he steps closer to Ivy.

There's something poignant about the tentative but determined way he tucks his arm around Ivy's waist, as if he's still not sure he could be allowed to show her that much affection. The scholar has also had a long journey toward believing anyone could want *him*, I suspect.

"If Signy's men could handle sharing between a trio, I'd imagine we could figure out a way too," he says, and presses a kiss to her hair. "You've spent too long with no one you can count on."

The corner of his mouth crooks upward at a sly angle I'm not used to. "And three lovers opens up even more… intriguing possibilities."

Ivy arches an eyebrow at him, but a hint of a smile crosses her lips. "You and that poetry book."

"There's nothing wrong with wanting to see you happy— and satisfied."

I beam at both of them. "I couldn't agree more. And to get started with that…" I swipe at a little smudge of dirt at the corner of Ivy's jaw that the scourge sorcerers missed in their hasty clean-up effort. "You spent the night in a cave. I think the first step to getting you good as new is a nice soak in a bath, don't you?"

Ivy's blush darkens.

"Just a bath?" she asks, sounding amused.

Remembering how the first bath I set up for her ended sends a quiver of desire to my groin. I lean in to claim a quick kiss.

"Whatever pleases you, Kindness. I simply want you to know we're here for you however you need us."

Alek lifts his chin. "Agreed."

Ivy looks down at herself. "Getting clean would be a relief—I'm sure about that."

"Then I have just the thing. You two wait here while I

make the arrangements. I'll step through the cords and escort you back when I'm ready—it shouldn't take long."

I slip her cord into the pouch on my belt and step through my own ring. After a moment of disorienting darkness, I'm back in my dorm room in the Domi.

A few of my dormmates are chatting in the common room, one who's training to be a dancer doing stretches on the floor, another who's about to start an apprenticeship as a bard strumming casually on her lute. I give them all a friendly nod and head out into the hall to check the reserved bathing rooms.

The companionship division has ten private bathing areas for our exclusive use, in consideration for the services some of us provide and the extensive cosmetic preparations many of us require. I breeze past the smaller options like the one where I brought Ivy last time.

This time, I don't want the experience to feel like something I'm presenting her with. I want us all on the same level, like real lovers rather than anything resembling courtesan and client.

And having additional space for whatever other activities we might engage in would be ideal too.

The first of the larger rooms has the eyes closed on the face carved on the door, indicating that it's locked for use. The second is open.

I slip into the cream-tiled space, survey it to confirm it meets my expectations, and secure the door. With practiced efficiency, I move through the room—turning on the tap on the massive bathtub built partly into the floor, pouring in an oil for relaxing sore muscles and a bubbling powder with a soothing scent, setting three plump towels on the bench for ease of access.

Then I spread Ivy's cord on the floor in its circle and step back through to the meeting room.

Ivy and Alek are leaning against the table, his arm still around her and their heads bent close together. When they look up at my arrival, it's clear I've interrupted a quiet conversation.

A pang shoots through my heart like the sensation that hit me when I walked in on them kissing in the side room the other day. Like a wordless admonishment telling me that I can never have quite the same shared affection.

But maybe I can. Maybe it isn't too much to ask that I have a woman who wants *me* to be happy as much as I want the same for her.

Because as content as Ivy looks in Alek's embrace, her face lights up at the sight of me.

She's an incredible woman. I'm still serving both my godlen and my purpose on this earth by catering to her pleasure.

Who could deserve more than the woman who's putting herself in so much danger to protect us all from divine retribution?

"Come with me," I say, and quickly add when Alek starts to hesitate, "Both of you."

We emerge one after the other into the bathing room. Ivy looks around at the sprawling, tiled space and lets out a laugh. "It's not just a bathroom—it's a bedroom too."

There is indeed a large, four-poster bed with covers the same ivory as the frame standing at the opposite end from the bathtub.

I grin at her. "Sometimes people want to relax in a drier fashion once they're clean. We can accommodate all preferences. If you simply want a comfortable sleep, you're welcome to it."

A sigh escapes her. "I might take you up on that. But first…"

She walks up to the bathtub, reaching for the lacing on

the basic silk gown the conspirators dressed her up in. So much more confident than the last time.

It warms me to see her assurance growing.

I move to join her, loosening the ties with experienced fingers. "I thought the three of us might enjoy a soak together. I'm sure both Alek and I could use a chance to unwind after all our worries about you while you were missing. And then you'll have proper company."

Ivy hums. "Sounds fair enough."

She casts a sideways glance toward the scholar, and I follow her gaze. At his awkward expression, I realize I may have miscalculated in my hurry.

"Only if you'd like to," I say to him, unsure of the best approach. Alek has always seemed like a rather private person. "I shouldn't have assumed—"

"It's all right," he interrupts with a crooked smile. "I'm glad you counted me in. It's only— My mask…"

He gestures to the leather shape that covers most of his face—not a good material for dampening.

Of course. I should have been prepared for that concern.

I scan the room, considering the possibilities. "I'm sure I could find an appropriate substitute if you're not comfortable removing it completely…"

Ivy turns with her dress slipping partway off her shoulders. "Or you could go unmasked. You know I think you're just as handsome without it. And I'm sure Casimir won't judge."

There's a tenderness to her voice that I've never heard with anyone else. An understanding between them that I'm not privy to.

At her words, Alek practically glows with adoration in return. He touches the edge of his mask, weighing the options.

I dip my head in acknowledgment of Ivy's remark.

"Whatever you're covering, it only reflects how your life has shaped you. There's a beauty in all experience, good and bad —in still being alive to show what we've been through."

Alek's throat works. Then he reaches for his tunic. "All right. It shouldn't matter anyway."

He sounds certain enough that I leave him to his undressing and shed my own clothes.

Ivy shimmies out of her undergarments, her wiry body drawing my eye as it always does. She unties the ribbon she wears around her arm in memory of her sister and rests it on top of her pile of clothes.

Then she clambers over the low edge of the bath and sinks into the bubbly water, sitting on the ledge along its wall. With a deep breath, she slides a little deeper. Her eyelids dip and her hair fans out into the water.

An ache fills my chest all the way to the base of my throat. She's so lovely—and so unaware of that fact.

A bath is hardly anything to compete with the horrors she's faced in the past day—gods, in the past several weeks. I wish I could wash all the stress and pain she must be carrying away.

I wish I could stop her from having to experience any more of it.

But how in the realms could a courtesan do that?

I can't keep her safe. I can't take down the scourge sorcerers in her place.

Pampering her to the fullest extent of my ability is the best thing I can contribute... but compared to what Stavros and Alek can offer, it feels like barely anything.

A niggling voice in the back of my head pipes up that I'm being selfish by focusing all my energy on this one woman, that I don't deserve to even try to devote myself to her, but I tune it out as well as I can. What I can give her is better than nothing.

I ease into the bath and sit kitty-corner from her. Alek pauses at the edge of the tub, stripped down to his drawers.

There's plenty to recommend itself about his tall, lean frame. The toned definition of compact muscle shows beneath his bronze skin across his chest and arms. He has nothing to be shy about there.

He grips his mask and pauses. Visibly girding himself, he peels it off his face.

The mottled flesh beneath, stretching across his forehead and nose and down his left cheek, tells a story I don't know the details of. I can see it was some kind of injury, one that dug too deep to be fully healed.

But he did survive it. Ardone teaches us that beauty can be found in all things. There's beauty in the interplay of colors amid the scars; beauty in the unusual shapes they create on his face.

Beauty in the fact that he was willing to share it with me at all.

I smile at him, hoping he can tell that I'm unbothered by his appearance. "It's an honor to have you trust me with your full self."

Something in Alek's stance loosens. He tugs off his drawers and scrambles into the tub.

"Oh," he says as the water envelops him. "That is nice. Now I'm thinking I've never actually had a proper bath."

Ivy shoots me a fond grin. "Casimir elevates them to an art form."

I tip my head back against the edge of the tub. There's so much space we can all sit without bumping up against each other. "Anything can be an art if you give it the proper attention."

Just because we don't have to bump into each other doesn't mean I want the distance. I scoot over so I can stroke the side of Ivy's face. "We can't change the hurt you've been through. But you can know that you never have to worry about where *we* stand. We want to see you safe and well. There's so much joy waiting for you when you reach the end of the mission you're on."

Ivy's smile tightens a little, but her eyes shine bright. She looks from me to Alek and back again. "You know... when I was in the tower, after Wendos injured me... part of what helped me keep standing up to him was thinking about you. How you'd already been there for me even then."

The ache gripping my chest melts into a heady warmth. "Any strength I can give you is yours to take, whenever you need it."

"And if you ever need more than we've thought to give, just ask," Alek adds, his voice gone a bit hoarse.

Ivy ducks her head with a hint of shyness. "I wouldn't mind help washing my hair."

I reach for the soap. "It would be my pleasure."

As I massage the suds into Ivy's scalp, Alek takes a little soap and washes away the smudge on her jaw I noticed earlier. As he works his way down her neck and along her arm, I feel the tension releasing from Ivy's body. She hums encouragingly.

We dunk her hair together, running our fingers through her wet locks on either side. Alek watches my movements closely and mimics them with careful precision.

Ivy sprawls out languid between us, her eyes closed. "Maybe we need to send an army of courtesans to deal with the scourge sorcerers," she murmurs absently. "Anyone would give up just about any information when they're getting this kind of treatment."

Alek chuckles, but the offhand remark pierces right through the center of me.

I've found out everything I can from my past clients and my leisure activities around the college. None of the bug club members we're keeping an eye on have been in the habit of hiring anyone from the companionship division.

But that isn't the only place we might find useful information. Ster. Torstem has been taking his accomplices out of the college—out of the city—for all those bug club expeditions and who knows what else…

The image floats through my mind of my mother's friend Laselle. Stopping by every month or two to lounge alongside my mother, her loose white-blond curls bobbing with her expansive movements as she gossiped about her clients.

Laselle has been in business for decades now, catering to the counts and provints on the estates closest to the capital. The conspirators won't have been able to go *too* far abroad.

It's possible they've left behind evidence of their dealings that someone has noticed and commented on.

My stomach tightens up at the idea of seeking Laselle out. The last words she ever said to me still ring out from the memory—that brief conversation at my mother's funeral.

I hope you make something of yourself, Casimir. A good woman was ruined to bring you into this world. You'd better do her legacy proud.

They used to make a game of it, her and my mother, having me perform for them and criticizing every tiny error. At the age of six, I once pinned and re-pinned Laselle's hair until my fingers started to bleed while she sneered at every effort I made.

Gods only know what she'd make of the man I've become. Of the quest I've devoted myself to that's nothing like what my mother expected of me.

But what does her opinion mean compared to the chance to make Ivy's task easier? If I can dredge up a clue that'll help us expose the conspirators' plans sooner, extricate her from their grasp before they harm her even more…

That would be worth just about anything.

Ivy teases her fingers along my chin and tugs me into a kiss. My pulse hitches eagerly as I drink in the sweet heat of her lips.

Apparently we are going to have more than just a bath—and I certainly won't complain. I've been longing to feel this woman's body against mine since our first and only full encounter weeks ago.

When she turns her head to seek out Alek's mouth in turn, I nip her earlobe and flick my tongue along her jaw, earning myself a gasp.

I know I can be everything she needs. I can bring her pleasure and a way out.

It could be a dangerous journey. I'll need to travel the estates alone to track Laselle down while keeping my true purpose hidden, and a courtesan on the roads can draw the wrong kinds of attention.

And that's fine. Why shouldn't I risk my life when Ivy already has and will again, over and over, until we see the scourge sorcerers fall?

Twenty-Nine

Ivy

I thought being enveloped between two stunning men in the meeting room was a thrilling experience. Finding myself pinned between them in the steamy water of the bathtub, our naked skin softened by Casimir's oils, is so overwhelming I might be drowning in delight.

It'd certainly be an incredible way to go.

With every brush of their hands over my body and every collision of our lips, the anguish of the past day melts away. I tug Alek even closer, arch back into Casimir's caresses, longing to lose myself in the pleasure of this moment as deeply as I can.

So much of my life right now is out of my control. It's barely mine at all.

But this—the unexpected connection I've found with these two men that I can hardly believe is real—is all mine. I want to own it, revel in it.

I shift around to reclaim Casimir's mouth, and he strokes his hand over my bare breast. As I gasp into the kiss, Alek

slides a tentative but no less eager hand down my side to my hip.

My head is spinning with the heat of the water and their bodies, with the sensations flooding me from both sides. Julita drew back into the farthest depths of my skull sometime after we got into the bath—I can barely sense her presence.

But through the blissful haze, a thread of uneasiness wriggles into my awareness. The memories of Benedikt's face revealed beneath the shroud, of his smirk when he raised his bow to shoot at me, linger on.

If even he would betray us…

I hesitate, and Casimir notices my reaction immediately. He eases back to catch my gaze. Alek goes still at my other side.

I sink back down onto the ledge so I can look at both of them. My hands instinctively reach for theirs. "You know you never have to worry about where *my* loyalties lie, don't you? I still think the scourge sorcerers are maniacs and criminals. I have no interest at all in buying into their mad philosophy, no matter what I've done to convince them."

Casimir chuckles and trails his free hand down the side of my face. "Of course. I never even considered it."

Alek is frowning. "Have we done or said anything to make you think we don't trust you?"

A lump rises in my throat. "No. Nothing like that. I just — You knew Benedikt for longer than you've known me, and he startled all of us. I figured I should make my position clear."

Alek's fingers tighten where they've intertwined with mine. "I've never worried either. You of all people would be able to recognize harmful magic when you see it."

Casimir dips his head to kiss the peak of my shoulder. "And every time you've talked about their initiation rituals, it's been obvious how uncomfortable you were with them. I hate that you've had to go back to them at all—I know you'd rather never deal with the conspiracy again."

The fleeting panic that gripped me unwinds from my gut. I relax into their combined embrace again, but the doubtful part of me—the part that's having trouble understanding how a street-rat thief won a brilliant scholar's and a noble courtesan's devotion—insists on one final clarification.

I glance at one and then the other. "And you're really okay with what we're doing here? With me being with both of you? I never would have expected—I wouldn't have asked—"

"I think we both know that too," Casimir murmurs, releasing my hand to tuck his arm around me. "I'm not the jealous type, Kindness. The happier you are, the happier I'll be too."

Alek's smile twists. "I never thought I'd be able to have anything like this at all. I know you caring about Casimir doesn't take anything away from whatever we'll have together."

He pauses, his gaze sliding to the other man with a hint of shyness. "And maybe Casimir will help me ensure I'm making you as 'happy' as I possibly can, since I can't say I know what I'm doing in that area all that well."

Casimir beams at him. "I can always offer advice. We should look at this as a collaboration, just like our investigations. We each bring our own approach and talents to the task at hand, and we're better for combining them."

I narrow my eyes. "Now you're making it sound like work."

The courtesan laughs and tugs me close against him. His voice drops to a murmur by my ear. "I can assure you what we're doing here is nothing but a pleasure. And I'm looking forward to seeing how much pleasure we can bring you."

He nibbles a path down my neck while teasing his fingers along my inner thigh. Alek leans in for another kiss, and just like that, I'm lost again.

I want them to feel good too. I want them to know just how much I cherish the affection they're offering me. How much I cherish *them* and everything they've brought into my life.

I stroke my hand over Alek's toned chest and across his stomach. He hums approvingly against my mouth.

My ass has settled into Casimir's lap—against the rigid length of him that tells me how much he's already enjoying this interlude. Shifting my weight, I rock against him in what I hope is a provocative motion.

It must work, because Casimir's breath hitches. He groans, and his hand slips up my thigh to cup the most sensitive part of me.

At the bolt of pleasure that races up from my core, I can't restrain a whimper. Alek lets out a hungry sound and kisses me harder, massaging my breast.

I trace my fingers over the lean muscles of his abdomen until they graze the jutting length of his cock. When I wrap my hand around it, he bucks into my grasp with a groan of his own.

Casimir swivels his thumb over my clit and delves his forefinger inside me. The pressure sends bliss pulsing through my nerves.

As my head tips back with a gasp, he nips my shoulder and starts to adjust our position. "There's one talent I'd like to bring to bear that I haven't gotten a chance to yet. And this is the perfect place for it…"

He lifts me out of the water, Alek adding his arms to the

task when he realizes what the courtesan is up to. Together, they set me on the smooth, wide edge of the tub.

Casimir motions to the scholar with a tip of his head. "You should get out too—I'd love to know someone's keeping her satisfied up above while I see what magic I can conjure down here."

He winks at me with an impish grin—and nudges my knees apart so he can lower his head between my legs.

At the first press of his mouth against my sex, the jolt of pleasure shocks a mumbled curse from my mouth. "Fuck."

I've heard women talk about this act, even seen it performed once, but none of my previous, momentary lovers were attentive enough to try it.

Gods above, I never imagined it could feel so good.

Casimir laps his tongue across every sensitive bit with exquisite care, as if he's charting my most private domain with his mouth. Each flick and swipe sparks even more of the heady delight now flooding my body.

I moan and clutch at Alek, who's followed Casimir's suggestion to clamber out next to me.

The scholar embraces me from behind, branding my neck and shoulders with heated kisses, caressing both of my breasts with his agile hands, tweaking my nipples to set off sparks through my flesh. His breath has gone ragged as if he's as affected by the sight of Casimir's attentions as I am by receiving them.

The courtesan curves his tongue between my folds. Then he sucks on my clit with just the right force to make me shudder with need. My fingers dig into Alek's arm.

A strained noise escapes the scholar, and then he's scooting back around me. "Can I— I'd like to do that for her too."

Casimir grins up at us with a lick of his lips. "It'd be selfish of me to keep this treasure all to myself."

As Alek sinks into the water, Casimir eases onto the side of the pool next to me. A pang resonates through my body at the loss of contact, but Alek wastes no time taking the courtesan's former position.

He considers me with his intense gaze. His bright brown eyes have never felt more penetrating. As he runs his thumb over my clit, they light up with an enthusiasm that might be academic as well as passionate.

"I've read about techniques," he says, lifting his gaze to Casimir. "But I wouldn't be surprised if you know better than any account I've happened across in the library."

Casimir's smile only grows. "Take your time. Enjoy every part of her, and she'll enjoy it too. Put your whole head into it, build up the pressure and a rhythm. And follow her encouragement."

He nuzzles my cheek. "Why don't you set one of those clever hands on Alek's head? Give his hair a tug to show him when he's doing particularly well."

I reach out to tangle my fingers in Alex's thick locks. Casimir helps me keep my balance, looping his arm around my waist to stroke my belly and palming one of my breasts with his other hand.

The first few swipes of Alek's tongue are tentative, but in my sensitized state they're giddying all on their own. I urge him toward me, and he captures my sex in the most thrilling sort of kiss. The coarse texture of his scarred cheek rubs against my inner thigh with unexpectedly delicious friction.

As he works me over, gaining confidence with every gasp and whimper he provokes, he glides his hands against my thighs. Somehow that touch amplifies the pleasure of his mouth beyond anything I was feeling before.

"Very good," Casimir murmurs, tweaking my nipple between his fingers in time with the rocking of Alek's head. When his fondling stirs another moan from my chest, he brings his skillful mouth to the crook of my jaw as if in reward.

At my tugging of his hair, Alek exhales roughly across my sex. He delves in deeper, picking up the pace of the movements of his tongue.

There's no doubting his devotion to the task now. He devours me as if he's intent on conjuring every bit of pleasure he can from my body, and all I can do is arch into his mouth.

The bliss that's been building inside me swells higher, tingling through every limb.

"Focus on her clit now," Casimir instructs, his voice roughening. "Stroke the rest of her with your fingers."

Alek complies, clamping his lips around that point of pleasure and flicking his tongue. His fingers massage my folds in time.

A choked sound escapes me. My fingernails dig into his scalp, and then I'm coming, unraveling, washed through with a blaze of ecstasy that leaves me shaking.

When I come back to myself, Alek is gazing up at me with an expression both pleased and a little dazed. He's so gorgeous in his delight at my release that all I can think of is paying him back in kind.

"My turn," I say. "Let's take this out of the water."

I help Alek climb out of the bath and usher him over to the bed, tugging Casimir with us. The courtesan raises no complaint when I scramble onto the covers, dripping, and pull Alek with me.

As the scholar sprawls out on his back at my urging, I take a moment to appreciate the full expanse of his trim form. He watches me, excitement bringing a ruddy tone to his bronze cheeks.

His cock bobs, rigidly erect, drawing my gaze. I lean over him and slick my tongue up his length.

Alek's hips jerk with a stuttered breath. Emboldened by his response, I smile and take him right into my mouth.

His cock has the same cool tang as the rest of him, sweetened by the lingering scent of the bath oils. I'm not really sure of what I'm doing, but I figure Casimir's advice probably applies to this act just as well.

Take my time. Enjoy every part. Build up the pressure and rhythm.

Gradually, I work my way down Alek's shaft, lapping my tongue against him and tightening my lips by increments. Each groan spurs me on.

Casimir strokes my back and offers a murmured suggestion. "Apply extra pressure beneath the head of his cock. Then swirl your tongue right around his shaft."

I suck and flex my tongue, and Alek outright shudders. As I feel his response, renewed arousal pools between my legs.

"It feels so good," he rasps, alternately caressing and clutching at my hair. "So good, Ivy. Casimir, you should be making her feel good too. Fill her... Fill her all the way."

I wonder if that's one of the arrangements from the Woudish erotic poetry book he's become so fond of. I can't complain about the suggestion it's inspired. When Casimir kneels behind me and squeezes my ass, I push into his touch approvingly.

He'll get at least as much out of this act as I do.

As I pump my head over Alek's cock, Casimir guides his shaft between my folds. My first climax wore me out, but part of me clamors for more—to be stretched, to be fully claimed.

"Fuck," Alek mumbles. "Ivy, I can't— I'm going to—"

I simply suck him down harder, willing him to let go. Casimir thrusts into me with a burst of pleasure, I moan around Alek's shaft, and the scholar bucks up to meet me with a breathless grunt.

Then he's coming, hot salty fluid coursing into my mouth as Casimir pulses into me from behind. The almost desperate sounds of Alek's release and the courtesan's practiced strokes send me spiraling faster than I would have thought possible.

I duck my head against Alek's thigh with a gasp. Alek trails his fingers over my hair, murmuring a stream of tender words, while Casimir plunges into me ever faster.

I clench around his cock, my second release crackling through me hard enough to white out my vision. Casimir's breath fragments as he grasps my hip.

He slams into me with even more force, setting off fresh sparks behind my eyes, and spills himself inside me.

As the courtesan rocks to a gentle stop, Alek sits up to guide my mouth to his. I kiss him, long and lingering, and then twist around to capture Casimir's lips in turn.

A warm, mellow sensation has spread through my entire body. I squirm against the sheets. "I just want to curl up here and drift to sleep."

Casimir pecks my cheek. "You can do that. Would you like us to stay?"

A flicker of panic rattles my pulse at the thought of them leaving after the intimacy we just shared. "Yes. Please."

He smiles. "I'll leave Stavros a note, then, so he doesn't go on a rampage trying to find you. Give me a minute, and I'll be right back."

He slips into a robe and heads for the ring of cord we arrived through.

Alek eases me down on the bed and aligns his body with mine. "I wish I never had to be anywhere else."

The raw honesty of those words hits me right in the

heart. "Me too," I whisper, feeling oddly shy about the words even though I'm only echoing his sentiment.

How could I ever have dreamed I'd find joy like this here in a den of vicious nobles?

The scholar runs his fingers lightly over the scars across my shoulder blades. "You deserve a life where no one's trying to hurt you. Where you're surrounded by people who want you to thrive. With all the books in every language, all the horses to ride, all the best knives."

I don't know how to answer the tenderness in his voice at all. My throat closes up, and then I manage a dry remark. "It might be a while before I get that if the scourge sorcerers have anything to say about it."

Alek leans in to nuzzle my hair. "I'm going to do whatever I can to make sure you're free of them soon. I've researched all the quarries producing significant amounts of clay across the country—I'm going to start traveling to the closer ones to take a look around."

My pulse hiccups. "If they notice and suspect why you're doing it—"

He kisses my temple. "I can come up with a good excuse. A scholarly one. It'll be a new 'research project.'"

If anyone could frame the investigation the right way, it's Alek. His tone is casual as he talks about it. But a knot forms in my stomach at the thought of him venturing out into the unknown, poking around in the places the conspirators might be hiding their most closely guarded secrets.

I have to crack those secrets from within—*soon*. That's the only way I can protect Alek and the other men from the dangers they're taking on too.

If I can't… I don't even want to think about the price I might have to pay for having this brief bit of happiness.

Casimir returns as quickly as he promised and settles himself onto the bed at my other side. Despite my worries, I find myself lulled into a doze between the warmth of their bodies. It isn't as if I got all that much sleep last night.

Somewhere in the midst of their own slowing breaths and soft caresses, I slip right into slumber. When my eyes flutter open again, I don't know how long it's been.

Alek and Casimir are asleep on either side of me, their bodies relaxed, their breaths even. A renewed glow of joy lights inside me.

I'm about to close my eyes and see if I can get a little more rest when Julita's presence stirs.

What— You're still— It's been hours.

I don't understand why she's upset. I open my mouth but hesitate to answer her for fear I'll wake my lovers.

Julita lets out a sound that's almost agonized. *Why am I even here? They don't think about me. I don't matter anymore. They only see you.*

My pulse lurches. "Julita?" I say under my breath, but my sense of her in my head has already contracted again. I don't think she even hears me.

THIRTY

Ivy

"**Y**ou can have a bit of a break now," Stavros says to me as we step into his quarters. "The next class today isn't until the fifth bell."

"And I have so many wonderful things to do with my free time." I roll my shoulders, which have gotten a little stiff from standing at attention during his lecture, and move into my now-automatic circuit of the room.

I can't even hope that I'll run into Casimir or Alek someplace we could talk a little. They've both been away from the college pursuing whatever leads they think might get us closer to exposing the scourge sorcerers' plans.

I haven't been able to contribute to that goal at all in the past few days. Since my trial with Benedikt, my palm has stayed blank. There hasn't been so much as a peep from the conspirators.

Maybe they're simply being cautious, giving me plenty of time to reveal ulterior motives before they call on me again.

Or maybe they've decided keeping me around is too big a risk, even if the gods appeared to favor me over Benedikt.

Stavros's gaze follows me around the room with a weight of concern that itches at me. He's probably wondering whether *he* made the right choice in backing me if I'm going to be useless to the cause now.

His voice comes out dry but mild. "I'm sure you'll have plenty of company to occupy you again when—"

A quiver of magic races through my nerves from somewhere along the wall. I jerk my hand up to cut off Stavros's remark.

His mouth snaps shut, his brow furrowing. I hold still by the side table I was passing and then carefully crouch down so I can peer beneath it.

The trace of magical energy guides my gaze. It still takes me a moment to spot the fat brown beetle hiding between one of the table's legs and the baseboard.

Ugh, Julita murmurs. *That's an unwelcome sight.*

The impression of sorcery is definitely coming from the bug. And what an appropriate creature for the members of the entomology club to have sculpted.

Frowning, I study it. The beetle stays where it is, unmoving. Nothing about the energy leaking off it shifts.

We still don't know what purpose the conspirators have for the creatures they've been creating out of clay. My riven soul might react to magic in the air, but I can't identify the specifics of what's been cast.

Julita lets out a huff. *What are you waiting for? Squash the vermin.*

My hand balls. I'd very much like to smash the bug out of existence. But beneath my first instinct, another idea is tickling up through my thoughts.

If the conspirators are using their creations to spy on people somehow... we could use that fact against them.

Offer them more proof that they should trust that my attitudes align with theirs.

It's worth a shot.

Stavros can obviously tell that I've discovered something, and he knows what I was looking for. He stands silently as I back away from the beetle.

I make a vague gesture that I hope he can understand is encouragement to play along. "I don't want to hear any more about that. How can it not bother you having the royal guards swarming the college day and night?"

The former general's eyebrow ticks upward, but he gamely matches the irritation in my tone. "They're keeping us safe."

I snort. "Keeping us safe or keeping us within their tight restrictions? The daimon were trying to tell us something isn't right, and they've silenced them. It's not like *we* can say anything for ourselves without risking getting arrested."

"I don't think anyone wants to hear the kinds of things you've been hinting at," Stavros replies, letting his voice darken. "Least of all me. Don't shame your family by talking like a traitor."

"Isn't it more traitorous *not* to speak up when something's wrong with the world?"

He scowls at me, getting right into character. "I don't want to hear another word. If I have to drag you to the guards to make sure you're not doing anything more than spouting off senseless rhetoric—"

I stomp toward the door. "Oh, quit acting like you've got the moral high ground here. I'm sure I can find better company than you."

As I grasp the doorknob, I catch his gaze. He offers a slight nod to indicate we're still good, that he knows it was all a pretense.

A pretense I need to follow through with. I stride out

into the hall and hesitate there, smoothing my hands down my skirt.

I don't know if our mock argument accomplished anything at all. The beetle could be in Stavros's room for any number of other reasons, not picking up on what we say at all.

At least I tried.

I'll have to make sure it's gone when I get back. Or maybe Stavros will contrive to discover it before then and do the squashing for me.

The peal of the palace bell rings through the Domi's walls, and I find myself remembering another afternoon when I was looking for ways to investigate. My pulse kicks up a notch with a spark of inspiration.

I set off toward the stairwell with renewed determination. No one else is around, so I risk a soft murmur. "Today would be a hunt day, wouldn't it?"

Julita shifts. *I believe so. You'll be able to tell quickly at the stables. But didn't you hate the last time you went?*

I shrug. "I can tolerate the embarrassment if it serves a purpose. I seem to remember a couple of the bug club members participated before..."

Oh! Yes, you're right. Were they from the group Alek thinks is part of the conspiracy?

I think back to the scholar's sketches of the members he considered most suspicious. "One of them was for sure. And even if they don't join the hunt this time, word might get around."

I need to do something to feel like I'm moving our mission along. Who knows what the conspirators have been planning while I wait for them to reach out to me again?

Julita goes quiet as I descend the stairs. I've just reached the ground floor when she speaks up again, in a wistful tone. *I wonder how Alek is getting on with his clay research.*

The hint of melancholy to the comment draws me up short with a prick of guilt in my gut.

We haven't talked about how close my relationship with both Alek and Casimir has gotten or about her mournful complaint when she returned to find us all in bed together the other day. I've been waiting to see if she'll broach the subject in her own time… but she's pretended as if it never happened.

Instead of heading straight to the stables, I take a meandering route that leaves me in the courtyard apart from the other roving students. There, I stop to pluck a flower that's sprouted between the blades of grass.

When I hold it to my nose as if to smell it, my hand hides the movement of my mouth. "Julita, if I'm handling anything in a way that upsets you—if it's uncomfortable for you to have to be here with me when I'm with Alek or Casimir—"

It's fine, Julita breaks in, too brusquely for me to believe her. *I can pull away—I told you. They want you; you want them—it's good.*

I swallow thickly. "I'm sure they still remember you, think about you."

Not while they're doing that *with you. And they shouldn't be. I never meant that much to them, and I know it, so there's nothing more to say.*

I don't think that's all she meant with her remark about them not seeing her anymore. It's true that none of the men have referred to Julita inside me as much as they used to— and Alek vehemently rejected her attempt to talk to him directly.

"We're friends, right?" I say, giving it one more try. "And friends should be able to talk about—"

There's nothing to talk about, Julita insists. *Everything is*

*good. You'd better hurry up, or you'll miss the start of the hunt.
Oh, gods smite us, there's that pushy guard again.*

I think she's only attempting to change the subject until I
shift my attention beyond the flower and realize the
ridiculously handsome guard who badgered me while
stargazing is marching straight toward me with a stern
expression. Although even when he's making a face like he's
got a stick up his ass, those blue-green eyes are fucking
breathtaking.

I bet the rest of the Crown's Watch hates this guy.

He comes to a stop a few paces away from me and tips
his head toward me. "What are you doing wandering around
over here?"

I twirl the wildflower between my fingers. "Can't a lady
stop to enjoy the flowers?"

He knits his brow at me beneath his chocolate-brown
curls, as if he's trying to figure out how flower-picking could
be a questionable act. The tingle of magic wafting off him
reminds me to be wary of his unknown gift.

Then he asks the last question I'd have expected. "Are you
all right?"

I blink at him and scramble for words. "Quite. Even
better now that my nose has enjoyed this lovely scent. But
now I have places to be."

I hustle on toward the stable, willing him to return to his
post.

Thankfully, I haven't missed the hunt. Pampered nobles
aren't known for their sense of urgency.

A couple dozen students are milling around the yard
outside the stable, most already mounted but a few not even
having claimed horses yet. It looks like the hunt master's
assistant has only just started handing out bows.

I spot several familiar faces in the bunch: my former
bully Anya and a couple of her friends, my rival Romild

taking a bow into her arms like it's an extra limb, Petra the distant royal off to the side with her usual reserved distance —and not one but two faces I recognize from Alek's profiles and my own investigations of the entomology club.

Restraining a smile of relief, I hustle into the stable to get my steed.

Toast huffs at the sight of me as if admonishing me for neglecting him. I rub his nose as I lead him out. "Who else would give you a chance at all, huh? You'd better behave, or maybe I'll pick a new favorite horse."

The temperamental stallion stomps a hoof, but then he walks out behind me without more than a brief shake of his reins.

As I mount him, Anya arches her eyebrows at me. "Really? You're riding that beast again?"

I aim a wry grin at her. "We've formed an understanding, and now we get along just fine. Thank you for introducing me to him."

The haughty noblewoman looks as if she's bitten back some caustic comment, probably remembering the understanding the two of *us* reached that ensures Stavros doesn't have her arrested.

Petra catches my eye briefly with a flicker of a smile I pretend I don't notice. She did suggest that I join another of these hunts, didn't she? Does she figure I'm here to kindle a friendship with her?

I'd imagine it's best if the probable conspirators in our midst don't get the impression I'm cozy with any member of the royal family, no matter how minor.

I accept the bow and the sheath of arrows the assistant offers me and wield them with a little more skill than the first time. With a subtle twitch of the reins, I send Toast ambling away from Petra, closer to the bug club members so they'll have a clear view.

If I really had been touched by the gods in my stand-off with Benedikt, I'd be startled by the unexpected talent I seemed to have gained. I might hope my improved skill was permanent.

I stroke my fingers along the wooden curve of the bow and adjust my position in the saddle, giving my best impression of a noblewoman eager to enjoy her newfound ability.

I can tell before the hunt master even directs us into the woods that I'm going to be clumsy as ever with the arrows. If I could throw knives at the conjured targets that appear along the forest path, *then* I'd be showing up the spoiled elites around me.

Instead, I let my face fall with disappointment more and more at every arrow that misses its mark. Partway through the trek, I pause and stare down at my hands as if I don't understand how they could be failing me now.

Great God help me, let the scourge sorcerers be watching my performance. Let them be thinking about how well the gods must have guided me the other day for me to have bested Benedikt then, how much faith they must have in me.

Otherwise I've acted like an idiot for nothing.

I've just prodded Toast back to a trot when Petra draws up beside me. She glances sideways with a purse of her lips. "Have you been getting on well, Ivy?"

I force a chuckle and waggle my bow. "It doesn't seem to be getting on with me."

She shakes her head. "No, I mean… in general."

A trickle of uneasiness winds through my stomach. What is it with people thinking I'm not okay? First that guard, now a royal niece-twice-removed or whatever exactly Petra is.

Do I *look* like I'm in some kind of trouble?

As I debate how to answer, I notice one of the bug club members has turned her head our way. My pulse stutters.

If they get the impression that I really am friends with Petra, any point I've managed to make with my disastrous archery performance won't matter at all.

I lift my chin as if I'm offended that she asked. "I'm sure you have better things to do than worry about *my* well-being."

Before she can respond, I apply my heels to Toast's sides. He breaks into a canter.

Now I have to hope that Petra isn't so offended she complains about me to the king. This is a nice pickle I've found myself in.

Not for the first time, I miss the simplicity of ripping off corrupt merchants and dropping coins on window ledges. At least as the Hand of Kosmel, I always knew exactly where I stood, exactly what needed doing.

I manage to stay ahead of Petra for the rest of the hunt. I also manage to nick the edge of one target, to Julita's excited cheer as if I hit it dead center. Which I guess with my aptitude is about the equivalent.

I keep up my show of being disgruntled with my pitiable skills while I brush Toast down and head back to the college buildings, however much good it's doing. My gut feels heavy.

How much longer will I have to keep up this whole charade?

The question nags at me through Stavros's afternoon class in the field, through a lonely supper in the dining hall, through a quick wash in one of the shared bathing rooms that aren't half as fancy as those in the companionship division.

Then, as I'm toweling myself off, a prickle spreads across my left palm.

I jerk my hand around. The glowing words crawl across my skin.

Midnight. Same place. Come alone.

I stare at my palm for a few seconds longer after the message fades away, waiting for relief to wash over me. All that rises up is a vague sense of trepidation.

I got what I was looking for. But I also wish I could be doing anything other than walking into the woods at midnight tonight.

THIRTY-ONE

Ivy

I arrive fifty paces into the woods with a cool autumn breeze nipping at my arms. As I peer through the darkness, I tug my cloak closer around me.

This time, the scourge sorcerers don't make me wait for long. It can't be more than a few minutes before two black-shrouded figures emerge from the thicker blackness between the trees.

Two black-shrouded figures… and a man in noble clothing whose smooth face still holds a touch of baby fat.

I have the vague sense I've seen his face around campus—he's got to be a first year, only eighteen.

I only have two years on him, but seeing his wide eyes and the nervous set of his mouth, I suddenly feel ancient in comparison.

"Come along," one of the shrouded figures says, managing to sound gruff even with the magical warble altering her voice. At least, I think it's a her. "The ceremony will begin soon."

She and her silent companion usher the nobleman and me through the woods at a brisk pace. I sneak glances at the guy, noting the resolve in his shoulders and the set of his jaw.

I'm pretty sure he's a potential recruit just like me. Why are they bringing us together now?

Why are they letting us *see* each other? When Benedikt accused me, they let him stay hidden until they started to doubt his story.

I guess I should be glad that their leaving us on equal ground probably means I'm not about to face another accusation of treachery.

Maybe it's yet another different test. The scourge sorcerers don't want to risk letting us identify any of the established conspirators, but if we turn on our fellow candidates, they'll know we can't be trusted to hold our tongues.

The young man whose name I don't know keeps quiet, so I do the same. I'm not sure what I could say that would be a good idea anyway. This isn't exactly a prime setting for small talk.

Fancy meeting you here! Lovely night to plot against the royal family, isn't it?

I arch an eyebrow slightly in a silent question to Julita. To my relief, she catches on despite the tension that's seeped into our interactions lately.

No idea who he is, she says. *If he's a first year, he's only been at the school for a couple of months. He mustn't be in the leadership division, and he can't have done anything all that noticeable.*

I continue studying him, attempting to commit his face to memory. Dark hair, narrow nose, knobby chin, top-heavy body with broad shoulders but narrow hips.

If I can describe him well enough to the other men, hopefully one of them will have some idea who he is.

After several minutes of tramping through the brush, I develop a suspicion of where we're headed. Sure enough, we reach the back wall.

One of our escorts raps on the stones with a low muttering, and the shadowy opening appears in front of us.

The woman who spoke earlier prods me through, her companion and the nobleman following behind. We emerge to find one more conspirator dragging the concealed boat onto the river.

Apprehension prickles down my spine. I hardly feel safe *on* the campus, but my situation is even more precarious when I let these psychopaths guide me beyond the college's walls.

But any hesitation is dangerous. Benedikt proved as much with his confession—he said he only balked briefly at making the sacrifice they demanded before they decided he wasn't committed enough.

An odd twinge passes through me, thinking of him and the last time the scourge sorcerers brought me out here. There's a jab of anger, but also a twinge of grief and guilt.

I hate that Benedikt was selfish enough to turn on me to try to save himself. I don't understand how he could have bought into this madness.

But I also hate that we made him feel inferior, however inadvertently.

I clamber onto the boat with the shrouded conspirators and the nobleman. We glide across through the darkness without so much as a peep from the guard patrolling the back wall.

Maybe the pretty boy who keeps hassling me should put his gift to better use and catch the actual bad guys around here.

On the far bank, we hike for another short distance to a

horse-drawn cart. Five more figures are waiting for us there—
only two of them concealed by black shrouds.

I eye the other three as I climb into the cart. They study
me with equal suspicion.

These must be potential recruits from elsewhere in the
city. They're at least middle-warders by their clothing—
quality fabrics and clean, no patches or darning.

One is really just a kid, a girl of maybe fifteen or sixteen,
but the other two are significantly older than me. I think the
woman, whose mousy brown hair is twisted back from her
face in a tight bun, must be in her thirties, and the man
maybe a decade older. The moonlight catches on the silver
flecks in his hair.

Then one of our escorts pulls an arched canvas covering
over the top of the cart. A tiny bit of moonlight filters
through, but no one will be able to see in… and I won't be
able to see where we're going.

These fiends are cleverer than they have any right to be,
Julita mutters.

Two of the conspirators take seats at the front of the cart
to start the horses trotting down the rough track. One of the
others sits in our midst.

"We have friends ensuring that our travels stay safe from
those who'd oppose our hopes for Silana," she tells us. "If a
cry to take flight goes up once we've reached our destination,
run straight to the cart. We'll have plenty of advance
warning, and the gods will protect us from discovery."

The gods? More like the conspirators' deranged magic.

No wonder it's taken so long for anyone to stumble on
the scourge sorcerers. Even Julita only did by chance, because
of her history with Wendos. They take every possible
precaution to keep themselves hidden.

Even if I called on my men for help, it sounds as if I'd be
whisked away before they could reach me.

As I suppress the jitter of my nerves, the shrouded woman retrieves a bottle from beneath her shroud.

"Everyone take a gulp," she says, handing it to the nobleman next to me. "It'll open your minds so you can fully embrace what's ahead."

I don't like the sound of that.

The nobleman makes a face after his swallow and passes the bottle to me. I take a quick sniff, but I don't recognize the sour earthy scent.

Well, I do have plenty of tricks up my sleeve, sometimes literally.

I make a show of filling my mouth and pass the bottle on. Then I raise my arm to swipe my hand across my mouth.

Before I can finish the gesture, the cart bumps on a rut. A dollop of the liquid jolts down my throat.

I spit the rest down my sleeve, silently cursing the lumps in the dirt. At least I didn't swallow a full portion.

As the cart jostles on, a faint fizzing develops beneath my thoughts. It's hard to judge the full effect when I'm just sitting here, but my gut clenches with uneasiness.

I have no idea how long the cart ride lasts. We candidates sit in tense silence. The shrouded figures among us intone in the thick, muddled syllables of the arcane dialect I heard Wendos using, so quietly I'm not sure I'd understand them even if I'd learned the language.

The cart jerks to a halt. Our escorts draw back the canvas to reveal a wide clearing surrounded by sparse forest on all sides.

Nothing I can see stands out as a potential landmark to identify this spot. No doubt that's by design.

There's a big dark heap off at the other end of the clearing, only a jumble of lumps in the darkness. The conspirators don't make any move toward it, directing us in front of the cart before leading the horses farther to the side.

When I walk, my mind seems to list as if I'm a boat on a wavy sea. I swallow thickly, the sour aftertaste of the drugged liquid lingering in my mouth.

If I'm feeling out of sorts, how badly will it have affected those who swallowed the entire mouthful?

Then one more shrouded figure steps into the clearing across from us, leading a man who has his hands bound behind his back and a golden crown on his drooping head.

At the first glimpse, my heart lurches. The crowned man has the same dark hair and strapping build as King Konram.

Julita gasps. *They couldn't really have—*

No, they couldn't. She cuts herself off when he raises his head, and we both see a face similar but not the same as the king's. The nose is large, but more bulbous than hawkish; the eyes are squintier and wider set.

Just a stand-in. But the implications are clear.

They become even more so when the shrouded man leading him lifts his voice.

"This king hasn't proven himself worthy of ruling over us," he says, projecting his words out into the stillness of the night. "All those who wish to lead must be properly tested. Rise to the challenge and make him confirm his might."

I've spent a significant part of the past few days observing Ster. Torstem whenever I could, wanting to make sure I could recognize him if I encountered him in this guise again. It only takes a couple of sentences before I'm sure this is the law professor's authoritative tone, even with the magical warbling disguising it. His cadence sounds just like it does when he's at his lectern.

Before I have a chance to wonder how we're going to "rise to the challenge," one of the other scourge sorcerers presses a knife into my hand. I stare down at it, my fingers instinctively curling around the hilt.

It's a plain one, but I can tell it's sharp from the way the faint moonlight hits the blade. My stomach flips over.

The woman from the city glances around, clutching the knife she was handed. "What are we supposed to do?"

Torstem shoves the false king toward us. "Deal a blow. Cut him deep. If the gods are with him, he'll endure."

Great God help us, Julita mumbles.

My magic flickers in my chest, but aimlessly. I'm braced for danger, but my riven power can't tell where the threat is.

In this moment, technically the threat is me.

I adjust my grip on the knife, willing down my queasiness.

I can handle this. I know my way around a blade.

I can make a strike look fierce while avoiding any vital organs or major blood vessels. A superficial wound.

The drug gives me even more of an excuse. They can't expect me to aim properly when my balance is off kilter, can they?

The shrouded figures around us raise their voices. "Test him! Test the king! Find out what he's worth."

The teenage girl darts forward and slashes with her knife. She clearly isn't experienced, but she slices through the man's silk tunic so blood wells against the fabric.

The nobleman lunges forward next, with a breath hissed through his teeth. He stabs the false king in the chest just below his shoulder.

As more blood spurts out, the man grunts. That's the only sign he's affected by the wounds.

I'm next. I grit my teeth and push myself forward, honing my mind as well as I can through the partial haze.

Whip out my hand. Hit him right *there.*

The blade glances off a rib, just as I intended. The impact reverberates up my arm, and the false king wobbles.

I bite back the apology that leaps up my throat and stumble to the side.

The woman from the city steps toward the stand-in, her knuckles pale where she's clutching her knife. She stares at him, at the blood staining his clothes. Her body sways.

Her voice comes out slurred. "I don't... To attack the king..."

Torstem makes a swift motion. Two of the other conspirators grab the woman and drag her away.

"Wait!" she cries out. "I can do it. I could. I just—I just wanted to be sure."

"If you aren't sure already, it's too late for you," Torstem announces, his voice booming through the clearing. "The gods will decide where you belong."

In a grave somewhere with no one knowing what really befell her, no doubt.

My innards lurch between the impulse to leap in and defend her and the need for self-preservation. I hold myself still, telling myself this is the right choice.

Would saving her be worth blowing my entire mission? She's been on board with everything the scourge sorcerers have asked of her until now—how reasonable a person can she really be?

My rationalization doesn't alleviate my growing nausea. As one of the scourge sorcerers clamps a hand over the woman's throat and they disappear between the trees, I avert my gaze.

The older man hurtles at the false king as if determined to show how very willing *he* is in comparison. He rams his knife into the other man's abdomen at an angle that might pierce the liver.

I restrain a wince. That's it. We've all shown our dedication—or not.

Now they'll bring out their healer woman and—

Ster. Torstem strides up to the false king from behind. "It's too late for this king. He's betrayed us all with his claim to the throne. Now we bring him down!"

He slams a dagger of his own right between the man's ribs, deep enough to pierce the heart.

I only just catch a yelp of alarm before it bursts from my throat. My power flares fiercer.

That's the threat. That's a man who'll kill just to make a point.

As the false king staggers, raising no more protest than a groan, my magic tugs at me to heal his wounds. To cast away the villains who staged this vicious "ceremony." To—

No. No, I can't.

I yank it in, and my head spins. A burning sensation spreads across my skin as if my power is trying to sear its way out.

I fumble to suppress it, and I think it senses my drugged weakness. It lashes out with a sharper pain straight through my lungs. I have to clamp my mouth shut against a grunt.

One of the shrouded figures drags the false king into the woods in a different direction from the woman who failed the trial. I swing myself away from them, tensing every muscle in my legs to hold them steady against the onslaught.

I let a little magic free only a few days ago. Gods only know how hard it'd be hitting me if my power wasn't partly sated.

Oh, gods, Ivy, I'm sorry.

Julita's sorry? What for? She sounds honestly anguished.

I sputter a puzzled guffaw, which hopefully sounds like derision toward the false king.

My ghostly passenger squirms in the back of my head. *I thought I recognized the smell—Borys and Wendos used a potion like that sometimes to supposedly help them tap into the 'power of their inner mind' or some rot like that. It simply made them act like idiots. I would have warned you, I just— I figured you could deal with it yourself. You handle so much else without needing my help.*

Despite her apology, resentment taints those last words. But between my unsteady mind, the magic I'm still grappling with, and a sudden blaze of fire before me, I can't focus on Julita right now.

The shadowy heap I noted at the far end of the clearing is a big heap of firewood. One of the scourge sorcerers has set it alight. The flames surge up toward the sky, warbling like their disguised voices.

Torstem waves us toward the bonfire. "Come! Let us treat the traitor king the way he deserves. Offer him up to the gods whose will he ignored!"

Great God smite us, he doesn't really mean—

Even as horror wrenches through me at the thought that we might be burning the man he fatally stabbed before the fellow's soul has departed, three of the scourge sorcerers drag a figure far too big to be any living human toward the fire. The wavering orange light glances off stitched together clothes stuffed with straw and a crown that looks like it's made of painted wood tied to the sagging burlap head.

Nice to know the psychopaths draw the line at burning a man alive. For the moment, anyway.

They really aren't hiding their intentions now. There's no mistaking the clear message: they want King Konram dead.

They tried to kill Prince Jacos too. I still don't know if they murdered his older son, Prince Dunstam, years ago.

Maybe I can find out at least one vital fact while they're in a sharing mood.

The shrouded figures motion us new recruits over to haul the straw figure the last few paces to the bonfire. I picture the flames leaping out to catch on their shrouds with an uncomfortable sense of satisfaction and clamp down on my magic when it wriggles up to offer its services.

As I join the others in grasping the straw-stuffed cloth, I let my legs sway a little more, my head loll with our movements. The drunker I seem on their drug, the less they can blame anything that comes out of my mouth on my conscious intentions.

"Death to the unworthy king!" I holler for extra credit, and heave at the figure in time with my current comrades.

The fire roars around the straw figure. In a matter of seconds, body, head, and crown are completely consumed by the flames.

I step back from the heat that prickles at my face, letting a wobble creep into my steps. "There he goes!" I babble, and turn to one of the shrouded figures. "Is this what you did to Prince Dunstam? Gotta get rid of them one by one, right?"

Ivy, Julita says nervously, like a warning.

But the scourge sorcerer just chuckles without revealing anything definite. "Everyone will get what they deserve in the end."

I lean closer, tilting my head to the other side and slurring my words. "But really. That *was* you—us—what we're doing here— He didn't really get sick. You took care of him, didn't you? We should celebrate that too!"

A hand claps onto my shoulder, followed by a voice that makes my pulse hitch.

"We should look to what we can do in the future, not dwell on the past," Torstem says.

Which doesn't answer the question either. I don't know whether they're trying to cover up their crime or take subtle credit for a "victory" they can't actually claim.

But with the leader of the conspiracy standing over me, I'm not going to push my inquiry any farther.

I aim a goofy grin at him. "Of course! Let the king burn!"

This one, anyway. What have they done with the living one? *Is* he still living?

Maybe if I can figure out what they've done with his body, that'll be another useful bit of proof.

I lean into my drugged act, playing up my dizziness to maximum effect. I've watched plenty of drunken louts all through the outer wards to know what effects an intoxicant can have on the body and mind.

I raise my fist in the air. "The other fake king should burn too! Let's send him to the gods. Where is he?"

When I stumble off toward the woods, I'm prepared for one of the conspirators to drag me back. But they must assume I won't remember much—let alone be able to do much—in my current state.

Or maybe they trust my loyalty enough now that they don't care what I see.

I stagger between the trees, allowing myself to trip on a root and sprawl in the dirt. Twigs cling to my skirt when I push myself upright.

"Ouch," I mumble, keeping up the dazed act for anyone who might be keeping watch.

Two tiny, darting presences whip past me with a tingle of agitated energy, tossing my cloak over my head. I yank it back in time to spot a faint glint flitting off through the forest.

Daimon. The spirit creatures don't appear to have enjoyed the scourge sorcerers' ceremonial burning any more than I have.

Which direction did the villains take the false king in? I fight through the real haze in my head to solidify my sense of direction.

I think… that way. I meander toward it on a rambling

course, as if I'm weaving through the forest mostly at random.

Of course, the conspirators might have carted him off in another direction once they were out of sight. I'll just have to keep roving around, playing the fool, until I stumble on his corpse or they call me back.

I scramble over a log and bumble through a clump of bushes. Then the toe of my boot hits something that makes an odd clinking sound.

Like... like *pottery*.

I do my best not to freeze up. Instead, I act as if I've tripped again to give me an excuse to end up on my hands and knees.

My fingers close around shards of fired clay.

In the darkness, I can barely see them, but I feel more chunks everywhere I touch. Far more pieces than a snake or a rat would break into.

My fingers close around a nob that feels like the shape of a nose. A chill sweeps through my body, turning my blood icy in my veins.

Gods help us all... Are the scourge sorcerers conjuring entire human beings?

THIRTY-TWO

Ivy

The first glow of the dawn has just reached the horizon when I slip into Stavros's quarters.

The drug the scourge sorcerers gave us still muddles my thoughts and throws off my coordination alongside a growing fatigue. I managed to make my way to the fourth floor quietly enough, but I push the door closed a little too hard, with a thump that resonates through the room.

A grunt and a sharp breath carry from the bedroom. Stavros charges to the doorway and scans the living space with eyes both bleary and panicked.

He obviously fell asleep during the long time I was gone. His dark red hair and the dress shirt he never changed out of are rumpled. From the urgency in his expression and the tense set of his mouth, I think I might have startled him out of another nightmare.

A nightmare about me, no doubt.

My hand flies up. "Wait!"

I teeter around the room feeling for magic, but the beetle must be gone, and nothing else has taken its place.

I collapse onto the sofa to ease my dizziness. "It's okay," I tell Stavros. "I haven't caused any catastrophes. The scourge sorcerers, though—"

Images from the chaotic night flash through my mind. I leap back up with a lurch of my own panic. "We should meet right away. I need to tell everyone—they're making people. They want to burn the king. We stabbed a man—"

There's too much I need to say—it's all colliding. I grope for the right words and sway on my feet.

Ivy, I think you should sit down again, Julita says in a nervous tone. *You've been up all night. It's not like they're staging a coup right now.*

Stavros has already marched across the room to set a steadying hand on my shoulder. "Are *you* all right? Did they hurt you?"

I shake my head, which unfortunately makes my head spin harder. "No. There was a drugged drink—I tried not to swallow—the stupid cart, ruts in the road…" I stop and force myself to inhale and exhale slowly. "I learned a lot. I should tell everyone."

Stavros's grip on my shoulder tightens. "Is there any immediate danger to the royal family or the city?"

"It didn't seem like it. But I don't know. If they have a lot of clay—and they threw the dummy in the fire."

I'm aware that I'm not making a great deal of sense, but I can't seem to keep my thoughts in coherent order.

Stavros nudges me toward the sofa, keeping his hand firmly in place until I've sat down. "I don't think you're in the best condition to explain what happened at the moment. You must be exhausted. Get a few hours' sleep, and then you can tell us everything."

I'm abruptly aware of how heavy my eyelids have gotten. I swipe at my eyes and peer up at the former general.

All the confusion I've felt in the past week swims to the surface, straight past my internal filter.

"Why are you being nice to me now?" I demand. "You should want the scourge sorcerers to murder me. Then you wouldn't need to worry anymore."

Stavros's expression tightens with what might be horror —or guilt. "Ivy, I'd never want that."

I scoff. "You hated me. My soul's still broken. I give you nightmares."

His mouth twists. "I didn't—I didn't hate you. I was afraid of what you might be capable of, but I know I was wrong. I shouldn't have needed to test you to figure it out."

I wave my hand vaguely. "You don't need to feel guilty about it. I'd have wanted to strangle me too. I'm afraid of me —how can I blame you?"

Stavros pauses with an audible swallow. He rests his hand on my shoulder again, gentler now. "You don't have to worry about *me* anymore. Lie down and get some rest. I'll be right here if you need anything."

I have the ridiculous urge to grasp his hand and pull him down on the sofa with me, so he really will be "right here." To sink into the heat of his body and his peppery scent, wrap myself in all the strength that emanates from his massive frame.

Of course, he wouldn't fit lying down on the sofa with me because of that massive frame. I doubt he'd want to be *that* close anyway, no matter what Casimir says.

I shouldn't want him to be either. He probably does still hate me somewhere underneath. He might decide to put another rope around my neck, and even if I can't totally blame him, I do generally prefer being alive.

Stavros lifts his hand to stroke his fingers over my hair—

a fleeting caress, but it makes my pulse skip a beat. "If you want to have that meeting, then sleep. We're not going anywhere until you've rested."

I let out a disgruntled huff, but I oblige him by lying down. My eyes close automatically. I'm not sure anything has ever felt as wonderful as these sofa cushions.

I think Stavros is still standing there, watching me—standing guard, like he thinks I might run off again if he doesn't. I can't find the wherewithal to care.

The fog rolls over my mind, and I drift away.

I wake up to a bitter taste in my mouth and a dull ache in the back of my head. But when I sit up, blinking in the bright daylight now streaming through the window at the other end of the room, my head doesn't reel. My body remains steady.

Stavros stands up where he was seated behind his desk. I don't know if he slept more, but he's wearing a new, unwrinkled shirt with an embroidered jacket over it, and he's put on his hand-shaped prosthetic over the stump of his left wrist.

He speaks in a familiar wry drawl, but his gaze fixes on me intently with a twitch of his head. "You've returned to consciousness. Do you have a story that makes a little more sense now?"

I can't remember exactly what I said to him when I first arrived this morning, but enough of our conversation—especially the last part of it—comes back to me that my face flushes.

I glance away with the excuse of grabbing a new dress. "I'll get changed, and then we should signal Alek and Casimir to come to the meeting room. Assuming they're around. It'll be easier to tell all of you at once, and they might know things that'll fill in the missing pieces."

Stavros nods, his tone darkening. "I have a little news of my own."

With that ominous statement hanging over me, I duck into the latrine and hastily swap my grass-stained gown for one more befitting the lady I'm pretending to be. As I fumble with the laces, it occurs to me that I'm going to need Casimir to bring me yet another replacement.

I seem to go through dresses like most people go through dinner.

I bustle back out to find Stavros waiting for me with his cord already looped on the floor and a plate of bread, cheese, and sliced meat in his hand. "I picked you up a little food when I went down to breakfast earlier. Nothing meant to be hot since I didn't know how long you'd sleep."

He's matter-of-fact about his generosity, but a fresh prickle of heat still creeps up my neck as I accept the plate. My stomach lets out an approving grumble. "Thank you."

Julita gives a laugh that sounds a bit stiff. *I obviously should have prodded him more to bring out this unexpected generous side.*

I lift my shoulders in a slight shrug to indicate that I didn't ask for any of this and wolf down the food in approximately five seconds flat.

Stavros waits for me to take my own cord out of the drawer in the sofa-side table where I've been keeping it. Like he's making a show of the fact that he's letting me handle it now.

Am I supposed to thank him for that too? He only handed it over because Casimir asked.

I lay it out in its ring hastily and step through at the same time he does. The magical passage into the palace meeting room hits me with a little more dizziness than usual, but the effect clears the moment I'm on solid ground again.

I prowl the edges of the room to confirm no unwelcome creatures are lurking. Stavros takes his locket out of his pocket and taps it to signal the others.

The sight of it gives me pause. I hadn't fully thought through the part of the plan where we alerted the other men. "Are you sure it's safe to use that? I mean, Benedikt had one too…"

Stavros's jaw tightens. "That problem has already been taken care of."

I'm about to ask him what he means when Alek emerges into the room with a warble of the air. "Is Ivy all—" he's saying before he's even steadied himself. Then he sees me, and a relieved smile springs to his lips.

I step closer to catch his hand for a quick squeeze. "I was summoned by the scourge sorcerers again last night, and it was pretty… intense. I thought I should fill you all in as quickly as possible. And you can tell us about your investigations too."

Alek's mouth slants downward. "There isn't much to report there so far, unfortunately. Plenty of clay quarries and few ways of narrowing them down without taking the trip to visit them."

Stavros dips his head to the scholar. "It's good that you're looking into them at all. None of the rest of us would be able to invent a suitable excuse."

Alek's smile comes back at the former general's praise. "I want to pitch in however I can. All the responsibility shouldn't fall on Ivy."

I mean, it's not as if you're out there alone, Julita mutters.

A twinge of guilt runs through my stomach. "At least I've got Julita with me no matter what happens," I say.

Alek blinks, as if he really had forgotten about the ghost who's taken up residence in my head.

Stavros lets out a stiff chuckle. "And we're still glad for any help she can offer, as limited as it might be in her current situation."

Julita lets out a disgruntled sound. *Limited? I've had plenty of useful observations—*

Her rant is cut short by Casimir's arrival. The courtesan steps out of his cord and swipes his disheveled hair away from his eyes, his outfit of dress shirt and trousers looking hastily pulled together. "Sorry. I was still sleeping. I had a late night plying people for information over drinks."

"So did Ivy," Stavros says dryly. Despite his tone, he lifts his hand to rest it on my back long enough to set my skin tingling, guiding me toward the table. "It sounds as though we've all been busy. Let's sit, and our Lady Thief can start by telling us what madness the Order of the Wild has pursued this time."

I settle into one of the chairs, my stomach knotting. But now my mind is clear enough that I can give a cohesive account of last night's events.

As I lay out everything from meeting with the other candidates to our journey across the river to the drugged drink we were given, the men's expressions turn increasingly tense. They barely speak other than sounds of sympathy or protest. But when I describe the young man who also came from the college, Casimir knits his brow.

"I might know him. That sounds like one of the newer students in the companionship division—he's specializing in poetry."

"See if you can arrange to point him out to Ivy in the dining hall or elsewhere so she can confirm," Stavros suggests with his commander's airs, and motions to me. "Where were they taking you?"

My gut only gets heavier as I tell them about the ritual in the clearing. Alek's stance goes rigid when I mention Ster. Torstem killing the false king, and Casimir pales at my description of the burning effigy and the remarks the law professor made.

"They've all but stated outright that they intend to see the royal family dead," I finish. "I don't know how soon they plan on making a move or how they'll do it, but I think we should warn the king of how passionate they are about that goal. And that might not even be the worst of it. I went looking for the body of the false king while the bonfire was still going... but what I found was a bunch of clay shards."

I have the sense that Alek's forehead has furrowed behind his mask. "They killed several of their conjured beasts too?"

I wet my lips. "I don't think so. I think the *man* was conjured out of a sculpture. That must be how they got him to look fairly similar to King Konram. And why they didn't have any qualms about killing him just for a trial."

Stavros's eyes have widened. "Bringing small animals to life is shocking enough. This was a totally convincing person?"

I grimace. "Yes. I mean, he didn't say anything, so I have no idea how much of a mind he had. But I had no suspicion he was anything other than an actual human being until I found the mess of clay."

"Great God help us," Alek says faintly. "If they could be making a horde of supporters..."

Stavros pushes back his chair with a rasp of the legs against the floor. "I think I'd better inform the king of all this as quickly as he can see me." He pauses. "I've already had some other news from the Crown's Watch."

My heart lurches at his tone. "What?"

The former general's eyes have gone stormy. "Benedikt's body was found yesterday evening. In the harbor, made to look like he was wandering amid the boats after having too much to drink, fell in and hit his head and drowned."

He catches my gaze. "He had his locket on him, probably because the conspirators didn't know the significance and wanted to avoid the death looking like a crime by involving robbery."

That's what he meant when he said we didn't need to worry about signaling the men.

Oh, Benny, Julita murmurs.

I hug myself, queasiness bubbling up through my chest even though I expected an outcome like this. "At least... At least he can't harm the royal family now. I hope it was a quick death."

Casimir taps his fingers down his front in the gesture of the divinities, his expression downcast. "However much of a scoundrel he decided to be in the end, I hope the same for him too."

Alek stiffens. "You don't think—if the scourge sorcerers can make *people* out of clay—could everything with him have been a trick?"

I stare at him, my stomach flipping over. *Could* it be true...?

But in the first instant I consider the idea, as much as part of me welcomes it, a conflicting certainty rises up. "I don't see how. The replica of the king only sort of looked like him—it doesn't seem the scourge sorcerers can make exact copies. And how would they have known I've got any connection to Benedikt for it to make sense as a trick? Unless they figured out I'm working against them, I guess, in which case they'd have already killed me."

"Not to mention that in every account we've had of the conjurings so far, they've changed back into clay at death," Stavros adds. He pauses, his tone turning even more solemn. "I saw his body myself to confirm. The poor prick."

Alek bows his head. A moment of silence passes between us—the last thing we can offer the colleague who betrayed us.

Then Stavros stands with a nod to Casimir. "Have you discovered anything I should bring up with King Konram as well?"

The courtesan makes an apologetic expression. "No. I'm still chasing down leads that I hope will turn up more concrete information."

"Then I'll make my report now." Stavros pauses. "Ivy, wait here until the next bell. If I'm able to speak to the king right away, he may want to hear more details directly from you."

A shiver runs through my nerves at the thought of facing the king, but I bob my head in agreement. Stavros strides to his ring without hesitation.

When he's gone, Casimir tugs his chair closer to mine and reaches to caress the side of my face. "Every time those fiends call on you, they ask something horrible of you."

I smile tightly. "We knew it'd probably be that way when we came up with the plan. I'm surviving."

Alek makes a face. "You should be able to do more than just *survive*."

When I look at him, I find I can smile more openly. "I have been, though. Mostly thanks to the two of you."

The scholar's piercing eyes soften. He touches my jaw and leans in for a kiss.

At the brush of Alek's lips against mine, Julita lets out a disgruntled sound. *Well, there's my cue to remove myself again.*

I jerk back, meaning to reassure her, but I can already feel that the tingle of her presence has faded to almost nothing in the back of my head.

"What's wrong?" Alek asks.

"It's not you," I assure him quickly. "It's…"

All Julita's remarks over the past few weeks bubble up to the surface. An ache wraps around my heart, but I know the right thing to do.

I grip Alek's hand to try to soften the blow. "Julita's been feeling discarded now that we've gotten so close. I think she's regretting chances she didn't take when she was alive and having trouble coming to terms with the fact that she won't get to take any chances like that again. It hurts her, seeing us together."

Casimir knits his brow. "That isn't your fault, Kindness."

"No. But if I'm going to live up to that nickname… we should tone down the physical closeness, at least. For now." I don't even know how much longer she'll end up staying with me. "She feels like she has to pull away every time we get at all intimate, and it sounds like she's stuck in this vague dark space when she does that…"

Alek twines his fingers with mine. "You know you haven't done anything wrong, don't you? None of us were involved with Julita that way."

He glances at Casimir, who inclines his head in confirmation. "She never engaged my 'services' as a client or as a friend. Occasional flirtation isn't any kind of claim, even if she were still alive."

"I know." I swallow thickly. "But she's the first real friend I've had. She's helped me through so many of the things I've faced here. And I wouldn't have met you at all if she hadn't trusted me with her mission. I don't want to make her last days here, however few they might be, totally miserable."

From the way she talked during the last trial, she's started to feel as if even I don't really want or need her around.

Casimir offers me a tender smile. "And that's why you do deserve the nickname. We can hold off on the physical displays of affection for the time being. As long as you know it's not for lack of interest." A sly glint enters his eyes.

I laugh. "If I start to doubt that, I'll give you the opportunity to remind me."

Alek still looks pensive. "I know this would be a difficult situation to bring up with her, but at some point you'll need to talk about—"

A flash of light blazes from the mirror in the corner, and his mouth snaps shut. I get to my feet, my pulse thumping faster.

The light must have been some kind of alert that the mirror's magical purpose was activated. It fades away to reveal an image of the king, standing in what looks to be the same room as when we spoke to him right after the attack on the city.

King Konram studies me for a moment in silence. My skin crawls under his scrutiny, but I hold my posture straight and clasp my hands in front of me to stop them from fidgeting.

"Ster. Stavros has informed me of your continuing work infiltrating the scourge sorcerer group," he says abruptly. "From what he describes, they've shown a particular animosity toward me."

I give a slight bow. "I'd say that's accurate, Your Highness."

"I'd like you to give me your full account of the recent ceremony that included my likeness. Leave out no details."

"Yes, of course."

I drag in a breath and go through the story again, pausing here and there to make sure I haven't forgotten anything. When I get to the most violent aspects of last night's events, my lungs constrict, but King Konram doesn't do anything more than frown.

The most reaction I get is when I mention my attempts to uncover his eldest son's fate. His stance stiffens slightly.

He makes a gesture to stop me. "You shouldn't pursue

that line of questioning any further. I've confirmed that scourge sorcery had nothing to do with Dunstam's death."

How did he manage to confirm anything about a death several years ago?

But it's hardly my place to debate with the king. I continue on to the end of my account.

"They continue to conceal and obscure everything they can," Konram says when I'm finished. "You still haven't heard any specific plans they intend to carry out?"

I shake my head. "I'm sorry, Your Highness. I'm not considered a real part of their 'order' yet—I suppose they don't trust me enough. But now that they're meeting in larger groups, there'll be more chances for me to identify people. Or, if soldiers could reach us after I send a signal, to take several into custody to interrogate."

The king gives a pensive hum. "From what you've said, they've become very skilled at evading discovery. Given the magic they can wield, I'm not sure any of my people could slip past their sentries unnoticed in order to apprehend the others—especially a large enough squadron to be sure of overpowering them."

My stomach sinks. And what magic might the scourge sorcerers have ready to throw at those soldiers if they did make it close enough to attack?

"I'll try to learn more about their defenses as well," I promise.

"Well, perhaps it's better this way. Even if we could apprehend them, they're far more likely to open up to a supposed ally than an officer of the law, don't you think?"

"That's why we took this course to begin with."

"Then I think we should continue it. We can't even be sure yet how far the conspiracy reaches. I have plenty of guards to see to my immediate protection." King Konram peers at me more closely. "Do you feel *you're* in any significant danger if you stay the course?"

I hesitate, startled by the question.

The king goes on before I need to speak. "My loyal general appears to be rather concerned about your well-being. Do you have any concerns about pushing onward with your mission?"

Gods smite me, has Stavros been trying to appeal to the king on my behalf?

Of course, it'll be as much to ensure I don't fall apart and lose all control over my powers as about my personal safety.

My stomach lurches, but I bob in a slight curtsey. "I'm glad that I can serve the royal family and my country in this way. Also, it would likely be at least as dangerous for me to attempt to withdraw at this point as to stay the course."

King Konram's lips curve into a thin smile. "I appreciate your commitment. It is vital that I know their strategies to fully defend myself, my family, and our country. Do whatever you can to find out what definite actions the miscreants intend to carry out. The risks you're taking will be rewarded."

THIRTY-THREE

Alek

T he midday sun beats down on me from the cloudless sky. It's warmer than I expected for an autumn day, or I'd have dressed in a lighter shirt.

I wipe the sweat from the back of my neck and restrain a grimace at the prickling of perspiration beneath my mask.

Ivy would point out that I could simply take it off. The memory of her hand against my cheek, the affection shining in her eyes when she took me in as I am, still sends a giddy thrill through my chest.

But I've faced enough looks of horror and disgust from other people that I'd rather not risk it. I don't want to give the employees of this clay quarry any reason to hesitate about welcoming my visit.

The sprawling building I'm approaching is appropriately covered with glazed clay tiles to form a mosaic: an image of Creaden, the godlen who presides over construction as well as leadership and justice, raising a temple from the ground

with a sweep of his hands while the first king of Silana applauds.

To the left of the main office entrance is a doorway to the on-site shop, a feature I've discovered is common at the clay quarries. The businesses ship most of the materials they dig up elsewhere for craftspeople to work with, but they also like to show off the end product that can be created.

To the right, I note a few wagons of varying sizes around the side of the building. I'd imagine there are storage and equipment rooms at that end.

This is the fourth quarry I've visited in the past week, a little farther from the capital than the others but still close enough to make a day trip of it. I've developed a pattern of investigation that seems to serve me well.

First, I step into the shop room. The woman supervising it bobs her head to me, her gaze lingering on my mask for a few moments with obvious curiosity. "Welcome to the Earthshine Quarry. I hope you find much to enjoy in our wares."

I nod to her in turn, pushing my mouth into a smile despite my self-consciousness. "I can already see the clay produced here is of excellent quality."

I turn toward the display shelves, taking in the variety of dishes, vases, and figurines, some fired plain, others glazed or painted. "Were all of these made on site?"

"Yes, our master potter likes to show off all the many styles that can be applied to our clay."

As I meander along the shelves as if browsing, I draw a small piece of broken pottery from my carry pouch. It's a shard from the snake Ivy captured and Stavros killed.

I've studied the color and texture of it so closely that I can see it when I close my eyes, but I examine it again to compare it to the examples of plain fired clay before me. My heart starts to beat a little faster.

My sample has the same ruddy brown hue as the clay produced here, with an equally fine grain. I rub my thumb over the shard and then touch one of the bowls.

They feel much the same too.

At all of the past quarries, my hopes dwindled at this point as I saw the differences in the materials. But this—this could be the clay that the scourge sorcerers used to make their conjured creatures.

And conjured men too, if Ivy's observations are correct. Knowing her, I'm inclined to think they are.

Suppressing the nausea that pools in my gut at that thought, I tuck the shard away.

"Can I help you with anything or make any suggestions, good sir?" the shopkeeper asks.

I shake my head. "Not at the moment, thank you. I've actually come from Sovereign College with an academic purpose rather than to buy. But it's been helpful seeing the finished product. I'll be sure to recommend this quarry to the artists at the college."

The last comment appears to please her even though I'm not a paying customer. She smiles brightly as I head out again.

I amble over to the office area as casually as I can, attempting to give every impression of a diligent but not overly invested scholar. If this is the source of the conspirators' clay, I don't know how tangled up the employees might be in their schemes.

They could know nothing about what purpose their materials are being put to… or they could answer to Ster. Torstem and the others. I can't give them any reason to suspect that I have an ulterior motive for being here.

As I reach the door, I give my hands a furtive wipe against my trousers, drying the sweat that isn't only because of the day's heat. My heart is still thumping twice as fast as it ought to.

I have no idea how Ivy manages to stay so cool under pressure, dealing with the unnerving trials the conspirators have forced on her. I'm nervous enough just having a chat with a quarry manager.

But maybe if I can handle this conversation well, she won't have to endure any more of those trials. The evidence of the scourge sorcerers' ultimate plans could be right here.

I knock on the door. After a moment, a burly man with a face nearly as ruddy as his clay opens it. His expression flickers between respect for my refined clothes, wariness at the sight of my mask, and a general air of confusion.

"I'm sorry to interrupt your work," I say quickly but smoothly, willing any sign of my nerves out of my voice. "I'm Aleksi Antoniek of Dovia, a scholar from Sovereign College, and I'm conducting a study of mining activities in Silana now compared to under Darium rule. I'd simply like to ask a few questions and take a quick look around—I won't interfere. I have a letter from my supervising professor if you'd like confirmation."

I fish out the small scroll and hold it out to the man. He takes it and scans the contents.

His gaze sweeps over me again, and my skin itches with the sense that he's assessing me as not much of a threat. He rubs his jaw, his eyebrows lifting slightly. "Our operation could be part of a royal study? That's pretty impressive. Come on in. I can give you a few minutes."

He motions for me to follow him into the building. Just beyond a small fore-room, he steps into a large office with a boxy wooden desk. The papers scattering its surface in apparent disarray have my fingers curling against the urge to straighten them out.

The rest of the space is filled by several shelves of paper

records, a few books, and various odds and ends that I can now recognize are parts of mining equipment. Probably saved as mementos to mark significant milestones of the business.

There's only one chair, behind the desk, where the burly man promptly sits. Even though he's now much lower than me, he gazes up at me with an imperious air. "My name is Nomar Pavelek, and I'm the manager of the Earthshine Quarry. Worked here for nearly three decades now, manager for two of those. What do you need to know?"

"I'd love to take a look at a few months of sales records to get an idea of where most of your materials end up," I say, with not a little relief at the idea of being able to dive into written accounts rather than trying to cajole information out of a person. "And it'd be helpful to know if there have been any particularly notable transactions or incidents during your time here."

Like, say, a new client suddenly demanding huge amounts of clay materials for some mysterious business they haven't clarified.

I can't say that last part out loud without potentially raising his suspicions, though.

Nomar leans back in his chair, his eyes going distant. After several seconds, he shakes his head. "I can't think of any 'incidents' that'd be of scholarly interest. It's a pretty steady business, not much in the way of dramatics. But I don't mind you taking a look at our books. We don't keep sensitive information in the ledgers, only names and amounts."

I offer an ingratiating smile. "That's all I'd need."

The manager propels himself out of his chair again and strides across the room. He pulls a sheaf of loose papers off one of the shelves and hands it to me. "That covers the first three months of this year. I'd prefer it stayed in this room."

"That's totally fine," I assure him. "I'll look through it and take whatever notes I need to right here."

I retrieve a paper, a small quill, and a tiny pot of ink from my carry pouch to look appropriately scholarly and sit on the floor with my back against the wall as if it wouldn't have occurred to me that I'd need a desk. Nomar goes back to whatever work he was taking care of in his own seat, shooting occasional evaluating glances my way.

Unfortunately, for all my hopes, the ledger papers don't reveal anything particularly enlightening. There are regular shipments of various amounts to the craftsmen's guilds in a few different cities, to a couple of townships presumably for building materials, and to an assortment of smaller clients.

Nothing jumps out at me as reason for concern, although I jot down all the names to look into later. But as I tabulate the figures in my head, my forehead furrows.

I wouldn't call myself an expert after seeing a grand total of three previous quarries, but I've noted certain patterns. This particular operation—the size of the building, the number of vehicles, and the sprawl of the quarry itself—gave the impression of being larger than the other three.

And yet it appears they've been sending out significantly less clay than those others, at least in the past few months. Strange.

I look up from my reading. "Would it be possible for me to examine a ledger from, say, ten years ago?"

Am I being paranoid, or does the manager hesitate for a second before answering. "I don't see why not. Let me find it…"

He skims through the records and offers me another sheaf after I return the first to him. When I scan the new set of figures, certainty congeals in my gut.

There are several substantial clients listed here who were no longer receiving shipments in the more recent records.

Some of them might no longer have any need for clay... but a few I recognize from the list of current clients at the other quarries I visited.

"It appears you've lost a number of customers in the past decade," I say in an off-hand tone.

I'm almost certain Nomar's posture goes a tad rigid at the remark. "Oh, our production has slowed a little over the past several years. And tastes change no matter how good our product is."

I suppose that could be the true explanation. I don't know how to prove it *isn't* by talking to this man. He's obviously not going to appreciate me accusing him of lying.

The scourge sorcerers have proven incredibly adept at hiding all evidence of their activities—even the sacrificial accomplices they've mutilated to bolster their magic. I have to handle my investigation with all due care, or a lead could slip right through my fingers.

Pretending to accept the answer at face value, I jot down a few more notes and then return the ledger to its place.

"Thank you so much for your help," I tell the manager. "Would it be a problem for me to take a quick look around this end of the quarry? I promise I'll take care not to fall in."

It's not much of a joke, but it gets me a chuckle out of Nomar. He waves me out. "Take your time. I don't know how interesting it'll be for a scholarly type, but we're proud of the work we do."

Outside, I wander around the side of the building where I saw the wagons. A couple of men are hauling sacks that are presumably full of the clay base onto one of the smaller vehicles.

I amble over to them, my mouth going dry as I scramble to think of how to approach a conversation. I didn't see enough reason for suspicion at any of the other quarries to feel the need to chat with the lower-level workers.

Why would manual laborers want to reveal anything to a privileged scholar from the capital city?

My thoughts trip back to the moment when Ivy presented me with that very provocative book of poetry—to her embarrassed remarks when I told her what it was. Her fear that I'd think she was stupid for making an overture to a noble.

But I assured her that I wasn't a noble in the first place.

I'm not, after all. I'm the son and grandson and great-grandson of merchants.

I might not have any idea what it's like to make a living digging minerals out of the earth and loading them into wagons, but I know a fair bit about goods and customers, production and distribution.

I do my best to loosen my posture as I come around the wagon, letting go of my meticulous academic airs. One of the men heaves the last sack into the back of the wagon and wipes his hands on a rag, peering at me.

With the sort of wry grin I saw my brothers often make when they spoke with the smiths my family employed, I pat the side of the wagon. "Another load about to go out? I hope it's a customer who gives more compliments than complaints."

The other man snorts. "Oh, they all find something to complain about now and then. This one's not so bad." He lifts his chin toward me. "You have some business here?"

I make a flippant gesture with my hand. "I'm just learning about the clay business—finding out how it's changed over the years, what goes into it, that sort of thing. You do important work. It should be recognized. And I know dealing with the clients is probably the hardest part of the job, not hauling the materials around."

The first man lets out a wary chuckle. "You're not wrong

about that. Do you have clients to deal with too?" He takes in my fine clothes with obvious skepticism.

"Not recently," I admit. "But I grew up in a family of weapons merchants. Never heard my dad curse so much as when a customer came to him asking him to replace half the merchandise because the shine wasn't quite right on the steel or some other absurd excuse."

To my relief, it seems as if my gambit is working. The worker's stance relaxes a little as he gives a more open laugh. "There are always a few with bizarre requests like that. We had someone last week try to return an entire shipment because they found a pebble in one of the bags. And then there's the client who's so concerned about keeping the purchases quiet that—"

His colleague cuts in with an urgent sound. "Jevam, that's enough."

Jevam shuts his mouth with an abashed expression that only fans the flames of my curiosity.

Someone buying the clay who's being secretive about it? That sounds like exactly a subject I should pursue.

I let out a guffaw as if I'm not taking any of it too seriously. "I wouldn't have thought clay would be a product requiring much secrecy."

The second man waves off my statement. "It's not. He's just exaggerating." He narrows his eyes at Jevam. "We should get back to work. I'll bring the horses around."

He stalks off toward another building that must be the stable. When he's disappeared into the building, I raise my eyebrows at Jevam. "Seems like he's all about keeping things quiet too."

Either I'm not being convincingly uninvested about the topic or his colleague's admonishment has really gotten to him. Jevam simply shrugs. "Not much to tell about it anyway."

I can't let this opening go. I grope for the right way to loosen his lips. "A case like that could give me a new understanding of the trade. That's the whole reason I'm coming out to talk to people like you."

In an instant, I realize I've made a misstep. I've separated us into people like me and people like him.

Jevam's mouth tightens, and he glances away. "Like I said, there isn't much to tell."

Maybe if I show I can relate to his situation, that'll smooth over my stumble? "You can probably imagine we had a lot of hush-hush dealings in the weapons business. I don't know how many times we supplied someone and then the next day armed whoever our first customer was going to go up against." I raise my hands in the air. "That's business for you."

"Yeah," Jevam mutters. "It doesn't make much sense to me when it's just clay."

But then he clams up again. He rubs the back of his hand, pushing up the loose sleeve of his shirt from his wrist, and I notice a ruddy, almost scaly patch of skin there. The thin cracks rippling through it shine an angry pink.

A twinge of sympathy resonates through my gut. That kind of skin condition would only be exacerbated working in conditions like this.

The words spill out before I've really thought them through. "You know, there's a technique that's gone out of fashion for treating painful dryness of the skin. It was common in the time before the Darium invasion. You boil some yimmerbush leaves and bark, which isn't hard to find, and let them steep in the hot water until it cools into a gel. Spread that salve on the spot twice a day, and it might start to clear up."

Jevam blinks at me. "Really? I never heard of that before."

I shrug. "Like I said, it's gone out of fashion. But pre-Darium history is my specialty."

And when I first arrived at the college, I was particularly interested in every possible cure for potentially healing one's skin.

The man looks down at his wrist and then offers me a smile that's almost shy. "There's a big yimmerbush that grows near my house. I'll have to try that. Thank you."

I find myself smiling back. "I hope it helps."

Jevam pauses and then leans in, his voice dropping. "I don't know how it'd help *you* much. But the client I mentioned—we've been bringing clay to them for a couple of years. Lately it's been twice a week. The crazy thing is, they have us take the wagon to a spot about an hour from here, where there's nothing around, pick up the wagon we brought last time that's empty now, and leave the full one. I have no idea where they take it from there."

A shiver runs down my spine. "That is awfully odd. And the manager agreed to that arrangement?"

He grimaces. "They got some special deal for 'discretion.' That's what I heard, anyway. Apparently the guy who came to negotiate it showed the king's seal, and Nomar felt he had to go along with royal authority."

The shiver deepens into a full body chill. I resist the urge to hug myself, releasing a rough laugh as if I merely find the story amusing.

Someone made the arrangements for these secret, escalating shipments of clay using the king's seal.

Someone among the scourge sorcerers was able to gain enough access to the palace to steal that emblem. And if they could do that... who knows what other havoc they might wreak right within the royal family's home?

THIRTY-FOUR

Ivy

When I slip into the dining hall late in the evening, it's nearly empty, as I was counting on.

I wasn't counting on my employer being one of the few figures lingering around the tables.

As Stavros saunters over to intercept me on my way to the counters, he arches his eyebrow. "Didn't you get your fill during our dinner earlier? I seem to recall you shoveling quite a healthy portion into your mouth."

The dry teasing somehow sets me more off-balance than any other attitude I've gotten from him in recent weeks. I know how to brace myself against his hostility, and I can accept his contrition and his aggressive protectiveness even if I find both a little baffling.

This… This feels like the old Stavros. The banter that started to take on a hint of affection rather than criticism in the last few days before the battle in the All-Giver's Tower exposed my magic.

I don't see how we could ever really go back to the way things were. But hearing the warmth in his drawl makes my pulse flutter no matter how much it shouldn't.

I decide it's safest not to look at his stunningly chiseled face directly. Instead, I focus on the last scattered appetizers from the dinner spread.

"*You're* back here too," I point out as I pluck up a couple of delicate pastries, a spiced egg, and a half-roll topped with frothy cheese. "I don't recall your plate being particularly sparse before you polished off the meal."

"I'm not here to eat. I had a student ask if we could discuss her progress while she had her own late dinner."

Ah, that'd probably be the brawny woman I passed on my way in, who marched out looking like she was ready to conquer an invading army all on her own. I guess Stavros gave her a good pep talk.

I add one more tidbit to my plate. "I'm not going to eat either. These are for something else. I had an idea."

Stavros folds his arms over his chest. "Now I'm intrigued."

I cast my gaze past him to our few other schoolmates who are taking their evening meal late. This isn't the place to discuss my ideas about tackling the scourge sorcerers in any detail.

"I'll fill you in if it gets me anywhere useful," I tell him. "I promise it doesn't involve anything death-defying. Now if you'll excuse me…"

I bob in a curtsey that's purposefully mocking, because we are supposed to be at odds as far as the rest of the school is aware.

Stavros takes the supposed insult in stride. "Just make sure you're not out so late you're groggy for our morning class."

I let sarcasm color my tone. "You have my full dedication."

I hold my head high as I carry the plate through the doorway.

The royal guards are so used to bizarre but innocuous behavior from spoiled nobles that neither of the two stationed by the front gate remarks on my cargo. They don't care where I eat my apparent late-evening snack.

As I head down the road between the college's walls and the Temple of the Crown, I tuck the small plate close to my side under the fall of my cloak. A few worshippers leaving the temple glance at me on my way up the steps, but none of their gazes linger.

What I'm doing isn't against any law or standard of propriety, but it is a little unusual. I'd rather not encourage questions.

The vast inner worship hall still overwhelms me when I step beneath its looming ceiling. I swallow thickly and push myself on toward the base of the central tower, the thick column that extends from the ground floor to high above the rest of the roof.

The tower where I sealed Wendos's fate and in some ways my own as well.

I haven't set foot on the spiral staircase since that evening. Girding myself, I begin the climb.

Julita's presence stirs. *Are you sure this is the best place to reach out to the daimon?*

I shrug. "We know there were some up here when Wendos was orchestrating his plans. And they're divine spirits, right? They probably like hanging out in temples in general—when they're not making mischief elsewhere."

Let's hope they don't decide to hassle you too badly.

"I don't think we need to worry about that." The city's

wandering spirit-creatures haven't disturbed anyone at the college since that night. I doubt they *wanted* to fling around glass during the ball or knock down part of the Quadring—it was the scourge sorcerers imposing their magic on the invisible beings.

But my brief encounter with a couple of them in the woods near the conspirators' bonfire reminded me of how much they might still be affected by the tactics inflicted on them. The scourge sorcerers manipulated them before—and maybe still are in some way we haven't uncovered.

The daimon might be able to reveal things I haven't learned through other means. Anything I can do to bring our investigations and my cozying up to the scourge sorcerers to an end, I'm all for.

I keep climbing until I reach the first slightly wider platform above the level of the roof. Narrow marble pillars frame an alcove with three arched windows. The floor is bare, but lingering traces of wax speak of previous acts of worship.

I set the plate in the middle of the alcove and kneel next to it. No one's sure that daimon ever actually consume the traditional food offerings people leave for them, but I hope they at least appreciate the gesture. This is a finer spread than the scraps of meat and fruit they'd typically receive.

Bowing my head, I extend my senses to check for any trace of magical presence. Nothing catches my attention, but that's not totally unexpected. The spirit-creatures roam all through our world, but I've only noticed traces of their energy when they're particularly riled up.

I inhale slowly, listening hard to confirm there are no human lurkers nearby, and launch into my plea in a low voice.

"Daimon of the city, I offer these delicacies in thanks for the peace you've given us in the past few weeks. I know you were forced to harm us. I'd like to make sure that never happens again. If there's anything you can show me about the people who manipulated you so I can expose them and stop them, I open myself to your help."

Closing my eyes, I will my breath to even out. Will the tension out of my body, as much as I'm capable of it.

If I'm too tightly guarded, who knows if the daimon will be able to convey anything at all?

For the first few minutes, there's only the cooling breeze drifting through the windows and the pang spreading through my knees from my position on the hard floor. Then a quiver of sensation brushes past my arm.

My pulse hiccups, but I hold myself still and calm. The quiver grazes my skin again, tickling over my neck and across my scalp. Another faint impression glides over my hands.

An emotion that isn't my own seeps into my chest: a pang of regret that feels like an apology. Then a tremor passes through my mind, giving me a flash of that high tower room, my fall on the steps, the pressure of the spirits pinning me down.

A lump rises in my throat. "I know it wasn't your idea to hurt me. He was controlling you. Do you know how he managed it? Or what else the people like him were hoping to do? Who else was working with him?"

The memory fractures into a blur of jumbled images that I can't make any sense of. Maybe that's the daimon's way of indicating they've got no answers to my questions.

I settle my nerves as well as I can and give it another shot. "Are they leaving you alone now, or are they still trying to push you around?"

That question results in an immediate jolt of distress. A rush of heat sweeps through me, tightening around my body.

Behind my closed eyelids, I catch a glimpse of billowing

flames. But it's dark inside the fire, so dark and cramped, like my very soul is being squeezed—

The sensations fall away, leaving me gasping. My eyes pop open of their own accord, but I can't make out the daimon in the dimming light around me.

"What was that?" I whisper. "What are they doing to you?"

Either the spirit-creatures can't answer me or they're reluctant to. Or they've fled completely at the signs of an impending interruption.

Voices are carrying up the stairs, along with the distant rasp of footsteps. My heart skips a beat.

I'm not doing anything wrong, but I'd rather not have to answer to a devout—or worse, a cleric. And if it's anyone with ties to the scourge sorcerers, they'll wonder why I of all people would be attempting to appease the daimon.

Not for the first time, I'm grateful for my scrawny frame. I tug the plate off to the side of the alcove where it'll be less noticeable and then tuck myself between the wall and one of the columns. There's just enough room for me to pull all the way back into the shadows beyond the nearest window.

I can't see much other than the alcove now, but there is a narrow gap between the column and the wall that gives me a view of the stairs. I peer through it, waiting to see who's bothering to climb the tower this late in the day.

A member of the Crown's Watch appears first, making me even more grateful that I decided to slip out of view. Then my gaze catches on the ornate silk robes of the figures following him.

There's Hessild, the royal family's lead magical advisor, looking as poised and polished as when I saw her during Sabrellia. Next to her treads the unnervingly lopsided man who's a secondary advisor—Lothar, Stavros said his name is. Along with warning me of the man's hatred of the riven.

The third advisor, Tinom, strides along behind them, a little faster to keep up with his shorter stature.

They're in the middle of a conversation. Lothar sighs as he passes my column. "I simply feel it's questionable to put just as much money and energy into celebrating a woman who isn't even Silanian as we do honoring the godlen."

Hessild tsks her tongue. "Signy is an important figure to the people—a symbol of our freedom from our former conquerors. If we had a hero from Silana who'd made anywhere near as much impact, I'm sure—"

She goes on, but my mind stops processing her words when I see who's following behind the three advisors.

There's no mistaking the chocolate-brown curls or elegant features of the guard who's taken to badgering me. As he passes by, bringing up the rear of the procession, a trace of the magic he always seems to be emitting pricks at my skin.

I go even more still, holding my breath.

The advisors proceed on up the next flight of stairs without a glance into the alcove, still debating the merits of the festival for Signy that's happening in a couple of weeks. The guard pauses at the base of the steps and turns toward the alcove.

I can only see a sliver of his pale face—only one of those unsettlingly bright blue-green eyes—but I can tell he's noted the offering plate. He cocks his head.

His gaze skims the alcove and comes to rest on the shadowy nook where I've tucked myself.

My heart thumps faster. My magic twitches in my chest, eager to thicken the shadows and ensure he doesn't see me.

But does it really matter if he does? Is he going to arrest me for skulking in the tower? There aren't any laws against that.

It's certainly not worth risking whatever magical backlash I'd cause.

His mouth twitches with what might be... a hint of a smile? Before I can decide what to make of that, Tinom calls down to him. "Everything all right, guard?"

The guard whips around and hustles up the steps. "Yes. My apologies for falling behind."

I wait in my hiding spot until I'm sure the tower's other visitors are well out of hearing. Then I ease out and crouch by my offering again.

Any serenity I'd cultivated has scattered with my thoughts. I take a few deep breaths and try to return to my meditative state, but I'm too aware of the possibility that I could be interrupted again.

No more images waver through my mind. No tingles of magic pass over my skin. The daimon might have wandered off anyway.

I leave the plate behind in case they decide they do want a snack, however exactly ephemeral beings who don't have mouths or stomachs would consume noble appetizers, and dart down the steps the way I came. I'd prefer to be gone before the advisors make the same trek.

As I hurry back to the college, I contemplate what the spirit-creatures did convey to me. It seems as if the scourge sorcerers have continued meddling with the daimon, just in some new way that has different effects.

They're being trapped or caged somehow? In a place with fire?

Maybe the conspirators are gathering a whole bunch of them to unleash on the city all at once? If they can control a whole horde simultaneously.

But I have no proof of that or anything else they might be plotting. It's mere speculation based on the vaguest of impressions.

I'm just passing through the college gate, charting my path through the conjured maze to this week's obnoxious phrase—*Leering freaks return for rotted lunch*—when my palm prickles with a burst of warmth. I jerk my hand up and catch the brief message as it glows across my skin.

Welcome to the Order of the Wild. Be ready for the call to your initiation.

THIRTY-FIVE

Ivy

Alek paces the meeting room with uncharacteristic agitation. "We have no idea what they'll throw at you now that you're supposedly one of them. *Anything* could happen at the initiation."

I lean against the side of the broad table. Tension's been coiled tight around my gut since I got the message from the scourge sorcerers a couple of hours ago.

But I still have to say, "That's been the case every time I've answered their summons. It's always been a risk. At least this time, they trust me enough that I might find out what I need to ensure that I *don't* have to go back again."

Casimir has maintained a warm presence at my side, his hand tucked gently around mine, but a thread of uneasiness winds through even his soothing tone. "This is what you've been working up to. But they didn't tell you when the 'call' would come. Do they expect you to run off to the woods at a moment's notice?"

I shrug. "That's how it worked when Benedikt accused

me. They want people who'll be obedient to them above any other duty."

My gaze veers along the empty table. A pang of melancholy resonates through my chest at the thought of the man I believed I could count on as much as the three around me.

The man who was willing to see me dead so he could join the scourge sorcerers' ranks. The man who met a shameful death of his own because I fought back.

The conspiracy is like a poison, tainting everything it touches.

The second Alek pauses in his pacing, Stavros begins his own restless prowl of the room. "We can hope that there'll be a large group of the conspirators together for the initiation. You should signal us with your locket once you're all together —I can lead a squadron of the Crown's Watch to arrest them. We can put an end to this and see you safe all at once."

The determination in his tone sets off a different sort of pang in my heart. He sounds honestly concerned about my well-being.

I still don't know how to wrap my head around his renewed protectiveness.

"The king didn't like that idea when I suggested it to him the other day," I point out. "I'm guessing he'll like it even less now that he wants me to find out who's gotten a hold of his royal seal. And we have no idea if it would even work when the conspirators are guarding their rituals so closely. If I'm the only one being initiated, as soon as a sentry warns of soldiers on their way, the scourge sorcerers will know I'm the one responsible."

And gods only know what they'll do to me then, before any squadron can reach me.

Alek's mouth slants at a miserable angle. "They might find out even before then, depending on how much access the conspirators have to discussions in and around the palace."

Stavros exhales sharply. "If the men King Konram sent to spy on the clay quarry catch the next secret delivery in time—"

"Then maybe it won't matter," I break in. "But we don't know how long that'll take or how soon they'll call me. We have to assume I'm going."

A growl escapes Stavros. He glowers at me, but his expression looks more anguished than angry. "I could follow you on my own. Act as a secondary witness. Be ready to jump in if they threaten you in any way."

My throat constricts. I think he means it. He'd jeopardize the entire plan so that he can act as my personal bodyguard.

Does he feel *that* guilty about how he treated me before? Or… does his interest actually run much deeper than that, the way Casimir suggested?

I don't know what to do with that possibility. It hardly matters when I have no idea how long his current dedication to my safety might last.

I manage to keep my voice nonchalant as I set my hands on my hips. "And how far do you really think you'd get before they noticed you? Maybe you could convince them you were tracking me without my knowledge, but they might not want to take the chance and slaughter us both regardless."

Stavros's hand moves to rest on his sword. "I'd slaughter plenty of them first."

I barely restrain myself from rolling my eyes. "Yes, well, true as that might be, I'd still prefer *not* to get slaughtered in the end, no matter how many of them we'd take down with us."

The former general grimaces, but he knows I have a point.

Casimir lifts his head. "There's another possibility we could revisit. Ivy's already needed to use her magic in unplanned ways to protect herself and win over the scourge sorcerers. It's the greatest weapon she has against them."

My power quivers in my chest, bringing to mind visions of the uses I could put it to. Freezing the conspirators in place so they're helpless while the soldiers ride in. Yanking the details of their plans from their mouths.

I brace myself for Stavros's angry refusal, but he's lapsed into a pensive silence instead. His gaze slides to me. "Perhaps it is time we took that step."

I stare at him. "Are you serious?"

He's claimed that he's come to terms with my riven magic, but I never imagined I'd hear the day when he gave it his overt approval.

The former general grimaces. "It isn't my preferred strategy. But we've run out of those. I think it's clear that we can trust your abilities more than the fiends you'd be inflicting your power on."

Alek speaks up, quiet but emphatic. "And it's going to start hurting you again if you keep denying it when you're in danger, isn't it? They're putting you in worse situations than the students here ever did."

I haven't told him how much my magic has already been punishing me. I wet my lips, grappling with a barrage of conflicting emotions.

"I don't... I don't know what would happen if I let it loose on that large a scale," I admit, my hands clenching. "I don't know if I can count on Kosmel to guide the consequences if my life isn't directly under threat. I *could* cause a total disaster."

Casimir strokes his thumb over the back of my hand. "I'm sure it couldn't be worse than what the scourge sorcerers are planning."

"Who can say?" A ragged laugh escapes me. "I don't even know what'll happen to *me* if I give in to the magic that openly. Somehow the middle of a scourge sorcery initiation doesn't seem like a great time to find out just how easily a riven soul can go insane."

Pointing out the danger I could be putting myself in gives all three of the men pause.

"Maybe not," Alek concedes after a moment. "But you have the option. If the situation becomes dire—if you see an opening you can't pass up—"

I can't picture any circumstances where I'd happily give my magic free rein, but I dip my head in acknowledgment. "I'll keep my locket on me too, in case it does seem worth signaling for help."

"You should carry more knives when you go," Stavros says. "You can justify it by saying you wanted to be prepared for anything—they have asked you to stab people in the past."

Casimir gives my hand a quick squeeze. "I should touch up your false godlen brand regularly."

I touch the spot between my breasts where he reapplied some makeup just a couple of days ago. "It's fine for now, but if I haven't been called on in a couple of days, definitely."

Alek perks up. "And I can find some almreed tea for you to start drinking regularly. I don't know what would directly counteract the drugs they'll use without knowing what those substances are, but almreed has a general anti-toxin effect. It'll at least lessen the effects of anything reactive that you ingest."

Julita sighs. *I'm sorry I don't know what drug Borys and Wendos used. They didn't want to share their actual secret "knowledge" with me.*

That's not her fault. I smile for both her sake and Alek's.

"I'll do my best to avoid the ingesting, but that'd be great to have as a backup plan."

Stavros rakes his hand through his hair. "All right. I'll keep thinking about additional measures. If anything occurs to the rest of you, call us to this room or pass on the message however you can."

Casimir bumps his shoulder softly against mine, but his gaze lingers on the other man. "I'm sure Ivy knows that we're doing everything in our power to protect her."

Something about those words and the look Stavros shoots the courtesan sends a wobble through my pulse.

The former general steps away, his gaze sweeping over the three of us in our closer cluster. "It's settled then. I'll go on ahead in case there's anything you wanted to… discuss in more privacy."

He steps into his cord and wavers out of view in an instant.

Heat blooms in my cheeks. What exactly does he think we're going to do in his absence?

What does he realize we've already done in the past?

Julita's presence squirms at the back of my skull, but both Alek and Casimir clearly remember what I said to them last time. Alek simply takes my other hand. Casimir gives me a quick but tender peck on the cheek.

"We really will do whatever it takes to see you back here safely," Alek says, his bright eyes flashing with resolve. "And if they hurt you… I won't rest until every one of those pricks is dead and buried."

I grip his hand tightly in return and manage to summon a teasing tone. "Bringing out the violent side beneath the straightlaced scholar. I like it."

Casimir gives my knuckles one last caress. "I'd be right there with him. But in the meantime, I'll pray to all the godlen to watch over you while you defend *them* from this menace. Now you should get some rest. We don't know when you'll be called on."

Alek tugs me into a swift hug that wrenches at my heart. "We'll talk more tomorrow," he says firmly.

After they've departed, I lean against the table for a few moments longer. I want to gather my emotions before I have to face Stavros again.

That's all? Julita speaks up in a puzzled tone. *A kiss on the cheek and a hug? You'd think with the danger you're about to charge into, they'd have a little more affection to show.*

A quiver of exasperation runs through my nerves. Now she's complaining that they aren't fawning over me *enough*?

"I told them we should cool off that side of our relationship for now," I say. "It was obviously making you uncomfortable."

Julita hesitates. *I was all right. I never expected—*

I break in before she gives any more of the reassurances I no longer believe anyway. "I know. But you've lost a lot, and I don't want to rub it in your face. I don't want you to feel like you have to hide away in the dark constantly. Having you here matters a lot to me too, in case I haven't made that clear enough. Besides, I've got an awful lot of other things to focus on right now."

I had no idea— Well. If you think that's best.

I notice she doesn't protest all that emphatically. Which is fine. I wasn't waiting for her to talk me out of my decision.

"Let's just get through this initiation, and then we can worry about the rest."

She lets out a strained laugh. *We can only hope it'll be so simple.*

When I step through the ring of cord into Stavros's quarters, I find the former general standing by his chest of prosthetics, removing the wooden hand from his wrist harness. He startles at my arrival and turns to face me as I make my now-habitual circuit of the room.

"I didn't expect you back so soon."

After confirming no conjured vermin are lurking around, I offer him a tight smile. "We'd already said almost everything that needed to be said."

"Ah." The former general hesitates, the set of his broad shoulders looking strangely awkward. "I don't know the specifics of what's developed between the three of you, but I hope that neither of them are concerned about you continuing to share my quarters."

"You've managed not to murder me so far, so I suppose they've decided you're not that great a threat to my continued existence."

Stavros's chuckle sounds awkward too. "I didn't mean as far as that... There aren't many who'd like the idea of their paramour living with another man."

I can't suppress the snort that escapes me. "Oh, they're probably happy about that part. They seem to have gotten it into their heads that I'm going to be the next Signy, and I need a full set."

The words have barely spilled from my lips before I realize that I've said them to the last person I'd have wanted to admit it to.

I snap my mouth shut, my cheeks flaring, and shoot Stavros a pointed glance. "Not that I agree with them or have any designs along those lines."

I won't mention the flicker of heat that washes through my veins when he gazes at me with as much intensity as he is right now.

The corner of his lips curves upward in a hint of his usual cocky grin, the one I haven't seen much of in recent weeks. "Duly noted. I'm glad to hear there aren't any issues of jealousy, in any case."

"Nothing to worry about." I pull myself away from him, my skin still thrumming with unwelcome heat, and head toward the sofa. "I guess we should both get some sleep while we can."

"It has been in rather short supply."

A trace of discomfort in Stavros's voice brings my gaze back to him. He's looking at his bedroom door now, with an expression as if he's dreading climbing under the covers.

A weird sense of guilt knots my stomach. Or maybe not so weird when I know it's nightmares about my possible crimes that have been disturbing his slumber.

After the protection and trust he offered me during our meeting, I can give him a little something in return, can't I?

The suggestion tumbles out before I can think better of it. "I could read some more from our book first. It might help settle my mind too. If you'd like that."

Stavros seems to waver for a moment and then shoots me a self-deprecating smile. "Who would have thought the great General Stavros would need a bedtime story? But thank you —if you aren't terribly tired already, I'd welcome it. Let me undress on my own so I don't offend your modesty. Join me in a few minutes."

As I wait for the rustling from the next room to quiet, I remove my belt and my boots so I'll be able to sit more comfortably while I read.

You shouldn't feel that bad for him after the way he treated you before, Julita says tartly. *He hardly needs coddling.*

"It really might help me sleep better too," I murmur back.

She lets out a skeptical hum.

When Stavros accepts my knock on the bedroom door, I find him sitting up at the far end of the vast bed, leaning against the headboard. The loose short-sleeved undershirt that covers everything but his head, neck, and arms leaves whatever modesty I possess completely unaffected. I do my best not to wonder what he might have on—or not—under the covers tucked around his torso.

As I go to retrieve the book from the table where I left it, the former general clears his throat. "Since it doesn't sound as if it'd cause any issues with Aleksi or Casimir, I was thinking —and you can absolutely say no, not that you've ever had any trouble with that before—I would feel even better if you spent the night in here rather than on the sofa. Simply so I'll know immediately if the scourge sorcerers call you away during the night."

I blink at him. "You want me to sleep in the chair?"

The crooked grin comes back. "I was thinking the bed has rather enough room. We can stick to our own ends without imposing on each other's space at all. I'd imagine it'd be more comfortable for you than the sofa."

My fingers tighten around the book. I know from past experience that his mattress is close to divine—he brought me in here after Esmae nearly murdered me.

But his bed didn't have *him* in it then.

I want to say yes at least as much as I want to say no, and I'm not sure I'd like the reasons why if I looked at them closely.

"Won't that be worse for your nightmares?" I say instead. "Having the monstrous riven sorcerer right there beside you?"

Stavros stares at me for a moment, some of the color leaching from his light brown skin. Then he swipes his hand over his face. "Ivy… You're not the villain in the nightmares I've been having lately. And I'm never quite fast enough to save you. So I'd say having you close at hand would help deflect any bad dreams too."

Julita makes a sound like a sucked in breath. The book wobbles in my hand. I can't find my words.

Even after all his apologies and attempts at amends-making, it never occurred to me that he could fear for my well-being on such a deep level it'd infect his dreams.

In my silence, Stavros makes a dismissive gesture. "It's all right. You clearly don't like the idea. Make full use of my chair for the reading, and—"

"No." My heart is beating very fast, and I'm not totally sure why. I don't know if I want the answer to that either. "A bed definitely beats a sofa. If we both stick to our own sides."

Stavros halts, and a softer smile touches his face. My racing pulse manages to skip a beat as well.

"We stick to our own sides," he says like a promise. "You can sleep on top of the covers if you prefer—or I will. Whatever makes you most comfortable."

I swallow thickly. "I'll stay on top for reading, at least."

Stavros nudges one of the plump pillows closer to my side. I prop it up against the headboard and sit gingerly right at the edge of the bed.

He's far enough away that I'd have to lean over to touch him. This really isn't that big a deal.

Insisting on that to myself, I tug on the ribbon to open the book to our last page and focus on the story. "They thought that was the worst of the journey, of course, until they stumbled on the village in the hidden valley…"

THIRTY-SIX

Ivy

I jolt out of sleep at an unexpected pressure around my waist.

I tense instinctively and realize it isn't just my waist. There's solid warmth all down my back that matches the weight on my side.

Stavros. He's drawn himself against me on the bed and looped his muscular arm around my belly in a loose embrace, his smoky spicy scent wafting over me.

I don't think he's aware of what he's done, though. The soft, slow rasp of his breath behind me tells me *he's* still asleep.

The heat of him courses right through to the center of me. I'm starkly aware that there are only a couple of layers of thin fabric separating our bodies.

How in the realms did we end up like this?

After he drifted off in the middle of the second chapter I was reading, I set the book aside and tried to doze off where

I'd been sitting on top of the covers. But the lacing of my dress felt too constricting.

He has seen me in my chemise and drawers before—including much shabbier ones than what Casimir has supplied for my noble role here at the college. I decided it didn't matter if he happened to see me again and wriggled out of the dress.

But then it was chilly in the open air. And he hadn't stirred from his end of the bed—he'd actually rolled away from me.

I thought it'd be safe enough to tuck myself under the covers at my end. It did help me get to sleep.

Until now.

Julita lets out a faint chuckle. *So much for sticking to his side. He's more interested in sticking to* yours. *Who would have known Stav is a cuddler when he's asleep?*

I can't tell whether she's annoyed as well as amused. I drop my voice to a whisper. "I definitely didn't. This isn't what I agreed to."

Hmm. You did put all those ideas about Signy and her lovers in his head.

She's definitely teasing me. I guess that's better than bitterness?

I grimace. "I didn't mean to say that. And I told him it wasn't my idea."

It seems he had ideas of his own.

A lump rises in my throat as I sort through my groggy thoughts. He *is* asleep—he's never shared a bed with me before.

"I doubt this has anything to do with me anyway," I mumble. "He must be used to sleeping with someone else."

How many lovers has the exalted general taken in his time? How many stuck around long enough for him to develop any kind of bedroom habits with them?

Those questions shouldn't stir a twinge of jealousy deep in my gut.

"What should I do?" I murmur to Julita.

I get the impression of her presence shrugging. *He made the move. I can't imagine it'll be easy to detach him unless you want to rouse him. It might be more fun to let him wake up on his own and become horrifyingly embarrassed, if you don't find his nearness too distasteful.*

I don't find it distasteful at all. My body is tingling with eager exhilaration.

Which might be a problem in itself.

But I'm too tired to worry about that right now. Why not enjoy the protective warmth, even if it's not entirely meant for me?

My ghostly passenger isn't wrong. It will be pretty satisfying to see how Stavros reacts when he realizes he snuggled up to me. I'll be able to hold it over his head for *years*.

The thought gives me a strange sense of contentment. I press my head deeper into the pillow and close my eyes, willing the giddiness of my pulse to slow.

If his body is looking to cuddle, I can at least assume he isn't having any nightmares. And maybe the show of supposed affection will convince my mind for one night that he isn't any kind of threat either.

I'm just starting to drift off again when Stavros shifts his position against me. His hand slides down... and dips right between my legs.

Oh! Julita exclaims alongside the spike of arousal that shoots up from my core.

In an instant, my sex is aching, my breath catching in my lungs. A gasp stutters out of me.

And Stavros wakes up.

I feel it in the hitch of his chest and the tensing of his

muscles against my body. His words come out in a hasty mumble as he yanks his hand away. "Ivy—I didn't —Gods—"

He's started to pull away from me when his frame freezes up even more. A husky note enters his hazy voice. "You're wet for me."

I'm pretty sure my drawers are outright drenched from his unconscious groping. The evidence of my arousal must have lingered on his hand.

I should say something to break the moment, but need is still humming through my body. My lips part, and all that comes out is a whimper that sounds like a plea.

"Fuck," Stavros mutters, so raw a heady shiver ripples through me.

He shifts toward me again, setting his hand on my hip like a question.

This is absurd. I shouldn't want this.

But the only thing I'm certain of in my sleepy haze is how much I do.

My head tips back encouragingly as if of its own accord. My hips give a slight rock, guiding his hand forward.

Another guttural curse spills from Stavros's mouth, his breath hot on my hair. Then his fingers slide back to the place where I craved them most.

I bite my lip but can't quite restrain a moan. Stavros echoes the sound with a ragged breath and ducks his head to brand his mouth against the crook of my neck.

He strokes his hand between my legs, setting off pulse after pulse of pleasure. I open my thighs a little wider to give him more access, and he makes a strangled sound.

"That's right. Want to make you come apart for me. Gods, I want to feel all of you."

He releases me to a whine of protest that I haven't finished before he's delving his hand right beneath my drawers. The caress of his fingers against my most sensitive skin brings another gasp to my lips.

Stavros molds his body against me as he has his way with my sex. His forefinger circles my clit in a spiral of blissful sparks and dips lower to explore my soaked opening. When he curls it right inside me, I shudder with a swell of delight.

Even through the daze of mingled fatigue and pleasure, I notice the bulge nudging against my lower ass. If the strain in his voice and the eagerness of his touch weren't enough to convince me, that'd be plenty of proof of how affected my unintended lover is.

I can't let him keep all the control here, can I? I'm not going to be selfish.

As my hips sway with the rhythm of his hand, I reach behind me. At the graze of my fingers, Stavros growls.

The rocking of his hand speeds up. A second strong finger dips between my folds, parting them, stretching me in just the right way.

As the heel of his hand starts to rub against my clit to giddying effect, I drag my fingers up and down his rigid cock through his drawers. Gods smite me, there's a lot of him.

I guess I shouldn't be surprised if that part of him is as massive as the rest.

Stavros buries his face in my hair, his urgent breaths tickling over my scalp. I'm too lost in the pleasure to figure out where the waistband of his drawers are, but I curl my fingers around his length as well as I can amid the fabric to pump him properly.

With a groan, he bucks into my grasp in time with his pulsing hand. The wave of pleasure is building inside me, already fogging my vision.

Even as I press into his touch, desperate for the release I can taste, I'm determined to bring him with me. I grip him tighter, work my hand faster, reveling in the broken panting that shows he's as lost in the moment as I am.

Stavros plunges his fingers even deeper into me with a graze of my clit, and a dam inside seems to burst.

I come with a rough cry and a clench of my sex around him, the final surge of ecstasy searing through my body. But even as my muscles shake with my release, I manage to pump him harder in turn.

Stavros groans again, how much because of my climax and how much my touch, I don't know. Either way, his hips jerk behind me.

In an instant, his drawers are as damp as mine, the hot spurt of his release soaking through to my wrist.

He withdraws his hand slowly to rest it on my belly, and mine drifts back to my thigh. As our breaths even out and the final shivers of bliss dissipate, a sheen of ice creeps through my chest.

How much did he really want this intimacy with *me*, rather than whatever woman his bleary mind imagined in his sleep?

Will he think I prompted the interlude somehow? Lured him in with my riven wiles?

What if this is the moment that tips him back over the edge to reviling me?

I hate the ache that lances through me at the thought.

I tug myself away over the short remaining space to the very edge of the mattress and flip around to face him. "This wasn't— I didn't mean for this to happen."

Stavros peers back at me, his damaged eyes unfocused in a way he doesn't usually allow them to appear when he's fully alert. He knits his brow. "Of course you didn't. You barely even wanted to sleep in the bed."

The tension keeps constricting around my ribs like a vise. My swallow brings back an echo of the burn of the rope around my throat. "I stayed on my side. I didn't even realize you'd moved until you were already right there."

He frowns and seems to stir himself into greater wakefulness. "I'm not upset. That was—" His head twitches to sharpen his vision. "Curse it all, Ivy, don't look at me like that."

My hands ball between us. "Like what?"

"Like you're fucking terrified of me."

My mouth opens and closes again. I stare back at him, and the only honest thing I can say spills out. "What if I *am* scared of you?"

I don't think I'm imagining the pain that flickers through Stavros's expression. He shifts his hand toward me but stops before it touches my face, maybe noting the stiffening of my posture.

"I've told you how sorry I am," he says hoarsely. "I swear I don't see you as a threat anymore. Gods above, I trust you... as much as I trust anyone in this place."

And there it is. My lungs constrict so tightly I can barely breathe.

I push myself into a sitting position, every part of me braced to run. "But you don't trust me completely. Or you wouldn't feel like you needed to qualify that statement."

Stavros gives a ragged laugh. "This is how I was trained. I don't trust anyone completely—not even myself. It doesn't matter."

The bottom of my stomach has dropped out. I scramble right off the bed, snatching at my discarded dress.

"Of course it fucking does," I retort. "You can laugh about it, because it doesn't matter to *you*. But what it means to me is you could change your mind back again at any moment, after any mistake, and I'd find myself with a noose around my neck after all."

"Ivy." Stavros jerks upright in my wake, but I'm already darting past the bedroom door.

I haul my gown down over me as hastily as I can and toss my cloak over the undone laces. Grabbing my boots, I tuck them under my arm with my balled underskirt.

Every motion, every brush of my drawers against my sensitized parts, reminds me of what an idiot I was just a few moments ago.

With a thump of the covers, Stavros's footsteps barge after me. "Ivy, you have to listen to me—"

No. Listening to him is how I ended up in his bed to begin with.

I bolt for the door and flee down the hall with my cloak flapping around me.

THIRTY-SEVEN

Ivy

From the bathing room I ducked into, I hear the creak of Stavros's footsteps stalking by down the hall. He doesn't know where I've gone, though.

I assume he stopped to pull on trousers before he rushed out of his quarters after me, and that gave me a decent head start.

He's not so indiscreet as to bellow my name and wake half the school's staff. After several minutes, the footsteps retrace their path.

I catch a rasp of a frustrated exhalation. The distant thump of a door closing.

Then there's only silence.

I can't quite rouse myself into action until the palace bell peals through the night—just one ring. Stavros and I turned in pretty early, but I've barely gotten any sleep.

Oh, well. That's typical these days. I'm sure as shit not going back to Stavros's quarters tonight, not even to take the sofa.

I don't love the idea of hiding in the bathing room all night either, though. Everything around me is hard and cold. But I'll need to be properly dressed before I venture farther.

As I set down my boots and straighten out the loose pants of my underskirt, I drop my voice to the faintest murmur. "Quite the mess I've gotten into now."

Julita's voice doesn't lift with a wry remark. It occurs to me that her presence has dwindled to only the slightest tingle in the back of my head.

Of course. She's always been uncomfortable witnessing any sexual intimacy between me and the men she once considered hers.

I can't restrain a wince at the thought. I told her I was cooling things off on her behalf, and then I went and did the exact opposite just hours later.

She probably pulled back into the blankness beyond my awareness as soon as she saw that I wasn't going to reject Stavros's attentions. Maybe as soon as she realized he was offering them at all, consciously or not.

I'm entirely alone.

The knowledge weighs on me as I shimmy the underskirt on over my legs and then reach behind me to tighten the laces of my gown.

I can't go back to Stavros, not after what just happened between us. I can't reach out to Alek or Casimir—even if it wouldn't put them in danger for me to openly seek them out, I wouldn't know where to find them beyond the general area of the dorms.

I couldn't even signal them to a meeting room. I left my locket behind in the pouch of my belt.

As I slip on my boots, I find I'm missing a different sort of weight. I removed my thigh sheaths with their knives when I was stripping down for sleep a few hours ago and didn't manage to catch them up in my hasty grab for my discarded clothes. They're lying on the floor in Stavros's bedroom right now, no doubt.

I have my favorite blade in my left boot, and that's all.

It's served me well enough on its own plenty of times. But remembering that doesn't stop a sense of gloom from washing over me.

I straighten up, fastening my cloak around my neck, and attempt to take stock. My assessment only leaves me more depressed.

I let desire get to my head and all but fucked a man who wanted to see me hung just a week or two ago. I drove away the one person who's been by my side more than anyone through this entire ordeal—not that Julita's had a whole lot of choice in the matter.

And now I'm adrift in this college where I don't even belong, with nowhere to sleep, nothing to do, and no one to turn to while the most dangerous part of my association with the scourge sorcerers looms on the horizon.

Blast it all from sea to sky.

I hug myself against the tightening of my chest, and my mind latches on to the possibility that there is still one figure left I could appeal to. The one who insisted I stick on this path.

Girding myself, I ease out into the hall.

The Domi's common areas are dim, the sconces put out. The streaks of moonlight through the windows at either end of the hall offer just enough illumination for me to find my way to the stairwell and out into the courtyard.

I pull my cloak's hood up over my head, but as usual, the guards don't raise any concerns about my leaving the security of the college. I guess it only really matters whether the people coming *in* have the right to.

The streets of the inner wards are nearly as quiet as the campus, although voices filter from a pub at the far end of the large square outside the temple. The temple's lanterns are still burning, of course, welcoming worshippers through the broad doorway at all hours.

The huge worship room feels even vaster draped in the dense shadows of the night. I halt on the threshold, momentarily overwhelmed.

I've approached Kosmel's statue enough times that I could head straight toward it blindfolded. But my gaze catches for a moment on the voluptuous marble form of Ardone at the other side of the domed room, her perfectly proportioned body poised in a come-hither stance, her full lips curled in a seductive smile.

Maybe I should be asking the godlen of love and sensuality for advice this time.

The thought has barely passed through my mind when I'd swear the statue winks at me.

My pulse hitches. I stare at Ardone's beautiful carved face, but none of her features shift again in the shadows.

It could have been a trick of the light. Or it could be one of those subtle ways the gods like to communicate with us.

I'm not sure which I'd prefer.

I tear my gaze away and stride over to Kosmel's cloaked form. The lanterns' glow turns the trickster godlen's smirk crueler than it's appeared before.

Kneeling by the base of his statue, I bow my head. I pitch my voice as low as when I spoke to Julita, wary of any devouts or fellow worshippers who might be lurking beyond my view.

"I'm tumbling even deeper into this insane game. I'd like to make it back out again. If there's anything you can tell me or show me that will help me through, I welcome it."

I try to open my mind to whatever his divine presence might want to bestow on me, though my gut stays knotted.

My muscles brace in anticipation of a message I won't actually welcome all that much.

Nothing comes. The temple remains silent.

The tension in my belly creeps to the base of my throat. The memory rises up of the reassuring touch I thought I felt when I prayed to Kosmel in the cave in the woods, and sudden tears prick at the backs of my eyes.

Have I somehow strayed too far from what he wanted from me, and now he's cast me aside?

I shove down my emotions and reach for one of the dice scattered around his marble feet. A simple yes or no answer. Surely he'll grant me at least that much.

I ask my question only in my head. *Should I keep playing along with the scourge sorcerers?*

The die rattles from my fingers. It bounces across the platform... and comes to rest against the side of Kosmel's boot, tilted at an angle so both the five and the six face equally upward.

I stare at the die for a few thumps of my heart. It doesn't budge.

A rough guffaw travels up my throat.

He might as well have said, "Fuck off, little rogue. You've got to figure this part out on your own."

I push back to my feet, uncertain of my destination. At the same moment, a prickling sensation spreads across my palm.

Oh, no.

I have to look. I have to watch the three letters gleam against my skin in the instant before they fade away.

Now.

I've gotten the call to my initiation.

THIRTY-EIGHT

Ivy

The message didn't say where to find my supposed co-conspirators, but I've only ever met up with them in one spot. They must figure if I can't work out where to go at this point, I'm not worth initiating after all.

I hustle the last short distance to the campus woods with all the stealth I can bring to bear. My magic unfurls in my chest, niggling at my nerves. Not demanding release yet, but testing me, stirred up by my apprehension.

Julita's presence is still faint. I don't know what the godlen who's pushed me this far wants from me next. None of my allies in the college have any idea I've been called on.

I don't even have the extra knives I meant to bring along for this event.

But the *Now* that glowed on my palm didn't offer any room for argument. I assume they're giving me a little grace so that I can get to the meeting spot from wherever I was before, but not much.

They could be watching me already, taking note of any diversions.

So I stride straight down the path between the trees, fighting the urge to shiver as the cool shadows swallow me.

It's windier than usual today. The gusts of breeze whip my cloak to one side and then the other, whirling through the panels of my skirt. The leaves hiss overhead.

Either the male student who joined me last time didn't make the cut or the conspirators have whisked him away from someplace else. I come to a stop fifty paces in alone. Immediately, one of the shrouded scourge sorcerers steps from the depths of the forest to receive me.

The figure doesn't speak, only beckons me to follow. I catch a faint rustling behind me that might be another conspirator bringing up the rear. Making sure *I'm* not being followed?

But no one has any idea I've been summoned. Even if one of my men was going to ignore my protests and try to watch over me, they never had the chance.

We pass through the back wall again and traverse the river on the concealed boat, the second shrouded conspirator joining us there. Like last time, my guides lead me to a cart, though only one other person is waiting—the teenaged girl who was part of our expedition last time.

As the horses set off, she studies me with wary eyes. Our escorts still haven't spoken to us.

It seems wisest not to break the silence. I'm not sure what I'd say anyway.

At least no one's pressed a cup of mind-addling drugs into our hands.

I close my eyes as if to get some more rest, which honestly I could use. But instead, I do my best to chart every shift in direction, every slight sound that reaches my ears from beyond the cart.

As far as I can determine, we're heading on a northeasterly course from Florian. As we leave the city farther behind, the cart veers more to the east, and the driver taps the horses to a faster pace.

The cart jostles, my tailbone jarring against the boards. Would it kill these people to give their newest recruits a cushion or two?

We must travel longer than last time. We're still moving when I pick up the second-hour peal of a bell from some distant temple, and we keep going for long enough after that I start listening for the set of three peals.

The cart slows. One of the scourge sorcerers ducks into the covered part of the cart with us, carrying a lumpy bundle.

"Put these on," he says, handing part of the bundle to each of us. "You'll become part of the Order of the Wild by tapping into your most primal self. Welcome to the salvation of Silana."

These murderous assholes do think highly of themselves, don't they?

I restrain a derisive snort and paw through the objects I've been given. There's a black cloak, thinner but longer than my own, folded around a simple clay mask designed to cover the upper half of my face.

A quiver of magic radiates off the mask into my soul. It's been enchanted in some way.

The consequences of refusing to put it on are almost certainly worse than the consequences of wearing it, though.

I ease the mask over my eyes and fasten it in place with the two ribbons that wind around the back. Then I swap my brown cloak for the black one.

The billowing wool fastens down the front with a series of clasps, covering my clothing completely. I pull up the hood instinctively.

The girl across from me has donned her own costume of

sorts. I can't see any magical effects from the mask on her. Perhaps the vibe I got had to do with how the clay was sculpted rather than any continuing impact it might have on the wearer.

The cart continues on for several minutes longer, until I do pick up the bell for the third hour. Moments later, the wheels jar to a stop under us.

I hear the fire before I see it. We step out from under the cart's covering to see an enormous bonfire crackling only twenty paces away.

It wafts not just heat but prickles of magic as well. The conspirators are probably using their sorcery to conceal the light. I can't even imagine how much power that's taking.

Power they mostly stole from their sacrificial accomplices. Are some of them here too? How soon will they reveal that horrifying part of their practices to the new members?

A softer tingling of magic flows down over my body. I tense instinctively, just as the girl next to me lets out a gasp.

When I spin toward her, her form has changed, and not merely because of the eerie, wavering light from the bonfire. Her mask appears to have stretched and morphed, covering her whole face and jutting up above her forehead with the pointed ears, mottled fur, and yellow eyes of a wild cat.

She's staring at me with as much shock as I feel. I touch my face, but can't feel anything strange about my skin. My mask is still where it was before.

Oh. Her mask won't have changed either. Her new "face" must be an illusion, triggered by our arrival.

More cat-like features sprout from her cloak—furry stripes and a sinewy tail, a flash of claws when she reaches her hand from between the folds. A little of the light shines through those surfaces, confirming that they're illusionary rather than solid.

What creature have the scourge sorcerers concealed me as?

My skin itches at the idea that their magic is all over me. But our guides usher us forward, and I push myself toward the fire.

Now that my vision has adjusted to the blaze, I take stock of the ring of figures around the fire. Some twenty figures are waiting for us, all dressed in the same black cloaks we are, their faces obscured with images of wolves and bears, owls and falcons.

Tapping into our inner wildness. That's what the conspirators told us in the cart.

Which means I still can't see any of my new colleagues. How long are they going to keep us new recruits in the dark about who we're actually working with?

Where have all of these people come from? There are far more than can be just from the bug club. How many are past students, how many other followers Torstem drew in from across the city—and who knows where else?

I have no way of knowing when I can't see their faces.

When I glance at our escorts again, they've drawn back the lower part of their shrouds' hoods to fix their own masks in place. One appears to be a stoat, while the other looks like a snake.

It takes all my self-control not to shudder.

"Join us!" The call goes up from the figures already around the fire, first from one and then echoed by a dozen other voices. We hustle over to fill the space that opens in the ring.

The fire's heat crackles against my face through the illusion. Sweat trickles down my back beneath my gown.

A particularly imposing form whose illusion makes him look like a hawk steps closer to the fire and walks along the inside of our ring of bodies. He holds up a large clay carafe.

They might be casting illusions on our faces, but they aren't bothering to disguise voices any longer. I recognize Ster. Torstem's authoritative tone the instant the first word leaves his mouth.

"Greetings to the newcomers and those already initiated! Tonight the Order of the Wild joins together in our worship of the gods and the old ways that have been forgotten. We'll tap into the essence of who we are and what the world should be. Let us Wildings drink to that!"

He stops by my companion from the cart first and taps her chin. The girl tips her head back, farther at his second nudge, her lips parting.

Torstem holds her chin in place as he pours a dollop of the liquid in the carafe down her throat. My stomach twists, watching.

She has no choice but to swallow. Even through the illusion, the bob of her throat is visible. And Torstem doesn't release her until it happens.

He turns to me next. My magic flares between my ribs, urging me to propel him away, to knock the whole lot of them down.

Would it be enough to destroy this group? Is everyone important here? Could I put an end of the conspiracy just like that?

Even if I could, what would happen after? I don't know where I am, don't know what's nearby, and have no way of communicating with anyone who'd care.

Maybe it shouldn't matter, but images from the stories of evil riven who slaughtered entire villages flash through my mind. I balk, and Ster. Torstem's hand comes to rest against my jaw.

My head tilts automatically, away from his touch. I force myself to open my mouth.

If I can manage to swallow only a little and spit out the rest after…

But the sour liquid sloshes into my mouth so forcefully it's either swallow or choke. I gulp, half gagging, and an unsettling lightness sweeps through my body before the stuff has even hit my gut.

The law professor pats my shoulder approvingly and lets me go. I clamp my mouth against the urge to vomit.

If I did, I suspect he'd come back to insist on another dose.

As he prowls on around the circle, distributing the drugged drink to disciple after disciple, my head spins. The figures around me expand and distort, like monstrous versions of the animals they're hiding behind.

They are monsters. All of them. If I'm going to be a monster, wouldn't slaughtering the lot of them be the most honorable kind of viciousness I could carry out?

Kosmel, I think, as loud as I can. *What do you want me to do? I can't unleash that kind of power without you guiding the backlash. I don't know what other disaster I might set off.*

Killing one man years ago left all the gardens in the surrounding neighborhood decimated by the explosion of insects. What would happen if I killed twenty?

How would I explain the end result to King Konram? I'd have gone against his orders. I haven't discovered who infiltrated the palace's defenses or how yet.

No answer feels right.

My stomach turns, and not just because of the toxins working their way through it. My body sways forward and back like a sapling in the wind.

The godlen of luck remains silent. He's left me to take my chances on my own.

Torstem finishes his circle and tosses the clay vessel into the fire. He lifts his arms, turning to take us all in with the fire warbling at his back. "The Order of the Wild remembers the wildness of our past! We will live as humans were meant to be!"

The other figures around the ring raise their hands too. "We will be wild!"

I realize us newbies are supposed to join in too. There are a couple of others who hesitated farther around the ring.

On the second iteration, we all lift our fists and our voices alongside the others. "We will be wild!"

Torstem strides around the ring at a faster pace, urgency creeping into his voice. "We will throw off the taint left by the empire and the usurpers who thought to rise up in their place!"

"We will!" the rest of us echo, though my heart skips a beat. The usurpers?

He leaves no doubt that he's talking about the current royal family with his next statement. "The Melchioreks barged in when the country was unsettled and tried to make it their own. But we know their way is not how it's meant to be. We'll destroy them all and let the gods decide the rightful rulers of our country as they once did!"

I force myself to join the shout, even though my nausea has returned. "We will!"

"We'll hold trials to find the ones who are worthy, and never let the crown pass to anyone unproven!"

"We will!"

The whole world is blurring around me, but even through the muddle in my head, I remember Alek telling me about this sort of thing. How before the Darium invasion, there'd been kingship trials to determine who would inherit the throne.

He wasn't upset that the trials had stopped. He said they were barbaric, that people who would have been great rulers ended up injured or dead.

Of course, the Order of the Wild seems to be all for barbarism.

"We'll bring back all the old laws that were forgotten. We'll honor *our* gods, *our* people. We'll celebrate life by truly living, in all its chaos and savagery!"

"We will!"

Is that what all this fuss is really about? They think Silana was better centuries ago, before the Darium Empire's meddling and everything that's followed?

A laugh I can't totally explain slips out of me. It doesn't matter—others are laughing around the circle too, joyfully. So pleased with throwing away five hundred years that I don't think can all be bad.

But then, what has the stinking royal family done for me that's all that good? It's because of the king I'm here in the middle of this madness. I didn't *want* to be.

What am I supposed to make of anything?

My head reels, and my feet stumble under me. Someone strikes up a tune on a fiddle—a dissonant, jerky melody that only jumbles my thoughts more.

Most of the scourge sorcerers start to move with the sound, curling their fingers and arching their backs, scratching at the air and leaping like the wild things they believe they are.

I find myself joining the strange dance alongside them. My body wants to reach for something beyond this place— something to steady me, something to hold me down. But there's nothing but the chaos Ster. Torstem talked about.

We stomp and spring around the fire, my senses getting dizzier with each step. I grope for my convictions, for the solid sense of why I'm here at all.

I need to identify the conspirators. I need to find out exactly what they mean to do.

At the first thought, my power is already leaping forward

in time with the mad dance. My heart lurches, and I snatch after my magic with all my self-control—

But I don't have much left.

My riven power slips through my jumbled thoughts and flings itself at the problem I've identified. The figure just ahead of me staggers to the side.

He clutches at his face, too late. The mask and the illusion attached to it wrench away, revealing Olari's boxy features, taut with a mix of drugged haze and sudden panic.

A surge of triumph rushes through my own panic to contain my magic. I figured he was a part of the conspiracy, but now I know for sure. I can tell King Konram. I—

Across the fire, someone shrieks. I heave myself forward in time to see another of the scourge sorcerers hunching over.

She's clawing at her face—at the mask that seems to have melted down over her nose. It's clogging her mouth. Only a whistle of breath escapes her.

I spin around. No, I have to stop it.

They'll see the connections—they'll realize I'm riven—

A few paces down the ring behind me, another mask rips upward. I recognize the dark eyes and heavy brow of a women I've seen bringing out food in the dining hall.

Over by the carts, one of the horses squeals in pain. A gasp escapes my lips.

What have I done to the animal? Is its harness digging deeper into its flesh?

No, no, I can't let this happen. Startled murmurs are breaking out all around me, along with hysterical laughter from those too far gone to be afraid.

The horse cries out again.

I pitch myself to the side, farther away from the fire, and crouch down with my hands pressed over my mask as if I'm afraid I'll lose it too. As if I have no idea what's happening.

With my eyes pressed tightly shut, I drag my magic back

to me. I need to contain it. I need to make sure it doesn't rampage any farther.

I have to shut it away before it gets *me* killed.

My power jerks against my unsteady hold. It could do so much more. It could topple them all to the ground. It could fling them into the fire.

No, I scream at it inside my head. All that'll mean is more chaos. More damage I can't control.

There's a shattering sound—I think the breaking of one of the warped masks. A tendril of my magic escapes me and flits into the fire, sending a flame lashing out at the scattered ring.

More shrieks. I scuttle farther away with my hands tangling in the grass.

Ster. Torstem's voice rises over the furor. "The gods act in unusual ways! They want us to prove we're worthy. Perhaps there's one among us who isn't. Stand and present yourselves."

Fuck. I don't know if I even *can* stand up straight without falling right over again. I'm shaking with the effort to contain the rest of my power. My head feels like it's been tipped upside down and kicked across a field for good measure.

Footsteps rustle through the grass toward me. Can I even trust what words will spill out of my mouth in my muddled state?

In the midst of all the terror and anguish, a clear voice breaks through my whirling thoughts from within them.

Ivy? What's going on?

I can't tell Julita—I can't speak to her without them all hearing.

I lift my head, attempting to push myself to my feet, and lose my balance. Instead, I topple back on my ass.

Torstem is stalking toward me, the hawk illusion draped

over his face and feathering his cloak looking even more ominous than it did before.

I swipe at my mouth where a hint of the sour flavor lingers, the most answer I can offer my ghostly passenger who's finally returned. "Hard to... hard to keep everything under control," I mumble as if to myself.

Julita must be able to sense enough to figure out the gist of the situation. She speaks quickly but firmly. *Okay. We can get through this. I had ways of staying centered when Borys and Wendos would drag me into their rituals... Press your hands and your feet flat against the ground.*

I follow her instructions automatically, adjusting my legs so the soles of my boots brace fully against the earth, leaning my splayed hands against the grass on either side of me.

Focus on all that stability, Julita goes on. *Imagine you have roots growing all the way down into the soil, anchoring you there. Deeper than any drug they could have fed you.*

With every word, the image she's giving me solidifies. I drag air in and out of my lungs and feel those roots as if they've literally sprouted from my palms and heels.

For good measure, I imagine branches unfurling inside me too, weaving into a box to hold my power in.

"The professor's assistant, isn't it?" Torstem says, coming to a stop in front of me. "You look as though you aren't doing all that well."

My attempt at anchoring myself helps me fend off the dizziness. "I think perhaps I drank a little too much wildness," I say, managing to keep up my noble diction, and let out a laugh I hope sounds more breezy than hysterical. "I'm a bit of a lightweight."

He holds out his hand. "Let me help you up."

He's the greatest threat here. He's the one who's orchestrated all the pain and violence.

My magic sears at the imaginary bars of its cage, burning

through my veins with a sting so sharp I force another guffaw to cover a gasp. As I lift my hand to take Torstem's, my power flails madly with the desire to blast at least him apart.

Julita lets out an urgent noise. *Your feet are still grounded. Your skin is so thick, no cut you take could ever really penetrate you. Everything important is yours to keep.*

An ache fills my throat. The sentiment she's expressed would have had a much more literal meaning when her brother and his best friend were carving her open to spill her blood in their amateur sacrifices.

As the law professor pulls me to my feet, I will my skin to turn to armor, like the thickest bark in existence. I smile brightly and harden the rest of me.

My magic batters against the new walls I've created, but it doesn't find any cracks this time.

There are other ways I can defeat this man. More important things I need from him than his death.

"Thank you," I say, and turn my face toward the bonfire as if reveling in the heat. "Things seemed to get rather insane for a moment. Why were the gods angry?"

Torstem smiles back with a curl at the corner of his illusionary hawkish beak. "I don't think they were—they were only ensuring we stood our ground. All's well again. There's nothing to be scared of here. The wildness guides us, and the gods are on our side."

I feel his gaze studying me, but I've given no reason for him to suspect I had anything to do with the supernatural disturbances. The only good thing about the reputation of the riven is no one expects to meet one who seems perfectly normal.

I lift my hands to the fire. "How soon do we really begin? How will we get our true kings?"

"Eager to see the change? I like that." He turns toward the fire as well, releasing my hand. "You shouldn't have to wait long. We've been gathering our forces. Within a few weeks' time, we'll be able to cut straight through to the royal family. Everything will fall with them."

I tense my neck to stop my head from jerking around in surprise.

A few *weeks*, and the king could be dead?

"That's good," I coo, the drug slurring my speech without my trying. "So good. Where do we cut King Konram down?"

Torstem lets out a low chuckle. "Don't worry about it. We'll build our connection to the old ways until then. When the time is right, we'll have all the power we need to strike."

THIRTY-NINE

Ivy

I have the vague idea that I can grab my cord and my locket without rousing Stavros, leap off to the palace meeting room, and summon the others so maybe I'll have company before I have to face the former general again.

No such luck. I shoulder open the door to find him standing by the sofa in the thin dawn light that's seeping past the curtains.

His stance stiffens at the sight of me. "Ivy—"

"There isn't time," I blurt out, at least as panicked about the thought of having to discuss what we did earlier tonight as about what I've learned from the scourge sorcerers. I snatch my cord from the drawer and brandish it toward him. "We need to talk to the mirror."

I haven't had a chance to make sure there's no conjured creature lurking around this room, so I'm not going to mention the king outright.

Stavros can clearly tell what I mean. He tenses even more, his eyes flashing. "What happened? You're swaying."

I am. I grasp the shelf beside me, steadying myself as well as I can, and toss my cord on the floor. It takes a few jerks before I can get it in a full circle. "I'm fine. Just go."

I hop through the makeshift portal before he can argue.

What exactly happened between the two of you? Julita murmurs, sounding as though she isn't sure she wants to know.

"Nothing I feel like discussing," I mutter as I wobble into the meeting room.

In the seconds it takes the former general to set up his own means of supernatural transportation, I conduct my usual survey of the space. No quivers of magic penetrate my lingering dizziness.

The scourge sorcerers don't even know this room exists. We should be safe.

My heart keeps thudding. I slump into one of the chairs so the room will spin less.

Stavros emerges a few paces away, already gripping his locket. As he presses the inside to signal the others, he looks me over with a grim expression and a twitch of his head.

"You got the summons for the initiation," he says. "They drugged you again. You need to rest."

I shake my head and grip the arms of the chair harder against the vertigo the motion provokes. "This is important. The royal family has to start preparing right away, for everything. For anything."

I'm babbling like before. I shut my eyes and focus hard on the set of my feet against the floor, the arms of the chair in my hands.

Julita's presence shifts inside me. *I'm sure the Melchioreks will be all right for another hour or two. You need to look after yourself, Ivy.*

That's what I'm doing, as much as I can justify.

The grounding makes me a little more coherent. "I'll

explain to you and the others, and you can explain to the king. In a way that's more organized. I'm sure I can get it all out."

Stavros mutters something under his breath, but he isn't going to jeopardize the king's safety just so I can take a nap.

The second Casimir steps from his own cord, Stavros whirls toward him. "The courtesans must know all kinds of hangover cures. What can you mix for Ivy quickly that'll help take the edge off any kind of intoxication?"

Casimir's gaze flicks to me with a widening of his eyes.

"I'm *fine*," I insist. "Just... just hazy. Fucking sorcerers."

The courtesan turns back to Stavros. "I can grab a couple of things that might help. Give me a few minutes."

He vanishes, and now I'm alone with the last person I wanted to see again.

Stavros's jaw works. "Ivy, about—"

To my immense relief, Alek springs into the room before the former general can do more than start that sentence. "Did the initiation happen already? Ivy, are you all right?"

"Fine, fine," I mumble, but affection swells in my heart at his concern.

I am okay now, aren't I? I'm back with the few people in this world who care about what happens to me.

And maybe I can stay here. King Konram will have to take action after he hears what Ster. Torstem said, won't he?

No more playing scourge sorcerer. No more gritting my teeth and forcing myself through trials and celebrations I find equally awful.

Although, what will I do with myself after that? It's not as if there'll be any reason for me to stay on as Stavros's supposed assistant once our investigations have concluded.

I guess I'll go back to my old haunts... The king implied he'd give me a reward, which'll mean I can distribute even more silver than usual to the people of Florian who need it most…

"Ivy," Alek says from right beside me, and I give a little start. I got so wrapped up in my wandering thoughts that I hadn't noticed him approaching me.

The scholar sets his hand on my arm, and I smile up at him with a sudden tightness in my throat. *He* can't follow me to the streets. Does everything we've shared end here too?

I don't want it to.

The scholar peers down at me with his piercing gaze. "You look upset. What did they do to you?"

A ragged laugh slips from my mouth. "Not much. Shitty refreshments. Clay masks."

Stavros speaks up from farther down the table, where he's wisely keeping his distance. "I think they forced her to take even more of that drugged drink than last time. She definitely seems more affected, but she insisted that she needed to fill us in right away."

I thump the chair arm. "Yes. It's important. When is Casimir coming back? We need him too."

As if conjured by my request, the courtesan appears in his ring of cord just seconds later. He's holding a steaming mug between his hands.

"Here," he says gently, bringing the mug to me. "This should help settle your mind and ease the disorientation. If you don't feel much better afterward, I brought an herb you can chew as well."

I sniff the hot liquid, which gives off a creamy nutty sort of scent that isn't unappealing, and accept the mug. The first tentative sip sends a flood of warmth straight to my gut.

Cas always knows just how to look after a person, Julita murmurs.

The men watch, radiating tension as I down the drink as quickly as I can stomach it. By the time I've drained half of the mug, my thoughts are managing to stick in place rather than floating off through my mind before I can totally set them in order.

I keep sipping while I gather those thoughts. More sobriety could hardly be a bad thing.

"The scourge sorcerers had a huge bonfire more than an hour's cart ride east of here," I say. "A few of us new initiates and around twenty established members. Everyone wore masks with magic to totally cover their faces, so I still don't know most of them. Ster. Torstem was leading things, and I ended up seeing Olari from the bug club and one of the dining hall chefs—the dark-haired woman who focuses on the desserts."

"Willone," Casimir supplies. Of course he'd know everyone's name. He grimaces. "I never imagined... Well, I haven't spoken to her much at all."

I nod in general acknowledgment. "We drank the drugged stuff and repeated some things Torstem said about the Order of the Wild, and there was a lot of weird dancing —but what's important is what he said."

I shift my attention to Alek. "You told me before about the kingship trials they used to hold in Silana before the empire took over. Torstem said outright that he wants to destroy the current royal family and hold new trials so we can have 'worthy' rulers. And other things about going back to the old ways. They seem to think that all this wildness they keep talking about is how it used to be in Silana. That's why they think the gods would prefer it—because we behaved like that back then, but we stopped."

Alek frowns. "They can't have a very definite idea of what anyone did all those centuries ago. It's my main area of study, and even with all the books I've had access to, I've still only come across fragmentary mentions of what ordinary life was like. What's survived the empire's purges is mostly references to major events like the trials."

"The scourge sorcerers took a few pieces they liked and ran with them," Stavros mutters, "making the rest up to suit themselves."

I let out a rough chuckle. "Probably. I have no idea how they justify the scourge sorcery element—they haven't mentioned that part to me yet. But I asked Torstem how they were going to eliminate the current rulers, and he said they're almost ready. That they've been gathering their 'forces,' whatever exactly those are, and he thinks they'll be striking at the entire royal family in just a few weeks."

Even Stavros draws up short at that announcement. "A few weeks? How?"

I shake my head miserably. "I couldn't get him to tell me any more detail, only that we'd hear about it when it's going to happen. But I don't know how much advance warning a new initiate would get. I don't know if he might have been making a cautious estimate and it could be as early as a few *days*. The Crown's Watch needs to take some kind of action right away."

Casimir comes up at my other side and brushes a few stray strands of hair back from my face in a soothing caress. "You've done fantastic, Ivy. You went through all that, and you were able to find out the part of their plans we needed to know most."

I rub my face. "I just hope it's enough."

"It has to be!" Alek says. "You can't go back to them when they might drag you into an assassination attempt next."

Julita's voice turns tart. *I should certainly hope not.*

Stavros has started to pace. "Did Torstem or the others say anything else? I need to know everything, even if it didn't seem relevant."

I pry back through my muddled memories of the night. "Before he sent me back here, Ster. Torstem told me to come to the next entomology club meeting, which is tomorrow evening, and that from now on I'll come to the Order of the Wild activities through them. So we got definite confirmation that the club is a front. I'd bet the half of the group that Olari is in supposedly went on a field trip last night."

Alek's mouth flattens into a pensive line. "Did they say anything about the clay? Did you find out what the drug is?"

"No. I didn't want to question them too much about things someone who's actually invested in the cause wouldn't care about—or that I shouldn't know about anyway."

Casimir squeezes my shoulder. "That's fine. You needed to protect yourself while you were out there at their mercy."

I strain my mind, but nothing else comes to me. "The rest was all more of the same—vague statements about removing corrupt undeserving people from power, honoring the gods properly, blah blah blah."

"All right." Stavros stalks over to the mirror. He presses something on the back of it, and a faint thread of magic grazes my skin.

As he steps in front of the mirror, Stavros glances over at me. "I'll do the talking, but you might as well stay here in case the king wants to speak to you directly again. For now, relax and recover."

Casimir teases his fingers over my hair again. "When we're finished here, I think you need a more enjoyable escape. I can book a bathing room like the one we used last time."

I open my mouth to protest, with a pang of guilt both for the rejection I need to make and the fact that I didn't reject other overtures last night.

But the courtesan holds up his hand to stop me. "Just for you, Kindness. I'll see which rooms are available and give you the instructions for accessing it. You can have a soak and a sleep, in whatever order you wish." He aims his attention at Stavros. "As long as your 'employer' won't begrudge you taking a day off."

Stavros's jaw flexes, but he inclines his head slightly. "She needs it. And I only have one lecture today, so her absence won't be all that conspicuous."

His gaze sears into me, reminding me of all the things we haven't really talked about yet. All the reasons I'd rather not catch up on my slumber in his quarters, where I doubt I'll be able to relax much at all.

I clasp Casimir's hand with the most affection I feel comfortable offering while knowing Julita is watching. "Thank you. I can't imagine anything better after all of this."

And then... And then I suppose tomorrow we'll have to talk about where I go from here.

My gut starts to twist, but before my worries can expand very far, the surface of the mirror wavers.

King Konram's image swims into clarity on the glass. His crown balances perfectly on his dark brown hair; his royal jacket and trousers look as neat as if he—or his assistants— spent an hour smoothing out every wrinkle.

If we've summoned him out of bed, he's doing an impressive job of hiding that fact.

"Ster. Stavros," he says in an equally smooth voice. "For you to be holding a meeting at this early hour, I assume you must have a matter of some urgency to convey."

Stavros dips into a respectful bow. "Yes, Your Highness. Very much so."

He summarizes the key points of what I told him much more succinctly than I managed in my still somewhat hazy state. I might appreciate his ability to cut to the chase more if my pulse hadn't started thudding harder as I take in the king's reaction—or lack thereof.

Konram is a consummate politician. Only the barest trace of emotion flickers through his expression at the revelation that the scourge sorcerers believe they'll be murdering him within a few weeks' time.

When Stavros is done, the king is silent for a stretch, absorbing the information. Then he shifts his position as if attempting to peer deeper into the room. "Your assistant who's infiltrated their 'Order of the Wild'—she's still there with you?"

Stavros's stance tenses, but he motions to me. "Yes, Your Highness. She'd be happy to answer any questions you have."

Casimir's hangover cure has dulled the effects of the drug enough that I can walk steadily if a little slower than usual over to the mirror. Stavros remains off to the side, a couple of paces away, as if he thinks I need guarding from the reflection of his king.

I dip into the lowest curtsey I trust myself to manage without losing my balance. "I'm sorry to have brought such dire news, Your Highness."

"Better that I receive it than go unawares," the king says with a hint of dryness that makes me like him a little better. "From what you've observed in your interactions with this group, Ster. Torstem is the leader of the conspiracy?"

"Yes, Your Highness. Whenever he's been present, he's been the one ordering the others around. And he's the head of the bug—the entomology—club that's wrapped up in the group too. He's also the only one we know of who's been finding the orphans to use as sacrificial accomplices. And Wendos referred to him as an authority figure."

King Konram hums thoughtfully, his dark gaze turning more penetrating as he considers me. I'm abruptly aware of my hair hanging loose and probably tangled, of the wrinkles that've no doubt formed in my own clothing during my long night.

"You didn't find any new information about who might have exploited the royal seal?" he asks.

"I'm sorry. They're very careful about how much they say, and I couldn't ask about it directly without revealing that I know more than a regular initiate should."

"Understandable. I assume, then, that they still believe you *are* a regular initiate, loyal to their cause?"

Where is he going with this?

"Yes, Your Highness," I say. "Ster. Torstem even asked me to meet with the entomology club tomorrow."

"Excellent." The king folds his hands in front of him. "I'm sure you can all appreciate that this is a delicate situation. The threat is imminent but unclear. If we wait for the traitors to strike, we may not be fully prepared."

Stavros steps closer. "With your permission, I could rouse Ster. Torstem right now, arrest him and bring him to—"

"No." Konram draws himself a little taller. "It's clear we can't hold back from action any longer, but if we only have Torstem, his imprisonment and trial may simply rile up his supporters and lead to a worse outcome."

I frown. "You could have the bug club members we suspect taken into custody too."

The king's gaze settles back on me. "Stavros said you saw many more conspirators at the initiation ritual than could have been part of that club, didn't he?"

"Yes," I acknowledge. "There are seven members we're reasonably sure are working with Torstem, but I counted around three times as many people at the initiation."

"Then I think we need to strike while they're all gathered together. That will give us the absolute certainty that those we apprehend are guilty, and we can subdue most if not all of Ster. Torstem's followers in one swoop. It does us no good to quell a few of them if the greater portion are still plotting against the crown. And as soon as they know we're making arrests, those we haven't captured will become even more cautious."

Stavros lifts his chin. "What do you suggest then, sire?"

King Konram's attention remains on me. "You've proven yourself adept enough to assist in Stavros's combat classes. I understand you're quite good with a knife."

"I—yes." A chill creeps over my skin. "I can hold my own."

"And Ster. Torstem has allowed you to get quite close to him during these rituals of theirs?"

I remember the closing of Torstem's fingers around mine when he helped me to my feet just a few hours ago. "Yes, Your Highness, he has."

"Then I think the course of action with the best outcome is obvious. The next time his Order of the Wild goes on one of their excursions, find a moment to stab him in the heart or slash his throat. In the ensuing chaos, disable their means of transport and flee after signaling your colleagues by your usual means. Stavros can bring a squad of soldiers to round up the other conspirators. Their distress over Torstem's death should make them easy pickings. And any remaining followers will be lost without a leader to rally around."

My heart stops for the space of a few beats.

Stavros makes a rough noise low in his throat. "Your Highness—you're asking Ivy to assassinate—"

Konram's gaze slides back to his former general. "Let's not think of it as an assassination. That would violate the laws of fair trial. But I'm sure I could forgive, even reward, a subject who was caught up in a horrible uprising and found the strength to strike at the instigators before it was too late."

"I should be the one—"

The king shakes his head at his former general, his expression turning almost bored as if he's already done with the conversation. "I can't have Ster. Torstem slaughtered in the halls of the college. The Crown's Watch will be on guard, and if we have an opportunity to settle the issue sooner, we will. But surely you can see that this strategy allows us the most discretion while removing the primary threat entirely."

"She is only an assistant," Stavros insists. "It's too much responsibility."

"That's not how you spoke about her before." Konram studies me again. "What do you think, Ivy of Nikodi? Do you have the skills and the stomach to carry out this one final task to defend your country?"

Every part of me wants to scream *No*.

Images well up in my mind—my sister's limp body, the crumpled corpse of the man who attacked me years ago, Esmae bleeding out on the floor. My stomach churns.

The king's eyes pin me in place. Will he see me as a traitor too if I refuse him?

I've already cut off my own finger and stabbed a man on this terrible quest. Why wouldn't he expect me to accept this demand too?

This is what the godlen would want anyway, isn't it—the scourge sorcerers not just imprisoned but razed from the earth? That's how *they* handled the last bunch.

But King Konram wants to keep up the appearance of a fair and honorable ruler before his people. Of course he'd have some minor noblewoman from a backwater county carry out the dirty work rather than handle it directly.

For an instant, a flare of anger cuts through my horror. *This* is the ruler I've risked so much to protect? How would he fare in one of those kingship trials if he were put to the test?

The moment the questions flit through my mind, I jolt back to reality with another flood of cold that drenches me from head to toe.

I'm thinking like the scourge sorcerers.

As if any of us can say whether the royal families of the past were the slightest bit more righteous than the one we have now. At least King Konram bothered to ask rather than order.

I square my shoulders, swallowing down my guilt at the traitorous thoughts that gripped me.

Why *shouldn't* it be me with the blood on my hands? I'm more capable than the man before me has any idea of.

"I can do it," I say, with only the slightest rasp in my voice.

Stavros sucks in a breath, but the king smiles before his former general has the chance to speak. "Then it's settled. I look forward to hearing of your success."

"Your High—" Stavros starts, but the mirror is already shimmering back to our reflections.

A taut silence fills the room. I wrap my arms around myself, my fingers curling into the edges of the cloak I retrieved in the scourge sorcerers' cart.

Stavros spins toward me. "Why did you agree? You can't *want* to play assassin."

"Of course not," I snap back, unable to hold back the quaver from the words now. "But how under the gods' gaze am I supposed to say no to the king himself?"

Alek and Casimir come around the table to join us.

"You shouldn't have to," the scholar says, his tone raw with pain. "You're not a killer."

I force a shrug. "I am, though. And I said I wanted to see the scourge sorcerers destroyed. If this is the way to do it with the least damage to the people we're trying to protect, then that's the way it is."

"If they catch you in the act, they'll kill *you*."

His voice breaks with the last word. I clutch my cloak tighter. "I know. But that was always true, wasn't it?"

Except before I was doing everything I could to appease

the scourge sorcerers. Now I'm going in with the intention of committing the worst crime any of the conspirators could imagine.

If I can't flee quickly enough—

Dread pools in my gut. I don't want to think about that.

"Ivy..." Casimir's dark eyes flash. "I've tracked down someone who may have information that'll give us a bigger picture. It might not be necessary to go quite that far after all."

I smile at him with a twinge of gratitude, but I can't summon any real hope. "Thank you."

The courtesan touches my cheek and presses a quick kiss to my temple. "I'll see about getting that bathing room for you. You'll need that chance to unwind now more than ever. And if I can get you out of this awful mission, I swear to you, I will."

FORTY

Casimir

The carriage rolls to a stop. My chest constricts around my heart for just an instant before I nudge myself forward to open the door.

From an objective standpoint, there's nothing to be afraid of beyond that door. It's just a baron's country home, and I've visited more than a dozen of those in the past.

But I'm not here to entertain a court noble on holiday. In theory, I'm making a friendly call on an old family friend, though I can't say she was ever really a friend of *mine*.

And I'm not a man of objectivism anyway. My calling is all about matters of emotion, and this conversation is likely to stir up a whole host of those, no matter what guise it's under.

I step out into the crisp fall air. The leaves of the tree overhead gleam in brilliant shades of red and orange. The breeze carries the light floral scents of the last late-blooming flowers from the garden around the side of the sprawling house.

I only take the smallest enjoyment from the pleasant setting as my gaze latches on to the woman waiting by the house's gilded doorway.

Laselle stands shorter than in my memories, mainly because I haven't seen her since I was ten. I have a few inches on her now. Her presence still looms large, though—enough so that I have the instinctive urge to bow even though she no longer has even a passing authority over me.

She must be well into her fourth decade now, perhaps even reaching her fifth, but the creams and powders skillfully layered over her face turn her golden-brown skin perfectly smooth, her eyes large and bright, her rouged lips full nearly to the point of absurdity.

She and my mother both practiced the art of toeing the line, amplifying their beauty to the absolute limit before it became grotesque.

She's kept a figure Ardone herself would admire. A vast ruby-red gown embroidered with gold emphasizes her hourglass figure. Jewels glint amid her intricately whorled hair and around her neck and wrists.

Clearly, Laselle has been doing well for herself as she continues to ply her trade. The most adept courtesans can continue drawing high ranking clients well into their elderly years.

Her current clients are one of the wealthiest couples in King Konram's court. It's taken me this long to track her down because they whisked her off to Icar for a more exotic international trip.

She steps forward with a smile that doesn't part her lips. Her voice is the same resonant lilt that fills my memories, with just a hint of hoarseness. "Cas! So *lovely* to see you after all this time. And you've come all the way from the city—goodness. Come along. We have lunch waiting for us in the pavilion."

I dip my head to her, even though she hasn't offered me the same respect. "It's good to see you too, Laselle."

She sweeps through the garden without another word to me until we reach the rounded, open-air structure that could have held a luncheon for thirty. The chic wooden table and chairs set up in its center look oddly dwarfed by the empty span of floorboards all around it.

Laselle sinks into one of the chairs with perfect grace, and I take the seat across from her. Bread, sliced meats and cheeses, and pastries are already laid out on a few platters between our plates.

A kitchen server appears and fills our cups with a rosy liquid with the sour tang of alcohol. I nod to her in thanks.

My dining partner leans forward, her gaze trailing over me more intently now that we're settled in. "How long has it been? Eleven years? Twelve? Too long, really."

"Eleven," I say evenly, and ignore her last remark entirely. If she'd really wanted to see me again, it'd have been much easier for her to visit Florian than for me to track her down while she toured the country estates beyond the city.

And I wouldn't have welcomed those visits anyway. Her visits in my childhood filled me with even more dread than when I had only my mother's wishes to appease.

Which was unfair of me. Laselle and my mother only wanted me to fulfill my potential, to honor our god in every way I could.

But feelings are feelings, and there isn't much you can do to argue with them.

Laselle daintily picks up a piece of bread and gives me another of her restrained smiles. "And now you're fully grown. You look to have been taking care of yourself well. You must be almost finished with your education, I assume?"

"One year left before I can enter the courtesan's guild," I confirm. The thought combined with my uncertainty about how exactly I want to continue my intended career path sends a thread of tension winding around my gut.

"At this point, I hope you've been pleasing many patrons already." She takes a careful bite of bread and cheese, showing just the slightest hint of her teeth. Not enough to reveal the row of jeweled replacements at the back of her mouth, but I know she has four sapphires embedded there.

Half as many gaudy teeth as my own, yet the sacrifice I planned never seemed to be enough in her mind.

"I've been quite active since I started the college program," I say, avoiding any mention of my current partial hiatus. "They encourage us to put our skills to use for a lesser fee. You can never learn as much as you do with the actual people you're meant to please."

"Well spoken. Perhaps you've managed to fill part of the void your mother left." Laselle's eyes narrow. "But why are you serving your own pleasure with countryside visits when there must be plenty of others who'd enjoy your services? Or more learning you could be doing?"

I swallow thickly behind my own smile. Flickers of memories rise up of the cutting glares and sneering remarks whenever my mother caught me taking a moment of my own leisure.

I didn't bring you into this world for you to loll about baking in the sun.

Don't tell me you took a ride on your own. Of all the useless things...

If your head is too empty to think of anything you need to be doing, you ask me. I can think of plenty.

Where's your appreciation for the life I gave you? You want to ruin me all over again?

I make my tone as ingratiating as I'm capable of. "I was hoping I might learn more from *you*. After all, you were Mother's greatest friend. I haven't had the benefit of her guidance in so long. I thought hearing of your own recent patronages might give me further inspiration."

Laselle simply hums dismissively and nibbles at her bread. An ache spreads up through my abdomen.

She isn't going to tell me anything if I don't make the right sort of appeal. It's been too long since I knew her, and I had only a child's understanding of her interests then.

Well, my gift can help with that.

I press my replaced molars gently against each other in my mouth and draw on the magic Ardone blessed me with in exchange, holding my gaze on Laselle. What could I do that would make her happiest right at this moment?

As always, the answer my gift brings me comes in a current of images and impressions. The flavor of them makes the ache in my stomach expand.

Ah. So that's really what matters most to her after all, at least when it comes to me.

I suppose I shouldn't be surprised. My mother always talked as if she wanted nothing from me but accomplishment, but I've always felt as if it was something more like atonement she was looking for.

If it saves Ivy from having to put herself in the scourge sorcerers' hands again and carry out the king's murderous orders, a little abasing is the least I can do.

I push back my chair and sink to my knees, letting my head come to rest against the edge of the table. "Please. The truth is that I feel I've lost my way without your and Mother's steadying advice. I'm not living up to her wishes. I'm not the man she expected me to be yet. Speaking to you is my last hope. Let me learn what I still can from you."

Shame prickles across my face at the humiliating position I've put myself in, but I keep my head bowed to hide it.

Laselle tsks her tongue, but I catch a hint of appreciation in her chuckle. "Well now, that is quite a quandary you've found yourself in. I'm not surprised you've gone astray—it was always difficult for Yonata to keep you in line even with my assistance. I suppose I owe it to her to set you to rights if I can."

I will the embarrassed heat from my face and lift myself back into my chair, maintaining a hunched, humble posture. "Thank you, with all my gratitude. It eats at me every day to think I'm failing to fulfill her legacy."

That last sentence stings coming up. There's a trace of truth to those words.

Why *am* I here and not catering to a patron? Why have I let myself think I can do anything else well enough that it's worth spending my time otherwise?

My mother would have said I should stick to my calling. Pamper Ivy if she'd pay me. Seek out the highest ranked clients I can impress.

Bring about all the delight she can't anymore.

I ball my hands against the niggling doubts. I'm an adult now—I'm my own man. Which means I have the responsibility of deciding the best course of my life for myself.

Not that she necessarily was wrong.

I do my best to hold my uneasiness at a distance while I kowtow to Laselle and ask my simpering questions about her exploits of the past few years. With every tale she tells to teach by example, she manages to work in a jab or two: "You'd need to stretch your creativity farther than you ever bothered." "You have to give yourself completely over to their whims, not let any of your selfish inclinations divert you."

I nod, give my thanks, and make the exclamations of awe I know she'll expect, holding that smile on my face until my cheeks feel ready to crack. I wait until she's told enough tales that I think she could accept a less fawning inquiry, and then delay several minutes longer to be safe.

Laselle gives me a decent opening, tipping back in her chair with a light laugh. "But then, for all their grandeur, a lot of the barons and baronesses have relatively simple tastes at heart. That's why they come out here to escape the complexities of the city courts."

I keep my tone casual, as if this is just another question in the long line. "I've heard a few murmurings about some rather wild parties out in the countryside. Large bonfires, masks, dancing beneath the stars. Are any of your patrons part of that crowd?"

My mother's friend taps her ruddy lips. "I don't think any of the noble families take part in events like that. But I have caught murmurs of my own. When I was calling on Baroness Reginne several months ago, I paid attention to the staff gossip as usual. Apparently one of the house messengers stumbled on some odd traces when he took a shortcut through one of the more distant and little-used areas of the county."

I raise my eyebrows enough to show curiosity, not my full investment. My pulse skips eagerly. "What sort of traces?"

Laselle waves her hand vaguely. "I only heard bits and pieces secondhand. From what I gathered, there were a few scattered bits of burnt wood and something the messenger took to be bone. That was what unnerved him. It seems whoever was carrying on out there, they needed extra internal stimulation to enjoy themselves. He also brought back a strip of dried crozzemi mushroom he found in the same area, and the kitchen staff had quite a night after boiling that. I'd have tried some myself, but it always gives me a headache after."

"Crozzemi?" I repeat. "I didn't think those grew in Silana."

"I can't say I've looked into it. I suppose whoever's

indulging, they must have decently deep pockets even if they aren't noble born." Laselle's gaze turns more pointed as it focuses on me again. "I hope you haven't resorted to intoxicants of that sort to enhance your abilities. A true courtesan should be able to please his or her patrons without skewing their sense of reality."

I hold up my hands. "Of course not. I wouldn't touch the stuff or offer it to anyone myself. I was only surprised."

Her eyes linger on me as if she isn't entirely convinced. As if she's thinking it would be just like me to take the lazy route—and lie about it.

I switch to a different angle. "It can't have been much of a bonfire if all they left was a few bits of wood."

Laselle shrugs. "At least they clean up after themselves, whatever they're after with antics of that sort. The real upper class wouldn't lower themselves to messing about in the dirt."

No patrons worthy of us, she means.

It doesn't appear she knows anything more about strange meetings in the counties around Florian. I work in a few more leading questions between more requests for advice, but none of her answers leave me any wiser about the scourge sorcerers' activities.

Still, when I get up from the table, I can bow to her with a satisfaction I don't entirely have to fake, even if it's not for the reasons she'd imagine.

"Thank you for taking the time to share all this with me. I'll continue to do my best to live up to my mother's aspirations for me."

"You do that," Laselle says, and hustles me back to my carriage.

I sit in a stew of uncomfortable memories and anxious thoughts the whole journey back to Florian. When the carriage stops outside Sovereign College's gate, I walk through the steps of the password almost without thinking, my mind already on the conversation ahead.

I don't want to disturb Ivy with a summons if she's still resting from her ordeal, though. I head to the bathing room I reserved for her first.

Peeking inside, I find the bed covers rumpled to show that she's slept there but the room currently unoccupied.

Where else might she have gone if she wanted some peace amid all the pressures laid on her?

I know her well enough to be fairly sure of the answer to that question.

The stables are somewhat busy in the middle of the afternoon as students come and go with their chosen mounts. No one's bustling about at the end of the aisle where Toast's stall is, though.

I wouldn't know Ivy's there either until the faint rasp of a brush over horsehair reaches my ears when I'm only a couple of steps away. My first entirely genuine smile of the day crosses my face as I stop by the stall door.

Ivy looks up from where she's tucked herself away toward the back of the stall, rubbing down the stallion's haunches. Her face brightens with the pleased light that never fails to set my spirits soaring.

The usually irritable horse snorts at me as if expressing annoyance that I might interrupt his grooming session, but he lowers his head with an almost apologetic air when Ivy pats his side. I shouldn't be even a little surprised that she's brought Stavros around when she's managed to tame this animal who until recently was seen more as a curse than a steed.

He stays still when I slip in after her so no one passing the aisle will see us talking.

"Had enough sleep?" I ask, keeping my voice low.

Ivy's smile tenses. She goes back to her grooming, to

Toast's approving sigh. "As much as I could. I got restless, so I thought I'd pay this beast a little attention." She swats him teasingly.

"Well, the room is yours until midnight. So if you feel you need to escape back there later, don't hesitate."

"Thank you." She studies me with those brightly knowing eyes of hers, so alert to any sign of trouble. "How did the visit you were going to make go? Did you find out anything?"

I can tell from her tone that she isn't even bothering to hope that I can get her out of the horrible task the king has set her on.

Guilt forms a lump in my gut before I manage to answer. "A little. I think I know where the scourge sorcerers have been holding at least some of their bonfires. And I'm almost certain of what they've been using to drug you."

Even though my offering barely feels like anything to me, some of the tension releases from Ivy's stance. "That could be a big help. I'd love to be able to keep my head clear."

I wish I could promise her that much. "We'll have to see if Alek can track down a viable antidote. I'll pass on word to him as soon as I've finished speaking with you—probably I'll need to call a meeting, but I won't be saying anything I haven't told you now. You should keep relaxing."

I doubt she's been exactly relaxed at any point today, but it speaks to how much stress she's under that she tips her head in agreement rather than insisting on coming along.

Every particle in my body clamors to wrap my arms around her and comfort her the best way I know how.

To stir enough bliss inside her that she can forget her worries for a time. To demonstrate my devotion in the most concrete possible way.

But I hold myself back from doing more than setting my

hand on her shoulder. I've let myself forget that it's not just Ivy but Julita I'm engaging with.

And Ivy, for all she balks at my nickname for her, is kind enough that she'd forego her own pleasures to ensure the woman whose soul she's carrying doesn't have to experience more unhappiness before her ultimate departure.

How long will she bury her own happiness to support everyone else's? She's already taken on too many burdens.

I know there's no arguing with her about it, though. She'd think less of me if I did.

Ivy leans just slightly into my touch, deepening my urge to pull her close. It's not as if it'd only be for *her* pleasure. The feel of her against me stirs something in me that's so much more than desire.

Then she peeks up at me through her eyelashes, a hint of slyness mingling with her concern. "You didn't like having to go see whoever you were making the trip to. I hope they weren't too obnoxious."

I haven't hidden my discomfort quite well enough.

I manage a sheepish laugh and allow myself the luxury of a kiss to the side of her head, breathing in the sweet scent of her hair with the smoky tang of the bonfire still lingering in it. "It'd simply been a long time. I wasn't sure what to expect. She was a friend of my mother's. They both had high expectations for me."

Ivy raises her eyebrows. "I find it hard to imagine anyone criticizing your abilities as a courtesan. You said it's a family tradition, didn't you, so they obviously didn't expect you to take up some other career path."

"Oh, definitely not. They wanted me to do as well as possible, that's all."

"Your mother isn't around anymore?"

Gods above, I shudder at the thought of having needed to arrange a meeting between the two women who've meant the most to me. "No. She passed away when I was ten. But the courtesan families look out for each other. I always had people to stay with."

Ivy touches my cheek. "I don't know how she could be anything but proud of who you've become."

My throat chokes up abruptly. I force a guffaw to cover the swell of emotion, but it keeps burning inside me.

My mother would yell at me for coming out here at all, for spending any time on a woman she'd see as a nobody. And maybe I have been lax in my responsibilities, in the debts I'm not sure I'll ever fully repay.

But she'd be wrong about Ivy. Because I know as I gaze back at her, with a certainty that stretches right down the center of me, that all the desire and devotion, the aching and the burn, add up to one word.

Love.

I love her, like I've never loved anyone. Like I had no concept was even possible.

Maybe I shouldn't indulge in the emotion. Maybe it's the selfishness Laselle talked about.

But love is Ardone's highest purpose. This feeling is her blessing.

Nothing could be more honorable to the divine powers I serve.

And if I have to get down in the dirt or spill blood to defend that love, I know with every fiber of my being that I won't hesitate.

Forty-One

Ivy

I don't know what any of the salts and oils are meant to do, so I simply open the bottles and sniff until I find a scent I like. Then I sprinkle the powder liberally into the running water of the bath.

The resulting foam intensifies the soothing herbal smell. I strip off the rest of my clothes and climb into the massive tub.

As I sink into the hot, fizzing water, a long sigh escapes my lips. It's echoed by the voice in my head.

If there's one thing I miss, it's enjoying a good soak.

The corners of my lips quirk upward, although a twinge of uncertainty ripples through my gut at the same time. Julita hasn't said much since we returned from the initiation ceremony. I'm not sure how she's feeling right now.

I keep my tone light. "Have I not been bathing to your noble standards?"

She chuckles. *It isn't as if you've had time to indulge in a longer wash all that often. And when you have—*

Julita stops, probably not wanting to touch on exactly what I've been getting up to during my extended baths. The twinge inside me deepens to an ache.

I pick up the cloth I left on the side of the tub and start to rub the lingering grit and sweat from my skin. "Well, if there's any particular oil you'd appreciate or soap you'd prefer, now's the time to tell me."

No, what you've chosen is just fine.

There's a sense of reverse to her tone that I'm not used to —not so much as if she's restraining herself but simply subdued. I guess she might be tired too.

I don't push. I massage the soap into my hair, unable to stop a shiver of delight at remembering Casimir's lithe fingers performing the same act, and dunk my head several times to rinse it. Then I work in some of the cream that's supposed to add silkiness and shine to the strands, just for the luxury of it.

The middle-ward bathhouses I had access to before never supplied anything that frivolous.

Once I've rinsed the cream out too, I sit on the ledge at one side of the tub and absorb the silky heat of the water. The scent floods my lungs. Even the scars on my back seem to soften.

This *is* a luxury. But I can't totally relax into the indulgence when I'm aware of the presence at the back of my skull, shifting here and there with thoughts she isn't sharing.

"You've been quiet today," I say finally.

Oh, I've simply had a lot to mull over. And there hasn't been much for me to contribute anyway.

My throat tightens. "You know, I'm sorry about what happened with Stavros, after I told you— I think we were both still half asleep, and I got caught up in the moment— I shouldn't—"

It's all right, Julita breaks in. *If you wanted that, I shouldn't be stopping you from getting caught up. I... You've had to change how you're living an awful lot because I barged into your head, haven't you.*

It's not a question, but I feel compelled to answer anyway. "You didn't force me to come to the college. I made the choice."

I mean, you haven't had any privacy. You've constantly had to consider me as well as yourself. I know you were used to getting by on your own, so to have a stranger watching your every move, interrupting your thoughts with mine whenever I spoke up...

Even when she was bemoaning the men's focus on me, I've never heard her sound quite as defeated as she does right now. Where is she going with this?

"It's an awkward situation," I acknowledge. "But we've made the best of it, or at least we're working toward that."

And the situation should be almost over with. But I don't know how to say that part in a way that doesn't sound totally insensitive.

When I've seen Julita's quest to destroy the scourge sorcerers through, when their conspiracy has crumbled, there'll be no reason for her to cling to this last shred of life through me. At some point, we'll have to talk about her final death.

I'm just not expecting that conversation to happen immediately.

Julita makes a sound as if clearing her throat. *I was thinking... I haven't been all that helpful in the past week or two. So perhaps it's time for me to move on and let you have your life just for yourself again.*

I blink, momentarily startled speechless. "Why would you even say that? We aren't finished with your mission."

I get the sense of Julita's presence squirming a little before she answers. *If anything, I suspect I've been distracting you. I've obviously been too caught up in my own concerns to ensure I'm there when I* can *help. If I'm causing more problems than I'm solving, leaving would be better for the mission as well as for you.*

My mouth opens, but no words come to me. A heat that has nothing to do with the bath has flared in the back of my eyes.

Why do I feel like I'm about to cry?

Julita isn't *wrong*. My ghostly passenger has been pulling back more and more. It's been difficult trying to balance her emotions with my own desires.

But somehow the thought of her vacating my mind completely, leaving me as alone as I used to be, makes the bottom of my stomach drop out. The emptiness I picture sends a shiver through my veins.

I'd be facing the scourge sorcerers with no one at all by my side. No wry remarks to keep my spirits up. No expressions of concern when I'm struggling.

Does she really think she's troubled me that much?

Maybe hanging on has become too much of a strain for *her*, but she doesn't want to admit it.

"Do *you* want to move on?" I ask, fighting to keep my voice steady. "If sticking with me has become too uncomfortable, I obviously wouldn't insist that you stay."

Ivy… I've appreciated every bit of life you've let me cling to. The last thing I want is to overstay my welcome.

I think that's a no to my question.

I gather myself as well as I can. "You haven't overstayed. Obviously everything between me and the men has become a little much for you, and I don't blame you for needing some space. But you are still helping. I don't know if I'd have gotten through the initiation without giving away my magic if you hadn't talked me through it. You *were* there when I needed you the most."

I can almost see Julita hanging her head. *I should have been there sooner.*

"That doesn't matter. You weren't too late. I—I hate that I have to deal with those assholes at all. It'd be so much harder without a friend there with me."

Julita gives a rough laugh. *You still consider me a friend?*

I frown. "Of course. That's why I've tried to consider your feelings. You stood up for me before any of the men bothered to. You've had my back, and I want to have yours."

There's a long stretch of silence. When Julita speaks again, she sounds as if she's choked up too, even though she hasn't got a throat to hold a lump or eyes to spill tears.

I'm so sorry. I'm gone from their lives now, so it's not as if I could have any of them anyway. It's not as if I'd have let anything happen with them if I'd stayed alive. I was too careful about protecting myself... It's not your fault I can now see that closing myself off might not have been the path that'd have made me the happiest.

I wish I could give her a hug. It occurs to me, with the sweetest of bittersweet pangs, that this is what it might have been like talking with Linzi if my little sister had lived long enough to confront adult jealousies and regrets.

"I've messed things up in plenty of ways myself, making assumptions and hesitating to trust," I say. "It isn't fair that you never got the chance to change your mind."

I'd say it's much less fair that I've made it harder for you to enjoy the affection they've offered you. You never treated them badly, Ivy. It made sense that you were cautious given how they first treated you and the differences between your positions and... everything. I had no excuse.

My mouth twists into a crooked smile. "I think you did. Your brother was awful to you, and your parents obviously weren't paying enough attention to intervene... Of course you found it hard to trust anyone."

Well. I think both of us can be more than our hardships. Julita gives herself a shake that tingles through my scalp. *They truly care for you. Even Stavros. I got so caught up in missing what I lost that I didn't stop to think... This is the best I can have now. Celebrating their devotion to you. Getting to enjoy a little taste of the exciting parts before I give you your privacy... and perhaps an additional vicarious thrill if you'll share some gossip afterward?*

I can't stop a giggle from tumbling out of my mouth. "Are you sure you really want to put yourself through hearing the details?"

I have to look at it the right way. What I'm gaining instead of what I can't have. I shouldn't really be here at all experiencing any of this. She pauses, and her tone turns sly. *And I'm not sure I wanted to miss seeing Stavros finally, completely won over. Why are things so tense between the two of you again?*

I wrinkle my nose. "Everything you could probably tell was about to happen happened, and then I got nervous that he wouldn't be happy about it when he fully woke up. And he admitted that he still doesn't totally trust *me*. I didn't stick around to hear his excuses about why."

Julita lets out a humph. *That man. He's got to get his head on straight eventually. Do what you will with him once he does. And don't hold yourself back with Alek and Casimir anymore either. I should have argued with you when you first told me you'd backed off.*

And this—this is exactly why the thought of the ghost in my head departing sets my emotions off-kilter. We understand each other. We have each other's backs as well as we can, just like I said to her.

"I don't know about Stavros," I say. "But the others—are you *sure?*"

Absolutely. You should be soaking up all that adoration, and I'll enjoy the afterglow. It's more fun sharing your life if you're enjoying it too. I simply forgot that for a little while.

I swallow thickly. "Well, thank you."

I should be thanking you. You could have told me good riddance a few minutes ago.

The water is starting to cool around me. I stretch out my legs and inhale more of the herbal scent, and then reach for the lever to open the drain. "Hopefully we'll have time for a little more enjoyment before we get to the murdering."

Julita gives the impression of a wince. *You'd think King Konram would be grateful enough for everything you've already done not to lay that on you too. If I could—*

She halts, with a pensive silence that puts me on the alert.

"What?" I prod after a moment as I climb out of the tub.

I wonder if my gift would still work. If you let me take charge briefly again. We could call on the king, and I could tell him you're not going to be his assassin, and he'd have to accept it.

I wrap one of the fluffy towels around me as I ponder her offer. "We don't know for sure that your gift *would* still work when you're not in the body that made the sacrifice. If it doesn't, the confrontation could go very badly."

I suppose that's true. It'd be difficult to test since we don't know who would request something and be unwilling to accept a no unless I compelled it.

I rub the towel over my head and hesitate in front of the room's tall mirror. My pale reflection gazes back at me, my figure no longer quite as scrawny now that I've had the benefit of the college dining hall for several weeks of meals, although my elbows are as knobby as ever and the muscles

I've honed stand out against my sallow skin. Plenty of scars mar that skin even without my back in view.

I still don't look like a noble. I look like a woman who's had to see and do more than anyone really should.

And maybe that's okay.

I pull my posture straighter. "Someone has to deal with Ster. Torstem. It might as well be me. I *am* in by far the best position to handle him quickly and without causing a bigger ruckus."

You don't want *to perform an assassination, do you? I know you've hated having to kill before—even Esmae.*

"I have hated it," I say quietly. "But I didn't want to come to the college at all. I didn't want to take on any of these responsibilities. I just liked the idea of what might happen if I didn't even less. That hasn't changed."

Even if carrying out this final part of the mission gets me killed too.

Julita is quiet for a moment. Then she says, *I think I can see why Kosmel called on you.*

I snort. "If he ever bothers to speak to me again. *He* was totally unhelpful last night. Couldn't even give me a dice roll."

I suppose it's difficult to interpret the actions of the gods.

"I don't know. That felt like a pretty clear 'Fuck you.' But it doesn't really matter. I got into this mission without him, so I'll get out of it without him too."

By the time I've dressed, the restlessness that drove me out of the bathing room before has crept back in.

It's evening now. Stavros will be back in his quarters soon if he isn't already.

Casimir said I have the room until midnight, so I can't hide away here for the whole night. And the thought of falling asleep and having to be kicked out makes my skin crawl.

I don't relish the idea of talking to the former general about last night's encounter just yet either.

With a huff of breath aimed mostly at myself, I step out into the hall and make my way to the Domi's small back stairwell. Fresh air to clear my head can't be a bad thing.

I wander through the inner courtyard, but there are still too many students milling around in the descending dusk. I spot Petra emerging from the Quadring and all but bolt in the opposite direction.

A conversation with her seems like a bad idea too.

I end up meandering through one of the Quadring's halls to the larger outer courtyard. The dark sprawl of the campus woods looms at the other end of the field, but I don't let myself focus on it. I stroll through the grass, taking in the statues positioned along the tall stone wall.

The one of Elox tossing a rippling blanket into the air is a particularly impressive feat of carving. I'm admiring it so avidly that I nearly trip over my feet when I step past it and my gaze jars against the figure on the other side.

The guard with the too-beautiful face and the magical vibes is standing by the wall a few paces down. He's wearing his deep blue uniform, so presumably he's on duty and meant to be patrolling, but he's standing stiffly still, his attention fixed on the arm he's raised in front of his chest.

At a twitch of movement, I realize there's a butterfly perched on his jacket sleeve.

The insect's yellow-and-blue wings dip down and back up again. The guard stares at it, his expression uncertain, as if he isn't sure what to do about the situation and worries he'll make the wrong choice.

Does he imagine it's going to attack him? Julita murmurs with amusement.

It's a bizarre enough scene that I stall in my tracks rather than hurrying past him. Which means I'm still staring at *him* when he lifts his gaze and notices me standing here.

I expect him to snap at me for gaping at him, the way high ranking people tend to do if you catch them in an awkward moment. Instead, his eyes open wider, almost pleadingly. As if he's making an appeal for help.

It's ridiculous. He obviously doesn't actually need help.

But everything about the situation is so absurd I find myself walking closer. "Have you been assaulted by that butterfly?"

The guard's gaze jerks back to the insect. He adjusts his arm a little higher, but the creature keeps clinging to it.

"It landed on me a few minutes ago," he says, his voice as puzzled as his expression, and points to one of its wings. "I think it's hurt—it might not be able to fly any farther. I don't know what to do."

Is he that concerned about the fate of a butterfly?

An uneasy pang runs through my chest. Somehow I can't simply dismiss him when he's showing such an unusual display of compassion.

Most of his colleagues would probably have shaken the creature off or swatted it dead and been done with it.

I study the wings and note the tattered edge on the one he indicated. Can a butterfly recover from an injury like that?

I don't know, but we might as well give it a chance.

Glancing around, I motion toward the woods. "Let's bring it someplace it'll have shelter. If it's going to recover, it'll be better off in a spot where no predators will notice it. Assuming you're not going to carry it around for the next day or two."

"No," the guard says as if he's taking my suggestion seriously. "It might get more damaged riding on me."

"Then it's settled. Come on."

I stride toward the line of trees, ignoring the

apprehension that fills me at the sight of the woods after all the things I've done within them. The guard trails behind me, holding his arm steady so as not to disturb his cargo.

When we reach the nearest trees, I peer through the brush and point out a leafy twig jutting from a sapling. "Put it here. The branch right overtop should stop any birds from spotting it."

The guard eases the butterfly onto his finger gingerly. It grips his skin with its tiny feet, but when he nudges it against the twig, it springs onto the bark with a flutter of its wings.

Studying it in its new resting place, the guard's stance relaxes. He glances at me, and another tingle of that magic he exudes brushes against my nerves.

I do my best to hide the tensing of my muscles, but a small furrow forms in his porcelain-smooth brow. "I make you nervous. This place does too. But you helped anyway."

My chin comes up automatically. "I'm perfectly fine. You looked like you could use a little direction. I've got other things to do now."

I spin around and stalk off before he can make any other accusations, but I catch his voice before I put more than a few paces between us. "Thank you."

I walk on without looking back.

Julita chuckles softly. *Now he is a strange one. I suppose if he badgers you about stargazing again, you can remind him of his butterfly escapades.*

A hint of a smile touches my lips, but my heart isn't in it. I don't feel comfortable wandering around the courtyard anymore, not when I might run into the guard and his unknown magical abilities again.

He couldn't have any idea *why* the woods make me uneasy, right?

The last streaks of sunlight are fading from the sky. Sconces flicker along the walls of the college buildings.

I rub my arms, cast about for another option, and then resign myself to my fate.

I do have to talk to Stavros eventually. About *all* the things that happened last night that we haven't addressed yet.

Time to get the awfulness over with.

FORTY-TWO

Stavros

I wasn't trying to break the plate. I only brought it up to my room at all because the buzz of chatter in the dining hall was grating at my nerves.

So the dish happened to be sitting by the edge of my desk while I paced around the room, straining my mind for something I could say to my king to change his mind, some alternate strategy I could offer that would make Ivy's involvement unnecessary. And when I kicked the leg of the desk in frustration, the plate happened to hop off and shatter on the floor.

Naturally, Ivy returns while I'm muttering to myself and picking up the broken pieces.

At the squeak of the door opening, I freeze other than the upward jerk of my head.

Ivy slips inside. Her bright blue gaze feels especially penetrating as she takes in my position and the jagged chunks of ceramics on the floor around me.

"What did that poor plate ever do to you?" she asks, her

tone sardonic but her body tensed as if she thinks she might need to bolt right back out the door.

"It was an accident," I mutter, scraping the shards together as hastily as I can between my regular hand and the hooked prosthetic I put on for a late-afternoon workout—which did absolutely nothing to get my head on straight.

While I work, Ivy stalks around the room in her now-typical surveillance for conjured creatures. Apparently finding none, she steps tentatively to the sofa and lowers herself onto it.

Her posture still looks braced to flee.

It hasn't escaped my notice that she's been running from me ever since my blunder last night. She's left every room we've been in together as swiftly as humanly possible.

As I bring the mess to the waste basket, I shoot her surreptitious glances. Brief twitches of my eyes for as long as my vision will remain steady.

She's gazing toward the window rather than watching me. Her mouth is set in a line that looks pained.

Even though the moss-green hue of the new gown Casimir's provided sets off her pale skin and red-blond hair to impressive effect, it doesn't suit her quite as well as her sparring clothes. But the fierce strength of her spirit shines through all the same.

That spark in her set my blood thrumming through my veins long before I was willing to accept, let alone admit, the effect she has on me. Now, remembering the way she arched and shuddered against me in my bed last night—

No, better to remember the fear in her eyes afterward. Giving in to my hotter desires before we had a stable foundation to carry us through them is what landed me in this disaster.

I wash my hands in the latrine and return to the common room, half expecting our thief-turned-lady to have darted off in my momentary absence. She's stayed, sitting stiffly on the sofa.

I consider walking over but decide it's safest giving her plenty of space. As I prop myself against the front of my desk, my stomach churns with all the things I need to say.

Before I can even open my mouth, her gaze flicks to me. She blurts out the words in a rush.

"My magic got away from me during the initiation."

Ah. Perhaps it's not just my blunder she's been fleeing.

Not that I can take any comfort in that fact. Her body has somehow become even more rigid where she's perched on the sofa.

Even with my view of her blurring, I can feel her gaze burning into me with its intentness.

If I don't handle her admission just right, I'll prove myself exactly the enemy she's afraid I am. I don't know if we'll be able to come back from another misstep so soon on the heels of the last.

I keep my voice perfectly calm. "I can't say that surprises me, what with the drugs and the chaos the scourge sorcerers were encouraging. What happened?"

She shifts uneasily on the sofa cushions. When I give my head a twitch to get a clearer glimpse of her, it's obvious from the distant look that's come into her eyes that she's as much uneasy with her recollections as how I'll react to them.

Which only offers more evidence of why I don't need to be afraid of *her*.

"Everyone was disguised," she says after a moment. "I knew I needed to figure out who they were, that getting out of this whole dangerous mission depended on identifying the conspirators. So my magic decided it would start wrenching off people's masks, and it slipped my grasp a couple of times. That's how I saw Olari and the woman from the dining hall."

"I'm not hearing anything horrifying so far. We told you

that you should use your power if it would work in your favor."

Her hands twist together in her lap. "But there's always a backlash. Kosmel wasn't around to guide it, and I don't know how. It—it pushed in to balance out the pulling away. One of the scourge sorcerer's masks seemed to *melt* down her face and into her mouth. They had to break it to stop it from choking her. And my magic hit one of the horses too—something with the bridle hurt it. The woman might have deserved it, but the horse definitely didn't."

I consider her account. "Surely it wasn't a lot of harm for something as simple as removing a mask?"

"With all the magic on the things, I'm not sure removing the masks was 'simple.'" Ivy sighs. "It didn't seem as if the horse was outright wounded. But if I hadn't gotten a handle on my power when I did, I don't know who or what else it might have hurt."

"You did get a handle on it, though. Without any permanent damage done."

"I couldn't manage it on my own. I was too disoriented. But Julita helped me steady myself and focus."

Julita. It's gotten increasingly difficult for me to picture the coy, chestnut-haired woman who cajoled me into taking up her cause residing in Ivy's head. What has *she* been saying to Ivy about me?

Is Ivy here right now because of her or in spite of her?

The firmness of her tone suggests her declaration matters to her. And I'm not lying when I say, "I'm glad she was there when you needed her."

Ivy's fingers tighten around the edge of the sofa cushion. "She won't always be, though."

"And you won't always be socializing with scourge sorcerers." I pause, summoning all the conviction I feel into my voice. "Ivy, nothing you've just told me changes my opinion. I'm not worried about you or your magic. You went seven years without ever losing your grip on it before you stumbled into this situation, so I don't see any reason to think your incredible control won't work just fine once you're out of this mess."

"You don't see any reason so far."

There. There is the crux of the problem, the catastrophe I created.

She was willing to trust me once after I'd been an ass to her when we first met. And then I let prejudice and fear and —being honest—my own wretched insecurities about one part of who she is overshadow all the rest, and wasn't just an ass but a brute.

How am I ever going to convince her that I won't make another about-face on her?

I know I won't. So I'm just going to have to give this appeal my all, no matter how much shame I have to dredge up in the process.

I owe this incredible woman my full truth.

I drop my gaze for a moment, gathering myself. "Ivy… You never deserved anything I put you through. I was wrong, over and over again. There was *never* any reason, not in anything you did, not even in what you are, so now that I've sorted myself out, I won't imagine any more."

Ivy's tone is wary. "If it wasn't anything I am, then what was it about?"

The corner of my mouth crooks up at a wry angle, but my chest constricts around the words. I've buried these unsettling emotions so far down, hiding them under layer upon layer of confidence and authority and comradery.

I never wanted to let them out. Maybe I had the fanciful idea they'd rot and disintegrate like a corpse into the earth, but it hasn't worked. The stifled anguish has been eating away at me from the inside all this time.

"I have fucked up, so badly. *I* hurt so many people, so many more than you have, and I was so terrified of making an even worse mistake that I couldn't see I was fucking up all over again with you."

When my gaze flicks to Ivy, she's knit her brow. "You've killed people in battle, sure, but I don't think enemy soldiers count the same way."

"That's not—" A rough laugh escapes me. I rub my forehead. "I've already told you what happened with Michas. Approximately."

"A riven sorcerer murdered him," Ivy says quietly.

"And I didn't see the danger in time. When I *did* realize something was wrong, I froze up rather than getting Michas out of there, against every combat instinct I'd already been training in…"

The words snag in my throat. I force myself to go on. "I could have saved him. The riven man was just trying to avoid capture. He struck out at Michas because he was closer and then fled. If we'd retreated sooner…"

Sympathy I'm not sure I deserve resonates through Ivy's voice. "You don't know that. You don't know how many more people that mad sorcerer might have murdered if you hadn't realized what he was."

"I know how many people died because of the choices I did make. Michas was only my first fuck-up. I can't even count how many soldiers have fallen under my watch over the years."

Ivy lets out a dismissive sound. "I don't think any general manages to completely avoid bloodshed on our side. That's not how war works."

My jaw tightens. "I don't know. I don't know how many of those deaths were unavoidable and how many I instigated. Because—have you heard anything about my last battle?"

She shakes her head, still and silent. Waiting for me to go on.

My sight stutters and hazes with each blink. A flare of frustration sears through the tangle of guilt and shame, but the anger is directed only at myself.

"Like most gifts, I could only use mine so many times in quick succession before it'd start wearing on me. I'd be able to see less and less of what was to come, and I'd get a headache and have trouble thinking straight. Not a good state to be in when you're leading hundreds of soldiers into the fray."

"All gifts have limitations," Ivy murmurs. "That's why the godlen hate scourge sorcery—for trying to cheat the natural boundaries."

"Yes. So I had to moderate how I used my magic when a situation got intense. I had to decide when to look ahead at the enemies' next moves and when to hold off. We were clashing with a Darium legion, and I'd already seen them behave exactly as I'd have guessed a few times, so I got cocky. I assumed there was no need to strain my gift and look again when it seemed obvious how they'd strike at us next."

I find myself gripping the stump of my wrist where the prosthetic is attached to its harness. The spot where I gave the sacrifice I then dishonored, for the gift I can no longer use.

"They had a new trick up their sleeve that I hadn't predicted," I go on, my voice stiffening against the weight of the admission. "Before I recognized it and could regroup, they'd slaughtered half of the soldiers I was leading. Men and women who'd counted on *me* to guide them through the battle. One of the Darium soldiers hit me with the blast of magic that scrambled my vision."

"But you ended up pushing them back."

"With sheer brute force and desperation—and the help

of some excellent comrades. Nothing I can really take credit for. And then I was done, as I should have been for my idiocy anyway."

Ivy pulls her legs up onto the sofa to wrap her arms loosely around her knees. "I'm sure you're not the only general who's ever had a battle go badly."

I grimace. "I can't think of any others who lost their entire usefulness in the field in one swoop."

"You're not useless."

I can taste the bitterness in my words, but is there really any point in pretending it away? "Useless enough that my king sent me here to simply teach what I was meant to be doing. Useless enough that my fiancé couldn't stand the thought of marrying a disgraced general and called off the engagement."

Ivy's lips part in shock. "You were engaged?"

"Yes," I say brusquely. "To the daughter of one of the barony families in Konram's court. It wasn't an epic romance, but we suited each other and liked each other enough that I hoped it would become more of a love match over time. But I was no longer the man she thought she'd have, and I wouldn't have wanted to stay with someone who saw me as inadequate anyway."

Ivy hesitates. "Last night, when you reached for me in your sleep—were you thinking of—"

I cut her off with a derisive noise. "No. Not really. There was obviously some unconscious habit associated with sleeping next to a woman, and I apologize for that—it's been nearly a year since I slept next to anyone, and I didn't think it would affect me. But I knew who you were from the moment I woke up."

I'm not sure the old habits *would* have kicked in if it wasn't that I've wanted Ivy more than I ever longed to touch Neela, even at the height of our courtship. But I doubt this is the ideal time to mention that fact.

I barrel onward. "That's not what matters the most, regardless. What matters is I witnessed your magic in the tower, and all I could see after that moment was the catastrophe I might have instigated. I agreed to let you act as my assistant. I missed any signs of what you were. If you lashed out at the students or staff or, gods forbid, wreaked havoc on the royal family right next door, I'd be to blame."

Ivy's voice sounds abruptly small, so painful to hear it might as well be a blade to my gut. "That sounds like a reasonable concern."

"It wasn't." I smack the desk hard enough that the ink pot rattles. "I was so caught up in how horrible I'd feel, how horrible I'd *look*, that I lost sight of what I'd already realized. I have nothing to fear in you. You'd sooner kill yourself than let your power run wild. You hated even stabbing that wretched false friend who'd already stabbed *you*."

Ivy swallows audibly. "It doesn't seem as if the riven get a choice."

"Because they go mad. But I have to assume as you have that they go mad through using their power. Which you've been willing to cough up blood to avoid doing. You'd sooner let some lout strangle you than protect yourself with it."

"I *have* hurt people."

"When you didn't know you could. When you didn't have a choice. Who am I to judge you for that? Hundreds of people died on the battlefield in one day because of a choice *I* made, and no one's ever suggested hanging me."

I push myself off the desk and step toward her, but the tensing of her stance stops me halfway to the sofa. My hand clenches at my side.

"I'm sorry," I say. "I've told you that before, but it never seems like enough. You've put so much of yourself at risk to protect this entire country, and I was treating you like a villain. The gods themselves had intervened, and somehow I still thought my honor was the thing on the line."

Ivy ducks her head. "I never expected you to trust me."

"But I do. That's the point." I dare to take another step closer. "I didn't say it properly last night. I think you're the only person in this mess I truly trust. It's my judgment I've never been sure I could count on, and I took that out on you. That's the real crime I've committed here."

When I refocus my vision on her, Ivy's expression is skeptical. I reach for the right words to convince her of how much I mean this confession.

"You're the most honorable person I've ever met. With every act you take, every word you speak, you prove it again and again. Just now, you didn't have to tell me about your magic acting up during the initiation, but you did. You gave Julita credit for helping you master it. You've offered me grace and compassion over the awful things I've done even though I had none for you when you'd just prevented a city-wide disaster."

"I don't think you did anything all that awful. And it shouldn't be all that special just to tell the truth."

My chuckle comes out raw. "But it is. I think you know it is. Ivy…"

I take another step, bringing me to the end of the sofa. I can't tell if she'd tolerate me trying to sit next to her, but I hate the sense that I'm looming over her like the brute I've acted as.

After a moment's hesitation, I sink down to a crouch that puts us on eye level. I hold her gaze even as her face goes hazy in my sight.

"You said that Casimir and Alek have compared you to Signy. I don't think they're wrong, and not just because of whatever romantic entanglements you've gotten yourself into."

Ivy snorts, but I go on. "If anything, you're even braver than she was. You're facing down an enemy less predictable and more brutal, who could do more harm to this world than the empire ever did, and you're doing it on your own except for a ghost who can't offer you anything but her voice. We'll stop this threat because of *you*, whether the rest of the country ever finds out who the real hero was or not."

Her voice roughens. "I haven't been alone. You've still been here, no matter how much of an asshole you've been in that time. Alek and Casimir have helped."

"You're the one riding at the front of the 'army.' You're the one taking the blows. I would never have asked what you're doing of any soldier, but you've volunteered, again and again, when you had no reason to come to us in the first place other than the selfless generosity you somehow keep dismissing. It would be *my* honor to have you as my Signy."

Ivy draws in a ragged breath. I hold there, waiting for her response, wishing I could read her face for more than a second at a time.

"You really mean that," she says in a wondering tone.

I can't suppress the dry note that creeps into my voice. "I'm aiming for honesty too. I—I don't expect anything from you. You deserve people standing by you who never doubted you to begin with. I'm only hoping that you can feel safe in my presence. That you know I'll only ever leap to protect you, not to hurt you. I don't know how much that's worth when I've failed to save so many before, and that was when I could at least still fucking *see*, but—"

Ivy leans forward and touches my cheek. "Stop."

The feel of her fingers against my skin arrests me. I blink, trying to make sense of the command. "What?"

"Did you really fail before?" she asks, an unexpected tender note slipping into her voice. "You froze up when you were a teenager—if we're not counting my childhood mistakes, I don't think we should count that either. During that last battle, the surprise tactics the Darium soldiers turned to—would you have been able to prevent the slaughter if you'd seen their next few actions a minute ahead of time?"

I think back to the moment when the tide shifted. The sudden blasts of conjured explosions, the wheeling of the cavalry.

"I don't know," I have to admit. "It might not have been enough to recognize their full strategy and counteract it. But it could have been. I never gave the soldiers who were relying on me a proper chance."

Ivy's hand lingers against my face, the warmth of her touch coursing across my cheek. "You might have been able to save them. But you also might have seen the signs and adjusted your own approach, and the Darium army would have held off until they were sure they'd take you by surprise. You might have burned out your gift too soon and missed something even worse."

"I can only go by what happened, and what happened—"

"—wasn't a guarantee. It was a bad situation that *they* caused. Haven't you started telling me that I shouldn't blame myself for struggling with my magic when it's because of the scourge sorcerers' meddling?"

I make a face at her. "That's different. You barely hurt anyone. I had a job to look after those soldiers."

Ivy offers me a small smile. "And I'd be willing to wager good money that you did as good a job as you could with the information you had. In any case, it isn't your job to protect me. There's nothing to fail."

A growl creeps up my throat. "I failed to even stop King Konram from placing that wretched demand on you. I know how much you've hated every time you've taken a life. And the moment you do, every other scourge sorcerer there will be out for your blood. He shouldn't have asked it of you. He's got a whole army trained to kill for him."

Somehow her smile turns even more sad. "But none of them could make it to a meeting of the Order of the Wild."

The growl bursts out of me. I push to my feet with a surge of resolve. "I should put an end to this entire thing. March down the hall to Torstem's office and run him straight through."

Ivy catches my hand. "And then what? His main accomplices will have a chance to scatter and regroup. The king will have to put you on trial. It'll come out that I infiltrated their group, and then anyone out for vengeance will come after me anyway. How does that help anyone?"

I exhale in a rush, but I don't have an answer.

Ivy straightens her posture with an air of resolve. "At least if I do it myself, I can control the situation. I can probably take him down without the others even realizing the knife was mine. And then it'll be over."

She says the last three words like a prayer.

I shake my head. "And you'll have to carry that much more weight on your conscience because I'm too damaged to shield you."

The anguish of my latest dreams echoes through me—the dreams where I see her up on the hangman's platform from across the square, the executioner just looping the noose around her neck. The dreams where I run and yell, but my boots sink into the cobblestones like mud, and I'm still much to far away when the trap door drops beneath her.

Ivy shatters the image with a guffaw and gets to her feet. "Stavros, I've seen you spar. If it comes to a fight, I'd rather have you defending me than anyone else, even myself. If you were too 'damaged' to be a threat, I wouldn't have been scared of you. But we can settle this right now."

I'm distracted enough by her use of the past tense when she mentions her fear that I don't quite process her last statement. "Settle what?"

The next thing I know, the woman before me has whipped a knife from her boot and lunged at me.

If she could read my emotions in that moment, she'd know how true everything I said to her is. My pulse jumps with surprise and a little alarm, but nothing close to panic.

I know down to my soul that she isn't turning traitor on me. This isn't a real attack.

But that doesn't mean she'll shy away from jabbing me a little if it proves her point.

The tip of Ivy's blade skims the side of my hand just before I block her strike. A pinprick of pain tells me she broke the skin.

More than two decades of honed combat instincts kick in. I shift my posture, dodge her next blow, and check her stance for an opening.

I took off my sword belt after I came back to the room, so I've only got my hands to work with, though the metal prosthetic serves as a decent weapon. I snatch at her wrist to try to disarm her, but she darts out of the way just in time.

Her knife never stops flashing for an instant. She's no match for me in size, but she's so fast I barely have the chance to overpower her.

As we circle the sofa and approach the window, Ivy keeps me on the defensive, blocking and parrying. But I've fought difficult battles before.

I rap her shin just hard enough to put her off-balance and attempt to topple her with a shove of my shoulder. Ivy scrambles backward, but she's retreating now.

Her knife clangs off my prosthetic, and I wrench the curved metal loop around just in time to snag on Ivy's hand. With a twist, I send the weapon careening across the room.

I yank her arm toward me and catch it in my other hand. With a breathless laugh, Ivy squirms against my hold. Her knee rams toward my gut.

She doesn't have a hope without her blade. Tucking my other arm around her head to cushion it, I heave us both onto the floor and let my much larger frame pin her limbs in place.

"That's enough," I say. "What in the realms are you playing at?"

Ivy beams up at me, her hair fanned across my forearm, her grin so bright even the blurring of my vision can't hide its delight. "Not playing. Just proving why I don't have to worry about your protective abilities. Even when *I'm* attacking you, you manage to protect me as well as yourself."

I stare down at her, my stomach flipping over with a heady rush like nothing I've ever felt before.

Gods above, this woman is more than incredible. I don't have the words to describe her.

But describing isn't what I most want to do with her right now.

My head bows as if drawn by a magnet. Ivy tilts hers upward just in time for our mouths to collide.

How can this be the first time I've really kissed her? These lips have caught my attention so many times, but those glimpses of them is nothing compared to their softness against my own or the eager breath that spills over them with an intoxicating heat.

All of it feels right—the press of her mouth, the silkiness of her hair when I run my fingers over it, her lithe body beneath mine.

I lift myself up slightly so I can deepen the kiss, and Ivy slips her arm free. She wraps it around the back of my neck and teases her fingers up into my hair.

The simple gesture sets off a cascade of sparks through

my scalp. Fuck me, we've barely started kissing and I'm already painfully hard.

I can't rut against her like the animal I turned into last night. If I fuck this up, I don't know if I'm ever going to get another chance to show her what she means to me.

I break the kiss to peer down at her, with a twitch of my head when my sight starts to fail me. Ivy meets my gaze, flushed and still smiling, looking nothing but pleased with our current position.

Her hand leaves my hair to trail over my neck along the collar of my dress shirt. "If you're all so determined to have your own Signy, I suppose I'll give it my best shot."

A laugh sputters out of me, alongside a swell of emotion that hums through my pulse and condenses at the base of my throat.

I know exactly what I need to say. What's been becoming true for longer than I've been willing to admit it, and maybe that's why I've been so terrified.

Part of me wants to duck my head so I don't have to take in her response, but that would be a coward's way. I adjust my eyes with a little tick to the side just as I speak, so I'll see her face as clearly as possible in the first moment.

"I love you."

FORTY-THREE

Ivy

I gape at Stavros, everything narrowing down to the three words ringing in my ears. Did he… did he really say what I thought I heard?

In my startled silence, his expression shifts, his mouth tensing. He moves as if to push himself right off me, but I snap out of my daze in time to catch the front of his shirt.

I still don't know how to answer him, but my arms move of their own accord. They loop across his shoulders, hugging him closer to me instead.

Stavros bows his head so our foreheads rest together. I hear him swallow.

He manages to find the droll tone that's both amused and annoyed me over our weeks together. "I shocked the words right out of you. That's some kind of accomplishment."

My laugh comes out choked. I tilt my head to seek out his lips.

Somehow sinking into a kiss feels easier than saying

anything back just yet. My emotions are still roiling inside me, plenty of previous shock mixing with amazement and affection.

Can I really doubt his admission when he's opened up to me about so much else? He put all his regrets and weaknesses on display just to reassure *me*.

Well, Julita says softly. *That's not where I was expecting this conversation to end up, but I'm glad I got to see it. He's right in everything he said about you, Ivy. And I think I've played voyeur long enough.*

Her presence dwindles in the back of my skull. Stavros's heat still encompasses me, his body dwarfing mine though no longer trapping it.

He loves me.

I can't quite wrap my head around the idea, though every time I remember his voice saying those words, another giddy flutter passes through my chest. I never thought...

Well, I never thought I'd hear him say most of the things he has tonight.

My heart aches with all the things *I'm* not saying. But it's not as if I could return the same exact sentiment yet.

Less than an hour ago, I considered it possible he'd end up dragging me to the executioner someday. A person needs a little time to catch their balance when the ground they thought they were standing on tips over.

I've wanted him... for much longer than I've liked. I think I started falling for him that night after the catastrophe of a ball when he admitted how much he'd come to appreciate my dedication—and revealed a sliver of the anguish he's fully bared this evening.

Every movement of his lips against mine is delectable. Every inch of my body tingles with the awareness of his massive frame braced over me.

Even as I think that, Stavros eases back. He pulls himself

upright, drawing me with him so we're sitting facing each other.

Not exactly apart, though. My knee rests against his thigh. His hand lingers against my jaw.

His mouth quirks into a slanted smile. "I suppose the shock can't be that bad. You didn't run away screaming in horror."

I meet his blue-and-brown gaze, letting my hand settle on his other arm just below the jut of his prosthetic. "It's still sinking in. I'm sorry I can't— My feelings were already jumbled up from everything we talked about before—"

"It's all right." Stavros strokes his thumb across my cheek. "I haven't made it easy on you. And I wouldn't want you to lie to me. It feels like some kind of miracle that you're even willing to kiss me."

More heat collects low in my belly. I'd like to do a lot more than kiss him—that much I'm sure of.

The knowledge steadies me. We've covered some of that territory before. Hooking up isn't quite as fraught as declarations of devotion.

Maybe there's an easy way I can put us back on level ground and defuse the tension of the moment.

I scoot a little backward and wave my hand at Stavros carelessly. "I think we can do better than that. But first, strip."

His expression turns incredulous. "What?"

I give another flippant gesture, indicating the whole muscular expanse of him I've never really gotten to admire before. "Strip. I want to have a look at what I'm working with."

His eyes flash with the eager light that's drawn me to this man from the first moment I saw it flare in his gaze. A sly grin crosses his face. "Turn-around's fair play, hmm?"

So he's recognized the call-back to our first sparring

session, back when he thought I was nothing more than a thieving street rat.

I shrug, offering my most innocent smile. "At least I have the pure motivation of simply wanting to appreciate the view, no ego involved."

Stavros guffaws. "Pure?" But to my delight, he stands up, reaching for his shirt.

I do drink in the view as he deftly undoes the buttons with his one hand. I suppose having sacrificed the other to Sabrelle when he turned twelve, he must have gotten a lot of practice at doing all kinds of things one-handed. None of his prosthetics would be much help with more delicate maneuvers.

The triangle of bare chest shows wider with each opened button. Then he reaches the bottom and shrugs the shirt right off, leaving the full muscular expanse of his torso bared, along with the harness that keeps his prosthetic in place against the stump of his wrist.

I lean back on my hands while I study him. He might not ride off into battle anymore, but he's kept up a warrior's physique. Every inch of his chest, abdomen, and arms is sculpted into taut ridges of muscle.

Here and there, marks either paler or ruddier cut across his light brown skin. I'm familiar enough with certain sorts of wounds to tell a few are scars left by blades and at least one was a burn, but others must be from weapons I don't often encounter.

Or not weapons at all. It was a magical strike that damaged his vision.

In the midst of it all, the curving lines of Sabrelle's brand stand out at the base of his sternum. The dedication he took for a life he's been almost entirely shut out of.

I hope Sabrelle hasn't abandoned him for his injury. He served her well while he could.

I'm occupied enough with ogling that it takes me a minute to notice that Stavros has stopped undressing. He's watching me take him in with a gaze as avid as mine.

I arch an eyebrow. "I don't think you're finished yet. You had me down to my underclothes."

"That I did. Well, if the lady wishes it…"

He tugs off his boots without hesitation. I think a hint of a flush creeps up his neck as he loosens the ties on his trousers.

I've no doubt that Stavros has entertained plenty of women beyond the one he once thought he'd marry, but I'd guess most of them didn't ask him to put on a show for their amusement.

He'll be used to them seducing *him* with strategically revealed skin and flirty glances.

I don't see any need to be coy after everything that's passed between us. When he drops his trousers, I let my gaze rove over every bulge and shadow of his chiseled legs from thighs to calves—and back up again, to one particularly impressive bulge tenting his drawers.

Stavros kicks his trousers to the side, his gaze smoldering into me. "Do I meet your satisfaction, Lady Thief?"

I wasn't always sure I liked that nickname. Hearing it now in his old sardonic lilt, the cockiness returned to his voice with warmth twined through it, lifts my spirits with another flutter of my pulse.

I smirk back at him. "I suppose you'll do."

With a rustle of my skirt, I stand and saunter toward him. Stavros holds perfectly still other than the rise and fall of his breath.

I set my hand on one pectoral and skim my fingertips down to his waist. The slight hitch of his chest eggs me on.

The top of my head barely reaches his shoulder. But that

simply means that I'm the perfect height to press a kiss to one of those scars mottling his torso.

At the brush of my lips against his heated skin, a rumble of amusement that's a little ragged as well emanates from the former general's lungs. He cups my shoulder, gliding his thumb along the curving neckline of my dress.

Everywhere I shift my gaze, there's another nick or lingering line that I couldn't make out from afar. My lungs constrict at the sight of them.

I really don't have any concept of just how much this man endured during his years on the front lines of Silana's ongoing military squabbles. Has he skirted death even more times than I have?

With a sudden sense of urgency, I set my hand over the roughened skin of his dedication brand and kiss another of the scars. And another. And another.

"What are you doing?" Stavros asks, with a rasp in his voice he can't quite master.

I move my lips to the next scar, letting them graze his mottled skin as I speak. "Thanking Sabrelle for ensuring that none of these wounds brought you to your end."

A choked sound escapes him, and then he's tugging my chin up while he lowers his head. His mouth crashes into mine.

I've been kissed before by all three of the other men Julita brought together. Benedikt's kiss was merely a quick thrill, doused by his blasé attitude afterward. But Alek's can electrify me, and Casimir knows how to make me melt.

Stavros's kiss sets me on fire.

Even as the flames of desire dance beneath my skin, threatening to burn me up, I can't help leaning into him. Can't help wanting to absorb every bit of the scorching need we kindle between us.

This is the only kind of bonfire I want to worship at.

When he tugs at the laces of my gown to loosen it, I don't have a single protest left in me. I let the garment fall and wriggle out of my underskirt as well between kiss after addicting kiss.

I have to let go of him so he can pull off my chemise. He gazes down at me, now as bared as he is, with the familiar twitch of his head that makes me abruptly self-conscious.

I won't look anything like the pampered noblewomen he must be used to. No amount of living among them will disguise the effects of my childhood deprivations or the scars I've taken in different sorts of battles.

But Stavros traces his fingers down my sternum with a reverent expression. They graze the false godlen brand and continue to my belly button.

Then he lifts my arm and presses a tender kiss to the scar that slashes across my bicep from a blade I didn't dodge quite fast enough. The wider one on my forearm, where I scraped it on a window ledge fleeing the Crown's Watch at thirteen.

He trails a caress back up my arm and grazes the worst scars across my shoulder blades, his touch feather-light. His voice comes out low and raw. "The only one I can thank for keeping you alive is you. But Sabrelle herself would be impressed by the strength that's gotten you through everything you've endured."

I can't deny the admiration or the hunger in his tone. Before the surge of emotion can overwhelm me, I yank his mouth back to mine.

With one hand tangled in my hair and other arm a solid pressure against the small of my back, Stavros guides us both down to the floor with me straddling his lap. It's a good position for our mismatched heights, putting me where I can claim another kiss by bobbing a little up on my knees... or drop lower against him to create a friction that has us both groaning.

When I grind against him through our drawers, Stavros's arm tightens around me. He teases his hand down my front to cup my breast and cants his hips upward to pay me back in kind.

"Last night was good before I screwed it up," he murmurs between increasingly urgent kisses. "But this is so much better."

I make a noise of agreement that sounds embarrassingly like a whine of need and reclaim his mouth. As his tongue flicks between my lips, his thumb swivels over my nipple. I shiver with the pleasure flooding me from every angle.

A hard surface cooler than his skin strokes over my hip. I startle for a second before I recognize that—of course—it's his prosthetic.

Stavros pauses, glancing down at the hooked loop of metal against my leg. "I can take it off. I wasn't thinking—"

"No," I say quickly. "I… I like it."

A blush burns across my cheeks at the admission, but the look Stavros gives me in return sears away any shame I might have felt about unusual tastes. Like I'm the only person he ever wants to look at for the rest of his life.

A sudden fear squeezes my heart. I touch his face as if I need to steady us both against this question.

"Are you sure you're okay with—with me being with Alek and Casimir too?"

Alek suggested it to begin with, and I know Casimir has an open mind about romantic partnerships, but Stavros has never struck me as the type to be good at sharing. Does he think my giving myself over to this moment with him means I'm giving myself *just* to him from now on?

Before the fear can dig its claws any deeper, one of the sly grins that used to infuriate me curves the former general's lips. "I'll tolerate it. Because just one man couldn't possibly be enough for our new Signy."

I like him this way. The cockiness buoyed by the warmth of real assurance, no harsh edge of defensiveness souring his tone.

This is the man thousands of soldiers would gladly have followed into battle, knowing he'd subject them to no risk he didn't take himself. Knowing their well-being mattered to him as much as brilliant tactics did.

I don't think any of the men and women who died fulfilling his orders would have blamed him for it.

I tap my fingers against his cheek in the lightest of swats. "It seems to be the only part of the role that actually benefits me."

Stavros hums and dips his head closer so I'm flooded with his smoky, spicy scent. His voice is more a purr than a growl now. "I like seeing you a little bit selfish. Asking for what you want, taking everything you can have. If that means I have to make sure I keep proving myself worthy of you so you don't decide two is plenty, I'm not one to shy from a challenge."

A headier shiver travels down my spine. I run my hands down the impressive planes of his chest and let my mouth meld with his.

With each collision of our lips and caress of his hand against my breast, the throbbing need between my legs deepens. I rock against him, whimpering into our kiss at the feel of his hardness meeting my sex.

I delve one hand down between us and stroke him through his drawers.

"I want this," I mutter, with a flare of boldness. "Inside me."

A ragged chuckle escapes Stavros. "Then who am I to deny you, Lady Thief?"

He wrenches at my drawers, hooking his prosthetic over the waist, and I fumble with his at the same time. The second

I've kicked mine off, I sink down over him, letting his rigid erection graze my folds skin to skin.

I'm so wet with my desire that we slide together perfectly. Stavros groans, but he steadies me in his arms.

"We take this slow. I don't want you feeling anything but good."

I give a small huff in acknowledgment, but he's just as big as I remembered from last night. I pump my fingers up and down over the velvety flesh that's rigid as steel underneath and line us up to take him into me.

With the first stretch of penetration, both our breaths stutter together. He eases inside gradually but firmly, filling me with a heady pressure until it takes all my self-control not to slam the rest of the way home, knowing I'd probably regret it.

Stavros strokes his prosthetic across my ass and his hand up and down my back, careful of my scars. A rumble sounds from low in his chest.

"That's right. Take it all. Fuck, Ivy."

There's so much need in those last two words that I clench around him with a whimper of my own longing. It already feels so good that I have trouble imagining what it'll be like when we really start moving.

Sweat has beaded on my forehead. I lean it against Stavros's shoulder and rock just slightly up and down. Working him deeper inside with every iteration until my next exhalation comes out in a gasp.

"Good?" he checks with a note of concern.

"So fucking good," I mumble, and start to pick up my pace.

Stavros bucks his hips up to meet me, carefully and then with more force when I moan my approval. Every jolt of sensation inside me sends bliss radiating through the rest of my body.

I cling to him, my fingernails digging into his back, but he makes no complaint. His lips brush against my hair, murmuring praise and encouragement and then simply, "Love you. Love you."

He bucks into me with those words, sending me soaring toward my release. The rush of it knocks the air from my lungs and a choked sound from my throat.

I tilt my head to the side and graze my teeth against the crook of his neck as if I need to bite him to stop myself from spiraling away completely. Stavros's hips jerk upwards, his cock plunging into me at just the right angle, and I shatter apart.

I feel him come with me, his muscles flexing around me, his embrace tightening as he clings to me just as firmly. I careen through the wave of pleasure and come back to earth nestled in his scorching but tender embrace.

"Mmm." I tuck myself even closer against him, reveling in the strength his body emanates. "Remind me to be selfish more often."

A laugh hitches out of Stavros. "I wish you could be. Great God help me, I wish I could hold you right here until the end of fucking time."

Until there are no more scourge sorcerers to worry about. Until the king has to make some other plan without me.

It's a nice thought, but we both know there's no answer so simple.

I nuzzle his jaw and hug him for the last short while before I have to go out and face the murderous path I've set myself on.

FORTY-FOUR

Ivy

I'm just pulling on my leather sparring vest when a hand comes to rest on my shoulder.

"I can help you with that."

I peer up at Stavros through my eyelashes as he hooks the loops down one side and then the other, his fingers sparking tingles over my skin through my shirt. "I have managed to do it up just fine on my own all those times before."

He hums, a soft rumble that makes my nerves flutter even more. "I like that you'll let me." His head dips lower as his hand slides across my waist. "And it puts me in a perfect position to do this."

His mouth claims mine before I can say anything else, but at that point I'm not interested in arguing anyway. Being wooed by the exalted former General Stavros is an unexpectedly intoxicating experience.

And his ex-fiancée gave this up because he wasn't riding off into battle trying to get himself killed every other day? I

don't know anything about her other than her status, but I'm pretty confident in saying she's an idiot.

Julita giggles. *You know, I wasn't sure if Stavros would be all that talented at kissing. I'm glad I lingered long enough to be proven wrong.*

There's enough genuine glee in her voice that I don't worry she's bottling up more jealousy. The new biggest problem in our friendship may be having to decide just how much detail I'm willing to go into about the intimate parts she's withdrawn for.

That thought reminds me of all the other ways Stavros and I need to be circumspect about our newfound closeness.

I ease back reluctantly. "When we leave this room, we're going to have to pretend things are still tense between us. If anyone associated with Torstem realizes we might be colluding after all…"

Stavros nods before I have to finish my statement. "I'm not looking forward to it, but I can glower and grouse at you if it'll shield you from worse harm." He glides his fingertips along my jaw in one last caress. "As long as you remember it is all an act."

I grin at him. "I don't think my memories of last night are going to fade that quickly."

But there are plenty of other memories to cast a pall over the day ahead. As we step into the hall, keeping a careful distance apart, my gaze slips along the row of doors toward Ster. Torstem's quarters farther down.

How long of a reprieve will I get before I need to spill his blood or betray the king?

I have the sudden urge to shove Stavros back into his quarters, to signal Alek and Casimir and spend whatever time I have left soaking up all the happiness I can squeeze out of this life. I don't know how much of a life I'll have left once I've carried out King Konram's orders.

As simple as the king made the job sound, with every passing hour the knowledge weighs on me that there's no guarantee I'll be able to escape in the chaos after the assassination. Torstem's end may be mine too.

But I have to admit that one life to rid the continent of a new scourge sorcerer uprising seems more than fair. I knew the risks when I set off on this path.

So I simply clench my hands at my sides and stalk along behind Stavros as if resenting my duties, all the way down to the training field.

Assisting with the combat class isn't so bad. These students have sparred with me enough to grant me a little respect.

I throw myself into the moment, clashing blades with the opponents Stavros sets me against and tossing out snarky remarks as if I'm every bit the rebel. It's a better distraction than moping around the campus on my own.

When the former general's back is turned, Olari shoots me a conspiratorial smile.

Does he know I saw him unmasked at the initiation ceremony? Or maybe he's simply anticipating that I'll put the pieces together when I join him for this evening's meeting of the bug club.

Despite my feigned friction with Stavros, I do my best to put on a supportive face with the students. Most of them have nothing to do with the mess I've gotten myself into.

I don't need more enemies on top of those I already have to contend with.

Speaking of potential enemies, this is one of the classes Petra joins the military division for. I contrive to avoid facing her throughout the various exercises Stavros assigns, but the distant royal has an unfortunate stubborn streak.

When I've finished hauling our equipment back into the storage building at the end of the class, I emerge from the room to find Petra standing in the building's dim hallway.

There's no one else around. It's obvious she's waiting for me.

I debate going so far as to stride right past her, but such a blatant snub feels unwise. So I stop and give her my best blank expression instead. "Was there something you needed?"

Petra's dark gaze flicks around us, as if she's as alert to possible eavesdroppers as I am. She steps closer, pitching her voice low. "I wanted to speak with you—briefly. I won't delay you for very long."

I fold my arms over my chest with a conscious effort to keep them loose rather than defensively tight. "Speak to me about what?"

Petra studies me for a few seconds, her pensive gaze uncomfortably keen. "I understand why you've rebuffed and avoided me, and I don't blame you for it. I shouldn't have put you in an awkward situation to begin with."

My stomach knots, but I knit my brow with honest confusion. "What are you talking about?"

She makes a dismissive gesture. "That's not the important part. The main thing I wanted to say is… When someone asks too much of you, it's reasonable to refuse. The people with the most power aren't always right."

A sinking sensation ripples through me from throat to gut. She can't possibly know—surely King Konram wouldn't have discussed his secret assassination plans with his niece however many times removed, of all people?

I'm not sure I believe he'd even tell the queen.

I can't stop my voice from stiffening slightly. "I don't quite follow what you mean. Ster. Stavros hasn't asked anything all that immense of me. I'm happy to do my job."

It's the response she should expect from someone who

hasn't been given a different, horrible job by a figure with a lot more power than my employer, but the intensity in Petra's smooth face doesn't shift.

"Maybe you're not sure you can say no outright," she says. "But you can pick your own methods to achieve the same goal. Do it your way, the way that feels right to you. That's all the gods want from us. I'm sorry."

She turns on her heel and hurries out of the storage building without another word. Her last two words ring in my head.

Somehow the apology unsettles me more than anything else.

Well, Julita says in a doubtful tone. *What in the realms was she getting at?*

I lift my shoulders in a tiny shrug, but my stomach keeps churning.

It certainly sounded as if Petra knows what I've been asked to do. Even if she doesn't—would her suggestion still apply?

Gods smite me, why should I listen to some minor royal's opinions anyway? It isn't her neck on the line with the scourge sorcerers or the king.

But through the rest of the day, Petra's words keep niggling at me.

I'm already carrying out the king's command "my way," aren't I? I'll be using my stealth and my knife, the tools I've relied on so often in the past.

Of course, Petra has no idea who I've been in the past. Does she think her distant uncle instructed me on exactly how to kill Ster. Torstem, and there might be some other method of murder I'd prefer?

Or did she mean something else entirely?

And what in the realms would the god who's kept me

alive this far want, anyway? Kosmel is continuing to be frustratingly silent on that subject.

I have to push all those unsettling questions aside when I make my way to the entomology club's room in the Quadring. This time I get to enter it through the door rather than slipping through a window.

Having experienced the space before, I'm prepared for the mix of woodsy and sour scents and the ever-present rustling of the club room's smallest inhabitants. Still, my skin creeps as I step inside.

Although to be fair, the human inhabitants are at least as much to blame for that.

Olari looks up from where he's standing near a row of terrariums with two other students I recognize from Alek's sketches and my own furtive observations. He dips his head to me in acknowledgment.

Several other students glance over from their places amid the tanks and tables to take in the newcomer. Some I recognize as other likely conspirators. The others are probably innocent dupes who think this organization really is just about an interest in insect life.

And then, naturally, there's our valiant leader, Ster. Torstem.

The law professor strides over and beckons me farther into the room. "Ivy of Nikodi. I heard you'd expressed an interest in joining our little cabal here." He chuckles lightly as if "cabal" isn't actually a more accurate word to describe what he's been running than "club."

He told me exactly how to reply, even if he doesn't realize I know he was the one giving the instructions.

I offer an ingratiating smile. "I've always been curious about the smallest of our world's creatures. I heard you've collected several rare specimens."

"Indeed we have! Come in, come in. Let me show you a few that we're particularly proud of."

He sets his hand on my shoulder to guide me forward. In the back of my head, Julita's presence shudders the way I wish I could.

I don't approve of King Konram assigning you to be a murderer, she mutters, *but if you have to murder someone, I can't say I mind it being this slimy traitor.*

I can't help but share her sentiment.

Ster. Torstem points out a pair of beetles with iridescent shells that change color depending on the angle of the light, a moth that looks identical to the leaves on the branch in its enclosure, and a ruddy-shelled centipede as thick as my thumb and twice as long. I gamely ooh and aah over them while sending silent thanks to Creaden for the thick construction of the habitats' walls.

I wouldn't say I'm particularly squeamish after my years living on the streets, but if that last creature scrambled its many legs up my arm, I think I might scream.

Torstem introduces me to the other club members in attendance, focusing on Olari's trio and the others whose names I'm familiar with.

"I believe you'll be with our fields group to start," he says in a casually authoritative tone. "It's too unwieldly for all of us to make our expeditions together, so we've divided into fields and forests, switching things up halfway through the year. Luckily for you, we have a fields expedition coming up in just a couple of nights, if you're able to join us. It's right before break-day, so it shouldn't interfere with your assistant position."

A couple of nights?

A chill sweeps through my body, but I keep my smile plastered in place. "I'm sure I can arrange that. I'll look forward to the trip."

In just two days, I'm supposed to kill this man.

Torstem simply smiles back, oblivious to my true intentions. "Wonderful. You'll be a welcome addition to our team."

Even if my head is whirling, I'm supposed to make a show of having a real interest in the club. I wander along the shelves of tanks, watching the various insects navigate their manufactured habitats. I can't shake the feeling that the walls have closed in on me as tightly as those surrounding the bug club's many tiny prisoners.

At one table, a couple of the members who must be from the forests group are adding soil to the base of a large, open-topped terrarium. I gravitate toward them. It might be nice to talk to someone who isn't scheming to topple civilization as we know it.

"What are you setting this one up for?" I ask.

The guy pats down the soil around a small metal trough with pebbles along the bottom. "We're hoping to find a glowdid on our next trip out. They only show themselves for a few weeks during the early summer. The club's never had one before."

"They're awfully quick too," explains the woman next to him. "And of course we don't want to harm the one we catch."

"I think we have a good chance." The guy brushes his fingers over the small shrub planted at one end of the tank. "Glowdids only eat pilmetta leaves, and it's notoriously difficult to grow them inside. But we've gotten this one to thrive. Prospira must support our quest."

The woman sketches her fingers down her front in the gesture of the divinities. "I think we should take it as a sign of approval. Maybe not of catching one, but of our overall goal, at least."

A quiver of sharper alertness runs through my nerves. Those words echo back to something Petra said.

I cock my head. "Your overall goal?"

The woman nods enthusiastically. "We'd like to catch a couple of glowdids in order to study and even breed them. But the most important part is simply observing them and getting a better understanding of their behavior, even if it's only in their normal environment. Their numbers have been dwindling lately. We'd like to find a way to help their population stay healthy and secure."

Different methods to achieve the same goal. Another quiver races straight down the middle of me. "That makes sense. I hope you can manage it."

I meander on, my eyes turned toward the next set of terrariums but my mind drifted far beyond this room.

The king's goal isn't really to have me murder Ster. Torstem. It's to end the threat the scourge sorcerers prevent. He simply thinks their leader's death is the likeliest way to ensure that outcome, and I'm the tool most readily available.

What if there's something that could destroy the conspiracy *without* me having to stain my hands with all that blood?

FORTY-FIVE

Alek

W hen I step through the cord into the palace meeting room at our scheduled time and find only Stavros waiting, my pulse hiccups. "Isn't Ivy—"

"The bug club meeting ran a little long, but she's fine," he says from where he's sitting at the table, before I need to finish my anxious question. "She didn't end up eating beforehand, so she ran to grab something from the dining hall before she'll join us."

The momentary panic that gripped me eases. I walk over to the table, but I still feel too anxious to sit down.

Stavros's expression is grim. It's hard to relax when even a former general who's survived a hundred battles looks uneasy about a situation.

My fingers curl around the top of the chair. "Did she tell you anything about what went on with the entomology club?"

Stavros's mouth tightens even more before he answers. "A little. As usual, she wants to give us the full account all together rather than repeating herself."

He obviously isn't inclined to give me the little he does know, but after a pause, he lifts his gaze to meet mine again. "One of those clay deliveries you suspect is for the scourge sorcerers went out this morning."

My heart skips in a more enthusiastic fashion. "Was someone able to track it?"

"The two soldiers the king assigned to watch the quarry are particularly adept at stealth missions. They followed the workers at a distance and saw the hand-off with the buyer. Unfortunately, they only managed to stay on the buyer's trail for half a mile before the wagon and its driver vanished."

I frown. "'Vanished'?"

Stavros lets out a disgruntled sigh. "Simply disappeared from view in a blink, as the soldiers tell it. They hung back for a short while and then surveyed the area, but they couldn't find any traces of passage."

I push away from the chair to pace the length of the table. "We know from what Ivy's told us that the scourge sorcerers must have someone very skilled with concealing magic on their side. They're able to disguise their passage of the Starsil and the bonfires they worship around."

"Yes, we have to assume magic was involved. So we don't know *where* they were taking the clay, but I think we can consider it confirmed that it is the scourge sorcerers who are taking it."

His tone stays as grim as his expression. I can't summon a smile myself.

It's an awfully minor victory. We need so much more if we're going to free Ivy from the task King Konram assigned to her.

Casimir arrives a moment later, with the same worried

glance around the room I must have made on my entrance. Before he can even ask about Ivy, she emerges from her loop of cord too with a swish of her layered skirts.

Her face holds such a mix of foreboding and resolve that a pang reverberates through my heart even as my lips spring into a smile at the sight of her. She swipes a few stray strands of hair back from her cheeks and squares her shoulders.

But when her eyes meet mine, the emotion that sparks in them sends a bolt of giddiness straight through my nerves. With an answering smile, she walks straight to me and bobs up to press her mouth against mine.

It isn't one of the chaste pecks we've exchanged since she told Casimir and me that we needed to tone down the physical part of our relationship. The heat of the kiss sets my pulse racing with a flush that washes over my skin.

I hesitate only for an instant with a hitch of surprise, and then I clasp the back of her neck to return the kiss as eagerly as she's offered it. I don't know what's gotten into her, but I want her to know I'm right here with her.

Ivy draws back with a softer smile that lights me up from head to toe. "I sorted some things out with Julita. We don't have to hold back our feelings."

The relief that sweeps through me at those words is as much for Ivy as my own satisfaction. I can't imagine what it's like being at odds with another person who's residing right inside your head.

I squeeze her shoulder. "I'm glad you could come to an understanding." As I peer into her eyes, I try to picture the woman I knew before her watching me through them too. "Thank you."

Ivy breaks into a laugh, a hint of a blush coloring her pale cheeks. "She says you're very welcome as long as you make sure to take good care of me."

My own face heats even more, but my lips twitch with a grin. "I don't think that'll be a problem."

Casimir has been following our exchange with his usual serene composure, no sign of impatience or jealousy. But the second Ivy turns to him, he steps forward to meet her, beaming so avidly no one could doubt how happy he is to accept her embrace.

It's a strange sensation, watching the woman I've fallen for kiss another man. A wobble runs through the pit of my stomach, a sense of loss that I'm not sharing that moment with her as well. And yet exhilaration floods me to see her beam back at him, even happier now that she's reconfirmed her affection for both of us.

She's an extraordinary woman. I'm not sure I really could "take care" of her as thoroughly as she deserves on my own.

And there's no one I'd trust more than the courtesan to ensure she's never left wanting—in any of the ways I want her life with us to be better than what she had before.

My gaze slides to the other man at the table.

Stavros has remained in his chair, but his expression has shifted as he watches Ivy with us. Like he can't tear his eyes from her… and he isn't sure he'd want to anyway.

I'm not sure what to make of that or the slightly wary smile Ivy shoots him that relaxes when he chuckles in return. Something has changed in their dynamic. The tension that's shadowed this room so often in the past few weeks has lightened.

I'll count that as a win, whatever exactly has passed between them.

Then Stavros sits up straighter, the solemn cast returning to his face, and I'm dragged back to the full reality of our situation. This isn't a joyful reunion—it's a strategy session to send Ivy off to commit an assassination.

The happy glow that came over Ivy dims too, but she

speaks with the same steely resolve I saw when she stepped into the room. "I'm supposed to go on a 'bug club' expedition in two nights. Presumably it's actually an Order of the Wild gathering."

My breath halts in my chest. "Two nights? You were *just* initiated."

Ivy shrugs. "Maybe they want to get us initiates fully immersed quickly. It's probably for the best, since we want to make our move before they have a chance to strike at the royal family."

Casimir sets his hand on her arm. "Did they say anything about what you'll be doing on the 'expedition'?"

She shakes her head. "I doubt they'd want to even hint at their real purpose with the other club members around. But it'll involve at least all of the members who are part of the conspiracy—and I should have a chance to get close to Ster. Torstem."

Stavros pushes to his feet as if he can't bear to stay sitting any longer. "I can alert the king and make an excuse to visit the nearest posted squadron that night, so I'll be able to direct them to you when you signal me."

It's happening too fast. I can't stop myself from blurting out a protest. "You shouldn't have to do it."

Stavros's dark gaze swings to me. "None of us thinks she should. But if she's going to insist—"

"I'm not," Ivy breaks in.

All three of us stare at her. Now I feel as if the breath has been knocked right out of my lungs.

"What?" I manage to say, afraid to hope that she means what I think she does.

Ivy lifts her chin defiantly. "I'll kill him if I have to. But I want to try another way first. The king doesn't *need* Torstem dead by my hand, does he? All that really matters to him is overturning the conspiracy."

Stavros is studying her with open bemusement. "I'd say that's true. He seemed to think Torstem's death was a necessary component. Do you have some new plan for accomplishing that aim?"

She grimaces. "I'm still working it out. I was hoping the three of you could help. We need all the scourge sorcerers distracted and in disarray for the soldiers to be able to sweep in and apprehend them. If the king would like one of his people to then find a reason to murder Torstem—for resisting arrest, perhaps—it'll be out of my hands."

A vicious light sparks in Stavros's eyes. "I know at least one person who'd be happy to take up that duty. And who can assure King Konram that you fulfilled all the important parts of your mission, as far as I'm concerned."

My spirits have lifted, but the weight of doubt dampens my initial excitement. "We'd still have to get the squadron to the conspirators before they realize there's trouble and scatter. From what Ivy's said, it'll be awfully difficult to distract them enough that they'd disregard a warning from their sentries. They're so quick to turn on anyone they feel isn't standing with them... Anything Ivy does to upset them could make her a target."

Stavros glances at Ivy with a frown. "Yes, whatever you do would have to keep them too distraught to rally at an impending threat for long enough for us to reach you. The closest squadron is about an hour's ride from the region Casimir identified."

I nod miserably. "I hate to say it, but you'd be safer stabbing Torstem and then fleeing. I can't think of much that would affect them that strongly other than losing their leader. The fervor they've shown—they're so devoted to their cause and so convinced that they have the only true answer to calling back the All-Giver—"

Ivy's head jerks toward me. "That's it!"

I blink at her. "What is?"

"They're sure they're right," she says, rapping her hand against the tabletop. "But even with all their power, they're not. What if I can do something that makes them doubt the entire reason they've gathered at all? Turn them against each other thinking they've been led astray, that the gods are angry with them rather than approving?"

Casimir rubs his jaw, his eyes gone pensive. "You'd need to tread carefully. The gods could be offended by *you* pretending to speak for them too."

But the new idea has given me a renewed surge of inspiration. "They don't have to speak. Most people don't hear voices from their godlen anyway. They interpret dreams —well, I suppose that isn't likely to be applicable in the middle of a gathering—and signs that catch their attention. If you could create a significant omen that would look like disapproval without outright impersonating one of the godlen…"

Stavros clears his throat. "To make a big enough 'sign' to unsettle the scourge sorcerers, I'd imagine Ivy would need to use her magic."

An uneasy silence settles over the room. Ivy's mouth twists as she studies Stavros's expression.

"You're right," she says after a moment. "So maybe I can't attempt a different approach after all. I—I'd be willing to tap into my power if it means throwing the conspirators into disorder, but I don't know if I'd be able to control it well enough to avoid doing more harm than good. It's always been Kosmel guiding the consequences when I've handled it effectively, and he hasn't given *me* any signs in days."

The hopelessness that's crept back into her voice lances through my gut.

I grope for any tool I have to counter it. "I was able to find an antidote for the crozzemi toxin's effects. I've already arranged to pick some up tomorrow morning, so you'll have it in time. You'll be more in control of your reactions than before."

Ivy shoots me a grateful smile, but she still looks deflated. "Thank you. That'll make some difference, assuming it works. But even when I'm fully conscious, I've never been able to harness the backlash my magic creates. It seems to decide for itself."

Except when the godlen who appeared to have chosen her as his champion intervened.

I knit my brow. "You said Kosmel hasn't offered any guidance recently. What exactly has he said before when he's spoken to you directly—when you've asked him to regulate your magic?"

Ivy pauses, her lips pursing as she thinks back. "The first time, when I was dying, he talked as if he couldn't guide it unless I agreed. In the tower, he said he'd help as long as I let him in. And the last time, with Benedikt... He basically said it was up to me. That I had to decide how I wanted to handle the situation and he'd just back me up, essentially."

I consider that and what she said about her initiation. "Did you ask him to help you do something when you were struggling with your magic the other night?"

Her forehead furrows. "Nothing specific, I guess. It was more of a broad call for help."

"Then maybe that's the problem. The gods don't generally intervene all that blatantly in anyone's life—and it sounds like he's said you have to direct how he assists rather than the other way around."

Casimir lets out a thoughtful hum. "That does align with a lot of the philosophy I've heard and read from clerics and devouts. The gods will act through us but not for us."

"So if I decide what I want to happen and tell him

exactly what I need," Ivy says slowly, "maybe he'll show up? But I won't know until I try."

The courtesan offers her a wry grin. "That's why they call it faith and not certainty."

Stavros stirs on his feet. "Normally in a situation this dangerous, I'd say only trust what you can hold in your hands. But he's supported you multiple times before."

Ivy inhales deeply and seems to gather herself. "All right. I don't have to make the ultimate decision until I'm there. I'll prepare as much as possible, but I can still go straight to the stabbing if I don't like the looks of things."

The ex-general tips his head. "We may also be able to arrange for some supplies to be left in the general area, so possibly your magic could draw on something concrete rather than having to conjure every effect from nothing. If you have any idea what sort of effects you'd want to create?"

Ivy has always seemed awkward when anyone's complimented her appearance, but I can honestly say that when that shrewd yet hopeful light comes into her face, I can't imagine another person looking more stunning. I can see everything she's been through—and all the strength she's used to rise above it.

She wets her lips and glances around at us. "The scourge sorcerers like to use fire to destroy what they don't want. What if I could turn the flames around on them?"

FORTY-SIX

Ivy

In the moments after I've pressed the inside of my locket, I clutch the trinket tightly, waiting under the warm glow of the meeting room's chandelier for the men I've summoned to arrive. Despite all the sentiments we've already exchanged, I feel unexpectedly adrift when I think of why I'm here.

I need to say it. I'm heading out in a matter of minutes to try to take down a murderously obsessive conspiracy.

I don't know if I'll get another chance.

Here with no one to see me, I let my anxious fingers fidget with the folds of my skirt. I've put on the turquoise gown that's my favorite, its vibrant hue mostly tucked away under my cloak, in an attempt to boost my spirits in every way possible.

I can become a noblewoman. I can catch a man's eye.

I'm a force to be reckoned with, and I will wield my magic as *I* wish it tonight.

Casimir materializes first, his deep green eyes wide with

urgency. I hold up my hand and then clasp his before he needs to ask any panicked questions. "Nothing's gone wrong. I just wanted to see you and Alek one more time before I go."

I discussed this meeting with Stavros in his quarters—he knows to ignore the signal. He's already set off to join the squadron that'll hopefully be charging to my aid in just a few hours.

I don't need to explain anything more to Casimir. The courtesan's expression softens with a mix of fondness and concern that squeezes my heart even tighter than it already felt.

He knows the chances of my returning are much less than any other time I've gone off with the Order of the Wild. Maybe altogether slim.

Who can say whether we'll see each other again?

Alek emerges from his cord a moment later, with his dark hair swaying across the top of his mask and a similarly urgent air. I tug him close to me with a reassuring smile that I hope gives him more comfort than it's giving me.

"I needed a little company right before I leave," I say.

But that's not the full reason. It's just going to take me a minute to gather myself for the rest.

Alek slips his arm around my waist and Casimir tucks his around my elbow. The two men who first accepted me for all I am envelop me in their warmth and their different sorts of strength from either side.

If I were being perfectly fair, I'd speak to Casimir before Alek. He's the one who welcomed me from the very beginning, who won my heart when I was so afraid of losing it.

But knowing these men as I do now, I turn to the scholar first. Casimir has the certainty of his gift showing him how much he matters to me; he has the confidence of years of navigating tender emotions.

This territory is as new to Alek as it is to me.

I touch the side of Alek's face, and he leans in automatically to claim a kiss. The lingering press of his mouth against mine tastes bittersweet, as if he's hoping the gesture can keep me here away from danger. I choke up despite my best efforts.

When he finally eases back, his bright brown eyes shine with as much emotion as is whirling inside me. I find the words rise in my throat with no effort after all.

I smile up at him. "I love you."

Alek's lips part with a moment's shock. "What?"

It's even easier the second time. "I love you. I love how quickly your mind works and how much information you choose to fill it with. I love your dedication to every cause you take up." My smile turns sly. "I love how much you enjoy certain volumes of Woudish poetry."

A breathless laugh escapes him, and then he's capturing my mouth in another kiss, more emphatic than the last.

"I love you too," he murmurs after, still close enough that his breath grazes my mouth. "Everything about you, everything you bring to this world. Gods help me, Ivy, if I could ride out there with you and stand with you against the scourge sorcerers—"

I swallow hard. "I know."

When I shift my gaze to Casimir, he's smiling so brightly I have no doubt that I made the right decision. He looks as happy to see me declare the depths of my affection for Alek as Alek is.

Here's hoping I can make him even happier.

For all the confidence I've gained, the words still feel momentous on my tongue. I tighten my grip on his hand. "I love you. I love your boundless compassion and your commitment to increasing the joy in the world. I love the generosity you've spoiled me with and the ways you've let me spoil you a little in return."

The courtesan dips his head, his lips brushing my temple and my cheek before reaching my mouth. I'm tingling before we're even really kissing.

"I love you too," he says, sounding a little choked up himself. "And I look forward to watching your delight through every bath and ride and dance we share. Meeting you is the greatest gift I could have asked for."

I hug them both closer, willing back the tears that prick at my eyes. I need to remember this—all the faith they have in me, how avidly they'll be awaiting my return—through every moment I'm out there among the enemy.

My mind slips back to my last exchange with Stavros: the fiery kiss he gave me, the emphatic order to do whatever it takes to get away from the scourge sorcerers alive. His promise to be there to cut them down for me as fast as his steed can carry him.

I might not be ready to say those three words back to him yet, but I treasure his faith in me too.

"You'll take the antidote?" Alek checks.

I nod. "I'm going to chew one of the tablets you made from the powder before I leave, just to be safe, and have a couple more in my sleeve for after."

"Good. Two should be enough to offset a cupful, but it won't hurt to have three."

Casimir reaches into his carry pouch. "I bought this before we knew how soon you'd be going. I thought it'd make a perfect welcome back present. But seeing you in that dress now..."

He draws out a pendant with a gleaming teal gemstone, hung on a fine gold chain. "So you'll have something from me with you no matter how far away you have to go."

I have to start blinking away tears now. I fasten the chain

around my neck and slip the pendant under the neckline of my dress where it'll stay safe next to my heart. "Thank you. It's beautiful."

The bell sounds through the walls, marking the eighth hour. That's my cue to go.

Official club meetings don't need to be held furtively in the middle of the night like clandestine initiation tests do.

I pull away from my men reluctantly. "I'd better go. I'll see you tomorrow."

Let that be a promise and not a lie.

With a ripple of magic through my flesh, I step back through the ring of cord into Stavros's quarters. I take a second to pat my thighs and confirm my extra knives are in place this time, as loath as I am to use them.

Then I pop one of the three antidote pills Alek gave me into my mouth. Its bitter flavor coats my tongue as I hurry out of the Domi.

I meet up with a few of the bug club members including Olari on my way across the outer field. The nine of us heading out tonight congregate along the college's wall just beyond the gate, where two carriages are waiting.

We're traveling in noble style this time. I guess there are some benefits to foregoing anonymity.

Ster. Torstem ushers us into the carriages seemingly at random, but I end up squeezed into the back of one directly across from him. As I peer out the window at the streets we pass, I can't help wondering if the law professor wanted to keep a close eye on his newest college recruit.

Am I the only one from whoever he was considering at the school who passed all his tests? I haven't seen the young man who came along that one night among the bug club members.

It's possible he's made a strange disappearance or met an untimely death, just like Benedikt.

I glance up at the star-flecked sky with a silent prayer. *Kosmel, if you're still watching over me, I need you with me tonight. I've jumped in as deep as I can get... but I'm not sure I can get out again without your help.*

No divine voice reverberates through my head in answer. I catch a flicker of movement that might be a crow landing on a rooftop, but when I peer closer, I can't make out its form any longer.

A sign or just wishful thinking?

My fellow club members stay quiet until we've passed through the gate out of the city. With farmland around us and no chance of anyone overhearing, Olari speaks up. "Where are we going tonight?"

A thin smile crosses Ster. Torstem's face. "I have something a little special planned that I think you'll all appreciate. We deserve a chance to stretch the gifts we've earned."

My stomach flips over. What's that supposed to mean?

Julita stirs out of her uneasy silence with a snarky remark. *He won't like what your gift can do to him.*

She still sounds unsettled, though.

As far as I can tell from the stars and the turns in the road, we head east and a little north as expected. But about an hour into our journey, the carriages roll to a halt, and we disembark to find a large covered wagon waiting for us.

The other bug club members clamber inside without missing a beat. Clearly this is typical protocol.

I follow them, suppressing the apprehension that's swelling in my gut.

Beneath the stretched canvas, a small lantern smolders, casting its wavering light and an oily scent through the interior. Built-in benches set with cushions line the sides of the wagon. Still more comfortable than my past conveyances, not that I find the fact all that reassuring.

As the driver taps the horses into motion, I notice the wagon lurches to the left. I think it's heading southeast now. After a few minutes, it veers farther left again.

We're not going to the same area where Casimir heard there'd been evidence of bonfires in the past. Will we end up closer to wherever Stavros's squadron is stationed... or farther away?

Even with my hands tucked under the fall of my cloak, I resist the urge to clench them. Around me, the other would-be worshippers are starting to talk in eager voices, anticipation thrumming through the air.

They're looking forward to this expedition as much as I'm dreading it.

Ster. Torstem pulls out a small chest from beneath the bench. He produces several vials of a greenish liquid that he passes around to each of us. "Let's buoy up our festive mood! The gods deserve all our emotions bared."

With a few whoops, everyone else unstoppers their vial. I do the same and take a quick whiff.

It smells the same as the stuff we drank before. One small relief.

Feeling Torstem's gaze on me, I toss mine back with the others. I don't risk trying to spit any down my sleeve while I'm in his sights, but I do pop the other two antidote pills into my mouth under the guise of wiping it.

How do you feel? Julita asks, as if I can answer her right now. *Do you think the antidote is working?*

My nerves are still jittering, but none of the dizziness has come over me so far. Around me, my companions are laughing and swaying on their seats. I force a grin onto my face and giggle at a jolt of the wheels as if I'm equally ecstatic.

Avoiding the drug was the least of my many problems. What's this special something Torstem has planned?

In the midst of the growing clamor, someone pulls out a

sack of clay masks like the kind we wore during my initiation. I guess we college-goers still want to stay disguised from the rest of the Order of the Wild, wherever they come from.

Or maybe they see it as part of their worship, merging our humanness with animal forms.

I fix a mask over my face, the sense of concealment oddly reassuring even though I know everyone here is aware of who I am already. A quiver of energy tickles against my skin, but the illusions don't spring into being yet—they must be triggered by other magic cast near the place where the Order of the Wild carries out their rites.

It isn't much longer before I have the sense of the wagon tilting up a slope. We jostle against each other with more giddy laughter that I have to fake.

Did Torstem drink any of the drug? I think he might be totally sober too, though he joins in the laughter with a few chuckles of his own.

When the wagon lurches and stops, we scramble out onto a broad hilltop. A bonfire is already roaring away in the center of the grassy plateau, where three other covered wagons are parked nearby.

A figure whose mask gives the look of a weasel is just tossing more logs to feed the flames. At least a dozen others stand around the fire, cloaked in illusions of various beasts.

As Ster. Torstem ushers us forward, the heat crackles over my skin alongside a ripple of the magical energy that must be concealing it to more distant eyes. Some of the other conspirators start reaching their hands toward the flames and whirling around in chaotic dances.

"We open ourselves up for the All-Giver!" someone shouts.

More cries go up through the warbling of the flames. "Worship the wildness within!"

"Remember where we came from!"

"Honor the spirit at our center, the true life the Great God gave us!"

I spin and clap my hands as if thrilled to be there, eyeing the supplies around us surreptitiously. There are the four wagons, although I need to be careful of the horses. A couple of people have brought out crates, one holding a few bottles of wine and another a heap of apples. Several of the revelers have dropped their cloaks or jackets to bask in the fire's heat.

I have no sense of where the materials my men arranged to have stashed for me ended up relative to our unexpected diversion in route, but I think I have everything I need with me as it is. Should I ask Kosmel to guide my magic now or let the scourge sorcerers get even more caught up in their arcane ritual?

My magic stirs in my chest, and I instinctively balk against it.

What if Kosmel doesn't approve of the course I've taken? I don't even know how much might be at stake if I give my power free rein without any divine direction at all.

In my hesitation, Torstem waves toward one of the wagons and raises his voice. "Wildings, we have a special guest with us tonight! Throughout our realm, there are those who've sacrificed much to support our cause and enhance the gifts we've been granted. Please celebrate Ginelle for all she's given us and her deep devotion to our gods!"

A woman emerges from the wagon with a masked figure on either side of her. Or at least I assume she's a woman from her name.

A shroud—pale gray, unlike the black ones the Order has favored before—drapes across her from head to feet. But even with that covering, having seen people like her before, I can make out the signs of a sacrificial accomplice.

No hair fills out the folds around her head, where her

scalp will have been carved bald. No doubt she gave up her ears too. The fabric falls flat across her face, where she's probably sacrificed her eyes and nose.

Her entire body looks oddly slim, because she's had both arms carved off at the shoulders like Wendos's accomplices in the tower. Her lurching gait suggests she gave at least part of one of her legs as well.

And who knows how much they cut out of her insides.

Another one, Julita murmurs with a shudder.

My stomach churns. The current scourge sorcerers have tried to skirt the prohibition against claiming another's sacrifice for their own power by keeping their victims alive… but I don't know how how what those poor dupes are put through can be considered a life at all.

Torstem grooms them from childhood, seeking out orphans and maybe other vulnerable boys and girls as well. Telling them stories of the greatness they can help him achieve in the name of the gods.

Persuading them that mutilating themselves to the edge of suicide is the greatest offering they can make to the divinities and their country.

The shrouded woman drops into an awkward kneel and bows her head. From the hazy whispers around the fire, I'm not sure how many of my companions have seen one of the accomplices meant to support their sorcery before, even concealed like this.

Torstem points across the darkened land. "Over there lies a count's manor house. A despicable man who doesn't deserve the title. He gathers taxes for himself in the name of the false king and ignores the pleas of the peasants living under him. We can free them to pick their own master. Ginelle's gift will amplify our own. Let us show the false leaders of this world what the gods think of their arrogance!"

A cheer rises up from the revelers. I lift my voice alongside theirs, restraining a snort at the hypocrisy.

Arrogance? Has Ster. Torstem looked in a mirror lately?

"If you have any kind of talent that would allow you to move or project or send something to a destination, join us now," the law professor goes on. "Let's throw some of our fateful fire onto the count and send his manor home up in smoke as an offering to the gods watching over us."

I'm exempt from this act of sabotage, then. My gift is supposedly for forging replicas, not conjuring anything real, and an illusion of flames isn't what they're looking for.

That fact doesn't stop my gut from plummeting as several of my companions step even closer to the fire.

"Repeat after me," Torstem orders. "These divine words tell the gods that we want to merge our gifts with Ginelle's for their benefit. Say them and picture the house of corruption. Use whatever power you have to cast the flames toward it."

He points in the direction he indicated before and starts speaking the same disjointed syllables I heard from Wendos in the tower. Julita cringes back in my head.

The participating Wildings pick up the chant, some with the confidence of experience, others cautiously as they adjust to the sounds. The fire flares higher, a sharper heat washing over me.

My pulse lurches. Whatever I'm going to do, I'd better do it soon.

I delve my hand into my pocket, flick open my locket, and press my thumb to its inner surface.

The summons has been sent. There's no going back from this.

I ease toward Torstem, counting on the ritual to distract part of his attention. I want to be near enough that I can spring in with one of my knives if my other plan goes wrong.

Someone breaks from their chant with a triumphant shout. My gaze jerks across the darkness—and catches on a flicker of light that appears to have sparked on a rooftop.

Even as my pulse stutters, the flame fizzles out. But the voices around me intensify with eagerness as the scourge sorcerers see the first proof that their efforts could work.

A pool of icy horror forms in the pit of my stomach, setting my riven power banging at my ribs for release.

I don't know anything about the count who oversees this domain, but he won't be the only one in that house. He'll have a family, maybe children—there'll be staff and servants. Most of them asleep and oblivious to any threat.

I have to act *now*.

I take one more step in Torstem's direction but fix my gaze on the fire. Through the clamor of my magic, I open myself up to the divine touch that's come to my aid before.

Kosmel, direct the backlash of my magic away from any who don't deserve the harm. As I command the fire, steal heat where it won't be missed. Please.

He doesn't answer. But like Casimir said, this is about faith, not certainty.

The only thing I'm certain of is that I don't want to be a true murderer.

I loosen my hold on the power inside me and funnel it toward the flames. With a yank of my will, they shoot higher —and lash out toward the gathered figures around me.

The chanting sorcerers yelp and scatter, dashing backward from the fire that's turned on them. A tingling pressure forms on my shoulder, like someone has set his hand there, confirming he's with me.

You're doing it! Julita crows. *Let's teach these fiends a lesson.*

I'm not alone, inside or out.

But I'm not here to murder by burning alive either. All I

want is to sow chaos against the people who've encouraged it —and remove the scourge sorcerers' means of escape.

I fling the fire toward the wagon we arrived in, letting it lick across the discarded clothes on the grass in between. The lumps of fabric and the wagon's canvas covering burst into flames.

I yank their searing heat down toward the base and its wheels, holding it back from the horses and their squeals of panic.

Kosmel's wryly divine voice reverberates through my body. *Very good, my wayward rogue. A few houses that had caught fire in the next province over have found themselves abruptly saved so you could bring the flames here. I'm sure you don't mind.*

I have to hold back a laugh. Power vibrates through my veins.

I can do this. I can bend my own wild power to serve a good purpose.

Let the scourge sorcerers see the results of *their* arrogance. Let them think about why their worshipful fire might have turned on them.

I will another blast of flames toward the second wagon—

And they sputter out before they reach the arched canvas.

The heat sizzling through the air dwindles. The fire on the first wagon snuffs out too.

Julita gasps. *What in the realms…?*

My gaze flicks around the hilltop, understanding hitting me like a jab to the gut.

Something is countering my magic.

FORTY-SEVEN

Ivy

"**B**e calm!" Ster. Torstem calls out to the gathered worshippers in their animalistic guises, with a tingling rush of magic that prickles through my nerves.

The panicked voices fade. The fire droops lower.

Oh no, Julita murmurs.

As I stare at the law professor, Alek's voice filters up from my memory: "His gift on record is the ability to quell anger."

Plenty of people find ways to adapt the gifts their godlen blessed them with to broader uses than they were originally intended for. Esmae's talent with the wind was meant for carrying "messages," but she managed to twist it into flinging knives as well.

You could certainly see a fire's destructive blaze as a sort of anger.

It never occurred to me that Torstem might be powerful enough to deflect my riven magic. But that's what's so dangerous and reviled about both my power and the kind scourge sorcerers take on, isn't it?

He's not using only his gift but the benefits of Ginelle's immense sacrifice as well.

And he doesn't even need to worry about consequences. The sacrifices have already been made.

The Order of the Wild members start to chatter with awed relief, and I realize my attempt has even worse consequences of the non-supernatural kind. Torstem has managed to make it look as if his authority cooled the fire and prevented the destruction—as if the gods support him even more than his followers would have already believed.

Fuck.

My hand drifts to my side in a subtle gesture, braced over the knife beneath. I've already signaled Stavros—before the soldiers get close, I need the scourge sorcerers in disarray, too distraught to cover up their ritual and flee.

My way didn't work. So now all that's left is to kill the man in the bloody fashion the king asked for.

My ghostly passenger isn't ready to give up. Julita shifts in the back of my head. *Isn't there anything else you could ask your magic to do? He can't have the power to stop everything.*

As Torstem motions his followers closer to the bonfire again with an air of total assurance, bitterness courses through me. I don't know what else I could do that would set this bunch scrambling.

I'm not sure how much time I even have. With every minute I delay, I risk ruining the entire plan.

How ridiculous is it that this man has built his secret cabal of traitors by riling up anger against our rulers, while holding a gift meant to do the opposite?

The second that thought runs through my mind, my breath halts in my throat.

He *has* controlled his followers by stoking their anger—

with his words and his actions, not his magic. He was doing it just now, encouraging them to take out their frustrations about unfair rule on the nearby count's home.

But he also has the power to diffuse all that anger, more effectively than any word or action could.

No one could be better at draining the conspiracy of its might than the man who started it.

The orange light of the flames dances off the illusion covering Torstem's face, like it did off the straw figure of the king he had us throw in the fire weeks ago. After he ordered us to stab a man who was conjured out of clay to look like King Konram too.

The spark of inspiration sends a giddy rush through my veins. That's it.

When it comes down to his life or his schemes, he'll have to choose the former. What will any scheme mean if he's dead?

"If the wheels are too damaged, we'll simply crowd into the smaller wagons," Torstem is saying, his even voice dismissing the last of his lackeys' fears. "No doubt what we just saw was some defensive magic from the count's estate, meant to stop us from dealing out the justice that's due."

Oh, he wants to see justice done, does he?

I ease a couple of steps back, not wanting to be near him when I set my new plan in motion. For a few beats of my heart, I cast my gaze skyward, in case that's where Kosmel is watching from right now.

Please, I need your help again. I don't know what the exact consequences of what I mean to do would be. When I change him, whatever else changes to balance it out, let it do no harm to our cause or to anyone who deserves protection.

This time I get no response at all. But I remember the sense of a hand on my shoulder, the voice that resonated through my bones.

The godlen who's claimed me is here, working through me.

No, working *with* me. Kosmel has made it clear that I'm supposed to be calling the shots.

A strange warmth blooms in my chest. It frightened me when he first blazed his mark onto my skin… but I'm glad he's watching over me.

For the first time in my life, I'm embracing the divine attention I've earned. Kosmel has claimed me, and that means I have a place in this world, no matter how many cracks run through my soul.

I train my own attention on Ster. Torstem's form. I picture King Konram's face—the deep-set eyes, the imposing nose and jutting chin, the thin lips, the dark brown hair that tops it.

Then I nudge my magic toward the law professor to morph the illusion projected by his mask.

The same hawk-like visage Torstem wore during my initiation wavers and transforms into a replica of the king's appearance. With a quiver of energy from my soul, a gleaming gold crown materializes on his head.

Torstem, of course, hasn't got a clue what I've done to him, since he can't see himself. But the few followers who were looking at him freeze with expressions of shock.

I don't wait for the rest to notice on their own. With another backward step, I point at the leader of the scourge sorcerers. "Great God help us—he looks like the king!"

Gazes all around the bonfire jerk toward Torstem. In their drug-addled state, the Order of the Wild members launch into a flurry of murmurs as agitated as they are confused.

Torstem's hands leap to his face. "What? It can't be."

"He does!" someone else shouts. "That's exactly what

King Konram looks like—I just saw him up close at the Sabrellia festival a few weeks ago."

A girl near me reels on her feet behind her cat-like mask. "How could this happen?"

I drift behind a few of the other revelers so I'm partly hidden among them. "The gods must be sending us a message. Our leader has no more right to rule than he says the royal family does! He's been leading us astray, and they're warning us."

An off-kilter laugh carries from farther away. "Or maybe that is the king himself! Maybe the gods have brought him to us so we can do what needs to be done immediately."

I guess that interpretation will serve my purpose as well as the one I was suggesting. I raise my voice again, without the slightest twinge of guilt when I think about all the children Ster. Torstem has manipulated into carving themselves up for his gain. "We have to destroy him!"

Rumbles of agreement reach me from all sides. The gathered conspirators surge toward Torstem, swaying but intent on their goal.

The law professor holds up his hands, his eyes that look like King Konram's sweeping from side to side. He must be wondering who's responsible for this magic, calculating his odds of survival.

I doubt he's got enough humility to consider that the gods might actually be sending him a divine message.

"This is a trick," he calls out, projecting his voice over the warble of the fire and the increasingly aggressive muttering of his followers. "Our enemies are trying to deceive you."

"Our enemies aren't *here*," the fox-masked man in front of me retorts. "This is a secret meeting. It has to be a sign from the gods. If it wasn't, why haven't they shown us they don't agree?"

Another shout careens across the hilltop. "Throw him into the fire!"

Torstem backs away, but the conspirators are closing in on him from all around. With the fire only a few paces behind him, there's nowhere for him to go.

"Look at him, trying to escape the fate he's owed," I holler for good measure. "Not much of a leader now, is he?"

Torstem's gaze veers in my direction, peering through the hazy light. Has he recognized my voice, realized that the supposed Ivy of Nikodi must have played a part in this charade?

It doesn't matter. There's no easy escape for him.

He has to use his magic on the crowd. Persuade them that the sight of the king shouldn't anger them, that our ruler can have a calming presence.

Contradict everything he's spent the last however many years brainwashing them into believing.

The raven-like figure nearest Torstem snatches at his arm, but Torstem yanks it away. His voice has frayed. "It's still me. You know me. You've trusted me—trust me now. This isn't what it seems."

"What else could it be?" a woman beside him demands. "You have the face of the man who's forced all of us under his wretched rule."

Another man smacks his hands together. "It *is* the king. He's lying through his teeth like always!"

I risk one more shout of my own. "The gods have given us a sign! We have to show we've listened."

A harsh cheer goes up. "Throw him in the fucking fire!"

This is the moment when Torstem needs to act. I brace myself for the calm to wash over me along with the rest of the crowd, with all the power of his sacrificial accomplice magnifying it.

I can only imagine the confusion that will follow.

He can try to inflame their rage against King Konram again afterward, but it'll never quite be the same. Their certainty will always have been shaken—they'll never be as confident as they were before.

He'll have destroyed the essence of his conspiracy before I had to lay a finger on him.

But as the small crowd converges on the law professor in his kingly illusion, a strange shift comes over his body. His shoulders tense, and he lifts his head higher with a look of resolve I'd think will only infuriate his followers more.

He raises one hand as if for our attention. "The king must die. The royal family must fall. Let me continue to show you the way."

Then he leaps straight into the fire.

A cry escapes my throat before I can catch it. A couple of the closer followers grope after their leader and jerk their hands back with yelps of pain at the burn.

In the fire, Torstem's figure and the illusion wrapped around it crumple amid the flames. A hiss-like whine of pain penetrates the roar of heat, and his body convulses. I don't know how he holds back a scream.

"The king is burning!" someone shouts, and the scourge sorcerers erupt into ragged cheers.

They whirl around, resuming their revels even wilder than before. An elbow bangs my shoulder, and I duck farther into the shadows at the edge of the hill, horror clamping around my gut.

How could Torstem have done that? He sacrificed himself… so his followers didn't have to sacrifice the beliefs he cultivated?

Does he really think they'll carry on with his mission after he's gone?

Did *he* honestly believe in his cause that deeply?

I might not be drugged, but my mind is reeling. I crouch

down, my fingers digging into the grass in an attempt to steady myself.

Julita's voice carries through my mind, hesitant but clear. *Well, I suppose you accomplished what you set out to do, even if it wasn't quite what you expected. You killed Torstem. You fulfilled the king's orders.*

I drag in a gulp of the smoky air, and my stomach starts to settle.

She's right. I got rid of Torstem like the king wanted, but I did it on my terms. I didn't shed his blood. He decided his end.

I'm no more of a killer than I was before, and that's what matters the most.

As I watch the conspirators stumble and cavort around the fire, a small smile crosses my lips with the first flutter of relief. They don't know it yet, but their reign of wildness is over.

Stavros is on his way with a squadron of soldiers right now. They'll round up this leaderless gang of traitors, and the conspiracy will die tonight just as Ster. Torstem did.

It's already starting. A couple of the revelers pause, swaying as they peer around them.

"Where *did* our real leader go?" one of them mumbles. "Did he just… leave us?"

"He became the king!" another crows. "The king died!" Then she pauses. "So Ster. Torstem is dead…"

As confusion starts to spread through the gathering, I think I catch a distant yell where I'm crouched farther back from the fire. It's too faint for my drugged companions to have made it out yet.

Is that one of Torstem's sentries, coming to warn them of the incoming soldiers?

I have one more task to complete to ensure my mission's success.

With the conspirators so dazed, I hardly need much stealth, but I move as swiftly and silently as I can through the wavering shadows. A slash of my favorite blade here and another there sets the restless horses free from one wagon and then next. Swats of the knife's handle send them galloping away, eager to flee the vicious flames that nearly charred them.

Just as I reach the final wagon, the hollers of alarm become more distinct. "The army's coming! Gather everything and leave! Where's Ster. Torstem?"

I don't wait to find out how the traitors will answer. With one last swipe of my blade, I sever the harness straps holding the last animals in place—and launch myself off the wagon onto one of their backs.

I clutch my steed's mane and dig in my heels. We race away into the night, leaving the traitors to their fate.

FORTY-EIGHT

Ivy

The sound of voices filtering through a doorway rouses me. I shift beneath the covers and blink, recognizing that I'm somehow in Stavros's bed.

I found him near the hill after the conspirators were arrested and rode back to Florian alongside him, but as soon as we reached the trio of royal buildings, he sent me to the college on my own with a strict order to sleep. From what I recall, I crashed on the sofa as usual.

He must have carried me over here when he finally returned. Maybe he figured I could use a little extra comfort.

If he shared the bed with me, more chastely than the last time, he's already gotten up. His voice is the one reverberating through the door now.

"I don't want to wake her. Last night will have taken a lot out of her."

Who's he talking to?

I scramble out of the bed, still wearing the turquoise

gown I was too exhausted to peel off last night, and smooth out the wrinkles as well as I can on my way to the door.

"I'm already awake," I say mildly as I push open the door, and halt on the threshold. "What are you two doing here?"

Alek and Casimir smile back at me from where they're standing near Stavros, Alek a little sheepishly but Casimir with all his usual warmth.

Stavros offers me a crooked grin of his own. "I passed on word that last night's conquest was a success, and your admirers took it upon themselves to stop by to get all the details."

Casimir chuckles and swoops in to sling his arm around my shoulders. "The scourge sorcerer conspiracy is being dismantled. Ster. Torstem is gone. There's no more reason for us to hide our association."

He sounds so pleased, but the pang of uneasiness that filled my stomach after my initiation returns. There's no reason for us to hide that we're associating, no... but there's also no more concrete reason for us to associate at all.

I push that thought aside for later and let myself lean into the courtesan's embrace. My gaze returns to Stavros. "What have you gotten out of the conspirators you rounded up last night?"

His grin sharpens. "More than we even hoped. The villains were still addled with their favorite drug, and a few of them started babbling with almost no prompting about how they'd freed Silana by killing the king. We got confessions of their traitorous plans—not with much detail, but it hardly matters at this point—along with some rather bizarre stories."

A rough laugh jolts out of me. "Last night... didn't exactly go the way I expected. Were the soldiers able to confirm Ster. Torstem's death?"

Stavros nods, his good humor dimming a little as he

studies me. "We retrieved what was left of Torstem's corpse from the remains of the bonfire. There wasn't much. But with some of his followers collaborating your story that he jumped into the flames, no one has any doubt that it's him and that there's no crime to be punished for his death."

Thank the gods, Julita says with a relieved sigh.

A current of my own relief penetrates the tension wound inside me. "It's over, then? What about the other sacrificial accomplices Torstem was working with?"

"It'll take some time to tie up the loose ends," Stavros says. "The poor girl at the bonfire wouldn't say much to us, but gods only know how traumatized she is at this point. It's hard to tell, but I don't think she's more than fifteen."

I wince. "You have to find the others. I don't know how much of a life they can have, but they should at least be free."

"The Crown's Watch is already tracing all of Torstem's activities and travels. A couple of his associates from last night have given us some leads as well, though they clammed up once the drug wore off. We'll set the rest of it right."

Stavros reaches out to squeeze my arm. "You did well, Ivy. Incredibly well. No one's going to ask anything more of you."

Including the king, he clearly means.

I take a deep breath, not sure what else to say.

But Alek, naturally, is thinking as far ahead as I am. "Ivy can continue on as your assistant, can't she? There isn't any reason for her to leave the college." He hesitates, his bright gaze searching mine. "Unless you want to."

They want me to *stay*? To keep playing a noblewoman as if I belong here?

But neither Casimir nor Stavros raises the slightest objection to Alek's idea.

I open my mouth and close it again, groping for words.

There are all the people in the outer wards I meant to

keep helping. I haven't left my blessings of silver coins in weeks.

Is it possible that I could still be the Hand of Kosmel… while also staying on as Ivy of Nikodi, assistant to Ster. Stavros? I may not like most of my schoolmates or every bit of the work, but the role does come with some rather impressive benefits.

A tremor of hope rises through my chest.

Julita lets out a laugh that sounds like pure delight. *Of course you should stay on, Ivy. You can keep putting everyone who needs it in their places.*

"I believe the king intends to reward your service well," Stavros says. "You'd be able to fill plenty of pouches with plenty of coins for trips around the city's fringes."

He understands—he *approves*.

An even starker wave of relief washes over me. I swallow thickly and gather myself.

But before I can speak, a firm knock sounds on the door.

From his furrowed brow, Stavros isn't expecting anyone. He strides over to answer it.

When he yanks the door open, his massive form blocks most of the doorway. I catch a glimpse of a stunning blue-green eye and chocolate-brown curls, and my body tenses.

"Is this a summons from the king?" Stavros asks.

"No," a familiar voice says. "I was hoping to speak with Ivy of Nikodi. Is she here?"

Stavros hesitates, but I step forward.

The guard who's seemed to haunt me around campus stands in the hallway, his face as beautiful as ever but his jaw tight and his eyes wider than I've ever seen them.

He looks almost… scared.

My heart lurches with the sudden certainty that something is wrong, even if I have no idea what.

I hurry the rest of the way to the door. "I'm here. What's the matter?"

The guard glances at me, and a faint glow of hope comes over him. "You're the only one I could think of to come to. I need your help."

Stavros shoots me a puzzled look, but I'm equally bewildered. "Help? With what?"

The guard nudges past Stavros, who lets him enter but looms over him with a defensive air. The other man doesn't appear to notice, let alone mind.

His attention is fixed completely on me.

"I've broken some of their hold on me," he says. "I've been asking questions, challenging orders... and they've decided I'm no good to them anymore."

I stare at him. "Who are you talking about? Who's had a hold on you?"

"The ones who made this body." He taps his chest. "They built the form out of clay and put me in it, and now they want to shatter me and send me back to the state I was in before. But I don't want to go. I like this kind of living."

Behind me, Alek lets out a strained sound. "They made you... out of clay?"

I'm outright gaping now, but I don't know how to reel in my shock or slow the thumping of my pulse. "The scourge sorcerers made you. But who—*what* were you before?"

The guard who isn't really a guard shifts his weight on his feet. "I have been saying I'm 'Rheave.' It's the closest thing to a name I have. Humans call all of us 'daimon.'"

Understanding snaps into place in my head alongside my memories of my appeal to the spirit-creatures in the All-Giver's tower. The images they sent of flames and constricting darkness.

It could have been fired clay, closing in around them.

The conspirators switched from controlling the daimon

in their ephemeral form to stuffing them into physical bodies.

"That's how they created life," Alek mutters as the pieces click together for him too. "They didn't actually create it. They stole what was already there."

"Can I stay with you?" Rheave asks, his gaze darting across my men and back to me. "If they find me, they'll kill this body."

Casimir eases forward, speaking in a soothing tone. "You should be safe now. The leader of the scourge sorcerers is dead. The army is rounding up his—"

"What?" The daimon in human form looks at the courtesan as if he's grown a second head. "No, he's not."

I manage to stop gaping long enough to ask, "How do you know?"

Rheave's gaze swings back to me. His lips purse as if he doesn't like what he's about to say.

"He's just called on all of us nearby. We're to go to the palace and murder every inhabitant who has Melchiorek blood."

The Gods of the Abandoned Realms

THE ALL-GIVER (the Great God, the One) - overseer of all existence, creator of the godlen

THE GODLEN OF THE SKY

Estera - wisdom, knowledge, and education

Inganne - creativity, play, childhood, and dreams

Kosmel - luck, trickery, and rebellion

THE GODLEN OF THE EARTH

Creaden - royalty, leadership, justice, and construction

Prospira - fertility, wealth, harvest, and parenthood

Sabrelle - warfare, sports, and hunting

THE GODLEN OF THE SEA

Ardone - love, beauty, and bodily pleasures

Elox - health, medicine, and peace

Jurnus - communication, travel, and weather

Made in the USA
Las Vegas, NV
05 December 2023

82131358R00353